Encounter with Destiny

SEQUEL TO WAVE OF DESTINY

Encounter with Destiny

Martha Melahn

Authors Choice Press

San Jose New York Lincoln Shanghai

Encounter with Destiny

Authors Choice Press
an imprint of iUniverse.com, Inc.

For information address:
iUniverse.com, Inc.
620 North 48th Street
Suite 201
Lincoln, NE 68504-3467
www.iuniverse.com

ISBN: 0-595-13477-7

Printed in the United States of America

For Darby, Jules, Britt, Melahn, Faxon, Hadyn, Harley, Wyatt, Julian, Clayton and Faurest.

PREFACE

As in *Wave of Destiny*, all major characters are fictitious; they include Anne-Marie and Bart Ramsden, Tim and Consuelo Clayton, Rafael de Palma and David Doyle. Lesser characters: Esteban Navarro, May Doyle, Jason and Emily Frazier, Jared and Alma Russell, Zipporah, Concepcion, Captain Sands, Pearl and Dr. Burbury are also unreal. However, a number of minor characters such as Sylvanus Pinder, Mayor Henry Mulrennan, W.A. Russell, Ben Baker, Reverend J.O.A. Sparks, and nurses Aunt Hannah and Aunt Petrona were very real people who, at the time, lived in the interesting city of Key West and contributed much to life there.

The New York Stock and Gold Exchanges' crash of 1869, known as Black Friday, the history of cigar manufacturing in Key West, and the Cuban migration following the Bayamo Uprising in Cuba, are depicted, however briefly, as they happened.

Anne-Marie and Bart's experiences in Mexico and their conversations with President Benito Jaurez and General Porfirio Diaz are related as they could have occurred.

Consuelo and Tim's home is described at Whitehurst and Greene Streets in Key West, and is now known as The Audubon House. The house, built originally for Captain John H. Geiger, skilled pilot and master wrecker, who selected the furniture from cargoes of salvaged ships, was restored by the Mitchell Wolfsons of Miami and made into a museum in 1960.

The sprinkling of Spanish in menus, particularly should be pardonable when the meaning is clear and authenticity paramount. Every effort has been made to describe the life, travel conditions, and cities as they were at the time.   MM

CHAPTER ONE

The large manor house in southern New Jersey stood waiting, ready to take whomever within the family coming down the poorly maintained turnpike. The house, hewn from rugged, wind-blown, coastal timber, even by the current year, 1868, had softened with time. The outer shell of wood now concealed an easy, gracious sanctuary. The grown Frazier children and their spouses came, bringing their children, and the house was always ready to absorb them. After Anne-Marie, the last girl to marry, left, Emily Frazier told her husband Jason that she was ready to give up the big house for something smaller, but Jason knew better. Every few months a carriage turned into the long elm-lined entrance road and discharged a family laden for a protracted visit. The house— and Emily—took on new life. Several of half a dozen closed bedrooms were reopened, dusted and aired. Beds were made with gleaming, almost invisibly mended linens; day help was taken on; lamps were cleaned and floors waxed. Once again young voices, laughing, crying and sometimes shrieking reverberated over the sound of footsteps.

The young ones, relishing the space yet respectful of its elegance, began with the exploration of every nook and cranny. Taking the narrow servants' stairs that ran from attic to cellar, they snooped for treasure in unlocked trunks or in the secret compartments some master cabinetmaker had buried within Emily's beautiful desks and bureaus. There was, of course, nothing new to be discovered among the old clothes and bric-a-brac, yet each exploration brought excitement, fresh and familiar as Grandmother Frazier's candy canes and saltwater taffy.

Bart Ramsden, a tall, intense, fair young sea captain, was anxious to call the visit to an end. Fond as he was of his in-laws, he was too badgered by problems to relax. Still, he recognized his wife and daughter's pleasure with their family.

No sooner did he enter his in-laws' house than he tripped on a naked wooden doll carelessly dropped by his daughter Samantha. The stiff, awkward plaything, impervious to anything less than fire, skidded unharmed across the entry as Bart painfully regained his balance and uttered a few well-chosen expletives acquired through years at sea.

Small things, unimportant things grated. He had been through too many backbreaking cruel experiences, narrowly surviving too many close calls, not to realize that something insidious and corrosive was destroying his normal good nature. He had fallen into a pattern of tight-lipped frustration, swallowing annoyances, ignoring what was building up inside. Now he exploded.

"Samantha," he bellowed, meeting silence.

"Samantha! Come here this minute!"

When no child but two maids appeared, he vented a measure of his anger. "God damn it! Where were you? There are two of you to pick up after one child. Father Frazier could have broken his neck on this damn thing." Taking two steps he gave the doll a swift kick into a new awkward and more distant position.

Concepcion, his wife's Spanish maid, blanched while Zipporah, a newly hired girl, quickly reached for the offending toy and mumbled, "Yes, sir."

Bart glanced up to see his wife standing at the head of the stairs, drawn by the commotion below. She had been listening for the sound of her husband without much eagerness. Bart was becoming increasingly difficult to live with. With others present he was polite, even kind, but when they were alone he was withdrawn or unaccountably cross. Nothing seemed to stem his rancor for more than a few hours at a time.

Unflinching, the tall young red-haired beauty met her husband's stare.

"I'm afraid I'm to blame. Mother took the children on a picnic, and I've kept the women upstairs. There's a lot of packing to be done." A clutch in the pit of her stomach caught her breath announcing her troubled mind.

Bart would not have apologized to two servants, but he dropped his voice. "I'm going to talk to Captain Sands. I'll be back for dinner." Turning sharply he strode from the house.

A whisking autumn wind, warmed by a day of bright sunshine, had swept through the yard so studded with fruit trees that the litter of leaves and twigs cracked under the stomping tread of his boots. In that moment it struck him that he resented his wife's ship. Even that his wife owned a ship was awkward and embarrassing—like an unexpected stepchild. An angry knot swelled within him as he climbed into the waiting brougham. The vehicle was distractingly new and extravagantly appointed. He breathed deeply, drawing in the scent of soft, tufted leather, and determined to quiet himself before reaching the harbor. But, allowing himself one final expression of rage, clenching his fist, he came down hard on the sill and exploded. "Damn nation!"

*   *   *   *

Upstairs Anne-Marie entered her old room sidestepping open, half-filled suitcases. Once the room had seemed large and airy, more than adequate for a seventeen-year-old bride. Now, four years later, the voluminous wardrobe of a wealthy woman, a potpourri of delicate wools, velvets, silks and satins crowded the armoire and overflowed into an adjacent room. In a few days they would be departing for Key West. In separating a northern wardrobe from what would be needed in the tropical island city, colossal disorder had resulted. Bonnets with streaming ribbons perched on every available knob and bedpost, and, from the corner of her eye, it seemed for a moment as if the room were peopled with others—other than herself, a weird thought.

"Thank heaven Bart hasn't many clothes," she murmured, viewing the bed piled high with dresses. She hoped the two maids could restore order before her husband, a prince of neatness, returned to rail at the disorder—and the size of her wardrobe.

Carefully, weaving her way, she stopped before the tall, many-drawered bureau and drew open one of the topmost small drawers. There, neatly folded lay her wedding veil of white Alençon lace. Strange, she had not noticed it there before.

Mother must have put it here, she mused, thinking I might want to pack it. It could be a good fifteen years before her daughter Samantha might need it—as she surely would, an already promising beauty.

Anne-Marie thought of her mother with kind, tender, loving tolerance. At the moment the lady would be spearheading a search for berries, the picnic finished off within the first fifteen minutes of the expedition. The grandchildren enjoyed permissiveness denied her own children.

Still, the veil drew Anne-Marie, and she carefully draped it over her head, gazing into the mirror. A fine high forehead sloped gently to a mass of coppery hair, allowing the fragile lace to billow over curls with a sheen from copious brushing. Her eyes, large and dewy, were enhanced by thick long lashes and topped by eyebrows that rose high in a gentle arch. Her cheeks—without pinching—lit naturally to a rosy flush like the pink of a child's skin after a cold bath. But, she did not think of the reflection of beauty framed for a moment as a portrait, but of her wedding day.

She remembered a different Bart that evening, shyly slipping an emerald on a gold chain around her neck. She had worn it daily since. For her, it was more of a symbol than her wedding ring.

Now, from under the exquisite veil, remembering, she could also see a gypsy who had told her fortune, while in the church the wedding party waited. Astonishingly, the gypsy's prophecies had proved correct: she had foreseen danger and a mortal enemy in a dark haired man. The gypsy had also feared for her firstborn who had drowned. She had seen the unexpected inherited wealth. "You should not marry today," the gypsy had said. She had—anyway. Predictably, it had been a stormy marriage, either heaven or hell. The gypsy had also told her something she had banished from her mind: "I fear for your husband's children." The fact that his children would also be hers made the prophecy unconscionable. This part was totally forgotten as if it had never been said.

Their finances were now such that it was no longer necessary for Bart to go to sea for months and months at a time. She knew there were times when he missed it—though he feared it. She had even bought a shipping business on the condition that he would give up the sea. For one thing, they wanted more of a family, which had not happened.

There was a slight tyranny involved. She had married Bart knowing that there would be long separations. She had welshed somewhat, therefore, on their prenuptial understanding. She was sure this was not what was bothering Bart. Something else was, and he had not confided in her.

One point of contention, she was well aware of: he had been falsely imprisoned. This had had its impact on his character and personality. While in prison on Dry Tortugas, he had met Dr. Samuel Mudd, incarcerated on equally unjust conspiracy charges for treating the killer of Abraham Lincoln. Together they had battled one of the world's worst epidemics of yellow fever. Anne-Marie and her father—with proof of Bart's innocence in hand—had succeeded in obtaining a presidential pardon for Bart and his release.

Mudd's case was another matter. Pardoning Mudd would have insured President Johnson's impeachment. After weeks in Washington, knocking on innumerable doors and crowding interminable waiting rooms, it became clear to Anne-Marie that wealth and influence had their limits. Bart, enraged and bitter over being unable to help his friend, had taken some of his resentment out on her. This was a natural reaction, she knew, but she hoped that bone of contention had been laid to rest. Characteristically, Bart did not harbor grudges. His anger was explosive, but soon burned into constructive action.

The effort to help Mudd had been a debacle. After an argument they returned to her parents' home in New Jersey. Her unwillingness to beat a dead horse even one more day in Washington infuriated Bart.

"Stay here in Washington and fight this if you want, Bart," she had told him. "I have other concerns that will be a good deal more fruitful on which to spend my time."

"Mudd's case is a good deal more important than money." The red color in his face had died slowly.

"I was thinking of Samantha. Our daughter has been without us for over a month." She had turned to avoid his eyes leveled on her. Inwardly trembling over her defiance, she then ordered the maid to pack her clothes. "I'm going home."

He quieted, accepting his wife's realistic appraisal.

"Dearest, I know you are not used to defeat. In this world we can't always win."

"The surest way to remain a winner is to win once and then not play anymore. That doesn't happen to be your husband's way."

It was a minor victory for Anne-Marie, but not a happy one.

She did not doubt that she loved Bart, only that she could live with him in harmony. His handsome face with striking blue eyes, bluer than forget-me-nots; his tall, lithe strong body and unbending back that would always carry the scars of floggings at sea; the lightning quickness of his mind and the restless flow of energy, loomed in her mind as an indomitable force that could carry her up, up, up—or crush her. They were opposites—enormously attracted to each other.

*　　　*　　　*　　　*

Meanwhile. Bart, rumbling along in the cab, reviewed his relationship with his wife. He was franker with himself than usual. He had wanted a sweet, adoring simple girl willing to sit at home waiting, bearing his children, bowing to his wishes and reveling in his exploits while he was at sea. And, as one of the youngest sea captains on the Jersey coast, he was, perhaps the most successful.

What he wanted from life was normal for the time.

Anne-Marie had changed. She had matured into a forceful personality. She had more of a mind than he had dreamed of. Adolescent prettiness had ripened into an incredible tantalizing beauty. When she distanced herself, her beauty made her aloofness all the more unbearable. Her father did very well managing their money, understandably as he was a banker. Because Bart knew he could not have done better himself, he felt unsure of his position.

A grave injustice had been done to Dr. Mudd. And, in an effort to accomplish one worthwhile thing in his life, he wanted that wrong righted. Anne-Marie seemed unsympathetic to his goal to clear Mudd's name. Because of her, he had failed his friend.

Unfortunately, his career, once supremely important to him, had now become silly and pointless in the face of her wealth. He did not want to sit around living in a grand style unless at the same time he could make some significant contribution to the betterment of the world—if only in a small way. Life had to hold more than a round of theater, opera and balls.

Now something else had come up that troubled him greatly, which he hated to discuss with Anne-Marie, knowing what her reaction would be. Again, an old friend was involved, Jared Russell. Jared was married to a girl Anne-Marie carried a grudge against—with some reason. Jared and his wife Alma had two small children and were expecting a third. Working for Bart in Mexico, Jared had disappeared, causing Bart considerable worry. Through letters, Alma had been badgering Bart to do something. Lord knows, thought Bart, under the circumstances I would have done the same. Long voyages were difficult for women left for months without word. He remembered Captain Daniel Gifford, who returned to Barnegat from a trip to learn that all three of his children had died in an influenza epidemic. Alone, his wife had handled everything. Soon, he was going to have to do something about Jared, but what? The mission had obviously involved unexpected danger—which Jared had been willing to face.

Doing something about Jared came precariously close to doing something about Mudd.

Unfortunately, he felt, at this point in his marriage, that he was desperately in love with his wife. Of course, he had always loved her. But, at this inconvenient time he was acutely aware of it and desperately wanted a rapport that he had been unable to achieve.

What he did not realize was that he was incapable of subterfuge. He had a one-track mind. When he was troubled he was irritable. But, love his wife he did—now passionately. This recognition welled and erupted like a volcano. With an oath he abandoned his plan to see Captain Sands. "Take me home," he ordered the driver.

*   *   *   *

Anne-Marie stood looking at herself in the mirror, her dejection growing into an overwhelming sense of futility. The sadness released a flow of silent tears. Blessed as she had been with so much that others had envied, she had failed miserably in building a happy satisfying life such as her mother enjoyed, and it was not that she had not tried…

Finally, wiping her eyes on her veil, she looked up to see Bart standing in the doorway, silently staring. For a moment neither spoke.

A flow of tears was hardly what Bart had expected, and he immediately regretted returning. In a confrontation with a woman tears were infuriating—an unfair advantage.

"What's the matter?" he demanded, entering the room and awkwardly stepping over an open suitcase carpeting the floor. Regaining his balance but not his temper, he stood squarely in front of his wife. "Don't you have enough clothes?" The remark was unthinking, and he knew it.

"Yes, I have enough, and when I don't I'll buy more." Her voice was flat and unprotesting.

He had returned to the house to beg her pardon for his rude outburst, and here they were, off on the wrong foot again, so unintentionally and so alien to the spirit of his return.

"Christ!"

With a quick kick of his foot, he slammed the door insuring their privacy. In his desperate urgency he reached for her, pulling her into his arms. His usual grace was absent. The powerful grip took Anne-Marie by surprise. For a moment, she hung suspended, her feet not touching the floor. She, too, hated to be caught weeping.

Particularly, she did not want her depression revealed, and she also wanted no hasty judgments and decisions—as was Bart's way.

Hurting and angered now by his brute force, Anne-Marie pushed to free herself, only to be held more tightly. "Bart, you're hurting me," she managed.

Breaking her face free, she struggled, thrashing about in his arms. Her rising anger only spurred his determination to have her. Inflamed by her resistance and ignoring her attempts to beat his chest, he finally threw her to the bed atop a mound of finery and sprang on her. His voice, brimming with despair, cried out, "Oh, Anne-Marie, don't you understand how much I love you?"

The words struck a chord in her, unleashing a whole new set of emotions. Suddenly, she felt his torment, his frustrations, his subjugation—that would be intolerable to him—clearer than her own self-absorbing unhappiness.

"I love you. I love you," he repeated. His plight and the length and depth of its revelation, was shattering. He rolled from her, pressing his head close to hers.

"Oh, Bart," she cried, raising an arm, no longer to fight him off but to caress him.

His lips found hers, but then broke away to speak. "What happened to us?"

"My God, I don't know, but I don't like it any better than you do." Again, tears welled. "I'm sorry about the tears."

"I'm here with love for you, spilling it over you, and just for the reason that I can do nothing else. Do I have to explain that I'm as much in love with you today than I was the day we married?"

"Perhaps."

"And, there are times—I know when they come, because they frighten me—that show me I love you even more, much more."

"Don't try to explain. We have too many problems and we have solved none of them."

"I'm not used to being idle. I'm used to simple men jumping to obey my commands—not conversations with women."

"I'm sure the home of your in-laws grates. But, Samantha needed to get to know her family in the North. It's been a sacrifice."

"One I've been happy to make, believe me," said Bart.

Happy did not seem the right word. Feeling grateful that she had not shattered a tenuous rapport, she reached for her husband and held him close and long in womanly reflection. Then, rather than risk fumbling words, she tightened her arms about him as an expression of their reunion. Passionately, he made love to her.

Later she remembered how he had looked during an instant at the door, the distress on his face as he threw her on the bed, and then his collapse. There was also his tender self-consciousness as he left her. Somehow her dress had become torn at the shoulder. She viewed a tattered sleeve. Swiftly, she tossed the dress under the bed lest the maids see it. Later in the day she would slip it into the furnace—no matter that the silk could be cut up for quilts. She wanted no reminder of the day. She had silk to spare.

*   *   *   *

Besides Anne-Marie's family, the house welcomed Anne-Marie's sister May, May's husband David Doyle and their two boys, Clay and Whitney. The visit of the Doyles was timed to catch Anne-Marie and Bart before they departed for Key West. A post Civil War depression had included the ship building industry and had thrown David out of work with the temporary closing of a major yard. He was only an accountant and certainly it was no fault of his that the shipyard was in trouble. By making the visit to May's family they could weather the storm and at the same time kiss May's little sister Anne-Marie and her family goodbye.

The girls were genuinely fond of one another. May was plain, but not without charm. She had taken her share of life's problems good-naturedly, laboring under the influence of a too good-looking husband. David was considered gently grasping and diligently lazy. It was an accurate but incomplete appraisal. Nevertheless, the Fraziers thrust aside all such considerations and welcomed the Doyles.

The arrival of the David Doyles and the departure of the Bart Ramsdens would be marked by a party.

While Emily, back from the picnic, supervised the preparation of a big family dinner, excitement over the approaching party rose through the house as did the aroma of freshly baked bread. A long series of house-rites flourished.

In a great round wooden tub bound in copper in the laundry room the children were scrubbed to receive their Sunday best, easing the traffic in the house's one bath chamber. Anne-Marie's brother arrived from Princeton. Father Jason Frazier left his bank early. The Caleb

Ramsdens, Bart's parents, had been invited and were already turning in the driveway.

Jason Frazier no longer farmed the back acreage of his land, but instead rented it to a neighbor who, as part of the agreement, kept his household supplied with fresh eggs, milk, chicken, beef, and often on festive occasions, as on this day, a suckling pig. Cherry trees, flanked by apples, plums and pears, lent their fruits. The surplus was canned in summer for a dazzling array of pies all year long. Nearby a small cranberry bog afforded its tasty harvest. Emily Frazier clung to her small vegetable garden with its herbs—the last remnant of agriculture on the place. Not far afield lay the ocean and the many inlets along the Jersey coast rich in fish, oysters, clams and scallops. This bounty from the land and sea was presented on a table dressed with snowy lace and gleaming silver as richly rewarding to the eye as to the tongue. Under the soft flickering light of home-made candles, Jason's imported wines, fired into new life by hand-cut crystal and fresh, jubilant, uncorked air, released their spirits to buoy those of the gathered clan. Emily seated her guests.

"Thank God for a father-in-law who knows good wine," observed David honestly.

"Leave us first thank God that we are all together again," replied Jason, mildly chastising Bart and leading the family into grace. Normally, Jason's prayers were longwinded, but, with guests present, the hope of the everlasting paled before the immediacy of lively conversation bound to ensue.

Having heard Jason's brief grace, David Doyle, an opportunist, lost no time in proposing a toast to not only Jason's fine hospitality but to the young Ramsdens, so soon to depart for Florida.

"Leave it to David to butter his bread and then want to frost it like a cake," whispered Bart to his wife. Before the visit was over he knew as well as she that David would ask them for considerable money as an unsecured interest-free loan. Still, Anne-Marie hoped that Bart had not been overheard, and by the tone of David's next question to Bart, apparently he had not been. David brimmed with genuine friendliness.

"And, what have you been up to, Bart?"

"Well, for want of anything better, this morning I helped two neighbors build a new pound, horse-high, bull-strong, and hog-tight," Bart replied, turning to his wife with a smile that said the afternoon had been better spent.

"Oh, I meant in Washington," continued David.

"Washington was much less satisfying. Our politicians are a bunch of gutless wonders—including the President." Scowling, Bart absently downed a goblet of vintage wine as if it were a common grog.

"We had a difficult time," added Anne-Marie, finding Bart's eyes. "We went championing the cause of Dr. Mudd only to be rebuffed at every turn. Everyone was aware of the misfiring of justice in the case of Mudd, but nothing could be done."

"'Public opinion forces me to take this stand,' was all we heard. Not one lawmaker was willing to go out on a limb for a man falsely tried, falsely imprisoned, and who should have since, by his heroic deeds, become a national hero. It's disgusting," raged Bart.

"Here's to mud in your eye," punned David, raising his glass and startling everyone into inappropriate laughter.

"Seriously," interjected Jason, "it's a sad state of affairs."

All, embarrassed, agreed.

"But, President Johnson had a point that saved him in my eyes," said Anne-Marie. "He hopes to continue to steer the ship-of-state toward rebuilding the South. To pardon Mudd would mean certain impeachment by a hostile Congress. Johnson believes so strongly in Lincoln's policies of benevolence that he is willing to sacrifice Mudd. At least, that's what he said."

Bart growled.

Anne-Marie continued. "Supposedly, Mudd's imprisonment therefore benefits the South in that Lincoln's policies retain some support.

Johnson is hanging in there by his fingernails, using his powers as best he can. If he survives in office to end his term honorably—if you can call it that—he will pardon Mudd before he leaves. He promised us that, and he promised Mudd's wife, but he adamantly refuses to do anything now."

"Then Mudd is a scapegoat," said Caleb Ramsden, his eyes moving around the room.

"Exactly," replied Bart, squarely turning to his wife, speaking as if to her only. "I refuse to take things as they come and to moderate my pace to conform to the pace of our leaders."

Anne-Marie shuddered inwardly. The tone was polite, but his bottled up resentment was thinly veiled. Someway, she was blamed. "You want miracles of progress—that's all," she replied with a smile that softened a shrug. Was their earlier rapport so short lived? She wondered.

"It's hard for me to imagine my little girl meeting the President of this country," whispered Emily to Mother Ramsden, somewhat proudly.

Jason shifted the focus with a less highly charged comment. "Without doubt, rough times are upon us, and there's little help to be had from Washington." He thought of his daughter May and how difficult it must be for her to have her husband out of work. The atmosphere in the room thickened in quiet.

"Have you swallowed the anchor, Bart?" asked David, meaning retired from the sea.

"It may seem so. Time will tell. My wife would like me around a while. The shipping industry is going through many changes. There's no way that sails can compete with steam on short hauls. The big competitor is, of course, the railroads, where, happily my wife is well-stocked."

The pun was not lost on the group, ready for an honest laugh.

"That's what you said five years ago," returned David, looking around for approbation.

"I wasn't saying quite that or I would have bought railroad stock myself," said Bart. It seemed David could never get anything right. The discussion, on the surface impersonal, was bound and gagged by deep emotional turmoil. It went beyond his relationship with Anne-Marie—so precarious that it had shaken him—back to the dungeons of Dry Tortugas and his promise to Mudd that he would work toward getting his release and pardon. He reached for the wine carafe to solace the bitterness gripping his stomach.

"Let me tell you younger men something," said Caleb, drawing his son Bart back into the group. "Changes don't come as fast as you think. Big changes take more capital than is presently available. Steel—the Bessemer process—and the rails' expansion has drained our coffers. The large clipper ship is coming into her heyday. She with her sails is still beautiful and profitable. Last summer the *Surprise* sailed from New York to San Francisco with a crew of four mates, thirty able seamen, six ordinary seamen, two boatswains, four boys, two cooks and a steward, a sailmaker and a carpenter. She carried 18,000 tons of freight. She reefed her topsails twice on the voyage. It was a veritable pleasure cruise. After unloading, she sailed, in ballast, to Canton where she loaded tea at twenty-five dollars a ton. At the end of the voyage she had not only paid her **entire** costs including her construction, but she had made a profit of fifty thousand dollars. How's that for a 'surprise?'" Caleb ended his spiel pushing back his chair with a "Harrumph."

"No one is arguing with you, Father," said Bart. "But, we've seen the railroads expanding into the plains." He paused. "We're a nation of tea drinkers, and I don't foresee a rail line soon to China, so there certainly is a place for tall ships. It's the small captain, trafficking along the coast, the little businessman, who is hard hit, bringing down the small ship-builder with him."

"I take it you're talking about me, a shipmaster with a small fleet, but I'm ready to retire anyway," replied Caleb, his pride offended by his son who used the word small.

"The British composites have hurt us," interjected David. "Not having our wood, they turned to iron frames with wood planking, and got strength, rigidity, and increased cargo space while avoiding the problem of weeds growing on iron. So, I'm laid off."

"Naturally, we're sorry, David," said Anne-Marie. "We don't think it's your fault."

At the end of the table Emily looked confused, not by the technicalities of the conversation, but by the tension and mood of her son-in-law Bart. Anne-Marie had confided that she and Bart were having problems. "We will work them out," Anne-Marie had said, but her tone was unconvincing. Emily's soft gray eyes moved to her daughter, but Anne-Marie sat regarding her husband.

"Some reasonably effective anti-fouling compounds for treating the hulls of iron ships are coming into use," said Caleb to Jason, turning away from his disappointing son to an older kindred soul. "They don't make it any easier for the Americans to compete against British ships on a world market."

"He still doesn't get the point," grumbled Bart only for Anne-Marie to hear.

The talk of ships, of a profit of fifty thousand dollars after costs in only one year, had unsettled Bart, Anne-Marie knew. With the help of more than a little wine he had plunged back into a world of action and excitement. The lure of distant shores, the challenge of thunderous waves and masterful winds, the privilege of power, surely weighed on him. Had he forgotten the other side of the coin: the days of boredom, the luck that runs out, the treacherous storms at sea and the too long separations from family? She would have to talk to her father about a project for Bart. Jason had already intimated that he had run up against some perplexing problems that he wanted to discuss before they left for Key West. Perhaps her father had some project in mind that could catch Bart's interest?

"The *Thermopylae* has consistently clocked over three hundred miles per day," said Bart, emerging from a reverie, confirming Anne-Marie's suspicion that he had been off and away, dreaming of days at sea.

Bart did not relent. "She is certainly one of England's most remarkable clippers. And her value—apart from the sweetness of her lines—is in her speed and strength." In the end he was talking only to Anne-Marie.

She turned to the group, almost apologetically. "The sea is a hard mistress. Her spell over men is hard to break." Then she turned to her dinner plate and away from Bart. He had had too much to drink. Still, she felt reasonably sure that she was the only one present aware of that fact. Otherwise, she would have been terribly embarrassed.

Blessedly, the conversation turned to Anne-Marie's brother Francis and his progress at Princeton. Bart went upstairs early with the excuse of telling the children a bedtime story. In all fairness, Anne-Marie knew that Clay and Whitney, sitting at the head of the stairs in their night-shirts, had waited patiently for Uncle Bart.

"There are drawbacks to being a favorite uncle," said May with a knowing smile.

Bart did not come back downstairs.

Finally, Anne-Marie went to bed herself. Familial voices, sprinkled with laughter, drifted upwards, echoing through the stairwell into her room. The door to Bart's room from hers was closed for the first time. Lonely and tired, she undressed and slipped into bed. Then she remembered her well-brought up nephews who would have kept coming back to their Uncle Bart until faced with a closed door. Feeling better, she fell asleep.

CHAPTER TWO

Samantha was the first to disturb Anne-Marie's rest in the morning as she climbed into her mother's bed. Concepcion filled the doorway, a broad grin of approval lighting her face. Samantha was the joy of Concepcion's life.

Anne-Marie's first daughter, also named Samantha, had perished at sea. This child was as strong as the other had been weak. Having kissed and hugged, Samantha was off for her porridge. As Anne-Marie drifted back into sleep, Bart, a quieter visitor, climbed into her bed.

"What time did you get to bed?" he whispered, bearing no sign of a hangover.

"Late, very late."

He would not let her sleep further, she knew. He moved to embrace her; she did not resist him. A hand gently caressed her bosom. "I drank too much last night."

"I have forgiven you," she murmured sleepily, enjoying an exploring hand. "I was even thinking of buying you the *Thermopylae* for Christmas. What would you think of that?"

At first, the generous thought pleased him; then he had second thoughts. Now, in a thoroughly awakened state himself, his other problems came to mind, and like ballast improperly positioned, weighed, tilting him.

"You wouldn't be wanting to get rid of me, would you?" he asked, surprised and suddenly put on the defensive. As he spoke he lifted his hand from her body.

Now thoroughly awake, her eyebrows raised, she moved away from him slightly to eye him coolly. Her coppery hair, bronzed by light, tumbled.

"With you I'm damned if I do and damned if I don't," she replied, her voice more sad than angry. "You know as well as I do that there are no short profitable runs in the shipping business as there used to be. So, I've asked you not to go back to sea. Then last night you virtually lusted over the *Thermopylae*, weeping in your cups for the sea again. When it's within my power with the stroke of a pen to make this wish come true, I feel like a selfish harridan holding you back. So, if you want to go to sea for a year at a time, you can, Bart—believe me, you can."

Her little speech finished with a flat note in a minor key, she moved from her bed toward her negligee, but he pulled her back.

The same words spilled out in a rage would have disturbed him; in a calm deliberate mood they were frightening.

"Come, come. Stop running against the wind. Let's not fight. Don't pay any attention to drinking talk. If you think I'm ready to pull out for a year, you're crazy." His voice fell. "Please, believe me."

She lay back on the bed, hardly suggesting surrender although she knew that Bart would be drawn toward lovemaking. Such was her art, the secret of her tantalizing power over her impetuous husband. She could always, after the promise of a tender yielding moment, suddenly distance herself to stand slightly aloof and out of reach. Her suppliant sweet introduction became in effect a lure. Her retreat offered an irresistible challenge—as if to say, "Capture me." But she was not playing a game. It was inadvertent, yet she behaved in a wholly inticing manner. The waves of red hair that waltzed about her face, the flawless alabaster skin, the graceful impossibly long neck, and the soft wide eyes did not detract from the allure.

"I thought I laid everything bare yesterday," said Bart. "Such a profession of love should be good for two days." The thought brought a mildly crazy grin to his face that was infectious and Anne-Marie wanted no more sparring.

"I know that you love me." She raised a hand to touch his face with unfailing magic. The gesture, like that of a lady dropping a handkerchief or hiding her face behind a fan, appealed and comforted where words may have failed.

Responding Bart bent to kiss his wife and then moved his face near her ear where he could find the traces of the evening's perfume lingering, tangled with a jungle of hair. "Considering that I don't want you out of my sight for five minutes, I'd hardly survive a year, Anne-Marie."

In that moment, reassurance lay in the body of his wife. Tenderly searching, his hands roamed her body, finding a river. Carefully and deliberately he wrapped her in a mantle of desire to match his own, blotting out past friction while an urgency churned within them. Within moments the power was no longer in her hands, but in his. The previous day's imbalance had leveled. They could think only of the couple they formed together. They still had a new felicity to discover. Her hands on his back, finding the ridges, the criss-crossing scars of an insane captain's whipping, were part of a sea life that he could not share, just as he could never share all of hers. Finally, at her pleading the moment was to come. Out of their blinding search came a sweet moment of brief but total surrender when oneness, however fleeting, obliterated the separative distances besetting them—the ultimate moment of complete joinder.

"If we could just love and love," she whispered.

Downstairs a breakfast, comparable only to those of the English, awaited them. Alcohol lamps under silver chafing dishes warmed scrambled eggs, scalloped potatoes, oysters, sausages and bacon, hot breads, while platters of ham and cheeses, tented by monogrammed linens to preserve their freshness, stood beside stacks of plates. On a table nearby a samovar of coffee, bubbled to perfection, perfumed the room, befitting Emily's standard of excellence. Jason, always the first to arise, sat now at the dining table in the morning room. A sheaf of papers were at hand. Peering over his glasses he greeted Anne-Marie and Bart.

"I'm glad you made it before Francis. The amount of food that your brother can put away always astounds me."

"I can see Mother anticipates his appetite. But, I see you have something to talk to us about," replied Anne-Marie, placing a kiss on her father's cheek. "In fact, you look as if some new tax has been levied on something ridiculous—like income."

"Do I look that grim?"

"You don't look pleased, and I don't think it has to do with what Francis eats."

"You're right. I'm not exactly pleased. Get yourselves some food and sit here with me before we're disturbed by the others."

Giving his coffee a stir, Jason began. "I know you are aware of your silver mining interests in Mexico. Fortunately, they represent only a small part of your wealth. Still, in good years they paid as much as fifty thousand dollars, which is not to be sneezed at. Last year you received practically nothing. I feel bad about this because it's been so long coming to my attention. I should have caught it earlier."

"Father, please, don't berate yourself. I know how complicated managing property with so many foreign holdings is. Bart and I could not have handled it."

Jason Frazier was to Anne-Marie a living fortress, a pillar of integrity and solidarity to which she owed her sense of security. She and Bart had tossed their financial affairs into his lap without a by your leave and he had responded with characteristic generous service. Jason ignored her comments.

"There are a number of reasons for the decline, which, of course, I can't help. I can explain the reasons to you, but time has been unnecessarily lost, and this I regret. You two have profited handsomely through foreign investments during the last few years, but perhaps we have not stayed abreast of politics around the world as we should have. In a nutshell, the Mexican investment has gone sour."

Jason paused while Anne-Marie and Bart nodded in agreement. Deliberately, Jason looked to them both. "Politics and economics walk hand-in-hand. This is true because the government in any country is the country's biggest spender. By virtue of your wealth and subsequent power you should recognize a considerable obligation to society. The livelihood of hundreds of people depends on you and your financial perception. My dear children, money is very easily lost. You may think you have so much that you never need to worry about it. Let me tell you, you have so much you are obligated to worry about it."

Jason's lectures had been a part of Anne-Marie's upbringing. The knit brows, the quivering nostrils, the pursed lips—every gesture—formed a composite of Father-laying-down-the-law. Sometimes the lessons had been painful when his outraged decency loosened the eyeglasses from his nose so that they fell from his face. At such times, even their mother discreetly tiptoed from the scene. Although rancor was missing today, Anne-Marie hoped Bart would take her father's lecture in the spirit in which it was intended—that of simply informing. Apparently, Bart had.

"Being a banker, I've had a little insight as to Mexico's plight and problems," continued Jason. "Let's go back to 1859 when a Swiss by the name of Jecker headed the banking house of Jecker, Torre and Company in Mexico City. He arranged a 3,000,000-franc loan for the Mexican government from France on the issuance of Mexican State Bonds which would mature at an unbelievable value of 75,000,000-francs—the most outrageous loan that I have ever heard of. But Mexico could pay only a part of this loan. Jecker was bankrupt and could not conclude the transaction. He went to Paris wanting French citizenship and a means of salvaging something. There he turned to the Duc de Morny, offering to sell his Mexican State Bond Issue for ten percent of the loan, a juicy proposition since the loan carried with it the right to explore Sonora and Baja California for mineral concessions. Morny formed a syndicate to take the bonds off Jecker's hands, not because of the paper, but because of the silver concessions. Do you follow me?"

"Indeed, Father Frazier," said Bart. "Please proceed."

It had been on a joint venture in Mexico with Jared Russell that Jared had disappeared. Jared's wife Alma had been pestering Bart to rescue her husband. Naturally, the mention of Mexico peaked Bart's interest, but he had not discussed this with Anne-Marie.

Jason continued, "I have to regress a moment to explain that, at the time, Mexico was plagued with two Presidents: a no-good, sly General Miguel Miramon, a Conservative supported by privileged landowners and a Catholic hierarchy; and a second, Benito Jaurez, a full-blooded Indian, head of the Liberal Party." Jason shook his head dourly. "I guess this could happen only in Mexico."

"The U.S. supported Jaurez because the European powers favored Miramon. Morny's problem was how to unseat Jaurez to favor the man he could control. With Morny in charge of the French syndicate, joined by English and Spanish bondholders, the Mexican indebtedness was transferred from the stock exchange to the Palace. There Napoleon and Eugenie were seized with a fever-dream of an overseas empire and a massive resurgence of French influence over the New World. In what was called a 'bondholder's war' a coalition of European troops entered Mexico, a sovereign nation—we thought—and put a hapless Austrian Hapsburg on a 'cactus throne,' all in the name of protecting an investment."

"I can't fault them as opportunists," said Bart. "At the time—ten years ago—Lincoln had too many problems with the South to pay any attention to Mexico. That I remember as the shipping trade to Mexico ground to a halt."

"Indeed, and speaking of opportunists, after having stolen two-fifths of Mexico's territory when we took those areas called California, much of Arizona, New Mexico, Colorado, Texas and Utah, we now got upset when the Monroe Doctrine was ignored. But, that's another story."

"Napoleon put Maximilian and his wife Carlotta on the throne," said Bart.

"Yes, for what they weren't: French, Spanish, German or English. Moreover, they were not leaders. As puppets in the hand of all the European powers, the two fair young people were ideal." Jason rose for a fresh coffee, and then returned to his chair.

"Of course, their loyalty would be first to Austria, which satisfied everyone," Anne-Marie noted.

"Except us, I remember," said Bart. "But, we were lucky. France was forced to withdraw her troops from Mexico due to Prussia's defeat of her ally Austria, pulling the rug out from under Maximilian."

Bart's heart skipped a beat. Here was Jason, his own dear father-in-law, giving him an out—business in Mexico involving saving Anne-Marie's money—which would offer an opportunity to find out what had happened to Jared Russell.

Jason pulled out a newspaper clipping and quoted it, entranced with the rhetoric: "'Maximilian was cut off like some night-blooming vine whose scent had become cloyingly obnoxious even to those who nurtured it.'

"Carlotta went to Europe to plead support for their throne, but had a spectacular lack of success. In 1867 the Mexicans shot Maximilian, which was regrettable, especially considering how ineffectual he had been," said Jason, continuing.

"The poor man, so idealistic, too," added Anne-Marie, thinking of the execution.

Turning to Bart, Anne-Marie noted his contented expression. "According to the European tabloids, Carlotta is insane. They love to picture her, framed in a window of some dark Belgian castle, grieving for her Maximilian." Obviously touched by the sad fate of the beautiful, dark-haired empress, she hoped to muster some sympathy from Bart.

"They also shot Generals Miramon and Mejia with Maxmilian. The two Generals died instantly, but poor Maximilian was still alive and to be finished off with a *coup de grace*," murmured Jason.

"Oh, Father! Why think of that? It's too horrible in a civilized age. He was no criminal…"

"Mexican marksmanship leaves much to be desired," said Bart, hoping to discourage Jason from saying anything more about the dangers of traveling in Mexico.

"Last year, at just about the time that Bart was pardoned, the Austrians finally got Maximilian's body back. It then lay in state in the Hofburg. Jaurez is still President, but hardly. Mexico is in chaos. His reforms are destroying the old establishment, and that includes the Catholic Church. And, for over one year now, dear daughter, you and your husband have not seen one *real,* which is about twelve American cents."

Bart jumped on the opportunity like a cat on a mouse. "When you think of what once came in, that's a tremendous loss, especially when we know the silver is there, waiting to be mined."

"Have you written?" asked Anne-Marie.

"Of course."

"And what did they say?"

Jason picked at his scrambled eggs.

"For heaven's sake, Father Frazier," said Bart. "You've let us keep you from your breakfast."

"That's all right," replied Jason, rapidly finishing off his now cold eggs, and gathering wind. "Nothing! If you can believe it. A Señor Ramirez is a part owner and manager of the Taxco mines. He doesn't answer letters nor has he sent a year-end statement. I fear that your whole investment, which fortunately was not with Jecker but which soared after Jecker's collapse, may be lost. You—rather your estate—got the original investment back years ago, but that's neither here nor there.

You are the major owner in what was a tidy prospecting and mining company with concessions over a wide geographical area. As long as there is silver there—or gold or gem stones—a share of the profits of the company, if any, belongs to you."

"And that's all Mexico is, my dear wife—one great big mine."

"Must you say that with a faraway look in your eyes?" queried Anne-Marie with a wan smile.

Bart laughed. Very little escaped his wife, he noted. However, in his breast pocket rested a letter from Alma Russell imploring him to do something about finding her husband. *"D'ont think for a moment that I wouldn't go to Mexico myself if it weren't for the deplorable condition I'm in,"* she had written. About to deliver a child, in this respect the letter was shaming, and Bart felt his responsibility.

"Once Anne-Marie and I get to Key West, we are not far from Veracruz," said Bart.

"I know what you're thinking, Bart Ramsden," said Anne-Marie. "But, before you go traipsing across Mexico we are going to do some investigating. Due to the unrest, such a trip could be very dangerous."

Jason piped up. "You can talk to the authorities…"

"Excuse me, Father Frazier, but we have been talking to authorities for weeks. Even the highest, President Johnson, got us nowhere. I can learn more by talking to a Mexican sailor, believe me."

"You have a good point."

Further discussion of the Mexican holdings was cut short by a group of hungry relatives. "You know I keep banking hours," said Jason, extracting and then replacing his watch. "And, brief as they are, they are important. You might come to my office this afternoon as there are a few odds and ends I'd like to cover with you."

"We will be there when the bank closes, sir," said Bart, knowing they had received a command performance. One of the odds and ends would be a loan to the Doyles. It was certainly a move Jason could have taken without discussing it with them as Jason had been given a *carte blanche* to manage their affairs. Yet he would not have done such a thing.

"I have tremendous respect for Jason," said Bart watching the carriage depart.

"So do I." He had set a standard for men that his daughters shared.

By now the aroma of coffee had drawn Emily, May, David and Anne-Marie's sleepy brother Francis who nevertheless put away the equivalent of two meals. Accustomed to this, Emily turned to the mail.

"You girls can help me with something. Your Uncle Elbert is breaking up housekeeping in the big house. He's lonely since your aunt died, and is moving to New York City. He wants advice on furnishings he should keep. I think he's ready to give things away if you're interested. I hate to go alone missing a day of Anne-Marie's company. Will you girls go, too?"

Emily's pearl gray eyes that perfectly matched her jacket of French mohair moved from daughter to daughter.

"That would be fun," said May, brightening perceptively. "It's a dreary old house stuffed with monstrous furniture, but there might be something we could use. Couldn't we, David?"

"Use or sell," he replied.

"One shouldn't sell family things," reproved May, looking to her mother for support.

"Everything **used** is somebody's family things which have been sold. Sometimes one must sell things—or go hungry," countered David.

"Don't talk that way. Nobody is going hungry. Just look at this table…" cried May. The remark had been made, she knew, for her sister's benefit, and she felt suddenly embarrassed. Still, she would salvage her pride. "If only Auntie had lived in Boston—the Athens of America. Think of the beautiful things we would inherit. New Yorkers have no taste."

"Taste or not, it would only take a day or two at most," pleaded Emily.

Soon the maids cleared away the remains of breakfast. When they had left David commented, "Mother Frazier, your new maid is quite a beauty."

"Oh, you mean Zipporah. She's Anne-Marie's lady's maid, hired for Key West."

"Concepcion had too much to do caring for Samantha," Anne-Marie explained. "Zipporah claims to be handy with a needle and I like the way she does my hair. Don't you like my new coiffure, David?"

Anne-Marie was teasing, but at the same time smothered indignation. Her maids were none of his business. She left the room hearing, "It's ravishing, Anne-Marie."

"I don't see how Anne-Marie expects to keep a pretty servant like that around long," said Emily to her son Francis. "She'll be off married and gone before she's half trained. Hire the plain ones, I always say..." Privately, Emily added, especially if a husband admits to noticing women other than his wife, like David.

That afternoon Anne-Marie and Bart took the brougham to the wharves and Jason's bank. Both were struck by the reduced activity. Bart reached for her hand. "Do you remember the first time I shipped out after we were married? You seemed so forlorn watching the loading of the *Catherine.* It tore out my heart to leave you."

"I remember everything. Mother says I have the memory of Minerva." Silently, she added to herself the depressing truth—for trivia only.

"And the face of Venus, the grace of Terpsichore, and the figure of Juno, I might add—which is every goddess I can think of or I would name them all."

She turned to her husband, surprised by his uncommon effusiveness, both at the moment and for the last few days. He was trying hard to please her.

"I always tried to act for the best in whatever I've done. And you know, I believe it's what I shall turn out of have done, difficult as my beautiful wife is." He was teasing, of course. Still, she sensed that in a playful way he was trying to prepare her for the fact that he should go to Mexico. The message of the present talk had been different for each, but it had reinforced, reinforced even immensely, the effort of each to understand the other. Despite the fact they were in a public place, she pressed a tremulous kiss on his lips.

Upstairs in her father's offices the morning's discussion continued. From behind a massive mahogany desk on a sea of deep green carpet, unhappily Jason detailed David Doyle's appeal for a substantial loan.

"It's a pretty tricky situation—lending money within a family. Generally, such loans are unsecured, and even if they were, who would take over in the event of default? I don't care for his proposition because I don't believe it's based on sound economics. It's that simple. What do you think, Bart?"

Bart turned to meet his wife's eyes. Jason's query was in itself a compliment. "I see no way for small shipbuilders to compete effectively with the large yards in New York and Boston. If he were to manufacture furniture or anything else immigrants will want and need, I would be more interested. Backwoods areas are too much in decline. What do you think, Anne-Marie? The final decision is up to you."

Anne-Marie rose and stepped to the window overlooking the wharves where a forest of masts once stood. There were fewer ships, less harried activity, fewer people. Brigantines and schooners sat docilely like mother ducks while smaller smacks and ketches rocked like ducklings around them. Of course, there were whalers. These ship-rigged craft were easily recognized by their whaleboats slung in davits along their sides. But, as more and more cities had built gasworks for gaslight, the need for whale oil had diminished. Now gas came from burning coal, and coal was moved on barges, fat and squatty dowagers of the seacoasts. Aromatic fruits and spices of the West Indies were still to be seen, but more and more of this trade was going to the larger centers of population, cities burgeoning with immigrants. Bart had predicted the change.

"Father," said Anne-Marie, "give May a sum that will insure that the family will eat well and be properly clothed. Don't make it so large that David will be willing to sit back as a man of leisure. When he has a better proposition, we will consider it."

She had to help her sister. David would not be pleased, and she did not even know that May would be grateful. At best, it was a situation in which neither the giver or the receiver would be satisfied.

"I'll withhold your decision until just before you leave," said Jason, reading her mind. He hoped to keep the visits comfortable for all concerned.

"I think we should explore the Mexican situation," said Bart. "Before we leave, I'd like copies of your records as well as any notes you might have on the political climate—if you would be so kind."

"They are already being prepared for you."

"We will have to talk a little more about Mexico," said Anne-Marie to Bart, an unsure huffy note in her voice. So that was what Bart was leading up to outside in the carriage when he told her that he always tried to act for the best. Obviously, the idea of going to Mexico was in his mind, steaming like a pot of coffee that would soon boil over. Worse, her father was encouraging him. With a flounce of her skirt she left the many-paned window overlooking the harbor and ignored her waiting chair.

"I'll try to obtain some maps—perhaps in Atlantic City…" said Bart.

Anne-Marie's waiting stance was an invitation to depart that Bart could not politely ignore. "We won't take up more of your time now, Father Frazier. Thank you."

Anne-Marie kissed her father and wordlessly departed, Bart at her heels. Later in the carriage, her color rising perceptively, she silently gazed through a window, and then busily fitted her gloves. Finally, she blurted, "I wish you wouldn't jump at things. You seem endlessly plotting and planning a departure. It is so defeating—as if you want to get away from me."

"That simply is not so. I'm just trying to be useful, which is damned hard when a woman has everything."

"Everything but a husband."

"A desire for your presence, Madame, has little to do with my ability to have it and at the same time to live with myself. I have expressed my desire, and lately, rather frequently."

"What you have expressed and what you are planning are a Gulf of Mexico apart, Bart Ramsden."

An urbane fluency that bordered on a sharp tongue was something Anne-Marie had developed in the last four years, but which always surprised Bart. On one hand, he hated to see her angry, while on the other hand; he found her pique delightfully stimulating. What a good mind she has, he thought, ever mindful of her physical attributes radiating with a full, fierce luster beside him.

She turned quickly to the window in an effort to remove herself from the turbulence within the cab.

"Apparently you have been doing a lot of tall thinking," she heard him say.

"I feel it in my bones," she replied

"The situation could change overnight. Any number of hair-brained schemes might interest me, my dear, that I won't take off on. While I had the *Catherine*, once the business of getting underway was over, I always said to myself, 'What a fool I am to leave her. Life is too short for this.' But, I'm not a banker, or a cobbler, or a gentleman farmer. I do feel a need to be useful. Remember what your father said about an obligation of wealth? Maybe I feel that more than you, and that it requires action. But, please, relax. Don't take things so…personally."

Through the breath of the chilly, slightly damp southwest draft whispering through the carriage, brushing away the last vestige of a long Indian summer, she met his eyes without evasion. "I feel so adrift. I wanted a home and we are building one—but you will be gone. I should like to have a family with a husband around." She spoke with yearning. "I do not mean to be selfish or controlling, but I would like a normal existence. Doesn't that fit at all with what you would like?"

"Of course." He drew her near, and for the moment he meant it.

She knew differently. I love him too much, she told herself.

It was becoming increasingly clear that she had married a restless man, who would move from place to place, from study to study, from occupation to occupation and, terrible to contemplate, perhaps even from sweetheart to sweetheart. He would always be a soldier of fortune, romantic, versatile and something of a fighter. It was a disturbing revelation in that now she saw that Bart was so by choice.

*   *   *   *

The following morning Anne-Marie went to work early with Zipporah sorting and repacking articles that years before she and Bart has received as wedding gifts. It was a pleasant, nostalgic chore, but she noticed that Zipporah seemed careless with things that did not have much cash worth, but which for sentimental reasons she valued. Anne-Marie felt she had learned from her mother how to train servants. It was important not to become ruffled by failures. If you were explicit and kind, your suggestions were supposed to take root. As patiently as she could in the face of Zipporah's indifference and inattentiveness, she explained exactly how she wanted things done. It was only when Bart appeared that Zipporah's face brightened with interest.

"I have an idea. Let's take a train to Cape May. I'll tell your mother we won't be back for dinner."

"I haven't been there since I was a child," Anne-Marie mused, rising. "The weather has held so that there'll still be people but no crowds. But, the work here…"

"I'll handle everything, Madame," said Zipporah, now smiling sweetly.

"Well then, why not?" agreed Anne-Marie. "What a grand idea!"

"I know Zippoprah will handle everything perfectly," said Bart, flashing an engaging smile.

Cape May provided visitors from Philadelphia and New York relief from the sweltering heat of the cities. When the Frazier children were little, the family vacationed on the Cape.

"Father said three thousand visitors coming and going everyday were too much and we stopped going," said Anne-Marie in their compartment on the train. "So the pattern changed, but I think Mother was sorry and we children were, too."

"Men like the gambling."

"Father would have thought of that. Perhaps gambling had something to do with our quitting. A banker shouldn't look as though he's playing with some poor farmer's savings."

"No, indeed."

The resort had grown, now reflecting the lavish lifestyles of its summer residents. Wide porches, cupolas, etched and stained glass windows, turrets and lacey decorations fancifully topped the many new large houses, three and four stories high, lining the wide drive facing the ocean.

"It's a carpenter's heaven," remarked Bart, looking down an airy tunnel of porches toward the end of the block. Wooden icicles and curlicues were everywhere. "Would you like a summer place here? Take your pick. They're all within your reach."

"Mother would love one."

"Would you?" he repeated.

"It would be fun. Can't you see me, after a refreshing dip, sitting elegantly corseted in a white cambric dress on a wicker settee, while you, fashionably clad in a proper morning suit, try your luck at cards at the Mainstay Inn?" She could not contain a giggle.

"Having dipped my feet in the South Jersey surf…"

A rambling white hotel and a long tan carpet of beach lay before them, dazzling in the autumn sun. "It's colder than it looks," said Anne-Marie, looking beyond a string of large parasols that made colorful canopies of shade to the great blue and white ocean whose hard surf washed the shore. Her concerns of the past two days vanished and a chord of delight struck her. From close behind, Bart took her elbows in the palms of his hands and drew her against him as they admired the brilliant coast.

"They may have dancing at the Hotel Cape May," he said.

"Could we go?"

"Why not? But, look at the houses," said Bart, now leading her along Ocean Drive.

She pointed. "Here's Queen Anne, and there's Italianate. Someplace near is a Wedding Cake Gothic and a Steamboat Gothic."

"Preserve me from that. Please don't like that pink house dripping with lace trim. A man could hardly be comfortable there."

A number of distinct gingerbread styles with a fairyland air about them met their scrutiny. "Even if you were bored silly after three days of fashionable people. Buying here looks like a good investment," said Anne-Marie pensively.

"Unfortunately, I think so myself," admitted Bart.

After an elegant but early dinner they waited for the last train running north. "We could spend the night?" he ventured at the last minute standing at the station.

"I have no luggage, and remember the trip tomorrow to New York. I shouldn't disappoint Mother and May." She felt torn.

"You're right, I suppose…"

"I had been such fun. It was too good to last."

After the brisk air of the Cape, the warm soporific air in the train wooed them both toward sleep. Anne-Marie's head fell to Bart's shoulder, but the creaking and swaying of the giant iron cradle proved too much. Besides, rounding each bend, the train whistled mournfully.

"What are you thinking about?" she asked finally.

"Oh, nothing in particular."

"You must have been thinking of something…"

"I was thinking that your head is getting heavy."

"Why didn't you say so earlier?"

"It was worth the pain."

In truth Bart was thinking of several things, one of which was rather merciless: an older man had died leaving Anne-Marie a fortune. Rarely, in moments of great contentment, did he allow himself to think of that, still tonight he did. The man's name could grip him with jealousy. Gleefully he could enjoy the man's money; greedily he could relish the jewels spun like webs around his wife's throat. But, he, Bart, was alive. That, he supposed was the ultimate revenge, because he suspected that the benefactor had been instrumental in sending him to prison.

He was also thinking of Jared Russell, whom he had sent to Mexico. Years before, Anne-Marie had been jealous of his wife Alma, who had been nothing more than a friend, whom he suspected had a crush on him. Jealousy, he recognized, as a dangerous emotion almost impossible to combat, occurring as it did in another person's head. How much better if those green-eyed dragons were never summoned in the first place because it often took some extraordinary devotion to lay them to rest. Certainly, he would spare Anne-Marie what he had been through. Now, with Jason's help, it would be easy—he thought.

Chapter Three

The family and servants alike noted the fact that Anne-Marie and Bart slept in separate rooms. The perpetually open door between the two rooms was possibly not as convincing as the wall between the two rooms adorned by delicately patterned, yellow-flowered wallpaper.

Concepcion assumed that the rich, unlike the poverty stricken fertile Latins squeezed into crowded barrios, could choose separate rooms and, of course, would. Babies continued to be born to the wealthy although in lesser numbers. Considerate gentlemen with heavy sexual appetites often discreetly took their pleasure elsewhere in order to spare their wives too many unwanted pregnancies.

When Anne-Marie and Bart first married she purchased a book of hygiene. Perplexingly it stated: "Intercourse can be governed by no certain law. Yet experience has proved that it is far more satisfactory to have an interval of at least two to four weeks; and many find that even three to four months afford greater impetus to power and growth as well as personal satisfaction. Men who have great results in the field of science, invention, philosophy, religion and philanthropy have been those who led continent lives."

The book further mentioned continence during gestation: "During pregnancy women should be exempt from sexual relations. Motherhood should be a shrine unpolluted by selfishness."

Anne-Marie never questioned the authority of the printed page—any page.

Finding her experience with Bart dangerously unhealthy, she had read passages to him. For a few minutes he had dutifully listened, revealing disbelief. Then, with an eyebrow askant he had one comment: "Burn the book!"

"You can't really mean that?" she had replied, naïve eyes blinking.

"I certainly do," he said, not bothering to disguise his disgust.

She didn't burn the book, but read further where it stated: "To attain the highest purity, the riches of the continent life, first adopt a plain, unstimulating dict; avoid coffee, intoxicating drinks, highly seasoned food, oysters and eggs, and all animal food; and *omit the evening meal.*" She put the book away forever. There was no way to equate a hygienic married life with both their appetites. Nor was there anyway to equate her parents' happy marriage with the food served in their home.

Emily looked on the separate rooms with concern and a prayer. She said nothing, but her pursed lips caused Anne-Marie to explain. "Bart never sleeps more than four hours at a time. It's a habit established by many years at sea. Worse still, he thrashes in bed, wearing me to a frazzle. Besides, since he was imprisoned on Dry Tortugas, he's had howling nightmares. When he feels like it, he visits me, and when I'm lonely I go to his bed. It's the only solution to a difficult problem."

Anne-Marie's explanation relieved Emily who clarified the situation to Jason.

The new maid saw the sleeping arrangement as a sign of estrangement and an opportunity for herself. Her new master was certainly attractive with a vacancy in his life that it might be quite profitable and satisfying to fill. Knowing that she was pretty with curly lemon-yellow hair and a full, difficult to conceal bosom, she looked for opportunities to be of service where there might be an opening for closer contact. This Bart hardly noticed, being far from an underprivileged husband.

Cleverly, she made herself inconspicuous when others were present, but most solicitous whenever Bart was alone.

Her attentions—a brush of his coat to remove a bit of lint, fresh warm shaving water when the first was hardly cool, boots polished to a mirror shine—were ingratiating. The clever ministrations were all the more pleasing offered, as they were, in an easy friendly manner above suspicion. Such service Bart regarded as a requirement and perquisite of the rich. Instead of appreciating Zipporah, he credited Anne-Marie's training of the girl.

Tired after a day at the Cape, Anne-Marie retired early only to awaken during the night hungry. Quietly, she slipped to the kitchen for a glass of milk and a cookie. Her father was there on a similar mission.

"We missed you at dinner," he said kindly, belting a deep blue velvet robe about himself and proffering her a chair.

"We had a lovely time, and we may buy a summer beach house on the Cape."

"I like that thought," replied Jason. "We want you back every year."

"Key West is too hot in the summertime, but the winters are lovely. Don't worry, we'll be back."

"Changing the subject, I'm glad for this chance to talk to you alone. Do stop me if I'm being meddlesome. Judging people has been the essence of your old father's business. As you can imagine, some despicable characters can be good credit risks so I don't necessarily separate good from bad, but I do observe people. I think highly of Bart, and frankly I'm worried about your relationship with him. You don't appear to be as happy as you should be."

"True. I suppose it's the money."

"I don't think it has to do with money. Bart has a lot of pride. He can't stay idle."

"I know."

"He's a restless fellow. I wonder how one boat or one dungeon ever contained him." He smiled to soften his words.

Her eyes met his. "They never did for long."

"But you would like to rein him in?"

"That's not exactly it. I'd like him near—at least for a bigger family. Samantha is disadvantaged being brought up alone. I cherish my old family, and want my own. Bart is always dreaming of a new world to conquer miles from home. His idea of the future is never in the back-yard. That's our difference."

Jason nodded acquiescent understanding. His eyes traveled above her to the many polished copper pots and pans hanging above the great black iron stove. "No marriage is easy, my dear daughter. I know that's trite. Most truisms are. Your mother and I had our adjustments before you were born. You married Bart expecting separations."

"Yes, and he led me to believe they were out of necessity. Apparently, that's not the case."

"To roam was his nature when he chose that profession, dear daughter."

"Father, what you say is true. It still hurts."

"I think it would be wise for you to encourage Bart to deal with the problem in Mexico, even though you'd prefer to have him with you. Possibly, for as long as the two of you live you may have to let him go every few weeks. That's not too much. He needs some worthwhile proj-ect, some success, some *raison d'être*. Now, Anne-Marie, he has nothing to do!"

"I hoped we could simply enjoy one another."

"Try to be understanding."

She swirled the last swallow of milk in her glass as she attempted to conceal her annoyance with her father's suggestion. Her gaze was fixed on her father's bony stork-like ankles as he spoke. Two pale yellowish sticks they were, emerging from his slippers under a robe and night-shirt. On his head a long pointed wool nightcap kept out the night drafts, the perilous vapors that had plagued men for centuries.

"He used to say that he hated going to sea, saying that it was a hard unnatural life. I don't want to be another Penelope, spinning and weaving by day and unraveling by night, Father."

"You won't, my dear. Penelope never grew up."

"Are you telling me that I haven't grown up, that our problems are my fault alone?" The words, though without rancor, came out stiffly.

A bony hand with gossamer thin skin gently patted her shoulder. "No, my dear. I wanted to alert you to Bart's injured pride. Pride is the essence of every man. I can only advise you to take store and make allowances."

In that moment with some discomfort she recognized her father as a truly loving man. Occasionally, he did offend her, but his grasp of her problems and his efforts to make her strong were gratifying and illuminating. He cared. Even so, she was saddened by his advice. Childishly she wished that she could crawl into his lap to weep and be comforted. Self-sufficiency would take some working on, she knew.

"You would have made a fine judge," she said, finally. "Thank you for your help."

Shuffling indistinct noises in the servants' quarters indicated that the cook would soon be setting the fire in the great cooking stove. The servants would breakfast first.

She rose. "I'm going back to bed, and I'll try to be more understanding."

Jason seemed relieved and did not bother to stifle a yawn. "Your mother has a big day planned tomorrow."

Still, Anne-Marie did not sleep. She felt boxed in by her family. Her own father had told her to let her husband go. A man must prove his manhood over and over again and his wife must let him, whatever the cost to her, he was urging, wasn't he? It did not occur to her that she wanted a husband to lean on, or that her father had told her that, too.

The big problem is as I see it, she told herself as she was drifting off to sleep, maybe that I'm too young and too rich.

*   *   *   *

At the last minute the trip to New York was almost cancelled as May was convinced that Whitney was born in delicate health and against all evidence, remained so.

"Whitney has a terrible cough," said May. "I'm frightened to leave him."

The valises stood waiting in the hall. Zipporah had—with infinite care—wrapped several changes of clothing in tissue paper, insuring her mistress an unmussed wardrobe. Even the toilet articles, dainty mother-of-pearl utensils securely cased in leather, assured a soignée appearance.

"Concepcion will be here, May. You need not worry. She's a born nurse." Still, it was with reluctance that May was persuaded to trust her older son to a foreigner.

"It's not as if his father weren't here to oversee things," added Emily.

In truth, it was the unacknowledged lure of discarded treasures from Uncle Elbert that overcame May's fears. Finally, the women were off for two nights with all the equipage and ceremony befitting a month's absence.

"Don't worry. I'll have plenty to do to keep me busy," said Bart.

"Leave the loading to Captain Sands," cautioned Anne-Marie, working her fingers into her gloves. "He knows exactly how my things should be stored. We're not trying to get the last sardine into the hold."

Bart laughed. In the end she had to undo her veil to kiss him, and then tuck in her hair again. "Miss me," she whispered. "Please…"

Indeed, the business of loading for two weeks at sea would present storage problems any first mate would have found formidable. The vessel was neither passenger nor freighter. On the contrary, her ship, newly outfitted to the latest specifications, was a large luxury first-class yacht. *Regina de los Girasoles* or *Queen of the Sunflowers* had been built for pleasure cruising not profit. Ease and comfort were the first considerations.

Anne-Marie's parting thrust had its effect. Bart, a licensed captain himself, did not interfere with Captain Sands' handling of the loading. Consequently, accompanied by Zipporah and the boxes of possessions, both personal and household items, he made several trips by carriage to the ship. From what Bart could see, there was no way to find fault. It presaged well for the coming trip to Key West, he mused.

As soon as the women returned from New York, the Ramsdens would set sail on the long voyage. Barring inclement weather and no problems, they would be underway about two weeks. The small crew was well trained. Further, it struck Bart that if Anne-Marie's personal staff were as solicitous and efficient as Zipporah, life would be rosy.

There were moments when Zipporah came close to exceeding the bounds of propriety and her position, but because of their apparently accidental nature, only a pleasant titillation held Bart. In removing an armful of clothes from her grip, it had been necessary to run his hand under her voluptuous bosom, and she hesitated before transferring the burden. Once in the turning of the carriage, she was thrown close to him, her suddenly sparkling face dangerously close to his. His good-natured laugh sealed the encounter as a playful trick of fate, but Bart's self-possession was shaken and she knew it.

"Do be careful, Squire," cautioned Zipporah primly. "Leave that heavy box for some husky sailor to lift. You might spoil your beautiful suit or hurt your back." Her admiration was evident.

Later, when the girl should have been tired, her continuing diligence surprised Bart.

"I'd like to see as much done as possible before Madame returns," she told him. "Especially, I want to see that your things are put away right while I have the chance. Otherwise, you may be neglected—and I don't want that."

Zipporah brightened a chore-filled day, and Bart was newly aware that she was remarkably pretty—so remarkably pretty that his eyes found difficulty leaving her. Walking back and forth from the carriage to the gangplank, she swayed in a curious subtle way. Even the surefooted sailors on sighting her seemed to him uncommonly unbalanced. While silently staring, their work stopped.

"Get moving," ordered Sands, cutting off the break. His fleeting glance to Bart met with understanding.

With three attractive women aboard, Bart was certain there would be more time spent ogling than working. Riding with Zipporah back in the carriage, he thought to caution the girl about dallying with sailors. Women on a ship always meant trouble, so God help them. But curiously, words failed him. Her bosom, which was slightly bared due to her exertion, looked fresh and full as two dewy melons, and the sight was pleasing enough to derail his thought of warning. Moreover, his years of experience with underlings precluded any familiarity, and Bart assumed his customary air of distancing himself with silence. An afternoon's flirtation notwithstanding, Zipporah could not have involved Bart in a liaison.

That night the men enjoyed a bachelor dinner followed by cheroots and several rounds of aged cognac. The conversation was easy man-talk, warm as lamb's wool and uncensored as insight.

Twice Concepcion interrupted to tell David that Whitney was coughing considerably and that she had given him medicine; then later that he was sleeping peacefully. However, when the men retired, David noted that Whitney was coughing again. "I'm afraid he'll disturb you, Bart. Your room is next to his. Why don't we switch rooms tonight so that I can hear him and take care of him if need be."

Considering David's parental concern, Bart readily agreed. "Do have a good night," he wished. "Call me if there's a serious problem."

"I'll feel at lot better with this arrangement," replied David prophetically. "Thank you."

Another dose of cough medicine quieted Whitney and within a few minutes the house was still.

David had hardly dosed off in Bart's bed when soft, hungry lips met his. The unexpected sleepy pleasure of this unusual attention from his wife registered and he almost spoke, but instead drew her into his embrace. Soon he recognized a different and softer body, curvaceous and sensuous yet of short stature. It could be none other than Anne-Marie's maid. Zipporah had paid him no mind, he knew. To Bart, on the other hand, he had jealously noted, she was most engaging. Grasping the present situation as one of mistaken identity, he quickly decided to capitalize on his good fortune and avoided giveaway sounds that might terminate the delicious adventure. He and Bart were about the same height and weight. The months in prison had softened Bart's normally harder, muscular build. Their hair, although differing in color, was worn at the same fashionable length. Both were lithe, slim-waisted, long-limbed, attractive to women, even in darkness.

Her soft, unbound flesh yielded warmly to his touch, bringing a pulsating rush of blood through his loins. As Zipporah lowered to his side, his body swelled to face her, making the quilts rise like a tent ready for a breath-taking theatrical performance. Drawing her close under the covers with him, his hands explored her body, relishing the nakedness, finding the hills and crevices with the satisfaction of a man discovering some beautiful hidden rich terrain. A sweet demanding ache of rising waters imposed a feverish need for release. Still, he feared a too early deliverance and bided his time, restraining his own need—growing more and more precious every minute. He stroked until her ardor rose to met his, her body begging for him. Unyielding to her summons, he held back, permitting the explosions in her body to burst and quiet. Once relieved of her incessant demands, more calmly he began again, certain of being able to contain himself. Slowly he entered her with long, deep, steady strokes, lifting his weight from her to maintain his own rhythmic motion unimpaired.

David was well aware of his body and the exception length of some of its parts. He had adapted his style of lovemaking to fully take advantage of his fortunate build. He had developed a style—tutored by more women than his wife could have dreamed possible. Consequently, he was a lover of consummate skill. David had learned the rewards of offering sexual satisfaction when there was little in his personality to warrant attention. Once he had made his way into a woman's bed, he was assured of as many encores and invitations as he chose. That he achieved this in a publicly unflirtatious manner, secured him against suspicion.

It was only when women showered him with gifts such as jeweled cufflinks, tiepins, rings and expensive scent, which he hid deeply under his socks or in a desk drawer, which were eventually found by May, that he had a problem. Then he had no recourse but to admit that he had bought the offending article himself. Of course, May believed him although she found it strange that he never wore these things.

Knowing that Zipporah had been satisfied, he continued his love-making with the challenge of rousing her again, and permitting himself a little more abandon. The tempo had its effect, and soon in a frenzy of desperation for both, it was over. Sapped and subdued for a time they lay as felled oaks and as silent. Supposing him asleep, Zipporah slipped from the bed, fumbled for her dressing gown and like a wraith vanished from the room.

For some minutes David lay contemplating the event. Zipporah and Bart had spent the day together, a prelude to the act. Obviously, Bart had not expected the visit, else he would not have so readily exchanged beds. Possibly this would have been the first time, or Zipporah would have noticed a different technique. For the first time in his life he felt like a voyeur or as if he had vicariously experienced the sexual act of others at the invitation of one of the partners. The women would be away for another night and it would be wise and pleasant to continue the hoax. That Zipporah was a horny little slut he had surmised already. With an untroubled conscience, he fell asleep.

True to the night's resolution, the following day David made himself a constant companion to Bart, a fact that surprised Bart. Had David approached the subject of a loan, he would have understood. David might also have had in mind a discussion on the Mexican project. Instead, as the day fairly beckoned for outdoor activity, David suggested that they hunt a few rabbits. So, for some hours they silently, together but apart, stalked the fields. The air was crisp and cool and the trees, as if to make up for lost time, were fast turning gold and red. Although they managed to scare a few rabbits, none even died of fright.

"I do much better on water," Bart allowed apologetically. "We should have gone fishing."

David thought that Bart would have done much better at home in his own bed, but he stifled the remark. Bart, an innocent, would not have got the significance of that smart opinion.

Dinner that evening was much the same as the night before. At Bart's request Jason had made inquiry into houses for sale on Cape May. Jason said that one house in particular would please Anne-Marie. "Mind you, I haven't seen it, but judging from the price, I can almost insure that she'll like it."

"I must say, I admire my sister's taste," said Francis.

"The house should be one that the whole family would enjoy, with all the modern conveniences, and the ocean, of course," Bart warned.

"This one would fill the bill. The owner apparently over-extended himself in building. Having fallen on hard times, he wants out," continued Jason.

"David, Francis and I can look at it tomorrow," said Bart. "And, if it's as handsome as you say—and my committee approves—I'd like to make Anne-Marie a present of it. This won't come from her funds."

Anne-Marie's wealth was beginning to appeal to Francis's feeling for the family. He was particularly pleased with the new carriage and a driver to man it, of course. Now a new summer home would come into the family and be suitably staffed to boot. Anne-Marie did things grandly. Fortunately, for him the Cape was famed for summertime's pretty girls. Many of his friends from Princeton also had summer mansions or 'cottages' as they called them and adorable little sisters to meet and woo. Cut off, living in the country, he had felt disadvantaged. But, word of his sister's wealth had spread and doors were beginning to open. He would not need the buxom Zipporah he had coveted and stalked the last few days.

Francis, a nice-enough-looking young man, was still immature and unsure of himself so that all of his expressions dissolved into a vast ineffectuality except in the company of his peers. Early on Zipporah had recognized him as a snob who, although he was not above grappling with her in the pantry or luring her to a neighbor's barn, she would never get out of the barnyard with Francis. He would only be one more talkative inexperienced lover on a college boy's allowance—for her a dead-end. She was out for bigger fish and time was of the essence. She would concentrate on Bart. Here was where the money was.

Zipporah had even considered Jason as a recipient for her charms. Older he was, and distinguished, and more importantly, prosperous. A decided twinkle in his eye showed promise, but a recognizable integrity in Jason marked him as no easy prey. Under a mantle of conviviality he was too shrewd. No, Zipporah needed a man who was lost, a man whom she could snare while he was in a moment of weakness. This she had known instinctively with peasant shrewdness well beyond her years. Calculating as she was, she was also the victim of her own flesh. Here was the one chink in her armor against 'unsuitables.'

Throughout the day, David could think of little but the expected encounter that night. He didn't want his son to remain ill, but he would have to insist on Bart's room and only at the last moment. He planned to lie, if necessary, about having to get up the night before, "Lord knows how many times." At every opportunity he questioned Whitney about how he was feeling, and, had the power of suggestion been effective, the boy would have been delirious.

David's intense, smothered excitement was impeccably contained by his middle-class Victorian manners. He knew vaguely that he often said the wrong thing. Bart particularly had seemed to treat him with coolly polite disdain, unwarranted, he felt, and so, in his opinion only reflected Bart's arrogance. But, Bart had changed in the last few years.

His aggressive, swashbuckling manner had dwindled, perhaps due to imprisonment. The experience would take a lot out of a man, David reckoned. Possibly the fact that his wife slept in a separate bedroom indicated a breach disguised as friendship and only maintained while visiting her parents. If this were true, Bart would, indeed, be shaken.

Jason had told the family in utmost confidence—and only for their own good—that Anne-Marie was the richest woman in the state of New Jersey, and certainly Florida, and possibly the second richest woman in the country. "A good many unsavory characters will be creeping out of the woodwork wanting to be friends of the family. Worse, it is not inconceivable that a family member could be taken and held as hostage," Jason warned. "So, always be careful of what you say and to whom."

The money had enhanced the self-confidence of them all, but none so little as Bart. He was less sure of himself. It seemed to David that Zipporah's presence in Bart's bed was one more indication of withered self-esteem. After all, she was the kind of beauty that money can buy. Consequently, in a confused and excited state—studiously concealed—David survived the day. Again, it was late when the men finally retired.

"If you don't mind, Bart, I think we should continue the sleeping arrangements until the women get back. Whitney seems a little better, but he obviously misses his mother at night. I wouldn't want him to disturb you."

"It would hardly be an imposition," Bart replied honestly and generously. "You know, I'm very fond of both your boys."

"That's kind of you, but I know how annoying other people's children can be sometimes," insisted David. "Remember May's law: If children are going to be sick, it will happen during the night." The request left no room for refusal even had Bart minded.

"Have a good night then, David. Let's hope Whitney will be well tomorrow," Bart replied gathering his nightshirt to move to David and May's room.

Sleep eluded David. For hours he tossed and turned, listening for the slightest sound in the room. Occasionally Whitney coughed, but David dared not respond and appear in the hall on the off chance that he would come face to face with Zipporah and be recognized. There were moments in which he raged at women in general, his anger making sleep even more unlikely. Finally, slightly before dawn he dosed off. When he fully awakened, he realized that household duties now claimed the girl and she would not visit his room. Zipporah was staying away simply to tease, he told himself. Recognizing her little game, he kicked himself for allowing himself to become a victim.

The more David thought about it, the angrier he became. One way or another, he would get revenge.

A most pleasant day followed in which David was adequately diverted by a trip to Cape May. Bart liked the house. He, May and the children would also enjoy a summer place as guests of the Ramsdens. Emily would particularly enjoy the change and the social life afforded by the resort. The happiness of his in-laws at no trouble to himself pleased David mightily.

By the time the men returned, a telegram had arrived postponing the women's return for one more night. All three gentlemen put their seal of approval on the property Jason had found. Bart asked Jason to proceed with the negotiations and purchase. The decision made dinner a festive occasion.

"I promise you, Anne-Marie will be surprised," said Bart, looking vastly pleased with himself. "I would appreciate it if you do not mention the house until I have a chance to tell her of it."

"Of course," they chorused.

David capitalized on his lack of sleep, not bothering to disguise his yawns and dragging limbs. "I certainly was glad we exchanged beds last night. Children can play happily all day, but the minute a parent's head hits the pillow, the illness either starts or becomes acute."

"Amazing how a fresh snow fall can bring out a short-lived fever," added Francis with a smile.

There was no discussion about the sleeping arrangements. Exhausted from the lack of sleep the night before and uncertain whether or not Zipporah would appear, David soon fell asleep.

So it was without the shellac of anticipation that he felt a hand on his foot, working its way along his body, gently yet tensely guiding a bent figure toward a goal. A ghostly swath of fabric fluttered in the darkness and fell to the floor. Sleepily David threw aside the covers giving one naked form access to another. For a few minutes he relished the excitement roused by her practiced manipulations. Then pulling her face to his, he became the aggressor in control of his own field, that of lovemaking. The previous encounter insured her ready acquiescence. Some men, he knew, thought only of their own pleasure, missing—after the opening act—the main body of the play, being only interested in the ending. David liked a play with a long run; his theater was the bed.

There were moments when he yearned to speak to excite her further, but forbore, fearful that his voice would betray his identity. However, she needed no speech to incite her to ecstasy; already she was enraptured in uncontrollable quivering emotion.

Sure of his craft, he made her work for what she got. Downstairs in the hall the grandfather clock chimed the hour and once Whitney, talking in his sleep, brought them to a halt until the house was still again. Reassured they continued until they reached a thundering climax.

The two encounters with Zipporah had been enormously satisfying. Not only was Zipporah young, energetic, and well tutored, but she had been stolen from Bart. Afterward, she did not so quickly leave, but rested silently curled beside him, her breath steadying to measured drafts. Now satisfied, David remembered his earlier resentment over her failure to appear on the previous sleepless night. For a moment he considered taking her again, but it had been a while since he had heard the chiming of the clock. Considering the hour, he decided she should be taught a lesson, but he preferred one that would not involve him. He would have to act fast—now—as the women would be back today. The following day the Ramsdens and their household would be off to Key West. Changing the timber of his voice to imitate Bart, assuming at the same time a tone of disgust, low and vibrating, he rasped, "Get out!"

A shocked silence followed. There was no need to repeat the words. Zipporah leaped up and with the nervous rustling of a garment retrieved from the floor, fled the room. Telling himself that it had been a neat trick, David almost laughed aloud. The real fun would come in the morning when he could observe Zipporah's reaction to Bart's simple presence. There was certain to be a change in her attitude and doubtless Bart would notice and be baffled. Rolling over, he was soon fast asleep.

David was the first up and managed to disturb Bart by entering his and May's room on the pretext of getting an article of clothing.

"I'm sorry I disturbed you," said David, still fumbling with the drawer. "I was trying to be quiet."

"No matter. I should probably get up anyway. There's still work to be done loading, and we lost yesterday."

"I'll be glad to help," replied David, now set on a course again adhering to Bart's side.

Sleepily Bart made his way back to his own room to wash and shave. David soon followed wanting to be on hand when Zipporah appeared.

"Say," said David, entering. "Not long ago I remember reading in the papers about an archaeologist who used a camera obscura in Mexico and was looking for backers for further exploration. I realize this is not your interest particularly, but there may be helpful information on the side."

Bart's reply was interrupted by Zipporah's arrival, a pitcher of warm water at hand.

Bart's warm "Good morning," to Zipporah elicited only an icy low echo from her and a rear view of her disappearing back, starchly upright.

"I guess she got up on the wrong side of the bed," commented Bart obviously surprised.

Silently David corrected, "No. Wrong bed." Aloud he offered, "We can talk about the newspaper article at breakfast."

As soon as Bart sat down for breakfast, David continued. "Seriously, I don't mind giving you a hand today, and, by the way, we might try to find some Mexican maps and other material on Mexico."

David's interest pleased and intrigued Bart. "That's really what I would like to be doing, and there might not be much time. Let's go," Bart replied.

After a productive day in the bookstores of Atlantic City and the ship chandler's houses, David and Bart returned to find the women at home. They had had a capital time, they agreed. Anne-Marie had enjoyed planning her uncle's apartment for him, overseeing the placement of furniture, selecting paint colors, and talking with the upholsterers. Uncle had been delighted with the attention and results—despite the cost of Anne-Marie's taste. She had made some purchases for the house in Key West, too, unobtainable there. Silk flowers from France and some of the latest kitchen gadgets had caught her eye.

"May came out like a bandit," laughed Anne-Marie.

May had to agree, "You'll like everything, David," she promised. "And, Concepcion says Whitney's cough is better."

"He coughed at night, but that's to be expected with his mother away," he rebuked, anxious to move to another subject. "I like your dress."

"So do I. It's a farewell present from Anne-Marie. And, wait until you see some of the sweet old jewelry Uncle Elbert gave me. Of course, he held back for some of the rest of the family, which will include Francis's bride—providing some girl will have him."

Francis took the jibe good-naturedly.

"Would you believe David has more jewelry than I do," remarked May, turning to Anne-Marie. Then, turning back to David, she whispered,

"Guess what the large stores in New York are selling? You can't…Women's underwear! Imagine! Laid on counters."

"May was glad she went, David. And you should be, too," said Emily.

Indeed, he was.

Later that evening when the Doyles were not present, Bart again introduced the subject to Mexico. "I bought some books today on Mexico to study and on mining as well, particularly in Germany, in the eventuality that it might prove wise to make a trip there." He looked to Anne-Marie for a reaction.

She took the news calmly, not raising an eyebrow, and he wondered if her opposition was dwindling.

They were sitting in the parlor with Jason. Jason's driver had just finished banking the fire in the great fireplace, so the room was warm and cozy.

"If such a trip were necessary, would you think of taking David along?" Jason asked. "I don't know what good he could be other than another body, but that can be useful in a foreign country."

"Father Frazier, if I thought that David could be of any use to Anne-Marie or me, apart from our satisfaction in a charity to him, we would take him. But, it cannot be in any demeaning way."

Bart could not tell Jason what he really felt—David would be more of a hindrance than a help. Still, he could understand Jason's need to help May by helping David and this prompted him to add, "Don't think we won't keep David in mind."

That night Bart and Anne-Marie made love tenderly. He made her forget in a strange hinterland between joy and ecstasy that he might leave her again despite her wishes, with no economic necessity as an excuse. But afterward, she was tired, too tired for apprehension over her vagrant soldier-of-fortune that now he seemed destined to be. Sleepily it occurred to her that too much freedom could also form a prison of its own, and she just might let him learn that, if only to hold him.

"I hope you endorsed what I said about David tonight," murmured Bart.

"I don't think it matters."

"Are we having an argument?"

"No, I'm having an observation," replied Anne-Marie, still sleepy.

Bart did not reply. It seemed to him that sometimes it is easier to say soothing things to a stranger than to a woman one has known for years and years so that certain kinds of sentiment are false, no matter how much one is loved. Little by little he was coming to the realization that he was married to a powerful woman who could not be fooled by pretty words.

In truth, Anne-Marie was beginning to see that Bart's strange tendency to discontent, which he labored under, had nothing to do with his love for her, but it did contribute to a restlessness that ruled him.

In the darkness Bart moved to his own bed.

Meanwhile downstairs in one of the small servants' rooms, a woman silently raged with hatred for Anne-Marie's husband and a spillage toward Anne-Marie based on envy. Had Anne-Marie known, she would have fired the woman instantly so that she would never have to come within miles of her, much less to board the same ship with her.

Chapter Four

"If you don't want to shove off in a snowstorm, I suggest we vamoose," said Bart. There was more than a hint in the air that the earth was heading toward other weather; the late Indian summer was gone.

Anne-Marie did not anticipate an easy voyage; they were short of hands; there was a child aboard; the winter had set in abruptly. Bundled as for an arctic expedition, they boarded *Los Girasoles.*

One hundred forty-four feet of ship under square rigging demanded a large crew, but understandably Captain Sands wanted to man his ship with home-based Key Westers. Bart concurred, although he confided to Anne-Marie, "It is the sort of thing I that I would do myself, but there is some risk involved. Those extra men are around for a purpose."

"I see no problem with a skeleton crew if we're careful," said Sands, ship-proud and beaming like a boy with a new toy. The ship fairly shone with newness. There was no painting to be done, no rust to hammer, no torn sails to mend. Perforce, the crew would have to stand more watches, but better food, pay and space would compensate. The crew's quarters on a ship were usually crowded; lives mixed into a human tossed salad where every whisper, cough or expulsion of wind could be overheard by all. This voyage would be different.

One additional consideration set Anne-Marie on edge. *Los Girasoles* was her ship and her husband, a sea captain, would not be in command. He was arbitrarily an owner, but Captain Sands was the responsible ruler once they were at sea. Bart would undoubtedly adjust to the shift in roles. Certainly, he knew maritime law. After ordering *Los Girasoles*, Anne-Marie had hired Sands feeling that he was one of the best captains in the business. After years at sea, Sands was ready for a non-competitive ship. Bart knew Sands' reputation, but they had never sailed together.

Good-byes were short, yet familial embraces brought a spate of tears as the Ramsdens took leave of the Fraziers and Doyles. Anne-Marie felt the crush of her mother's silent fear that a long separation meant she might never see her daughter again. Finally, they were underway and soon the white handkerchiefs, little wet waving flags, disappeared from view. Anne-Marie wearily put Samantha down on the child's own feet. Then she reached for her again, clasping her to her bosom, as if clinging tightly to this Samantha insured the child's safety and her own mental well being.

"I'll take her," offered Bart, lifting Samantha from her.

"Young lady, may I have this dance?" He smiled down at the child while making a waltz step. Samantha was not tall enough to see over the bulkhead, and the brief dance transformed her surprised expression into a smile.

All eyes now followed the shoreline, a sparsely settled receding band of green.

"I hope you notice a few of the rivers we will soon pass, including the Delaware and Chesapeake," said Bart to his wife, seemingly to repress a laugh.

"And why do you say that?" She looked puzzled.

"Because you once told me that the Great Egg River and the Middle River came together to form the Atlantic Ocean—and I almost believed you."

"I must have been a five-year-old," laughed Anne-Marie, grateful for a break in the sadness of her departure.

Propelled by a good northerly, they sailed along the South Jersey coast to Cape May. "Do you see that large white house on the ocean?" asked Bart, pointing to the most prestigious residence on the coast.

"Yes. Why do you mention it?"

"Because it is yours."

"What do you mean, it's mine?" A quizzical smile curled on her lips while mild disbelief danced in her eyes.

"I bought and paid for it for you yesterday," replied Bart, shyly containing his pleasure.

She turned facing him, a beautiful sight, drinking in the delight of the moment. Then she turned back to the house, "I can see. It's beautiful. Perfect!" Moving to Bart, she stretched her arms to embrace him, drawing his head down to hers, ignoring others about the ship, she tenderly kissed him. Then, feeling he might be embarrassed, she pulled away. "A house coming from you means a lot," she murmured, crowded with emotion.

With that she turned to see Zipporah, standing on the forecastle deck, gripping the forestay, glowering at them. Her maid, less than composed? Why? The stare, loaded with hatred, was immediately erased, but Anne-Marie knew she had caught the girl in an unguarded moment and that something sinister had been revealed. It was frightening, so much so that she was ready to ask Captain Sands to put into the nearest port to put Zipporah off.

"What's the matter? Have you changed your mind about the house? You don't act as if you liked surprises." Disappointment crowded his face.

"Oh, it's not that at all," she replied turning to Bart. "I just caught a frightful expression on Zipporah's face as she saw us embrace—as if she hates us. She is evil."

"She's been in an awful mood. Something has upset her. I noticed it while you were in New York. Certainly, it's been nothing we've done."

"I'd like to have her put ashore."

Bart, not having caught the expression himself, did not take her seriously. "She probably was glaring at some fresh sailor."

His observation was quieting, but she resolved to get to the truth of the matter. She would have a talk with the girl to find out what was wrong. The episode, however brief, brought back memories of another tragic voyage. Anne-Marie's life had been steeped in takes of the sea; and the tales remembered were never happy ones. There was to be no enmity on this voyage if it were in her power to stop it—regardless of the time lost.

"Zipporah, please come to my cabin and do my hair," said Anne-Marie. "The wind on deck has made a sight of me, I'm sure." Zipporah was quick to comply.

Seating herself at the dressing table, clutching her silver hand mirror as if it were a weapon, Anne-Marie addressed the maid. "Zipporah, are you unhappy working for us?"

"No, Ma'am," replied the girl nervously.

"I saw a most unpleasant expression on your face as you looked at us on deck."

"It could not have had anything to do with you, Ma'am," avowed Zipporah, her eyes wide with apprehension. "I hope my work has been satisfactory."

Clearly, Zipoporah did not want her job terminated.

"Could it have had anything to do with my husband?" pressed Anne-Marie, her face unsoftened, hard as plaque, now looking straight at Zipporah.

"No, Ma'am," lied Zipporah quickly, anchoring several hairpins between her lips, so that Anne-Marie wondered if she were stalling for time. Finally, when the pins were in place, Zipporah elaborated more fully. "I've had one or two bad times. Sometimes I remember them, forgetting where I am."

Although slow in forth coming, the explanation seemed highly plausible to Anne-Marie. Surely recurring fears had marred her own face. "Would you care to talk about them?" Her voice was now filtered of all anger.

"No, Ma'am," said Zipporah, putting an abrupt end to the conversation.

Mildly satisfied, Anne-Marie let it go. She did not know the girl well, hardly long enough to establish a confidential relationship, and she was surely entitled to some personal feelings. She had tried to offer her help, perhaps prematurely, and it was rejected. Zipporah will bear watching, thought Anne-Marie, ostensibly examining her coiffure in the hand mirror, but actually focusing on the self-conscious servant.

*   *   *   *

Eighty feet up, a sailor gently swayed atop the royal yard. From the dizzying roost came the call, "Whales ahoy."

Clutching Samantha and Bart's hands, Anne-Marie hurried on deck.

Tinges of aquamarine in the gray-blue waters marked a pod of humpbacks. "They're a bit early this year," announced Sands to those gathered on deck. "Every year they swim two thousand miles from Newfoundland to the island of Hispaniola—divided into Haiti and Santo Domingo—where they breed. A year later they return to the same area to give birth. They feed in Newfoundland during the summer."

"Look at their size, Samantha," urged Bart, holding the girl high. "The whales are playing like pups."

"When they breach water, four to five tons of just one whale makes quite a splash. If we were drifting they would come a lot closer just out of curiosity," explained Sands to Anne-Marie, "But, we are moving too fast. It is quite a thing to watch their lobtailing somersaulting dance. The humpbacks are the most graceful animals in all of whaledom. I am fascinated by them."

"I've seen blue whales over ninety feet long," added Bart. "That's four times as big as the largest dinosaur that ever lived."

"I'm impressed," said Anne-Marie, taking over Samantha. "Come. I'll take you inside where it is warmer and tell you some stories about whales." She was thinking about the indomitable leviathan of Job; the whale that swallowed Jonah; and the giant mammal that doomed Captain Ahab. Making their way to the salon Anne-Marie realized that she was not wholly comfortable on deck, and no wonder, she thought. At the same time she hated sitting in the cabin missing the panorama outside. So, she must grit her teeth and relearn her love of the sea.

Her anxiety regarding Bart and Captain Sands she saw was needless. The two men spent much time exchanging notes as to weather, courses, other times and other ships. Quickly, they were cronies, happily trading stories about other salty sons of the sea and none of it lost any fat in the telling, they guiltily admitted.

Sands, in his late fifties, had captained a number of sailing ships, but he never mentioned unpleasant owners by name. With Bart, he was always ready to discuss design; and he shared Bart's interest over the advance of steamships over sail. Sands' ruddy face and gnarled hands reflected years of experience. A good many human foibles, stemming from as many stresses, had sharpened his discretion.

The Gulf Stream, the giant ocean river, emerges from some hidden womb in the South Atlantic; sweeps through the Caribbean between Cuba and the Yucatan Peninsula; tightened, seethes its way northward between Cuba and Florida in the Florida Straits; then finally surges onward north and east, widely past the long Atlantic seaboard, past Ireland and Scotland to disappear under floes of ice. For those traveling southbound off the U.S. coast, the force of the great northbound Gulf can nullify the winter's north wind, forcing traffic to hug the rocky shore, letting the ocean river sluice by on the port side. Under sail it is often a perilous course, especially where the coastline juts close to the stream, leaving only a narrow passage in which maneuverability is severely reduced. The worst of these passages, off stormy Cape Hatteras, justly earned a reputation as the 'graveyard for ships.' Once past the choppy waters at the mouth of the Chesapeake, the die for Hatteras was cast. From then on it was a straight run without refuge until the grave-yard was rounded or received another carcass.

Throughout the day the ocean was calm and the sky clear. *Los Girasoles* plowed placidly along, nautical miles slipping behind her glistening hull with regularity and persistence. It was on the third night out that *Los Girasoles* began to roll, waking Bart out of a sleep. He pulled on trousers and a mackintosh, and careening made his way top-side, wondering whether the last roll had been as steep as it seemed or had he been dreaming?

If so, he was no longer dreaming. On deck his fears were confirmed. They were in an incipient gale, soon stiff enough to whine through the lines, while black menacing seas mounted in the sky, shrouded from view by a blanket of darkness.

Sands himself was at the wheel. "The barometer is dropping, sir. I think we're in for a rough time of it."

Bart moved toward the bulwark and looked down at the sea. In the next moment he had to cling to it with all his strength to keep from toppling backward as the ship careened back and forth.

"She's riding well, Sands, but Christ, this is one helluva storm," shouted Bart, wondering if the women below had been tossed out of their berths. He guessed that they had been, and would be now on mattresses that had slipped from the bunks. They were in the safest part of the ship, and in any event, there was little that could be done for them. By now the forecastle remained inches deep in water. Water came boiling down the deck, finally sloshing over the side. The compass swung erratically.

"I'll be happy to see the light of day," grunted Sands. Bart shared the sentiment. He noticed that Sands had long since stowed the kites and shortened the sails down. In view of the reduced crew such foresight was necessary. There was little to do other than fight the wheel to hold her steady in a macabre dance with the wind. Often Bart had thought of a storm at sea as a riotous, exhausting ballet with nature. Measures with precise timing were called for in a lead-and-follow set of routines in which the rhythm of everything that happened was important. The wind and the sea always led, the ship followed. The roles were never reversed. Now Bart held his breath as *Los Girasoles* shuddered for several seconds on the crest of a long swell and then dropped into a deep trough. That drop would surely have shaken up the women, thought Bart, hoping devoutly that no one had been hurt. They were in extremely bad weather. It was all hands then with a vengeance. Within seconds sailors scrambled to carry out Sands' orders, "Down with the fore and main topgallants—and the spanker!" Still, both Sands and Bart knew the wind was capable of snapping off a mast as easily as a man's fingers could break a match.

"I'll be glad to take the wheel and relieve you," offered Bart, shouting. "You've surely stood a long watch."

"I'm fine," Sands assured him.

The reply was gallant, but hardly true, and Bart knew it. He had no idea how long the older gentleman had been at the wheel. Surely by now seeping, trickling, gelid water pressed by the wind had reached his bones. Bart himself felt frozen.

"Perhaps you should see that the Missus is all right. She and the other women may be frightened out of their minds," said Sands.

For a moment Bart was aghast at being relegated to checking out womenfolk while his concern encompassed not only the women but the ship itself and all hands.

Still, he knew his position aboard: Sands was the captain. Slowly he started to the deck, noticing that it was slanting steeply starboard, so steeply that he could not stand on it. Then, to his horror, he realized that this was not just as roll, the deck remained slanted.

Slowly the deck leveled again. Swallowing chagrin, Bart made his way below.

In the main salon, chairs and tables had piled against the bulkhead in a mountainous tangle. As Bart rushed to make his way through, they started sliding again, crashing to the other side. Cupboards had broken open, and their contents pitched about the deck. As the ship again came upright, he dashed for the master quarters. There in nightclothes Anne-Marie, Zipporah, and Concepcion clutching Samantha, on the floor on mattresses, braced themselves as best they could. In the faint gray light of dawn, only white figures were visible. Fabrics flapped and all hands scrabbled wildly for a firmer grip on anything firmly attached in a toppling world paneled in mahogany.

"My God, Bart," said Anne-Marie, "Will we survive this?"

"Of course, it's nothing but a storm at sea. You'll be all right. It'll soon be over." Unable to do anything for them, he hurried from the cabin, hearing only the wailing of the servants.

Once more the deck heaved and fell to starboard, and before Bart knew what was happening, he had tumbled through the air. Regaining the deck and his balance, and thankful that nothing seemed broken, he continued his way toward the main deck. There an unbelievably huge black wave loomed high over the ship and then came smashing down so that the ship careened heavily to port and began sideslipping over the swells, breaching to, and then straightening out again.

"It sounds like an insane asylum below, but the women are all right," reported Bart, screaming to make himself heard over the howling, shrieking wind.

Bracing himself as best he could, Bart stood watching the captain and soon found himself mesmerized. The captain, locked into position, was simply not reacting or perhaps he was responding so slowly that the effect was the same. The ship yawed shakily back and forth, and suddenly it occurred to Bart that the captain might have been scared out of his wits. *Los Girasoles* was a brand new ship, and Sands had not had time to learn the way she would behave in a gale. A short shakedown cruise under ideal conditions was hardly more than a polite 'How do you do?' with no reply expected. *Los Girasoles* was beautifully built, well designed, and supersensitive to a turn of the wheel. Very possibly she was balking under Sands' heavy handling.

"Christ Almighty!" cried Bart. "Let her ride a little looser!"

"It's…It's…It's hard to tell about a new ship," stammered Sands, collapsing.

Supporting Sands and grabbing the wheel Bart cried for hands who swiftly got Sands below. They no sooner disappeared than a monster wave came crashing down upon them so that nothing but white spray was visible. Jesus, thought Bart, I don't give a damn how she rolls, just keep us off those God damned rocks! To hell with a southerly course. We need to ride this mother out even if she takes us to China.

Butting, plunging, and then slipping, *Los Girasoles* was riding free again while the wind screamed and whined: a cold white foam, silvery in the morning light churned around Bart.

Suddenly, the sky opened up and in the distance the lighthouse beacon to the larboard, right where she should be, spelled out the perilous point, dimly but clearly.

A tidy battle had been won, but not the war. Bart and the crew knew that they could still end up at the bottom of the sea. Then the wind suddenly changed, solid and dreadful and the ship wore round; the rain poured; both binnacle lights blew out. The ship would not pay off. Bart had to get the ship before the wind again since it was now blowing directly on the masts and yards from ahead of them, and they were not stayed to take the strain from this direction.

Calling again for hands, Bart ordered: "Square the mizzen yards. Leave the fore and main aback." With this done, she canted herself without the helm, although the spray broke heavily about her. Then Bart canted her around until the afteryards filled, backing her into the wind so that he could regain control. For a moment she hung, then she began to gather headway. It seemed like a long time, but she came.

"She seems to know what's expected of her," said Bart to a mate nearby. With the after-sails filled, Bart could use the helm and run before the wind. The masts stood while they ran and ran and ran. "We're going to get out of this if it takes us to Africa," he joked.

In due time Bart was able to correct their course and at the same time review Sands' role. Capable and experienced as he was, he had stood a watch too long considering his age. Incredibly, considering the strength of the gale and the shortage of hands, they suffered little damage either to sails or to rigging, due chiefly to Sands' expertise. Now, worried about the captain and judging it safe to relinquish the wheel, Bart went below.

"How are you, sir?" asked Bart, entering the captain's cabin and seeing Sands awake.

"I'm going to make it, Bart. It's the old heart…She gave out on me."

"We're out of trouble, if you are, Captain," Bart replied. "Rest quietly. I'm going to check the women. The ship is in good shape."

Bart made his way to face the shaken women, knowing his long absence was blameworthy in their minds. He found then all sitting on the floor. "I'm sorry I've had to neglect you. You'd better stay right where you are until we hit smoother water. Sands collapsed, which will keep me busy for a while, but he should be all right."

"I've been so frightened that you'd be washed overboard," cried Anne-Marie, her eyes still distraught.

"I already have a rich mermaid," he joked departing.

Once again he checked on Sands who had taken his medicine and was now warmly wrapped in blankets. Ordering a sailor to stay with the captain and report any change in his condition, Bart returned to the wheel. In the early morning hour with a wind that still whistled through the lines, he felt a strange exhilaration. With skill and perseverance they had survived a deadly thrust of nature, ton for ton coming down on them, that by all rights should have pounded them to the bottom. Possibly two things had saved them: Sands' caution early on in getting the sails down, and later his own handling of the ship. He felt rightfully proud of himself and it was a good feeling. Now visibility had improved so that more than the sea was in sight. A bright light to the east was the sun. A sweet pain in his throat was one of joy that they were all alive. Shortly after, a long, dark, shape, hairy with weed, bobbed on swells some fifty yards to the port. Waves were breaking over it in showers of foam. Bart veered, for a moment thinking that it was a whale and wondering why it did not submerge. Then he realized that it was the bottom of a ship—and a big one at that. He and a mate stared in horror. Immediately he sent a sailor aloft in a harness with binoculars to look for survivors, but none were to be seen. It was a painful sobering experience. Bart mopped a stream of cold rain from his drawn and whiskery face. Peaks and troughs of water veiled by spray soon screened the remains of their shocked view. They needed now to concentrate on their own safety, still not assured. Gale gusts and high waters were to continue for the next few hours until finally safety seemed certain. *Los Girasoles* had turned out to be a sweet ship and out of respect Bart's secret, non-verbalized resentment toward her had died. Finally he felt secure in turning the ship over to a mate, and fearing exhaustion in himself, went below. Sailors, Concepcion and Zipporah had restored some order. Anne-Marie had taken over the care of Samantha, dispelling the child's fears as best she could. Taking Anne-Marie's chin in his hand, he placed a tender kiss on her lips.

"I'm sorry you had a difficult time," he murmured, then, "I need some sleep."

Anne-Marie gathered breath and pushed Bart into a bunk. Then covering him with a blanket, a meaningful gesture that he might know he was loved, she and Samantha left the stateroom.

On the deck the sun shone brightly. Bathed and swept clean, the ship glistened. Anne-Marie breathed deeply, marveling at the different world that now surrounded them.

Instead of blackness and perilous winds, light and power seemed to sweep along in harmony. Billowing clouds and bouffant sails, gleaming in their whiteness behind the delicate tracery of lines and stays, punctuated blue sky and deeper vibrant ocean. It was hard to see in the light of the sun and harder not to look.

Anne-Marie reached for Samantha, lifting her so she could see the great stretch of water. "Sometimes it is very rough at sea, but we really weren't in danger in our cabin. Concepcion and Zipporah are frightened of the sea, and of the Lord, and of the Devil, and of horses, dogs, witches, strangers, insects, darkness, and everything new. But we are certain of the people who are looking out for us. We don't have to be afraid. We are much happier when we know that."

Without whales Samantha was unimpressed. "I'd better go see about my dolls."

"Concepcion and Zipporah will see to them."

"Zipporah won't. She's mean," said Samantha.

Anne-Marie allowed the child to slip down to the deck. "I can't believe that." Mild disapproval colored her tone.

"She's always mean unless you're around. She's not even nice to Concepcion."

"Perhaps she doesn't feel well. A lot of people feel queasy on a ship."

"No, she's always mean."

"Are you sure you and Concepcion have not founded a little club, speaking Spanish, which she doesn't understand, so that she feels left out?"

"We didn't used to," replied Samantha, matter-of-factly.

Anne-Marie surveyed her daughter. Twenty-four hours in the day she was supervised. Samantha had a reserve, peculiar to children who have learned early not to laugh or cry with abandon, but to be content with a regime that kept them always occupied pleasantly or constructively. She was destined to be over-protected, but she could be taught to think.

They checked the dolls. Even those with beautiful porcelain bisque heads had survived the storm. "Well," said Samantha, "I hope they learned something."

Suppressing a smile, Anne-Marie turned Samantha over to Concepcion and thankfully returned to her stateroom. The hours of struggling to retain balance in the darkness, while being rudely tossed about, took their toll in aching muscles and bruises. Now that the excitement was over, her exhaustion was complete. Seeking comfort, she stretched out on her bunk, but found it illusive. A rising uneasiness over Zipporah added to her unrest.

Her staff, except for Zipporah, had been well trained. They valued their jobs and worked well together, uncomplaining. She hired Zipporah, a stranger to the town without recommendation, both out of compassion for the homeless girl and the knowledge that trained help was hard to come by among the proud, independent Key Westers. Apparently, she had made a mistake. The girl was disturbing. To dismiss her with an unscheduled stop at Charleston or Jacksonville would be costly in time. Bart would disapprove. Besides, children were often grossly unfair. The girl could have been fighting seasickness, homesickness, anything. Finally, she slept. When she awoke a rosy late afternoon sun streamed through the portholes so that the deep mahogany red paneling reflected two glowing balls of fire. Bart stretched languidly and beckoned for her to join him.

"My, you're all dressed aren't you?" he murmured, sleepily feeling the silk fabric.

"I stretched out for a minute and lost a whole afternoon."

"Take those things off. You'll dress for dinner anyway," he whispered, fumbling with her buttons.

Standing, Anne-Marie undid the ribbons which held her hair, then tossed her head so that the lustrous waves cascaded to her shoulders in a russet tumble of soft, warm, swirling light. She began to unbutton her blouse herself, turning slightly away and only gradually exposing her breasts. They were firm and round with nipples drawn tight by the cool air. She knew instinctively that the ritual of undressing was an important aspect of making love. Suspensefully and deliberately she let her clothing fall to a heap on the deck, savoring the childlike carelessness. Then, slipping into the space Bart provided, cozy and warm, she thrust her hips against him. "You haven't left me much space," she scolded good-naturedly.

"You have plenty of space. We're not kangaroos."

"Do kangaroos need a lot of room?"

"I guess so. They jump around a lot. But, I've never taken a kangaroo to bed," he replied, relishing the pleasant close contact, drawing out the thrill of anticipation now that he was certain of the greater intimacy to come.

"Oh. I thought you could tell me about it," she teased.

"No, you'd better talk to another kangaroo."

He kissed her to stop the silly talk, and in the closeness of the little room, the smell of her perfume and the warm softness of her body set him aflame. They made love.

For Bart, making love to Anne-Marie was unlike loving any other woman. It had always been so from the day they were married. She could always command from him, beyond the overwhelming sensations which rushed through him like liquid fire, a part of his soul. She could wind him, like the mainspring of a clock, into rapture like none other. At the same time, he knew that had he loved her less, he would have been a better lover.

They gathered strength to dress.

Not wanting to be in her way, Bart let her dress first. He stuck to his bunk, quietly watching her as she moved about the cabin. Leisurely, she selected a green velvet gown to wear for dinner. Then she sat down with her back to him so that he could hook her up.

"I'm not very good at this," he said.

"You're good at everything you do—making love, sailing ships…"

"The light is almost gone."

A chord of delight struck inside of her, drawn by the closeness and warmth of the present mingling with the supercharged remnants of the last hour. How much she loved this difficult man, she mused. He could never guess.

"I cannot fault your sense of touch," she said, smiling and tickling his ribs with two errant fingers. Playfully fearing retaliation by being tickled in return, she jumped to her feet and swept open the door as if to flee the cabin. There, in the companionway, a lamp in hand like some uncharted beacon, crouched Zipporah.

The girl was so near the door it seemed to Anne-Marie that she fairly fell into the room with the illumination.

"What are you doing here?" asked Anne-Marie, shocked.

"I was…. just about to knock, Madame…I knew you would be needing a lamp," stammered the girl, paling before the onslaught of her mistress.

"I'm aghast!" cried Anne-Marie, her eyes now flashing with anger.

Placing the lamp in its bracket, the girl rushed from the cabin.

Turning to Bart who still lay naked in bed but covered, Anne-Marie voiced her indignation. "That woman has to go! I'm not going to put up with eavesdropping. The nerve! Find some way to get her off this ship before I throw her overboard."

Bart could not help laughing. "I'm not arguing with you, but calm down. Possibly she was putting her ear to the door to learn if we were awake before knocking. Her timing was unfortunate. I think you scared her silly."

"She scared me—looming in the doorway like a ghost! I don't like her, Bart. I won't put her off this ship because it would be too much trouble, but her days with us are numbered."

"She's your maid, so you're the one to decide, but I wouldn't be too hasty."

Zipporah's later explanation was just as Bart had surmised. "Ma'am, I know it looked terrible," cried the red-faced girl, now wringing her hands. "But I had just put my ear to the door, listening for voices to learn if you were awake. I felt you would need a light if you were. It was past time for you to dress. The cook was distressed over holding dinner…"

Reluctantly, Anne-Marie accepted the apology, at the same time real-izing that she was swayed by Bart and the girl's tears. "I'll let it go this time, but you might as well know that you're skating on thin ice with me, young woman!"

Later, as Anne-Marie reconstructed the incident, she realized that several aspects disturbed her, and lingered to disturb her more: She had forgotten the glower on the girl's face the day of the departure—and this time there were no other people around who might have drawn her fire except herself and Bart; Samantha did not like her; and, for an instant there had been a malicious expression on the girl's face, erased immediately by shock, which Anne-Marie had caught but had been too angry to fear. In retrospect, the girl was frightening.

CHAPTER FIVE

The arrival in Key West was spectacular. A steady breeze from the southeast swept *Regina de los Girasoles* directly past the new house, now completed. Staunchly and majestically the house faced the sea. Two great wings, welcoming arms around a courtyard, rose to capture the prevailing breezes and afforded almost every room in the house a view of the water. None of the cliches found in dark, gloomy, fussy Victorian mansions applied here. The house was like a large Italian villa—high, wide and handsome. Anne-Marie knew the floor plan was open and informal, featuring bay windows and interior sliding doors, but she was unprepared for the size.

Not so Bart, he had seen it under construction.

"Apparently, this sets the tenor of our lives. I hope we can handle it," said Anne-Marie meekly, swallowing hard. Figuratively, a new door was opening, one that was ostensibly massive and secure, yet one that would demand a mastery over many aspects of their lives.

"It looks pretty elegant to me." Bart's eyebrows arched expectantly.

A large crowd of bystanders lined the wharves as the ship was secured in her berth. Many came regularly to watch the fishing boats dock and unload just as people in other small towns waited at railroad stations for glimpses of travelers from other places. Others came for the sunsets, among the world's most spectacular—the sea and sun conspiring to end each day in a riot of color. Now Key Westers were gathered for a new sight, their first view of a pleasure ocean-going yacht. There could be no doubt that this vessel was she: no commercial cargo would be carried in a ship so abundantly curtained, nor would a merchant ship be so beautiful in design.

The size of the audience drove the family from the deck into the salon.

"Consuelo and Tim will be here soon, I'm sure," said Bart. "I hope you're also prepared for reporters, and the mayor, and heaven only knows who else, because it appears that all of Key West is out there to greet you."

"I can't believe it!" cried Anne-Marie.

"I should have prepared you, but I simply did not think of it. It was the same when I arrived from Fort Jefferson. Whether you like it or not, my dear, you're a celebrity, a public figure, an object of curiosity."

"I can see. This could become an annoyance."

Within minutes Captain Sands appeared, his traditional dress hat in hand. As Bart had predicted, their old friends Consuelo and Tim Clayton were there, as were the mayor and a reporter from the *Key West Dispatch.*

"Tell the reporter that we'll talk to him tomorrow. Let the Claytons come aboard, and we'll greet the mayor on the top deck," whispered Anne-Marie.

Expeditiously and with considerable charm Anne-Marie handled Mayor Henry Mulrennan, giving him an invitation to dinner the following week. "If we're not in our new home, we'll be right here on the ship." Then she proffered her hand in a gracious farewell and flawless dismissal. Finally, they were free to greet their old friends.

Bart had first met Tim Clayton when Tim joined his ship, the *Catherine,* as his second mate. Tim, like Jared Russell, was a man Bart trusted implicitly. The Claytons were there for Bart at great risk when he was falsely accused of murder and gun smuggling and helped him clear his name. The two couples loved each other dearly. Then Tim had been charged with building the Ramsden's new home in Key West.

Aboard ship, as second mate, Tim's position traditionally carried a no-man's-land status. Bart rightly felt that Tim's quick mind and barbed tongue would and should command a respect general practice did not usually bestow. Tim's star continued to rise with his marriage to Consuelo, a wealthy widow. 'The Rock,' as they referred to Key West, now was home to both couples.

Because Tim was capable and willing to take on the construction of a house for Anne-Marie, she had turned the job over to him, naively feeling that by virtue of his upper class English birthright and fine education, he could produce a modern, elegant, tasteful mansion. Luckily, she had been right.

Anne-Marie gathered the Claytons in an encompassing smile. "I can hardly wait to see the house, but we can't possibly leave the ship until the crowd disperses. Right now we seem to be in a goldfish bowl with a thousand eyes staring at us."

"Our carriage is here. We can slip out later tonight. I believe I have followed your instructions to the letter," said Tim.

"I can see you've added a few gray hairs doing it," replied Anne-Marie laughing. "I'm sorry."

"I'm trying to look older than my child wife," teased Tim.

Tim was five years older than Bart. Slightly graying hair, lightened by the sun, framed his innocent nice face that often wore an engaging grin. His wife Consuelo, actually was a few years older, but few would have believed it. Exactly how many remained a secret the dark-haired beauty would not reveal.

"Marriage agrees with you both remarkably," added Bart, smiling with his guests was they waited for the crowd to dwindle.

"A bachelor is a public temptation, as you well know, Bart. I got tired of women fighting over me at every corner, and so, I finally married for money." Knowing another story, they all laughed.

"Seriously, give the credit for my connubial bliss to Consuelo. She treats all disasters as incidents and none of the incidents as disasters, as you well know," replied Tim.

"Indeed, she does," replied Bart, mindful of his own depression in the difficult period in which he was trying to clear his name. She, generating hope, had been his salvation. For a long moment his eyes rested on the vibrant dark beauty who had grown even lovelier. Tim could be credited with some of it, and him, none of it, although he had had his try. In the soft evening light in a butterfly-bright gown and opal jewelry, she seemed to shimmer before him. Anne-Marie noticed the stare.

"The trouble with marriage is that while women are mothers at heart, men may remain bachelors," said Anne-Marie in joking reproof.

"I think it's time for our announcement," said Consuelo, hastily. "I'm going to be a mother! Can you believe it?" She blushed.

"That's wonderful. You've got to have a son that our next daughter can marry. Congratulations to you both," said Bart.

Anne-Marie looked at Bart, totally surprised by his remark that he would be thinking of a future child for themselves. First a house on Cape May and now another child…He was trying hard to be nice…

"Kind people," said Tim rising. "I think the coast is clear now so that you can inspect your house."

The men were off to fetch the carriage, leaving the women to follow leisurely. "You will find motherhood a rewarding experience, Consuelo. It agrees with you already."

"Don't think I wasn't shocked at first, but now I'm accustomed to the idea. Besides, it may keep me young for my young husband," replied Consuelo.

The intimation of Consuelo's insecurity over the small age difference between herself and Tim startled Anne-Marie. Tim was so willing and ready to be possessed by Consuelo. Within seconds the men rounded the corner with the carriage. Bart descended to hand the ladies in. Anne-Marie stood by the horse, a brisk evening breeze whipped her hair as it had done on her wedding day, recalling now the gypsy's prophecy: "I fear for your firstborn." Why had she thought of that? The loss still pained—and probably always would. Before this evening Bart had never alluded to more children and perhaps that was it—that and the horse and the dark-haired woman by her side as then on that day— long ago now.

Anne-Marie's mood lifted as they entered the house. Proudly Tim lit the lamps.

The first floor rooms opened on terraces and a main loggia that would become the living room. A checkered black and white marble floor shimmered before them, now a great vacant space of polished newness. Above them massive beams supported the ceiling and floor upstairs, reached by a squared staircase. Two hand-carved mahogany figures, as on the bowsprit of a ship, graced the newel posts.

"How beautiful," cried Anne-Marie, in a rare speechless state.

"Absolutely first class," said Bart admiringly.

To the left was the drawing room with a great fireplace and inlaid wood floor, balanced by the dining room on the right, also with a matching fireplace.

"I suppose you could seat forty at one time here," said Tim, "God, the butcher and the cook willing…"

Beyond was a smaller dining room or breakfast room. On the second floor Tim led them to an upstairs sitting room and a broad hall leading to two bedrooms, each with dressing and bath chambers as well as walk-in closets.

"You have Consuelo to thank for this planning and execution," said Tim.

"I thought you would like what I have always dreamed of," said Consuelo. "A room just for clothes! What heaven! And I made Tim install bath chambers all over the house. You have one, Bart has one, the children and guests have one, and even the servants have a tub room." Five ample bedrooms and a bath followed on the third floor.

"This house should be livable all year," added Tim. "If there's a breeze, you'll get it."

"You've done a magnificent job. I love it," said Anne-Marie.

"There's still more to see," said Tim, leading them to a kitchen and pantry. In the kitchen a large copper sink had a drainboard, a contraption neither Anne-Marie nor Bart had ever seen before. While the men discussed the mortised rafters and joists heldtogether with wood pins, the women turned to furnishings.

"As you can see, I took things from your former home, but only the necessities. I knew you would want to select and arrange things," said Consuelo.

Still, more had been done than Anne-Marie expected. She had no sooner decided on the changes when Bart piped up, "Oh, I'm sure she won't change a thing. Everything is perfect."

"Now wait a minute, Bart," interjected Anne-Marie, anxious to avoid an embarrassing situation. "You know I love to move furniture about. I change things so often sometimes Bart gets up on the wrong side of the bed." They laughed. "Bart's opinion comes from everything in its place—after years at sea. There such rules mean survival. I don't think this house will sink because a locker gets moved." Again, they all laughed. Bart, understanding that he had put Anne-Marie in a difficult position was glad she had worked her way out of it.

"It's better to stub your toe in the dark than beat you head against a wall," said Tim. "The old order changeth, yielding place to new…"

"Oh, it's good to hear that beautiful English accent again," said Anne-Marie, happy to find a another subject.

One heard a potpourri of accents in Key West. The small island community was a Mecca for all kinds of people including the stragglers from almost every nation. They all came by ship, some accidentally, blown in either by a kind wind or a violent one. Like mangrove trees, that by their splayed roots caught the whirling sand in waves and tides building new land, people also took root. Key West's strategic location as a crossroad with a natural harbor insured a steady arrival of sailing vessels in need of drinking water and ships' supplies. A constant stream from the Bahamas, Cuba, England, Spain, Russia, Poland, Germany even France—the country least inclined to see its citizens depart—used Key West as a port of entry to the United States. One way or another the city accommodated the arrivals. Those who liked it and could, or would, stayed. A few had come under force, namely the Blacks.

Most of the Blacks came in 1860 when two U.S. gunboats, the *Mohawk* and *Wyandotte*, captured two slavers with three hundred Africans aboard. Several large barracks, called a 'baracoon,' were constructed at Whitehead's Point. These fronted the shore, and everyday the Africans would go *en masse* to bathe. They were fed by the city, and Consuelo remembered seeing them in groups of ten, seated around a large bucket of rice and meat, each dipping in with his own spoon, bite by bite, infection and cross-infection be damned. On their arrival the percentage of sick among them was enormous. Nearly all had opthalmia. Gradually and eventually, they were absorbed into the town, but they were severely restricted by the authorities. A nine-thirty curfew prohibited them from appearing on the street, whether they were free or not. Nor were they allowed to beat a drum, fiddle or make noise without written permission from the mayor or councilmen. Long before the end of the Civil War, they had all been freed by federal fiat.

A fine living could be made in Key West if one joined the burgeoning salvage industry. Oddly, although the business was in saving property, it was called perversely 'wrecking.' Many wreckers had built handsome homes and furnished them with salvaged goods from the world over. Their daughters and sons were educated in fine eastern schools or abroad. Consuelo was a product of this setting. Officers from Fort Taylor and the naval base, dashing and handsome men, assured the ladies of Key West a brighter social life than any city in the South after the Civil War. The colorful, unique, tropic city struck Anne-Marie as a wonderfully healthy place in which to bring up her daughter. Furthermore, Bart loved the town.

"Back to the ship for champagne," said Bart. "We should have brought a bottle along to crack over the doorstep."

"It might have killed the sunflowers Consuelo planted. Did you notice the carved sunflowers on the doors throughout the house?"

"I don't think one detail escaped me," replied Anne-Marie. "Just test me."

"All right. How many doors are there to the cupboards in the pantry?" asked Tim.

Anne-Marie closed her eyes, obviously thinking. "Thirty-six."

"By gosh! The woman is right," said Tim, satisfied that, indeed, she had missed nothing. Later he told Consuelo that he would have wagered a fortune that she would be right.

Back on the ship over champagne Tim broached the question of Bart's immediate plans for his own future.

"I'll have to get the household settled, which will include a few landscaping and mooring problems which we have discussed, and then there's a sticky problem in Mexico that I may have to look into," Bart replied, mindful of Anne-Marie's gaze. "Father Frazier is trying to untangle it. If worst comes to worst, I may have to tackle it."

"I just met a man from Mexico," said Tim. "Actually, he comes from Spain. He lived in Mexico and left with the Royalists."

"We'll get you two together with him at dinner," offered Consuelo. "His name is Rafael de Palma, and he's rather charming."

"That would be most kind of you," replied Bart. "I also thought I'd like to talk to a few Mexican sailors."

Anne-Marie tried to remain calm.

＊　　　　＊　　　　＊　　　　＊

Anne-Marie was not used to perspiring yet suddenly she felt uncommonly warm. She loosened the gold clasp of her aunt's ivory-handled fan that she was carrying and whipped the air about her face. She turned to notice a stranger's stare, one long enough to make her uncomfortable, despite his handsome Latin features.

The occasion was a dinner party given by Consuelo a few weeks after the Ramsdens had moved into their new home. Now Consuelo, with the stranger in tow, was weaving toward her.

"Anne-Marie, this is Rafael de Palma," said Consuelo, who was immediately distracted by another beckoning guest and forced to leave abruptly. "Excuse me for just a minute…"

The gentleman placed a kiss upon her hand.

"I have heard of you, of course," said Anne-Marie, meeting his dark, steady appreciative eyes. "I hear you've come from Mexico."

"Don't tell me my past precedes me," he replied, smiling.

Rafael de Palma, tall, slender, debonair, with dark wavy hair and eyes like deep pools, would have made an impression on any young woman.

"My husband wants very much to meet you. We have Mexican business interests," murmured Anne-Marie, turning her eyes from him to gaze around the room, seeking her husband.

"I'm distraught."

"Why?" she asked, determined to disabuse him of the thought that she was distraught and inviting a flirtation.

"To learn that you have a husband."

So, he did notice, thought Anne-Marie. "I'm sure you'll recover. The room is full of lovely ladies to aid you." She raised her fan to stir the air and enable her to gain breath for an appropriate laugh. For her husband and friends' sake, she did not want to be rude, but his romantic approach was discomforting. She knew his behavior was designed to be flattering, and perhaps Latin women expected it. She found it distasteful. "There are other foreign places that interest me more."

"Such as?"

"I have never been to Spain."

"I know."

"How do you know?" she asked, wondering what he knew and from whom had he heard it. Her fan now gently wafted the curls around her face.

"Spain would never have let you go."

"What charming compliments you Europeans enchant us with," replied Anne-Marie. "Our men are too sedate to employ such flattery. Or, are you all incurable romantics?" The man is insufferable, she thought.

"Why do you decry romance? There's little enough of it. American women have remained Puritan, too prim to enjoy male friendliness, fearful of gossip, no doubt," he retorted. For the first time his eyes left hers.

Anne-Marie met his charge. "More likely our women, descendants of pioneers, have had to be more business-like, since they've had to do most of the work—except for commerce, of course. That would tend to develop practicality in them. And," she paused, "also a sense of humor about men, for that matter. But, here comes my husband…Bart, may I present Rafael de Palma. I'm sure he knows everything there is to know about Mexico." Abruptly, but smiling, she left them, delighted with the opportunity to escape.

"I've been anxious to meet you," said Bart, "having heard from the Claytons that you recently left Mexico." Naturally, Bart dismissed Anne-Marie's precipitate flight. After all, she had been cool to the subject of Mexico.

"I would be more than delighted to be any help that I can. The country is in chaos."

"I'm aware of that. My wife has considerable holdings in Taxco, which she has had no return on for some time now. I have thought of looking into the situation myself, also having interests there."

"You would be in an ideal position to do so. Benito Jaurez looks with favor on Americans. As a European, I am a *persona non grata.* If I can advise you, don't hesitate to call on me. What little knowledge I have is at your disposal."

"That's most kind of you," Bart replied, brushed by swirling dancers. "It's hardly possible to talk here, but I would be honored if you would join us an evening for dinner. Perhaps Monday next week?"

"I'd be delighted. I've made Russell House my home temporarily. Here is my card. I am at your service."

The men parted, aware that they were expected to circulate. He seems like a forthright chap, thought Rafael. He's frank enough about his wife having the money. I have a feeling that it would be worth my while to get to know them better. He reasoned rightly.

Later in the evening Bart told Anne-Marie that he had invited Rafael de Palma to dinner Monday night.

"I don't see how you could have invited that insufferable Spaniard to our home,' exploded Anne-Marie.

"I'm sorry. I should have discussed it with you first. I thought he might be of value to us. I could have invited him to meet me on the ship—and next time I will. I had no idea you disliked him." Bart was embarrassed. Anne-Marie's discomfort increased.

"It's his arrogance that annoys me. He has a supercilious way about him. He's a snob. He will use us and look down on us. I know his type. Besides, his suit smells of camphor." She maneuvered her fan irritably.

"I did not see any of that in him. I found him uncommonly pleasant and decent."

Affronted by that judgment, Anne-Marie said coldly, "I felt he considered us prey. He is obviously impoverished."

"I'm amazed, especially to hear that you know **his type**," said Bart huffily. Her violent criticism of de Palma aroused his suspicion. "I'd like to know where you got to know **his type**! I felt I was the member of this family who had done the traveling, who has dealt with the Europeans…"

"I read, my dear, and as a Key Wester have met many slick types!" She raised her nose in elegant disdain. "Please, say no more about him. We will have him to dinner. I will not embarrass you. Learn from him all you can."

Her sudden resignation surprised him. "We will leave it at that then," he concluded exuding authority. Though mollified, he met her grand manner with his own.

*   *   *   *

Anne-Marie could not leave it at that no matter how she tried. She would be tolerant. Above all, she would present a superlative dinner, remembering feasts her mother's cook had prepared. Ignoring Bart's simple tastes—though she did not consult him—she selected a Key West epicure's dinner: turtle soup, pompano, shrimp, venison, pineapple sorbet to clear the palate of that last gamy treat, Southern beaten biscuits—two hundred whacks with a rolling pin in the kitchen—, rice, and finally meringues and coffee with accompanying appropriate wines throughout.

She did not appear herself until just before the dinner hour. Then in a soft gray silk dress, the most décolleté she had, bearing a necklace, a veritable breastplate of large square-cut emeralds, she paused in the doorway awaiting recognition. When it came she glided toward them, head high as if she were a queen. The men were speechless, their eyes fastened upon her.

She broke the silence extending her hand. "How delightful that you are dining with us."

"I'm afraid I cannot think of food at this moment." Rafael sighed and smiled as he turned to Bart. "You wife is very beautiful. I congratulate you."

"That she is," agreed Bart, noting that his wife had not smiled at either man.

The formal table, glittering under a many-tiered crystal chandelier, was as spectacular as her person. Heavy ornamental silver goblets and silver chargers, the finest English bone china crowning Belgium's best lace—the product of many years of toil by nuns—lent their aura. Liveried footmen stood behind every chair. A napkin used was a napkin removed. No queen's table could have been more opulent or better attended.

Bart had no idea his wife could arrange such a production, yet he wisely played his role of a mannerly gentleman as if they customarily lived in such style. Anne-Marie had complied with his wishes, but, Good Lord, it was overdone.

Despite her elaborate preparations and her plan to remain cool and aloof, Anne-Marie soon found the evening unlike the one she had imagined, and the fault, she knew, was entirely her own. Rafael was interesting. When her eyes traveled to his, her thought went on another journey, new and exciting, far from the confines of the room and her memories. He had gone to Mexico as a liaison officer between the English, French, Spanish and Belgian units under a Marshal of France, Achille Bazaine. "There I became a close friend of Maximilian and Carlotta. I saw them betrayed by Bazaine and lost most of my own personal fortune in trying to save them," he explained.

"Supposedly we live in an age of enlightenment," said Bart.

Rafael's eyes mirrored a loss that had caused him so much pain. "Because of the circumstances under which they came to Mexico—appointees of Napoleon III—they were doomed. The great tragedy lay in that they soon came to love their adopted country as their own. They were determined to see the people free, educated, relieved of corruption and their natural treasures preserved. Much of what Maximilian did was in this direction."

"I'm sure the gentle, kind man never could have imagined that he would face a firing squad," said Anne-Marie in a soft poignant tone.

"Perhaps a kinder fate than that of his wife," she heard him say, as once again his eyes fastened upon her.

In one moment she found the man kindly sensitive and in the next she was repulsed by him—as if he were a too-sweet sticky piece of candy.

"Have you written off Mexico as a potentially powerful nation?" Bart asked.

"I can say this," responded Rafael, returning his attention to Bart. "I doubt that Mexico will ever become a threat to the United States, despite the bad history between the two countries. There is incalculable wealth there, but it will always be in the hands of a very few. The land itself is ferocious. Just as an infant cannot become a man without a nurturing interlude of childhood, a people cannot become a nation without an intervening education. The Mexican is a mixture of two peoples: Spanish and Indian. Spain laid down the rules and methods, but Mestizo Mexico provided the artists and pastors. The result is neither of the two, but a unique meld, the Mexican. Jaurez cannot organize the country. The gap between the government and the people is too wide. Your property in Mexico can be preserved under Jaurez, who wants law and order, but I predict his regime will be short-lived. You should act fast. In Mexico everything belongs to whoever is on top. You must get on top—and time is short. Moreover, you must be prepared to do this over and over again."

Anne-Marie watched Bart drink in Rafael de Palma's words.

"What you have said is most interesting, and I'm honored to be the recipient of your informed and well-considered opinion," replied Bart, not daring to look toward his wife.

"I feel the wine had muddled my thinking, but I doubt it has muddled my husband's question box. Please, don't take offense, but I shall leave the fate of Mexico in your capable hands, gentlemen," said Anne-Marie rising, anxious to retire. Clearly, Bart was being led down a path that led to Mexico.

"Madame, I regret having bored you. Please, forgive me." Rafael looked genuinely pained.

"Quite the contrary. You haven't bored me at all. It's tomorrow's heavy schedule that I must meet. Nothing more." Her voice filtered uncommonly low as she met his gaze and proffered her hand. Then she turned to Bart as if he could save her from a new affliction. "You'll find cognac in the drawing room, dearest." She kissed her husband's brow without even a glance toward Rafael.

Upstairs she collapsed on her bed fully dressed. Under no circumstance did she want to see that four-flusher again. That finally resolved, she slowly unbuttoned her silk shoes with her shoe hook and then mindlessly wiggled her toes until the shoes slid off and fell to the floor. If Bart insisted on seeing the man they would have to meet elsewhere. Then she rang for Zipporah to help her undress, to undo the tiny buttons, dotting like vertebrae, inaccessible in the back of her dress.

*   *   *   *

"That was a splendid dinner you planned last night," said Bart. "You did yourself proud. Had you remained with us for the evening, I could have proclaimed you the world's greatest hostess."

Anne-Marie felt her instincts were on target; Rafael de Palma had told Bart what he wanted to hear. She responded in a voice less than warm. "I felt certain that you wanted to hear about Mexico and nothing more. De Palma always plays the *gallante* when ladies are within hearing, and a lot of small talk bores you—as it does me. He is like the cock that thinks the sun has risen to hear him crow. Besides, he always seems to be drooling down my bosom."

"My dear wife, there's not a man alive who wouldn't drool down your bosom when you expose it so. And, for such a short acquaintance I can't understand why you don't like him."

"I don't dislike him. I simply distrust him. He's too clever."

"He doesn't strike me as being the clever type at all—if what you mean is shrewdly clever or cunning for his own ends. As for his manner toward you, what you evidently see as an attempt at seduction, I see nothing but the accepted habit of the Latin male."

Bart was right, of course. She had been brought up with Northerners who looked with disdain on such forward social behavior. She did not want to be unfair or prejudiced. "But, you have found him interesting because he says what you want to hear, and I find him uninteresting because he says what I don't want to hear. That's it in a nutshell."

They were breakfasting on the terrace overlooking the ocean. The sun was already high in the sky and Bart could feel it on his neck and it stung like a collar of nettles. The water shone like a metal reflector billowing under white clouds so that Bart's golden face and white linen shirt blazed in the salt air. Anne-Marie moved toward the shade, partly as a defense against the blazing glare, and partly to shadow her face which might reveal to Bart her disappointment. She was fighting a losing battle against him when it came to his wish to go to Mexico, but she could hold out a little longer.

Then, perhaps with time and a little southeast breeze, her misapprehensions might blow away.

"Let's not argue. It's too beautiful here. You've done a marvelous job on the landscaping. How quickly everything grows." She reached for his hand. "There's no point in getting excited over Mexico until we hear from Father—and we should soon."

A flock of sooty terns and noddies swarmed high in the air over the ocean. Brilliant swirls and sweeps of color in shades of blue and green, topped by foamy opalescent white waves, held them both in pensive appreciation. Then a flock of vibrant pink flamingoes in a line slowly flapped their way along, bound for the ponds where salt was made. Their matchstick necks and legs were fully extended. "They fly low over water but high over land, don't they?" asked Anne-Marie, sensitive to Bart warming under her touch. "Wouldn't you love to fly?"

"I expect I would, but I'm wingless."

"Then all I would have to do would be to clip your wings," she replied laughing.

"You do that effectively anyway."

They both laughed.

"You are really a very attractive man. That I want you constantly is a compliment. If you decide that it is important that you go to Mexico, you should. I promise that I won't make it hard for you. You are such an elusive husband."

She wondered at her rash turnabout.

"And you are such a possessive wife," he returned, gaily relieved by her apparent surrender to his want and will, which she should have done in the first place, like any good wife, he thought comfortably.

Within the week the letter did arrive from Father Frazier stating that he had been unable to get any word from Mexico. He advised Bart to sail over with Captain Sands. *"The trip need not take much time. The French have built a railroad from Vera Cruz to Paso del Macho, which I understand the British have been lengthening toward Mexico City,"* he wrote. He did not mention that the French had built the stretch to rush their troops out of the yellow fever area, but he might not have known that, thought Rafael de Palma, as Bart read him the letter.

"I would appreciate it if you would join us again for dinner," said Bart. "I'd like to pick your brains, if you will permit me—now that the trip is certain." The two men were speaking in the lobby of the hotel Russell House where Bart had found Rafael.

"With great pleasure," Rafael beamed. "Come up to my room with me, and I'll give you some maps to study."

Bart sat in Rafael's quarters, a small suite, waiting as Rafael picked through papers in a desk. The one touch of elegance in the room was a magnificent French pitcher and washbowl, so incongruous to the setting it could not be missed. Rafael soon found what he was looking for and Bart was on his way. "Until tomorrow night, and thank you," said Bart.

Anne-Marie received the news of the invitation with mixed feelings. One day was surely enough notice for an elaborate meal, but her problem lay in her reluctance to enlarge her acquaintance with Rafael de Palma. She had taken care to avoid this by turning down invitations when she felt sure he would be present. A small conspiracy with Consuelo had helped. "Please, keep us away from that man, Consuelo. He can only mean trouble."

Consuelo found this stand baffling. Certainly Anne-Marie was experienced enough to handle his advances. The current predicament made Anne-Marie's posture rather childish in her mind.

"I'll do what I can," promised Consuelo. "Rafael's very much in demand at dinner parties, and hostesses are often reluctant to reveal whom they have invited. I can't guarantee anything."

"I know. I wouldn't want it to appear that his presence is unacceptable to me either. That would be unkind and unfair," Anne-Marie replied.

"What an enigma," said Consuelo.

When Bart announced the second invitation to Rafael de Palma, Anne-Marie evidenced only irritation. "Couldn't you have taken his to lunch? That I might have been able to escape. Dinner is impossible."

"I thought of lunch," said Bart, "but it seemed—well, not enough. I want something from the man."

The thought that Rafael could be helpful to Bart superceded her own considerations, and she resolved to be the perfect hostess in one final effort. Still, with no little chagrin, she found herself dressing as if for a man. It must be a basic female instinct, she decided. She wore no plunging neckline and cascading emeralds this time. A pristine throat embracing white lace collar left everything to recollection.

"Graduation Day at Wesleyan?" Bart smiled.

"I have to do something to avoid those lecherous stares," reproved Anne-Marie, pinning a cameo below her chin as she surveyed herself, satisfied, in the mirror.

"I must say, the man certainly made an impression on you," said Bart. "I give him credit for that."

"So would a gorilla," she retorted as he left the room laughing. "By the way, I also invited the Claytons." Giving herself a final glance, she noted that Bart seemed more like his old self. Key West was having a salubrious effect on his moods and disposition. The presence of Consuelo and Tim, like reinforcements, might steady hands that had on occasion felt moist and heavy as if Rafael's leering eyes had laid a weight over her wrists.

Because the evening was balmy, they dined on the hurricane lamp-lit terrace with alfresco elegance. Rafael was seated carefully at the other end of the table close to Bart. "So that you may talk more easily," Anne-Marie explained. Nevertheless, the flames from the lamp lit his face and sparkling teeth with curious lights, and although often she could not hear him speak, she wished she could. She also watched Tim from the corner of her eye. Dear, sweet Tim, she could also count on him as her guardian angel. She had come to lean so on his expertise. What did he think of Rafael? She would ask. But, she knew that Tim was too sensible, too strong, too incorruptible himself to accurately judge Rafael. Meanwhile, she sat talking to Consuelo about babies, exercise, diet, a table length from Rafael, grateful for distance.

Finally, she addressed him directly. "I would feel so much better about Bart going to Mexico if you were free to accompany him."

"To be able to do so would give me a great deal of pleasure, Madame Ramsden, but I'm afraid it is out of the question. I was forced to escape. Only forged papers, borrowed clothing and an English education—not to mention nerve—saved me from a firing squad or worse. Believe me, I would be a great hindrance to your husband."

"We would not want you to take any such risk on our behalf. After all, only money is at stake," she replied.

"And certainly not your last nickel," added Tim.

"But, you might justly call it my folly," said Bart, doing his best to avoid his wife's eyes.

"It has been said that a good folly is worth whatever you've paid for it," rejoined Tim.

Paid for in what coin? thought Anne-Marie.

"I have a good many misgivings about this trip, Consuelo," murmured Anne-Marie softly. "But, Bart is determined to go, and I can't stop him without becoming an ogre."

"Perhaps you are needlessly worrying, dear. Don't pay interest on trouble until it is due."

Indeed the following day Anne-Marie received a thank-you note from Rafael de Palma, which was dated, the **midnight** of the dinner. *"I cannot sleep without first writing you, offering myself at your service even at the cost of my life. Your wish shall be my command. I can refuse you nothing."*

Such was the tenor of the letter, not a thank-you note that eventually thanked her for the evening.

That's clearly a love-letter, ruminated Anne-Marie. How presumptuous of him to write at midnight! What nerve he has to write a married woman in that tone!

Thoroughly incensed, she sought Bart's hammock in the garden to cool down and relax. Rafael de Palma was capable of becoming a real problem. Charm, expertise, power, and unbounded purposefulness made him a compelling personality; but there was something sinister and unsavory about the man equally repelling and downright frightening. When Bart casually strolled into view, the thought of his departure pierced her heart. Springing from the hammock she ran to him, throwing herself into his arms.

"My dearest, I hate to have you leave," she cried.

His hand cupped her head to his shoulder. Over his back she could see the hammock still swaying.

"Woman!" he said simply. Holding her close, trying to allay her fears.

That morning Bart had received a letter from Alma saying that there still had been no word from Jared. *"I'm grateful for the money you have been sending—otherwise I would be destitute. Our baby is not here yet. I can only hope that my distress will not effect the unborn. I feel guilty. The whole business was such a mistake. Please do something. This will not make Anne-Marie happy, I know. Forgive my pleading, Alma.*"

During the last couple of weeks Bart's spirits had lifted somewhat as he saw the trip to Mexico materializing with Anne-Marie's acquiescence. Short of taking off himself, he had been badgering officials by letters and cables. He did not like to see Anne-Marie lose money—or himself for that matter—but this worry was nothing compared to his concern for Jared. Furthermore, Mexico being such a big lawless country, he did not know how to begin the search. Certainly, one step was learning the language, an approach Anne-Marie approved of. Anne-Marie had learned Spanish from her maid Concepcion, having seen that that woman, an exceptional servant, was one of the individuals incapable of learning another language. The only recourse had been for Anne-Marie to learn Spanish. She had become interested in the study and so had continued to expand her vocabulary even moving into the literature.

Bart regretted his duplicity without much guilt. Anne-Marie's attitude toward Mudd had convinced him that the course he was taking was the honorable one. Under the circumstances a man was entitled to a few secrets, especially in light of Anne-Marie's antagonism toward Alma.

*　　　*　　　*　　　*

Bart, Jared and Alma, school chums, were the same age, seven or eight years older than Anne-Marie. Possibly feeling jealous of Anne-Marie's beauty, Alma had teased Anne-Marie with statements such as, "I saw Bart last night." Well, so had a lot of other people walking down the street. The little barbs might have been easily forgiven had it not been for an unfortunate accident. Alma had given a party to which Anne-Marie was invited knowing her presence would add to Bart's enjoyment of the evening. Alma had been given her own horse, which Anne-Marie was anxious to see. The horse had not been stabled for the night, but was tethered outside the kitchen door.

"Of course, you can see it," Alma had said. "There should be sufficient light from the kitchen."

Alma had forgotten that on this day construction had commenced on an addition to the back of the house, and a small trench had been dug which only ran a few feet, and which the kitchen light did not reveal. Anne-Marie fell into the trench. Fortunately, she was not hurt, but her dress was soiled, her arms blackened and her hair thrown in disarray. In this condition she raced home, certain of Alma's evil intentions. After a few minutes when Anne-Marie did not return, Alma and Bart went to look for her. Because Alma almost fell into the trench herself, Bart became convinced that Alma had acted innocently. Alma's apologies fell on deaf ears. Nothing would convince Anne-Marie that Alma had at least hoped that Anne-Marie would fall.

Soon after Alma and Jared became engaged. Anne-Marie refused to enter the festivities. In small towns such rivalries flourished among the young, but usually softened in time with subsequent marriages, children and adult understanding. Jared and Alma moved away before the breach could be healed—if it ever would. Bart remained friendly with the Russells through correspondence. This Anne-Marie had no objection to as long as he did not drag her into it.

A few years later when Bart learned that Jared had fallen on hard times with a wife and two children, he attempted to come to his friend's rescue with a financial proposition that would benefit both families. Financed by Bart, a partnership was set up. Jared would go to Mexico getting sources for tequila, which would be shipped to the U.S. for bottling and sale. Then Jared disappeared. Bart's mistake lay in not discussing this with Anne-Marie at the onset. The longer he harbored the secret, the deeper his concern grew.

Now Anne-Marie felt Bart was anxious to separate himself from her. The money was not that important. Someway Bart's values were impaired. She was hurt. Only her father's stand—which had put her in the wrong—forced her toward greater leniency in accepting Bart as he was—or as she believed she was. She loved her husband, and the more she loved him the greater was his capacity to pain her.

Chapter Six

Captain Sands was examined by Dr. Burbury in Key West. "Exhaustion and cold brought on an attack of angina pectoris, but I see no reason for you to give up work as long as you're careful. There's nothing like a good chronic illness to insure a long life," advised the good doctor. So, with Captain Sands in charge, Bart sailed for Mexico.

Sands left Bart in the harbor of *Villa Rica de Vera Cruz* or the Rich Town of the True Cross as Cortez had named it some three centuries before. At Bart's insistence, Sands then returned to Key West. "It is pointless for you to sit here collecting weed off the coast of Mexico, exposing the men to yellow fever and the ship to piracy, waiting for me." Bart had promised to write Anne-Marie, although he hoped to finish his business and return in a month. It was March. By May, they hoped to be in the new house on Cape May. This gift from Bart had naturally grown appreciably in Anne-Marie's mind, representing as it did, a new attitude of Bart's regarding their future life together, finally somewhat in line with her hopes.

Unknown to Bart and Anne-Marie, his arrival in Veracruz had been anticipated. Several pairs of eyes had noted the arrival of the *Regina de los Girasoles* and Bart's disembarkation. Bart disappeared behind a high sea wall designed to keep out pirates, but which more effectively kept out the sea breezes and the sewage in, while encouraging mosquitoes that were infinitely more annoying than pirates.

At first Anne-Marie attended to the decoration of the house by attending auctions of salvaged goods so that time passed quickly. When after two weeks no word from Bart had been received, she grew irritated. Steadfastly, she had refused to see Rafael although his notes had become less personal. His invitations to luncheons and dinners went unanswered. While she was annoyed with Bart, a dalliance with Rafael—if only out of spite—was out of the question. Any charm and commanding presence had become lost on her once he became so thoroughly supportive of Bart's venture. Both men, as if in collusion, annoyed her. Finally, one afternoon she decided to call upon Rafael. At this point she was unwilling to bother Tim and Consuelo or discuss the errand.

Russell House was in easy walking distance. Rafael happened to be in his suite, where he received her. He was delighted by her visit.

"Please, excuse this intrusion, but I'm at wit's end over what may have happened to my husband," said Anne-Marie. "Have you any suggestions?"

"Of course," replied Rafael. "Please, sit down. Tell me what you have heard from him?"

"Why nothing! Nothing at all!" Gingerly, Anne-Marie took the edge of a seat, while Rafael rose, turned to a small *cellerette*, and, producing a bottle of fine port, poured two small wines. Anne-Marie's instinct was to refuse, but she knew she had treated Rafael badly, so this was not the time to scorn his hospitality. She sipped the wine.

"Go back then to the beginning, Madame Ramsden. Are you certain that he arrived in Veracruz?"

Suddenly feeling woozy, Anne-Marie set down her wine glass. Rafael caught her before she hit the floor. He then carried her unconscious through two French doors to put her down on his bed. Then he unbuttoned his trousers and lifted her skirts. There was no problem penetrating her by slipping aside her fine French satin underwear. Without putting his weight on her, smiling until the last minute, he deposited his seed. He then straightened her clothes, donned his hat and a cane, and went out for a stroll. Two hours later when he returned, Anne-Marie was gone.

Anne-Marie had awakened with a terrible headache. Remembering that she had come to Rafael's quarters, she surmised that she had fainted and that Rafael had gone to fetch a doctor. Realizing that she had made a terrible mistake in coming to his quarters in the first place, she beat a hasty retreat. Once home using her own toilet, unbeknownst to her, a goodly portion of Rafael's semen was lost, but not all of it.

As her concern for Bart matured into full-blown anxiety, she drew more and more on Consuelo and Tim for reassurance and support. Such statements as: "You must be sick of the sight of my face," "I know I'm a burden to you," and "If he's not dead, I'm ready to kill him for keeping us in the dark as to his well-being," became familiar refrains.

"Only the good die young," Tim had quipped. Certain that Bart had not been good by being inconsiderate, they had laughed.

"When Bart went to sea, he always refused to speculate on when he would return simply because he wanted the freedom to change his schedule without causing me any worry. I am well aware of the many things that can happen to delay a ship bringing him home," said Anne-Marie, trying to rationalize.

Telegrams to her father and to the State Department of both the United States and Mexico, of course, has been sent. "He may be furious and think that we're treating him like a child, but I'm furious myself," pouted Anne-Marie.

"Let's proceed as we think best. He may walk in tomorrow followed by six letters two weeks later, but if he doesn't, you'll feel better," said Consuelo.

"That calls for sending someone to Mexico," said Anne-Marie.

In a telegram to Jason, Tim suggested that distressing news, if any, be channeled through him, not wanting Anne-Marie to be alone should this be the case. Within the week Tim had to tell Anne-Marie that Bart had not entered Mexico. "The fact has been confirmed by the U.S. Ambassador himself." His worried eyes heralded alarm.

"Dear God, what do suppose has happened? We've gone over this a hundred times. I trust Sands. The crew confirmed him." Anne-Marie slipped into a chair, her knees weakened.

"We have to assume foul play. It's the only answer. I want to talk to Rafael de Palma. He could be of help. I'm sure he has friends there." Anne-Marie let the suggestion go, carried off by the breeze. He was to her an unpleasant subject, and she did not want the Claytons to know that she had already questioned him. She couldn't even remember what he had said…. The whole afternoon was hazy….

"Consuelo, in your condition you must not let this upset you," said Anne-Marie.

"You always think of others," replied Consuelo, rightfully touched.

"All right, ladies, let's be practical," cautioned Tim. "Bart has been in a good many tight places before. One way or another he managed to deal with them, and often to his greater advantage. I think it most likely that he is being held for ransom. It happens very frequently in Mexico now. And, before long we will receive some sort of a ransom note, posted from heaven knows where, to insure that the trail will be cold."

They were seated in Anne-Marie's loggia, facing the ocean. Anne-Marie turned to a window. Outside a schooner headed for the channel, while men, like ants, raced about the deck. The bit of action registered and then receded from her mind. "I'm trying to forgive myself for all the mean thoughts I've had over his negligence in writing. There's been a parade of them."

"Don't torture yourself. Jason will be pressuring the government. I hope the newspapers don't scent this." Tim's hands came down hard on his thighs. He turned to Consuelo as if to learn what she was thinking. She closed her eyes. Good lord, I hope she's not too deeply shocked, Tim thought, a small panic rising to unsettle him.

"Anne-Marie, we all care deeply for Bart, but please don't ask my husband to go find him, because with this baby, the most important thing to ever happen in our lives, due soon, I'm sorry, I cannot let him go."

Consuelo's words were like a caress, relieving the tight squeezing alarm in his chest. He reached for his wife's hand and the touch of her was a balm.

"Of course not!" cried Anne-Marie, now reaching to her friend now ballooning with child. "I wouldn't think of it."

"I'm going to ask Dr. Burbury to send you something tonight so that you can sleep," said Tim, once again in control of his feelings and thinking quickly.

"That's a good idea. How lucky we are to have such a good doctor on 'The Rock.'"

"Despite being overworked, he is always patient and understanding," said Consuelo. "He's always so gracious…"

Tim smiled over his wife's effusiveness. "I suppose if you want the hen to lay you'd better let her cackle. Anne-Marie, Consuelo will remain here with you, but I must go to the cable office and I want to talk to de Palma before running down Dr. Burbury."

"I can call on my brother-in-law, David Doyle. You might suggest that in the cable to Jason," said Anne-Marie, at the same time thinking of how Bart would shudder at the thought of his life hanging in David's hands.

The evening over, this thought was foremost in Anne-Marie's mind as she rang for Zipporah. She sat cogitating at her dressing table. Jason would be pleased that she was calling on David. She looked up, drawn back into the room by Zipporah's footsteps. Suddenly, she saw that Zipporah's walk was different. A second look that ripened into a hard stare, revealed that the girl was pregnant. A thickened waist, fuller bosom, and broadening of her back were the distinguishing signs.

The girl worked down the long tedious line of hooks and eyes as Anne-Marie addressed her. "Zipporah, are you expecting?"

"Yes, Ma'am."

"Who is the father or am I being rude to ask?" continued Anne-Marie, hesitantly.

"I'd rather not say, Ma'am," replied Zipporah after a long silence.

"I don't mean to be prying, but you are not married or are you?"

"No, Ma'am."

"I hope the father will help you, and at least support the child. He should."

Anne-Marie was not pleased with this development, thinking of another dependent, forthcoming lapses of service, and what this could mean in her household. A sense of responsibility surfaced.

"Do you think so?" the girl asked.

"Of course. For the last two thousand years it has taken two to make a baby."

"Then I'll tell you," said Zipporah, her eyes suddenly ablaze as her back stiffened. "The father is your husband. He raped me."

Stunned, Anne-Marie rose and wheeled about. "You're lying. I know my husband." Her eyes widened, looking precisely like marbles, glared with rising rage. "And when did this rape take place?"

"He's the father, I swear. I didn't want to do it. You were in New York. I couldn't fight him off. He was too strong."

"Get out of my room!" screamed Anne-Marie, her face growing red with rage. "I'll deal with you tomorrow."

Turning on her heels, yellow curls flying with the wind of her departure, Zipporah fled.

Drowning in a flood of outrage, Anne-Marie was left with a hammering in her chest, and subsequent pounding of blood through her veins. It was some minutes before anger dissolved into sorrow. Then she lay on her bed, stripped of all pride, tears smarting on her cheeks. How and why had Bart done such a thing? Was it brute revolt or a hedonistic escapade? Perhaps it was bitter retaliation against herself and her money. And, with a poor servant girl—or was she a flirting hussy? What difference did it make? She was a victim of both of them. Finally, she took Dr. Burbury's sleeping potion.

Downstairs in her narrow bed two hearts in the body of Zipporah beat with joy. What blessed relief. What luck that she had heard Madame talking with the Claytons and learned that Mister Ramsden was lost in Mexico. She had saddled him with the babe and it would serve him right! He'd been happy enough to have her warm his bed, and then nervy enough to throw her out. His high and mighty lady would pay, she thought, rubbing her belly. Yes, indeed. If by some miracle he did survive some Mexican jungle, the lady would still pay, and she would make him pay, too, one way or another. Anyway, she was saved. How easy it had been. But, he sure knew how to do it good. Never had it ever been so—good.

*   *   *   *

Anne-Marie breakfasted with Samantha, fighting to overcome the effects of a drugged night and the news it brought.

"Don't you feel good, Mama?" Samantha was troubled by her mother's frowning silence.

"Mama is worried about your father," replied Anne-Marie, which was, at least, partly true. "He has been naughty—he hasn't written."

"He will be happy about the plants," remarked the child, glad to speak of anything except the porridge she was avoiding. "Most are living."

"I suppose so," she replied dully.

Along one wall oleanders had taken hold. A transplanted sea grape with large woody leaves, round as saucers, defied sun, wind and spray with new growth. The coconut trees no longer needed their crutches and a riot of white and purple periwinkles flourished with a vigor matched only by the sandspurs. Sometime during the night leaf-cutters had gourmandized the bougainvillea. The gardener came through watering, making birds flutter softly in the minty orange jasmine; quail doves flew by, the brilliant metallic hues of their plumage gleaming on swift little bodies; butterflies chased each other; the bees—or perhaps wasps—hummed. After a painful night, nature's quiet scene helped her resolve the problem of Zipporah which had to be faced.

"What will you learn today?" she asked Samantha.

"Catechism and all the horrible suffering of Jesus Christ."

"I suppose that will be helpful."

"I can tell you about it now…"

"No, thank you, not now. I can see that you're not going to eat your porridge and you will go hungry before lunch. So, you will suffer. Now, go tell Zipporah I want to see her. You may be excused." The tone was firm but not angry, and Samantha went skipping off to the lessons of Galilee.

Within minutes Zipporah appeared, dressed in a fresh, stiffly starched uniform. Only the day before Anne-Marie had seen the maid as a porcelain doll who, she was sure, had been abused. Today she envisioned a calcimined slut. Under her plate Anne-Marie had an envelope.

"You may leave the uniform. Dress in your own clothes. Concepcion will supervise your packing." She produced the envelope. "Here is money for your passage north. After you have located out of this state, you will receive twenty-five dollars a month until your child is eighteen. The cash will come in postal money orders from a Johnny Jones, on the condition that you never reveal whom the father of your child is. If you ever so much as hint that my husband is involved, the money will end. Is that perfectly clear?"

"Yes, Ma'am."

"You may go."

Zipporah had heard words of the kind before: "Now get out," he had said.

The confrontation left Anne-Marie nauseous. Tiny beads of perspiration, miniscule eruptions, smarted about her eyes. As soon as she could raise her voice she called for Concepcion.

Before the morning was over, Consuelo and Tim arrived.

"Forgive me for saying so, but you look as if you had a terrible night," said Consuelo, noting the dark circles, strong as stage makeup, blackening her eyes.

"I slept a bit." She paused, "Probably I should not tell you, except that if something happened to me, it is something Tim would have to handle. More than that, I trust you both. I have had another blow." Her voice struck staccato notes.

"Wasn't it Milton who said: 'Evil news rides fast, while good news baits?'" asked Tim.

"Yes, and this bad news came fast. Last night I discovered Zipporah is pregnant. I should have seen it before, but I've been too distracted. She said Bart is the father and that he raped her," said Anne-Marie bitterly. "I threw her out with money to get out of state and the promise of twenty-five a month from a Johnny Jones until the child is eighteen. If Bart is lost and something happens to me, I would not want our families to learn of this although Bart's child might one day warrant recognition. It can't help being born...But, this would be left to your discretion, Tim."

Tim smothered his shock. "That does not sound like Bart, Anne-Marie. Does she know Bart is missing?"

A fresh flow of tears defied her attempts to contain them. "Probably, listening is a habit with her."

"So," said Tim. "It seems probable to me that Bart's disappearance has provided her with a scapegoat and a very easy touch. I fear you're going to hear more from that quarter. The seed of blackmail has been planted, and the harvest may be a peck of bitter fruit. Let's not hang Bart without a trial. When a man is not around to defend himself, it is easy to cry rape or anything for that matter. Right now Zipporah is the least of our worries. She'll be quiet for a while, anyway."

"Thank you, Tim," muttered Anne-Marie. "I felt like the blind man who walked up to a wall and thought he had reached the end of the world."

"Don't jump to conclusions, my dear. Worried as you are, that's easy to do—and probably unfair," said Consuelo, knowing better than Tim what a blow this must have been to Anne-Marie's pride.

"I know Rafael de Palma is not one of your favorite people, but I think you should talk to him. Let's see what he advises doing. He's our only authority. I've sent for your brother-in-law. We need all the help we can get. Besides, you should not be living alone."

"I'll do as you say. I certainly can't put up a social front."

"Unfortunately, our little society is the only distraction Key West can offer—and you need distraction."

"I'll have Rafael de Palma to dinner tomorrow night, and, of course, I'll expect you both."

A good many qualms surfaced as she wrote the invitation for Tim to deliver, but Tim had insisted. She would have to be very careful, that was all.

Anne-Marie's concern over seeing Rafael de Palma again proved ill founded. He behaved like a perfect gentleman, evidencing tender concern for her with no effort at seduction.

"Rafael," said Tim, "we feel the captain has been taken prisoner and yet Anne-Marie has received no ransom notes. Can you offer any suggestions as to what might have happened?"

"It's baffling. As I told Anne-Marie once, I'm sure very few tall, blond, young men spend over a month in Mexico without being noticed—and hardly the captain. However, there seems to be a terrible breakdown in the postal system. My mail is not coming through at all, which has caused me considerable distress."

"Certainly, that could be our answer," conceded Tim, looking at Anne-Marie.

"Letters used to come through regularly every two weeks. It's been two months since I've had mail. Due to the unrest there, naturally I'm concerned about my friends," added Rafael.

"We understand how you feel," replied Tim.

"I would suggest that we wait a little longer. Then if the captain has not been heard from we must formulate some plan of action," said Rafael.

"I'm so grateful. You've offered me a small ray of hope," said Anne-Marie, graciously.

During the next couple of weeks Anne-Marie threw herself into as many of the service activities as the small island community allowed. Mornings while Samantha was in school she offered her services to the Marine Hospital where she read to the ill and feeble, rolled bandages, and mended. She also found herself in a church controversy.

Hearing that many of the members of the Methodist church wanted instrumental music in 1868, Anne-Marie had offered to contribute an organ. Over thirty members took a great offense to this and severed themselves from the congregation, forming a new organization. Naturally, Anne-Marie felt terrible over the enmity her generosity had generated. A coterie composed chiefly of the Russell, Albury, Ingraham, Pinder and Curry families then got together to build a new church on the corner of Flemming and William Streets, called the Sparks Chapel after the Rev. J.O.A. Sparks, its first pastor. The deed gift of the land contained a clause prohibiting the use of instrumental music. Not wanting to offend anyone, Anne-Marie then donated heavily through Tim to the newly organized Royal Arch Chapter No. 21 of the Free and Accepted Masons. None of these contributions brought much satisfaction as her concern for Bart grew.

As might be expected, the Ramsdens and Claytons did not enjoy a wide circle of friends on 'The Rock,' although they could have had they wanted to. The town was small and few couples within their age group could be considered rich, although many of the elder citizens lived quietly on substantial holdings. They had sent their children north and abroad for fine educations. However, officers from Fort Taylor and the naval base had siphoned off many a belle during the Civil War, and many young men were prone to 'Rock fever' and left for wider horizons. Still, some women such as Mimi Lacrosse, a widow and Consuelo's oldest friend at forty, were remarkably well preserved and young enough at heart to be included in this circle of prominent young matrons. This group was not as dependent upon the churches for social life as most of the citizenry.

"I think we'd better have another discussion with Rafael," suggested Tim. "We must formulate a plan of action. I don't want to add to your unhappiness, but the time has come…"

"Bart's absence is beginning to cause ripples in town and I might as well admit what the problem is before malicious gossip starts. Besides, I need distraction."

Anne-Marie's dinners were always exquisite and this evening was no exception. The weather permitted them to dine on the terrace under a bright full moon and a sprinkling of starshine. For some weeks Mimi Lacrosse had been paired with Rafael de Palma at such dinners and Anne-Marie continued this arrangement. Young Judge Thomas Boynton and his wife and two other couples were included, as well as Major Pendelton who had recently been transferred to Fort Taylor and was awaiting the arrival of his wife. Brightly cushioned wicker furniture around two tables for six had been set up. At the hostess's table Anne-Marie placed Tim and the Major on her right and left; Rafael sat at the end of the table with Consuelo and Mimi.

To Anne-Marie's consternation, Rafael's eyes were always upon her, seemingly stripping her to nudity of a wood nymph while caressing her skin as deftly as an ocean breeze. He ignored Mimi, forcing Anne-Marie to direct an inordinate amount of her conversation toward the overly flattered major. After dinner, on the pretext of drawing a map of Mexico on a little piece of paper, Rafael drew his chair around to hers. There was little to do but ignore the move.

"Here is Veracruz, a terrible place, a stinking pit of humanity. From there one travels westward to Soledad, Córdoba, Orizaba, Puebla, Cholula, Mexico City and then south to Cuernavaca and Taxco," said Rafael, penciling in the cities with circles, his hand brushing hers. She quickly withdrew it, hoping the gesture had gone unobserved. Mimi's frigid stare told her otherwise. Anne-Marie rose from her chair.

"I think we should move inside so that the servants can put things to rights. I'm afraid it's going to rain. If you will notice, the stars have disappeared." Purposefully, Anne-Marie accompanied Mimi into the house. "I hope the conversation centering on Mexico did not bore you, but I'm terribly concerned about my husband."

"I'm sure you are," Mimi replied, with a sarcastic tone not lost on Anne-Marie.

Consuelo had hardly eaten a bite, allowing the others to do all the talking. Anne-Marie sought her out. She wanted desperately to discuss the miserable evening with Consuelo and get her help in placating Mimi, but this proved impossible—Consuelo looked uncomfortable. "Are you all right?" queried Anne-Marie. "You look very pale and you ate so little…"

"I feel queasy. I never heard of morning sickness at night, but I'm unwell. Do forgive me, but I should go home."

Tim, always sensitive to her condition, overheard and moved immediately to her side. "We'll slip out quietly not to unsettle your other guests," he whispered.

"I'll see you tomorrow," replied Anne-Marie giving her cheek a kiss and Tim's hand a squeeze. "Take care of her."

Not long after the other guests departed, including Mimi and Rafael. "Your husband will appear any day now, Anne-Marie. He has obviously run into problems, and, of course, you know the mails…" said the Major Pendelton.

"Let me know if there is anything we can do."

"It's important that you not worry…"

As graciously as possible Anne-Marie accepted their kind encouragement. She fairly ran up the stairs, threw herself on the bed, and wept.

*　　*　　*　　*

Mimi and Rafael had walked the short distance to the Ramsden's home. Homeward, Rafael's long strides barely kept up with Mimi's furious pace. Mimi was a tiny woman of French descent. She owned one of the most beautiful homes in Key West, and she had been the first in her circle to discover Rafael de Palma. As her escort he had been privy to her friends' hospitality as well as her own. Nothing steady had evolved in their relationship in Rafael's mind, but it had in hers. The five years' difference in their ages no one noticed. The foreignness in them both made them an ideal friendly pair. There was little in their behavior toward one another to indicate a budding romance. Behind Mimi's finely plucked eyebrows, beak-like nose and rosebud lips—and a prominent beauty spot—was a sharp Gaelic mind: pragmatic and perverse. Playfully, she recognized a fortune hunter, but proudly considered herself immune. She knew Rafael's physical beauty could command enormous wealth, but the bride would have to be of childbearing age to rebuild a dynasty on some remote impoverished Spanish estate. Now Rafael's obvious interest in Anne-Marie—after all she had done for him—brought out all the theatrics, jealousy and mockery in her temperament.

Well aware that Mimi was out of hand, Rafael grasped her elbow and whirled her around to face him. "Stop this ridiculous behavior!"

"Stop **my** ridiculous behavior! What unmitigated nerve! You say that to me after your behavior this evening! You ignored your partner, leered the entire evening at your hostess, and made such a fool of yourself that you made a fool of me!"

"Let's not talk about fools.... I had thought that you might be more magnanimous. The girl is desperately worried about her husband. She feels abandoned, helpless...Not one of your Bible-reading Puritan friends playfully gave her as much as a wink—which is what she needed. Have you no compassion? Surely, you should have known what I was doing. I thought our friendship strong enough to withstand an

obvious play for what it was! Mimi, you have wounded me deeply…"
He turned from her as bright opalescent eyes dimmed.

For a moment Mimi pouted. "I had no idea you were such a cavalier."
Her tone was less angry yet still haughty.

"You have been so good to me," said Rafael, now taking her hands. "I
have wronged you, but only to help another—perhaps foolishly." Her
hands in his lost tension and they moved to rub a heavy string of oriental pearls that hung to her waist. Her offense and defense had crumbled.
The battle was over. "Let's have a glass of wine," she suggested, taking his
arm to proceed at a leisurely pace.

Once inside her home, Mimi excused herself for a moment. She
returned to the sitting room to find Rafael standing with a glass of
wine extended to her. Nervously, she swallowed the wine, conscious of
drinking too fast, escaping into a warm light-headed luxuriance. Rafael
hid not hesitate. In an all-enveloping reach he swept her into his arms
and pressed her lips to his. Loosening one hand to reach between her
thighs, feeling through the thin tissues of her clothes, he began
stroking, immediately establishing an intimacy that could not be
undone. Like a master locksmith working with a key to the chamber,
his sensitive delicate fingers rhthymically and steadily maintained their
mesmerizing motion as her evening dress and slip rose higher and
higher. The lover's quarrel had been the prelude and all thought of
resistance failed her. He was now privy to the secret confines of her
body for the first time. He risked no interruption to climb the stairs for
more comfortable lovemaking, but drew her to the sofa where he
unbuttoned his fly. From his loins sprang a long fire-hot organ. While
his lips held hers with infinite tenderness and long slow drawn out
plunges he transported them both to a microcosmic flight into ecstasy.

When they finally straightened their garments, like closing curtains
to secret rooms, Rafael spoke. "Come lie with me once more and let me
make love to you properly. You were so needlessly upset, and you need
more comforting."

Instantly taking her by the hand, he led her upstairs, giving her no chance to refuse. The momentum could not be broken. Without severing his kiss, he undressed her. Then on her bed in a mountain of lacey pillows throughout the night with infinite charm and delight he continued to make love to her. Finally, when the first rays of sun filtered through the shutters and the blue jays began screaming over their vested interests, he dressed and departed.

Mimi slept late. Ever after she had awakened, and her maid had brought her a breakfast tray, she lay in bed remembering the night. The memory would be hard to erase, but she should do so.

*   *   *   *

Anne-Marie awakened to find a letter from her father expressing deep concern over Bart's disappearance. "*You must give credence to the fact that Mexican immigration officials may have extorted money from Bart on a thousand small pretexts. Once paid off, very probably they did not list him on their rolls. He may have written letters still sitting in some hinterland post office drawers. Such is the nature of the country. Even a small indiscretion in such a land, which we can both imagine Bart capable of considering his temper, could have serious consequences. I suffer over my part in this but such is the nature of your loving father.*"

Some small indiscretion, indeed. Well, through Zipporah Bart was to be a father again. The thought stung and then pained even more deeply when the gypsy's prophecy came to mind. At least this child to carry the curse would not be hers. Still, she shivered.

Later Consuelo's maid Pearl arrived with a dinner invitation. "*You must get out of the house. Tim will call for you. There will be no other guests. I hope my infirmity last night brought you no worry. We love you, Consuelo.*"

Toward evening flowers arrived from Rafael. His note said, "*Thank you for a most unforgettable evening. R. de P.*" Hardly an indiscretion there, thought Anne-Marie, remembering his eyes with discomfort. Mother would have found the note charming, although she probably would have connected it with trouble.

Consuelo and Tim's home was one of the handsomest in the city. It had been built by Consuelo's first husband, a man much older than she. The high wooden house stood fringed by a white picket fence. Porches ran on three sides, contained by railings and a comfortable scattering of white outdoor furniture. A profusion of ferns in containers on Victorian plant stands gave the house a lived-in quality, uncharacteristic of the times. Equally different was the garden backyard, secluded for dining and preferred over the formal Chippendale dining room with its pristine elegance. Outdoors one felt the full effect of the cooling breezes and only the summer rains and infestations of mosquitoes could detract from its enchantment. Night jessamine, roses, gardenias, and night blooming jasmine perfumed the air, suspended in penetrating soft nocturnal shadows.

Consuelo greeted Anne-Marie with a kiss. "You look a good deal better than yesterday. You've lost that green-around-the-gills-look. I suffered for you," said Anne-Marie.

"I hoped you would understand."

Later in the evening Anne-Marie mentioned her problem with Mimi. "I'm sure you noted Rafael's behavior which hurt Mimi and embarrassed me. I'm certain she thinks I encouraged Rafael, as she left my home furious with us both."

"I was so ill, I didn't pay much attention," Consuelo confessed. "I've known Mimi for many years. She's temperamental, but it blows over. Don't let it worry you."

"She was ready to scratch my eyes out. She's so powerful and well known in Key West that she could ruin my reputation. Actually, I was awake most of the night coming to terms with everything including a possibly errant husband. But, as Tim said, it is grossly unfair to accept the word of a servant girl both Samantha and Concepcion considered evil over what I know my husband to be. People like Zipporah are capable of poisoning one's mind. But, it may take me weeks to throw this off."

"A wise man once said, 'Keep you eyes open before marriage and half-shut afterward,'" counseled Tim. Then turning to his wife with a wink he added, "And, I devoutly hope you will. Married men are horribly tedious when they are good husbands and conceited fools when they are not."

"I will allow you to bore me, dear heart." Consuelo pinched his cheek. Her beauty seemed to crowd the garden. Tim flushed over the grip she tightened around his heart, which Anne-Marie could not miss. Nature seemed to compensate for the distorted pregnant figure by casting a special munificent expectant glowing beauty into the face.

"I've a good memory for forgetting," said Anne-Marie. "I'll try to keep an open mind. I must admit, I closed it for a while for repairs. After all, it is only my pride that was hurt."

"Pride makes awful fools of people, Anne-Marie," said Tim.

"More than money?"

"Money is hard to get and easy to lose. The opposite is true of pride."

"Tim, you are always so wise I could choke you," laughed Anne-Marie. "But, you are so dear I can't even do that."

"We must formulate an attack for locating Bart. We will have to work closely with Rafael. His inside knowledge of the country and his contacts are invaluable. The whole project as I envision it may call for some daring action, including an element of surprise. It probably will be costly."

After the mention of Rafael's name, Anne-Marie hardly heard the remainder of what Tim had to say. First it had been Bart throwing Rafael at her and now it was his best friend doing the same. How could these men be so blind?

"We may have to send an armed brigade to Mexico, Anne-Marie. That may probably be our last resort," said Tim, looking to her for a reaction.

"We'll do what we have to," she replied, shocked by that proposition.

Anne-Marie returned home to find a letter from Rafael waiting. "*Dear Madame, I have spent the day writing friends in Mexico. Possibly these private sources can learn more than the authorities as to what happened to your husband. I have asked them to leave no stone unturned and assured them that I will gladly bear all the costs involved. I am your devoted servant. How can I be otherwise to warrant your friendship. R. de P.*"

With a heavy hand and heart she replied, "*Dear Señor de Palma, Thank you for your most kind letter. Please understand that under no circumstances could I allow you to bear any cost in the search for my husband—nor would he permit it. This does not detract from my appreciation of your concern. Gratefully, Anne-Marie Frazier Ramsden.*"

Another letter in an entirely different vein arrived. It was from Zipporah. Exactly as Tim predicted, she had arrived in Charleston and would need more money to get settled. She could no longer get into her clothes. Destruction during the Civil War had produced shortages in housing, clothing, food—everything. After her costly travel, she could not survive with what she had. In her condition she could not work and faced hunger. Her needs were modest considering the way she had suffered and how she was suffering now.

Even though Tim had warned her, the letter reopened wounds. Her last dinner party had been a painful public admission that she faced troubles. Rafael was pushing himself upon her, and unfortunately she was obliged to use him. Mimi apparently had become an enemy.

She was rendered so uncertain by the events and letters of the last forty-eight hours that she was thrown into a pall of silence. For two days she stayed in her room. Then she looked in her mirror, faced herself squarely and, as was her way, started building her way back to where she wanted to be, a sense of her own worth taking over. She wrote a scolding letter to Bart and the mine manager in Taxco. Then she walked to the post office also to send Zipporah money.

"We never used to have mail from Mexico," said the postmaster. "Lately, I've noticed a lot of it."

Anne-Marie seriously doubted that anyone but herself and Rafael in the small city of Key West had been writing Mexico. Undoubtedly Rafael was working diligently on her behalf.

On March 11, 1869 Anne-Marie had noted that Bart's friend Samuel Mudd had been pardoned. He passed through Key West on his way north to join his family. What a shame Bart is not here for the moment, Anne-Marie had thought sadly. By June, 1869 the heat of summer bore down on Key West. Anne Marie thought of her family enjoying the beautiful new home Bart had bought her on the Cape. She was not only sad, but angry.

Her anger and despair were due to increase. During Bart's prolonged absence, she had begun opening his mail, paying his bills, and attempting to handle his business, if only through forwarding correspondence to her father. A letter from Alma Russell arrived, hating to bother him, but requesting money. The money he had sent had run out. She had had a baby girl, and was getting some help from her parents. There was no mention of Jared, her husband. The letter struck Anne-Marie as very strange, although Bart was certainly entitled to his own charities. Anxious for an explanation, she dug deeper in Bart's desk, discovering an earlier letter which had arrived shortly before he departed for Mexico. In this letter Alma had referred to **our** baby. Obviously, Jared had left her. Bart was supporting her. Alma even mentioned **the affair** and her guilt. Clearly Bart was a philanderer of the grossest sort. Tim had her convinced that she should look the other way as far as Zipporah was concerned—not to pass judgment when Bart could not defend himself. Now here was written proof of infidelity that possibly went back years. "Oh, how those men hang together," raged Anne-Marie.

Another situation came to Anne-Marie's attention. She had been missing her periods. At first she decided this was due to worry. She had not gained weight, but earlier there had been a few queasy moments. The marking of days on her calendar had only pertained to Bart's travel. I'd better talk to Dr. Burbury, she decided, not quite knowing how to accept the possibility that she might be pregnant herself. Prior to Bart's departure, they had made love a lot more than usual, ignoring precautions, rather hoping that she might conceive. Dr. Burbury's examination, done through her clothing, simply by poking, prompted the kind doctor to inform her that, "It appears that your friend Consuelo Clayton's condition was contagious, Anne-Marie."

CHAPTER SEVEN

Unknown to Anne-Marie, the heavy correspondence between Key West and Mexico had begun while Bart was still at home. Upon meeting the Ramsdens, Rafael de Palma had reopened a correspondence with Señorita Ramona Gonzalez in Veracruz. While professing his undying love for her, he also outlined a kidnapping plot, which could give them money to return happily married to his impoverished estate in Spain. She would have to find disreputable characters ideally situated and well-motivated to carry this out—not hard to find in the city. From Key West he could mastermind the whole operation with no risk. It made no difference how the operation in Mexico turned out. He would have either the ransom money or the rich Ramsden widow to marry. In the meantime, he could look forward to a pleasant interlude of being of solace to Anne-Marie. His letters to Ramona described Anne-Marie as a spoiled woman who could be parted easily with a good share of her wealth, she having no sense about money. Rafael always included a few crisp bills that would have made an impression on the poor girl. After all, in Mexico he could hire a man's labor for twenty-five cents a day.

Rafael kept up a steady stream of letters to Mexico, but to his acute distress, he received no replies, and there was no one in whom he could confide.

*   *   *   *

Even from the deck of *Regina de los Girasoles,* Bart could see that Rafael de Palma had been correct: the city of Veracruz was much improved.

Legend had called Veracruz the filthiest city in the Americas, a dismal tumbledown port with desecrated churches, unpaved muddy streets, and a barnyard stench. The city was built low with houses of stone dredged from the sea, there being no other stone available. A few scattered low ornamental cupolas—something like mosques without the elegance of minarets, broke the hovering skyline, and gave the city an almost oriental look. Changes had come, however, during the Empire. Baking in the hot, tropical, fiery sun, the stuccoed buildings looked to Bart freshly painted. A castle guarded the port.

Rafael had explained that the natives were of Spanish descent with remains of the old Spanish *grandezza* in their blood to assure a hearty heritage. "Their outlook is more European than Mexican," he had explained. Fearing nothing, happily believing in the fertile marriage of European and Indian culture now firmly meshed—according to Rafael—Bart bid Captain Sands goodbye so that the ship could profit from a rapidly gathering *Norte.* Boarding the tender in which he was rowed ashore, Bart felt good. He felt quite safe.

During the reign of Maximilian the city had prospered through trade with Europe, which had trebled. Contraband flourished. Vanilla beans, chocolate, tobacco, coffee, jars of powdery insect dye or cochineal, chests of indigo balls, lignum vitae, mahogany, tortoise shell, silver and even oriental porcelain and silk from the Philippines laboriously hauled by mules across Mexico, were shipped from Veracruz. A deep natural harbor, for centuries plagued by ubiquitous pirates, was now safely and regularly serviced by large ships; the plunderers had moved to the customhouses.

Bart's initial encouragement as he sighted the visible improvements was short lived. In the ugly, peeling, hot immigration offices and customhouse, there was considerable unnecessary delay. Over and over swarthy officials examined Bart's papers. He was frisked and finally accused of smuggling new clothes. After a series of conferences, he was fined, which amounted to the inevitable payoff. Eventually, he was allowed to enter the town.

Walking to the central plaza, Bart noted that the formerly filthy and often muddy streets, now newly paved, were cleaned of offal by the hoards of *zopilotes*, or carrion vultures. The birds of ill omen hung about, bleak and expectant, their feathers in perpetual disarray. Occasionally, they croaked in a chorus, flapping their black wings in the sultry air. The birds, the town's unpaid garbage collectors, were protected by law. Like Gothic gargoyles, they squatted on cornices of buildings or poised themselves with a macabre sense of line on the fluted columns of the organ cactus. Pedestrians, Bart soon saw, avoided their perches.

He began exploring the walled city from the southern end. Here an old cemetery adjoined a stinking slaughterhouse and at the same time withstood an encroaching jungle. To the north lay the snake-infested, yellow fever marshlands, another formidable boundary. Newspapers often referred to Mexico as a 'witches' cauldron,' and Verzcruz was hot enough to be just that, despite a northerly mosquito-laden breeze blowing in from the marshland. Beating off the voracious pests, Bart hurried back to the central square with a strong sense of having reached a point of no return. With understanding, he recalled that in 1519 Cortez, the *Conquistador,* had whipped up the courage of his men by burning his ships and sinking them in the harbor off Veracruz, cutting off a retreat. Not that Bart was ready to turn back from this alien land, but he would have been happy to have circumvented Veracruz with its tiny Sacrifice Island off the coast, and the whole of *Tierra Caliente.* It was just too damned hot!

Most of the improvements made by the French rightly concerned the possible need of getting their troops out of the area as fast as possible, but many were more permanent. The square, now paved with marble, was adorned by a park of shade trees. Surrounding shops and arcades included cafés and restaurants touting French food. Bart noted the posted menus with relief. He knew the Mexicans raised dogs for food, but today excellent fish, edible game birds, fresh fruits and vegetables were plentiful, which would spare him the more exotic native dishes. French wines were cheaper than in Key West. Everyone seemed to have money.

Leisurely, he strolled the central district, walking as far as the newly constructed railroad depot. Posted signs announced that there would be no train departing until the following day. Armed with this information, he looked for a pleasant inn with a café to await the dinner hour. Pretty women in Spanish shawls, their servants discreetly behind them, promenaded the square, in and out of shops. Plangent guitars echoed from doorway to doorway, interrupted only by braying donkeys and barking dogs. Heartened by his discoveries concerning food, Bart's spirits rose. His one valise was light. The dirty, evil-looking characters had been left behind in the narrow alleyways close to the docks. Thirsty and being more closely observed than he would have imagined, Bart entered an inn and ordered wine. A drink would allow him to look the place over before asking for a room. As he settled himself in a heavy wooden chair, for a moment he thought he recognized two men he had seen earlier, but then dismissed the thought. The men all looked alike to him. Only younger and older versions of the same dark, swarthy type, wearing short-beards, tight fitting trousers with numerous silver buttons running down legs or across chests, entered the room. Having drained his glass of wine, which had not been as good as anticipated, he felt dizzy. Soon after he collapsed, insensible.

He awakened in a large white cell, violently ill. He had been stripped of outer clothing and lay on a dirty pallet on a tile floor. One small iron-barred window admitted a blinding ferocious light. Access to the room was limited to a heavy wooden door. This he saw vaguely. Dark brown vomit, that he knew to be his own, ran in a caked stream from the pallet to the floor, a testimony to his stomach's rebellion against some powerful drug in the wine. He tried to sit up, but the effort was too dizzying to endure. His head throbbed as if a hundred minute demons were hammering at his brain. Carefully, he let himself down to gather his pounding wits.

First, he dimly thought that he had been shanghaied, but then he realized that, had that been the case, he would already be aboard some ship underway. Evidently, he had been taken captive for ransom. Escape at the moment was impossible. He would first sleep off the effect of the drug and then consider the possibilities for escape. Aware only that he felt awful, incapable of sitting, worse than he had ever felt in his life, he lay still until he fell into a blessed sleep. Once in the night he awakened to brush dozens of crawling cockroaches from his body. At dawn he noticed the ants carrying away their dead carcasses. But, he did not sleep off the drug or his illness. If anything, he was worse, he thought, burning hot. He could not get himself awake.

Sometime later, he was aware of three or four men in the room. A young woman forced water down his throat. Then the men returned. One, older and kinder, seemed to be a doctor, but Bart needed no introduction to his diagnosis. He had yellow fever, the dreaded *amarillo fevre*. It was the one disease with which he was familiar. The throbbing head, furred tongue, and feverish yellow skin, often were followed by a coma that preceded death. One consolation filtered through his delirium: someone considered him a prize and would try to keep him alive. From his stay throughout the epidemic on Dry Tortugas, he knew that the disease was not always fatal.

In semi-conscious moments he feared that the walls, towering, were crushing down on him, yet on the floor beside him stood a chamber pot, ornately decorated but with a wedge missing, never moving. Strangely, only because he seldom noticed such things, he remembered that he had seen that pattern before. It had been in the Russell House in Rafael de Palma's suite, of course. A matching pitcher and washbowl had been on a bureau. It was a small world. Ruefully, he thought of

Anne-Marie. What was she doing? She had not wanted this trip for him. He had to get to the police to make inquiry over Jared.

Eventually, Bart was wrapped in wet clothes and taken from the room. Then he vaguely knew that he lay in the back of a cart on a bed of wet-down cornhusks, and was jolted violently over hideously bumpy roads. Fortunately, he slipped into unconsciousness and for days remained so. Finally, his fever broke and he was still alive. The air was different—cool. He had no idea, of course, where he was. In an adobe room, again in a prison, his bed was made with heavy coarse sheets. Iron bars guarded the lone window, and a wrought iron door secured the sole entry. Whether it was locked, he did not know, but could not tell. He was too weak to do more than breathe.

Strange people came and were gone, but one girl remained in attendance. She forced bitter tasting water down his throat and even forced water into his intestines with a clyster pump. Cool juices by mouth had followed: lime, orange and papaya. Now a different doctor came.

Bart had been carried into the *Tierra Templada* or temperate land.

Orizaba, a snow capped volcano thrust into the sky, was in full view from the window. Bart easily recognized the peak. On the clear day that he arrived it could be seen from the Gulf of Mexico. The fact that it could be seen from such a distance reduced its value as a landmark.

Bart knew that there were villages in Mexico, inaccessible by coach, to be reached only by horseback. Also, he had read that there were hamlets, virtual eagles' aeries, beyond horses, to be reached only by foot. By the silence, Bart knew he was well isolated. Only a thin reedy whistle of the wind catching in the red tile roof broke the miles of silence.

During the first hours of emergence from his coma, Bart knew he would have to plan his escape, but he now was too weak to lift his head without assistance. He would have to rebuild every muscle in his body. This he would have to do at night, gradually, unwatched.

He did not know his captor, and he would have been astounded to know whom and what she was.

Ramona Gonzalez, born in Veracruz, had a trickle of Spanish blood in her veins, but the mainstream was Indian. This heritage gave her straight glossy black hair, a wide forehead, short sturdy stature—oddly stately. Orphaned early, she was taken to live with an uncle, a widower with four sons. So, while still a child, the girl became a servant in the house, a cook, laundress and maid, with no chance to marry. At sixteen in a casual encounter in the street, she met Rafael de Palma. She was happy when he promptly made her his mistress and slave to one instead of five; life was easier. Ramona was quite beneath Rafael in social standing, but because of the hundreds of soldiers in Veracruz, there was a great shortage of women.

Comfortable in the relationship, Rafael eventually took her to Mexico City. Predictably he had many affairs with ladies of quality, but Ramona laundered his shirts, pressed his uniforms, cooked his food, cleaned his quarters and kept his bed warm and ready. She dreamed of marriage, but knew that it would never happen, yet from time to time he teased her with the possibility. After three years in Mexico City the European forces were withdrawn. When Rafael was forced to leave Mexico, he could not take her with him. She remembered that he had been kind to her, and she loved him. When he wrote of the big 'fish' who could be kidnapped for a tidy ransom, Ramona knew any number of unsavory characters capable of carrying out Rafael's plot.

Ramona had arranged to be notified when Bart's ship arrived. The fleecing at the customhouse was prearranged—as well as the drugging. Rafael had written: "*Don't let your thugs kill him, at least until we have the money in hand. Those paying the ransom will want proof that he is alive. This you can get by having him write on a newspaper of a current date.*"

With Rafael's warning in mind, and his word as law, Ramona worked tirelessly to keep Bart alive, seeking aid when she needed it—as she had from the beginning of their venture. She had been terrified when Bart came down with the fever. Her great chance of happiness with Rafael was fleeing on the wings of a disease-carrying mosquito. Should Bart die, Rafael would never forgive her, as this was also his big chance.

With the aid of a pair of unscrupulous characters, Pepito and Jiminez, bandits who regularly held up the stagecoaches that departed from where the railroad ended, Ramona took Bart to their hideaway.

Pepito and Jiminez, frequently in league with rich *rancheros* in the region, indulged in the harmless sport of halting, undressing travelers, and ridding them of their jewels. After an exchange of courtesies, the ruffians took their liberties with the ladies. Meanwhile, the coachmen and aides, sat placidly on their perch, their eyes straight ahead. The sounds from the interior of the coaches where the ladies were, left no doubt in the minds of the men (under point of gun) as to what was going on. Even the mules were said to be able to gauge the exact moment when they might resume their trot. Ribald laughter and a rising cloud of dust ended the ordeal. Understandably, few were willing to report the horrifying incidents.

Ramona carried out her part of the plot exactly as outlined, but unfortunately Bart's unanticipated illness threw everything off schedule. Despite the lure of their promised slice of the pie, the bandits saw the danger of keeping Bart around for a long time. Rafael's admonition not to kill the prisoner seemed unnecessary to their simple minds.

"The *gringa* will pay, whether or not he lives," Pepito insisted. "I know the type."

Ramona conceded his experience with women was extensive.

"We've worked enough of these women over to know exactly how they'll behave," added Jiminez with a shrug.

"Don't be so anxious. Do you want to bring Jaurez and the whole Mexican army down on us? This is an important man. His wife will not pay until her advisors are assured that he is alive. I haven't even gone to Soledad yet with the ransom letter. He's been too sick to leave. And, it will take many days for the money to fly to us. Patience, my brothers."

Short stubby fingers straightened her skirt. The two *hombres* would be difficult to control.

"You'd better go soon," mumbled Pepito, his coarse features bearing a scowl.

"I will, just as soon as I see that he is going to live."

The men were then off, riding their horses to their camp, well sited as a lookout for unguarded coaches to plunder. Traffic had been slowed with the exodus of the Europeans, and it was becoming harder and harder to steal a living.

In the sickroom Bart's convalescence progressed. Fortunately, nurse and patient could speak together. Ramona had learned rudimentary English from sailors in Veracruz, and Bart had been working on Spanish from the time Jared had disappeared. Having won Jason's backing, Bart had submerged himself in learning the language. So when Ramona entered his room with a mug of juice and a spoon, Bart could whisper, "Thank you for saving my life," in Spanish with a voice that was more like a croak. Sunken blue bloodshot eyes looked into hers.

"Take this," she replied, the broad planes of her face revealing no emotion. Her sturdy arm slipped under his shoulder, lifting him so that he could drink. The mixture of juices and herbal tea heavily laced with sugar and an egg were hardly palatable. Swallowing was difficult, but he managed to get it down without gagging to disgorge it.

"Thank you for that, too," he whispered, falling back in exhaustion on the pillow, hoping desperately that his stomach would not have the strength to reject that last concoction. Aware of the problem. Ramona lingered until she was certain Bart's stomach had quieted. Then, walking straight and silently, she left the room. The process was repeated perhaps half a dozen times as day with almost no variation, except for an occasional wash.

After three days of absence, Pepito and Jiminez returned to the *rancho.* They gathered and talked with Ramona in the large kitchen, the one communal room in the house. Pepito swaggered to a table where a jug of *pulque* rested, and tipped the bottle to his lips for a swig.

Ramona called their attention to Bart's improvement. "We will have to put a guard on the door soon. He is waking up. One day while you are gone he could overpower me. Also, now I can go to the post with the letter."

Pepito hitched up his pants where they had dropped below his belly. "A guard! We will have to pay a guard money with our hard-earned pesos! I say be done with him. The man is an inconvenience."

"Relax," ordered Ramona. "You have already made a big profit on him from what was in his valise. That is only a small part of what is to come. What you've got from him already would cover four months in a first class hotel in Veracruz. He has paid that for a small bed in an adobe hut. Think of it that way," she advised.

"He's had maid service," replied Pepito proudly. "Don't belittle our accommodations. The floors and roof are tile."

"I have eyes, but you are not hurting. You have missed no stagecoach business because of him. From the beginning I told you that this would take time."

Secretly, Ramona was appalled at finding growing resistance within the group, and fought to stem it. The yellow fever delay cut seriously into the funds that Rafael had sent her and which once seemed more than ample.

Ramona spoke with the authority and confidence of an older woman. Her face, proud and stoic, carried a stare that added weight to her words. The ruffians, fortunately, listened. Of the three, only she knew how to read and write. With these skills came prestige and a superiority that they accepted, at least for the time being.

At first, with desperation not borne of consideration for Bart, Ramona had been a ministering angel. Slowly, she began to take an interest in her patient, not as a man, but as living evidence and product of her work. She had defeated death. As Bart began to recover, he displayed his gratitude as would a lonely child, and Ramona grew even more protective. Slowly, but inexorably a bond between nurse and patient grew, not withstanding that he now knew that she was part of a gang that had kidnapped him. She had saved his life—a fact that could not be discounted. Her kind attentions and caring attitude, regardless of motive, merited and won his appreciation. Brief and limited as their conversations were, neither wore blinders and the distance between them dwindled.

After Ramona finally composed and wrote the ransom letter, she rode to the post, there and back being a day's journey. In her post office box was a letter from Rafael, forwarded to her by a girlfriend in Veracruz. Impatient Rafael had written a demanding, uncaring, and offending letter. Ramona read it, and in a typically silent Indian protest to bullying, she retaliated by tearing up her ransom note. She would let Rafael worry and fume and wait. Eventually, he would suppose it to have been lost and would send another. Placidly, she returned to the *rancho*, moved as always by the beauty of her country.

As she rode, she met only a few landsmen, leading donkeys laden with vanilla, trotting down from the slopes of Oaxaca, their furry hides scented by the precious spice. Maguey plantations stretched for miles. Tapering, tall-stemmed white flowers rose from the fleshy spears of the maguey plant, the heart of which yielded stinking *pulque* and sisal even to her Olmecan Indian ancestors. The *pulque* could be distilled to make tequila that usually the rich enjoyed. Nowhere on earth could a bounteous nature have composed a more lavish landscape with its riotous savage flora. The cool, limpid air, the magnificent cerulean blue sky that turned purple with haze or topaz near the earth, wrapped benevolently around her. Here and there a little adobe hut, whitewashed with lime, beaconed with flowers, delighted her eyes and fed her soul. This was her land.

Ramona thought of her captive, a sweet wraith of a man, with the slowly growing beard of gold like the gentle Quetzalcoatl, who her ancestors believed one day would return from the exile forced upon him by Smoking Mirror, the war god.

Ramona had been raised in Catholicism with its pantheon of saints, but once outside the portals of the church, those saints could be dropped like a *serape* from her shoulders, should the need arise. Smoldering ancient legends about the gods of nature had more appeal, and faith had proved them more efficacious.

On returning to the ranch, Ramona lied to Pepito and Jiminez. "Now we need only wait." She moved slowly about the kitchen where long red chilies, green chilies, yellow chilies, braided strings of garlic, and ears or corn hung drying. A charcoal fire cut the night's chill. The men sat at the rough wooden table with the ever-present *pulque* in reach. Rings of dirt, like thin necklaces, marked their throats. The smell of sweat and horses mingled with that of the *pulque* and rose like a bubble around them. Their spirits were high.

"You've had a good day?" asked Ramona.

Pepito unfolded a cloth containing stolen rings, a few coins, broaches and watches, no pieces of great value between them. With a discerning finger she picked through the cache. "Only wedding bands the men were probably happy to be rid of and a few cheap cameos," she scoffed. "No one with enough sense to own good jewels travels with them anymore. By working too hard, you have killed the goose that lays the golden egg."

"Still, it's not a bad haul," defended Pepito. "Even if it only goes into someone's teeth." Jiminez laughed in appreciation, flashing a great gold tooth.

"Good luck," said Ramona, leaving with a bowl of broth for her patient. A sense of revulsion spurred her departure—one that would have to be concealed.

"Tomorrow I'm going to roast a turkey," she told Bart. "I think you're ready for solid food."

"That will be a pleasant change. My stomach no longer protests so much. I think I'm very hungry until I get the first swallow down, then the objections start."

She searched his face. "Your beard is beginning to grow, and your skin is not so yellow."

"You mean it no longer matches my eyes. What a shame!"

"You remind me of the Emperor Maximilian," said Ramona. "He, too, was very good looking."

"Don't tell me that. He had a weak Hapsburg chin. That's why he always wore a beard. Also, he died young. I hope not to do that."

"Then you must behave and make no trouble. My friends are not gentlemen."

"Thank you for the advice. I will lie here quietly. After all, I don't have much choice."

"True." Taking the empty bowl, she met his eyes. A heavy iron key clicked in the lock marking her departure.

As soon as darkness fell, Bart began an effort to regain his strength, at first sitting up, then dangling his feet. For a moment he was so dizzy he feared he would pitch forward to the floor. After a few minutes he lay back, rested, and tried the exercise again. Mere sitting up was exhausting. A dozen times through the night he took himself that far. During the day there would be no opportunity for exercise for fear of disclosing his progress. His eventual plan was escape, but in the meantime he knew he needed to avoid cankerous bedsores that were sure to form on his back unless he turned often as his circulation improved. He could already feel a few sore spots, soon bound to erupt. A program of surreptitious nocturnal gymnastics could be his salvation. He would try.

With genuine unmistakable warmth, he welcomed Ramona's visits, which broke the lonely, tedious convalescence. The food she brought was important, but it was her company—although it was brief—that was most appreciated. The sound of her distant footsteps announced her approach so that by the time she reached his door, he was beaming a welcome. As soon as he finished eating, she left, taking with her all his memory of her. Alone he thought of little except building back his strength by walking, Anne-Marie, and Jared.

There were brief fleeting moments when he came precariously close to revealing the progress he was making from sheer need to share his pride and happiness with someone. Discretion prevailed. He even worried about any telltale signs of dust on his feet, although Ramona kept the floor spotlessly clean. The coarse red tile floors were unwaxed and yielded fine a red powder, which, he feared, might betray him.

His presence, however, began to please Ramona. She sensed how genuinely glad he was to see her, and more importantly, how embarrassed and appreciative he was over the more unpleasant sickroom chores she performed. She was not accustomed to such feelings in a man. In truth, the gentleness she found in Bart was more a product of his weakened state than his normal nature, but this she did not know. Undivided attention and gratitude were flattering. Bart and his concern for her colored her thoughts. At the same time devotion to Rafael faltered. She frequently thought a lot about the ransom note she had not mailed. Rafael's rudeness had offended her. Now she thought of it only as a procrastination to extend a pleasant interlude that was gaining in interest. Happily, Pepito and Jiminez were enjoying productive times in their usual pursuit. Buoyed by their own successes and her good cooking, the pressure on Ramona was relieved. She was now spending more time with Bart.

"I wish you would tell me more about your country," said Bart. "I haven't seen much of it. By profession I'm a sea captain and I've seldom seen more than the ports of any country—too often the worst parts."

"What would you like to know?"

"Everything."

"That's more than I know. At least, Mexico must be the most beautiful country in the world. I've only seen pictures of other lands, but they seem pale in comparison. Other people have told me this also," she added proudly.

"I've heard that, too, and from a man who was not Mexican, but a friend in Key West."

Ramona did not need to ask his name. From him she had heard many fatuous promises, and no doubt Bart had also. So, Bart considered the man a friend. Apparently, to Rafael nothing was sacred.

"Perhaps we have the world's most complicated history," Ramona said finally. "My people are inured to suffering. Sometimes I believe we love pain. Often we act like barbarians, inviting trouble for ourselves. No wonder we get more than we can handle."

"The Mexicans have no monopoly there." Bart gazed at her immobile face, looking deep into her dark eyes fringed with topaz. He could never understand this woman behind a mask of olive skin, yet she was intriguing. The foreignness of her face, her body nourished by strange soil, the awkward accent on her tongue, became a mystery that dared solving.

At this point it had never occurred to him to make any intimate gesture toward her anymore than he would have been moved to pull Samantha's wooden doll into his bed. Suddenly, it struck him that the womanliness of her was within reach, and he had only to touch her to release some of its strangeness. Yet he did not. Much as he wanted to escape, he would not use her as a means. Like her people, the woman could be used and abused. An overblown sense of loyalty and willingness to sacrifice marked her as well as her ancestors. As soon as he regained his strength, he would find a means of escaping by overpowering the pompous asses who sometimes swaggered past his door, but he would not hurt her, he vowed.

Ramona roasted a turkey as promised and served it for the hearty Mexican noon meal. The sauce was a mole, a spicy combination of onion, garlic, chili, bitter chocolate, clove, nutmeg and broth thickened with *pipian*, a flour made of toasted squash seeds, too rich for Bart's squeamish stomach. Pepito and Jiminez loved it and ate and drank themselves into a stupor.

"I don't mean to be ungrateful, but I'm having trouble eating," said Bart. Like a great groundswell, a cramp gripped his abdomen, as he pushed the food away. "I'm sorry."

"Don't be. You can't help it. I thought your stomach was stronger. The fault is mine," she added, leaving, ready to assume the guilt life handed out, even from her prisoner. Later she returned with medicine for his pain, a strong drug which she knew also to be an aphrodisiac. As she left the room, he felt the pain lifting like a cloud.

With nightfall she slipped into his bed. Two minutes earlier she would have caught him standing, reeling, gazing out of his barred window to a field of blackness. Above a crescent moon and only a snow-covered mountain peak had glistened in the distance. Under the influence of the drug, he had lost all sense of caution. Hallucinating, he thought he was with Anne-Marie.

"How did you get here?" he asked.

"No matter," she replied, sealing his lips with her own as she climbed under his cover and upon him. Under the lambent riding motion of her body, he felt the first twinges of arousal. Then the vision of Anne-Marie faded and he sensed that he was with Ramona. With boyish naivete, he was surprised. He was not desirous of her, but he did not want to offend her with rejection. Having abandoned seduction as a means of escape, her presence was disconcerting. Then the drug took over again just as he was saying, "I doubt that I can perform," and he was back with Anne-Marie. The odd feeling that he was someway consorting with the enemy or betraying a sister evaporated. Anne-Marie was kissing him, but she had grown shorter. Strange that she would do that, he thought. Within a few minutes the soft calling of her flesh elicited a rush of blood to his loins and his body rose to enter her. As passion took over, he needed no more magic lanterns. The similar rush of blood within her body swelled the tissues that gripped him, wringing a searing excitation, nearly forgotten.

Ramona made no sound, remaining as non-committal in lovemaking as she was in feeding and bathing him.

Later, Bart remembered what had happened and hoped that it had been a dream. He had no idea how deeply Ramona was involved in the plot against him. Generously, he had assumed that someone had hired her after he had become ill. He resolved that under no circumstances would he accept any more of her medicine. Heaven only knew how careless he might have been under such an influence.

*   *   *   *

Gradually, Pepito and Jiminez were becoming more impatient. For days there had been no unguarded coaches to rob, or other thieves had got to the unwary victims first. "Tomorrow, Ramona, you go to the post. Word about the money should be there. I'm tired of my money going to feed that *gringo*." Pepito's tone left no doubt about his wish to take action.

"He doesn't eat much. You act as if I liked this—sitting alone, cooking for three men, emptying bedpans. He can't even walk to the latrine," clucked Ramona.

Pepito threw Jiminez a glance that she knew heralded trouble.

"There are other diversions we could practice," suggested Pepito, brusquely reaching for her bosom.

"Get your hands off me. This is a business proposition. I told you that when we came here." Her eyes narrowed to slits, cold in rejection. Pepito backed down. Ramona was not his type of a woman. Her bosom was too small and erect, her face and waist too broad.

"You're just an Indian," he sneered.

"That's right."

"Jiminez and I like ladies."

"Tomorrow I will go to the post. Obviously, something has gone wrong. Perhaps the ransom note was never delivered. That's the only explanation. I will write another—just in case."

"You'd better, unless you want to see your prize cut up and fed to the eagles," threatened Pepito.

"I have never heard of such a strung out kidnapping, and such a long, long illness. There must be something else wrong with him—unless he is just lazy or hopeful we will throw him out. The man's muscles must be jelly by now," added Jiminez, breaking his usual silence. He was the taller, the less energetic of the partners. Also, Pepito owned the small ranch. Therefore he had the louder voice.

"I will dictate a letter that will bring this to an end," swore Pepito, picking through a small writing chest that he had stolen, believing it to contain jewelry. Producing a quill, ink and paper, he ordered Ramona to write. She did, translating and making modifications for a clear message.

The next day, leaving Bart a large clay bowl of fruit to blunt his appetite, Ramona returned to the post. There a raving letter from Rafael demanding to know what happened awaited her. Where was the ransom note? Where was the captive? She took the letter back to show her men. It proved her right. The first letter had never reached him. But again she had destroyed the ransom note, this time one dictated by Pepito. She had done this for reasons of her own, motivated by stirrings within her mind and body, which swept over all other considerations; she had come to the conclusion that she was pregnant. Weighing the past and weighing the future, she came to decisions which had to be taken. Carefully, she buried the little scraps of paper. Pepito's threatening message was torn to shreds, and trampled into the earth. Her lungs burst for a moment in fear over the consequences. Then she returned home.

Changes had been made. Pepito had put a guard on Bart's door.

"What's he doing there?" Ramona asked.

"One of these days while we are away our prisoner is going to overpower you and escape. I'm taking a precaution."

Much as Ramona did not like the arrangement, she recognized what Pepito said was true. It would not be wise to combat Pepito openly on the matter, so she voiced agreement.

"Look at this," said Ramona, putting down Rafael's letter. "Exactly as I said. The first letter never arrived."

The two men gazed at the foreign paper that mysteriously carried a message that could be understood without being heard. A stream of curses ensued.

"Everything in this country takes time, Pepito. Save your breath, someday you may need it." Overwhelmed by her own dilemmas and in a torpor, she left the room.

*   *   *   *

The presence of a new guard complicated Ramona's life. When she went to clean the room or bring food, she was locked in, and the time of her stay was open to query. Without the key, she could not visit him at night. Communication with Bart was difficult.

Bart was no more pleased than she. He could do little but curse the fact that he had not moved fast enough. Rightly, he felt that he would need Ramona with him to escape. She knew the terrain, but more importantly, he could not leave her at the mercy of two enraged thugs. Once or twice he risked peering from his window and door during daylight confirming that there was nothing to be learned from the view open to him. He could promise her enough money to make a switch of allegiance worthwhile, if money was what she wanted. They would need two horses. He had no clothes. But, he almost had his strength back. Now everything was complicated by a guard. The guard, a heavy ignorant brute, might suspect some conniving—certainly considering some friendliness in their voices when they spoke to each other.

"We should have made the *gringo* himself write the letter," said Ramona to Pepito. "Perhaps they do not believe us." This letter would have had no more chance of being mailed as the others, but with a little paper she and Bart could exchange notes. She did not know how Bart would receive the news of her pregnancy.

"If we do not hear something soon, I may let him write the letter—or I may kill him," said Pepito.

"You might meet a firing squad for that. Don't be foolish. Robbing stagecoaches and raping fine ladies is one thing: murder is another. Jaurez is a man of law. You have survived only because most of your misdemeanors—if you can call them that—go unreported. The ladies' pride and shame save you."

"I doubt that there would be anyone around to turn me in," replied Pepito

Ramona understood. Without doubt, he was capable of killing her, if he thought for a minute that she could be dangerous to him.

Before she could make any plans she needed to tell Bart that she was carrying his child. His reaction would determine everything. The following day when she brought his food and began the cleaning, she sent the guard for more water. The errand afforded a moment to talk unobserved.

"I'm going to have a baby," she said, simply.

"Did I understand you correctly?"

"Yes, I think you understood. The child is yours." A long silence followed.

"I will take care of you, if I ever get out of here." Bart was stunned. It had not been a dream.

"We can plan an escape as soon as you're able."

"I am able, but we will need horses. I have no clothes."

"Give me a few days. I will need to go to the village for drugs."

"Have you any money?"

"A little. Where can we go? We cannot return to Veracruz," she said.

"We must go to Taxco. I have connections there."

When the guard returned, she was silently cleaning the room. Slowly he ate the prepared food. Out of consideration for her he had swallowed the shock over her news, but why should I be surprised at such a consequence? he thought. The money to take care of Ramona and the child would be no problem. What difference would it make? She would remain in Mexico. What sort of curious little creature would they produce together?

The thought of Anne-Marie was hardly to be borne. She would have to be protected from this.

Within a few days Ramona handed Bart a piece of paper. "Write your wife a ransom letter that I can take to the post and mail. Your hosts are growing impatient."

Ramona's news made Bart certain of one thing: he did not want Anne-Marie to receive a ransom note, pay and locate him until he could get his life straightened out with Ramona taken care of someway. He did not address the letter to Key West, but Ramona did not notice this.

"I will mail the letter myself," Pepito announced, taking the letter from her.

"As you want, but remember the ransom comes to me, and to me only, under terms which you do not know. Go mail the letter. You are only one link in a chain."

By Ramona's calculations they had about two weeks to clear the area. Because Pepito was taking the letter to the post, she had lost the opportunity to buy drugs, but she could find others in the countryside. Luckily Pepito and Jiminez were gone for two days giving her time to search and find herbs that would knock out three men in less than a lethal punch. She found what she wanted, however, Pepito and Jiminez returned with a startling discovery. A reward of one thousand gold dollars had been posted in every post office in Mexico for news of the whereabouts and safe return of Captain Bartholomew Ramsden. Pepito had seen the poster and recognized Bart's face. A stranger read it to him.

"I'm going to turn him in," cried Pepito. "One thousand in the hand is worth more than two thousand in the bush."

"Don't be a fool. That is nothing compared to what we will make," replied Ramona. "These are very rich people. The Señora is the richest woman in all of Florida. You will be arrested as a kidnapper and shot."

One thousand dollars was a fortune to Pepito. "I don't care. He doesn't know me. I can say he was delirious and we saved him. It's simple and it's true!" Arms clutched together, Pepito and Jiminez were hopping with joy. "What luck!"

Showing nothing, Ramona was devastated. Now she could never dissuade Pepito from turning in Bart. She would end up with nothing but a child. She and Bart would have to act that very night. She would drug the men, steal clothes for Bart, and they would make the break.

In a small backroom a cowhide bag, not unlike a large hammock, nailed to a long wooden frame, held the fermenting juice of the maguey that made the *pulque*. The smell of the white foamy liquid was gagging, but she filled a jug, grateful for the potent nature of the drink. In this she mixed a strong diffused concoction of bark, leaves and berries. With the men unconscious, she would be able to get the keys to Bart's room. She did not see how Bart could walk far, but they could take the horses. Would there be enough light on the precipitous mountain trail? She dared not think—much less calculate the hours they would have. By daylight she knew the way. Could she find it in the dark? What a fool I am to have run such risks…Did I now know them?

That day she prepared guinea pigs for dinner well fortified with garlic and a sauce made of tomatillos. Her two conspirators were delighted with the meal that lavishly celebrated their discovery. Soon the spiked *pulque*, jovially shuttled back and forth between the two men, had its effect. They were staggering to their beds unaware of the potent content and strength of their draught. The key to Bart's cell lay carelessly on the table. When their snores began to blast the night, Ramona stealthily moved along the portico or veranda toward the bedrooms.

The six bedrooms of the *rancho* were loosely knit by a series of breezeways, stables and storerooms in a line, not unlike a string of railroad cars. The covered verandah, decked with a tile roof, unified the disparate elements. Silently, Ramona slipped along the porch to the men's bedrooms, praying they had not bothered to bolt the heavy wooden doors. She would have to enter Jiminez's room first for clothes for Bart, he being more nearly Bart's size.

Feeling her way along, suddenly she reached rough wood that with a shove of her shoulder gave way. Squeaking hinges screamed through the silent night, more disconcertingly, she stepped down a few inches, almost losing her balance, to a dirt floor. She knew immediately that she had opened the wrong door, one to a storeroom. Hoes and shovels dislodged by her near fall, slipped to the ground with a frightening clatter. For only a few minutes she waited frozen for a thundering attack. Then, when no response came she stepped back to the verandah and continued to the right door that, blessedly, had not been locked. Once again the heavy iron hinges protested under the weight of the heavy hand-hewn door. Jiminez's snores halted for a long drawn-out terrifying minute, but finally picked up their reassuring, lumbering tempo, undisturbed even by their own noise. Gathering breath, Ramona slipped across the room to the usual pegs on the wall for clothing, an old poncho and a pair of pants. Accidentally, she stepped on a boot, causing it to rise against her ankle with a frightening movement until she realized what she had done. Stumbling on its mate, she grabbed the boots and with arms full slipped from the room.

Upon hearing the key in the lock Bart jumped from his bed. Immediately, he recognized the short whispering figure. "Quickly, get into these clothes."

The pants were short and too big in the waist. "A piece of rope from the stable will hold them up," said Ramona, bunching the bedclothes to appear as if a body was under them.

"The men?" queried Bart.

"Drugged—dead to the world until late morning."

Bart locked the door and moved toward the stables. "With my room locked we may gain a few minutes' time."

"Are you all right? Are you strong enough to walk?" she asked.

"I can walk, but you must lead. I have no idea where I am or what is underfoot."

Once in the stable they quieted the nervous horses. Bart could also work his feet into the boots which fit tolerably. Fumbling and fidgeting in the darkness they improvised a rope belt to hold up Bart's pants. Finally, they got the horses saddled and led them slowly from the stable into the yard, past the ranch house, single file to the trail. Only the scuffling of feet, the scurrying of rodents, and a distant hoot of an owl broke the stillness of the night. A transient moon shed a little light as they picked their way along the dangerous trail at what seemed like a snail's pace.

"Let's hope the drug keeps the men out of the way until late in the morning," said Ramona. "Then we can make some time with the first light of day."

"I'd like to race."

"No, we can't go fast, Bart," she cautioned. "Perhaps we should hide during the daylight. The men know the perches where they can watch the trail for miles. They know the terrain like the palms of their hands, while we can easily become lost. There are dangerous precipices everywhere. Honestly, we dare not hurry. Traps are many."

Doubtful despite her warning, Bart had to struggle against resentment over their slow pace. After months of confinement, he was anxious to celebrate the sweet air of freedom.

Fortunately, the darkness prevented the horses from the terrors they could not see. When the first rays of daylight, like a rising curtain, exposed giant boulders, sheer cliffs that dropped hundreds of feet, stumbling blocks of felled trees, and wide gullies that even a light rain could turn into raging riverbeds of cascading water, Bart was aghast.

"Ramona, I see no way that we can survive this by traveling only at night. Only by the grace of God and sheer luck are we still alive!"

"I did try to warn you," she replied. "It's a difficult land."

Appraising the situation, Bart did not see how they could survive, much less escape.

CHAPTER EIGHT

Anne-Marie's latest discovery—her pregnancy on top of discovering Bart's correspondence with Alma Russell, did not provoke great consternation. If Bart returned safely and proved to be innocent, as Tim felt he was, she would be happy about the child. And, if Bart was forever lost, she guessed that she would also be happy about the babe. She had cherished her family such that she had not wanted Samantha to grow up without siblings. Stressful as Alma's correspondence with Bart appeared, this time she decided to keep her findings to herself. The fact that her imagined rival, Alma, also was suffering, offered little solace. Anne-Marie was not mean. She would not dignify money with a letter, however. A postal money order in Bart's name would have to suffice.

She put on a dark dress that matched her mood, then changed her mind and put on another, bright enough for a festival. At least, I don't have to look like a victim, she told herself. She looked in the mirror and saw that her mouth looked like a wound. Sticking to her resolve, she looked at herself in the colorful frock. She drew back her heavy hair and coiled it. "I'll survive," she told herself out loud, reaching for a white lace parasol to shade her from the blazing sun as she walked to the post office. Someway looking good helped still the inner commotion—a little.

*   *   *   *

William Rosecrans, Envoy Extraordinary and Minister Plenipotentiary of the United States to Mexico under President Andrew Johnson, and his successor Thomas Nelson under President Ulysses Grant, who took office in 1869, were both sympathetic to Anne-Marie's cause. But the fact remained that there was no record of her husband having entered Mexico. Under the circumstances Mexican officials threw up their hands. Generously they allowed award notices to be posted in all Mexican post offices. Bart's tattered photograph joined those of dozens of 'Wanted' criminals and assorted outlaws in rogues' galleries—which no one paid any attention to for the simple reason that most of the viewers could not read.

Soon it became clear that she could expect little official assistance. Any illusions she fostered over the power and influence of money soon faded. She had influence in many places, but in that vast and primitive land of Mexico she had none at all.

Meanwhile, it had become clear to Rafael de Palma that as far as his business with Ramona was concerned, the plan had failed. To hell with her. There was money to be made in leading an effort to find Bart, which, he hoped, would not be successful; nevertheless, this was the new road he would take.

"Frankly, I see but one course of action," said Rafael, joining Anne-Marie for dinner at her invitation. "You will have to form your own army."

"My own army! I never heard of such a thing. It's preposterous."

"Not at all. Such bands are called *guerrilleros*. All large landowners have them to maintain control of their holdings. My dear, with one hundred well-trained men you could conquer the country. I'm exaggerating, of course, but you must see my point. We would enter legally in a band. I would need false papers, but they are obtainable. It's a marvelously simple plan."

"I suppose I should also build a navy to support and transport the army," said Anne-Marie, her sarcasm cutting like a broken bottle at his throat. A napkin crumpled in her hand.

Rafael was offended. "You're not taking me seriously." His eyes lowered. "Very honestly, I do not relish the appearance of your husband. But that does not mean that I would withhold my best advice to you. I have promised to help you. I am a man of honor. This is the only way that I can help you—unfortunately. My only fortune is under my hat." He spoke with apologetic hardness.

"I'm sorry. I apologize. Your suggestion is so startling, I could not believe it although I should have because Tim also once mentioned a brigade. Surely, you have an exaggeration of my wealth. But, if you and Tim find this feasible, I will write my father. How much money are you thinking of?"

Rafael had put her on the defensive, a spot she despised. Now she was turning the tables.

"Not much in the long run," he replied. "You would need to buy guns and horses, and both can be sold in Mexico for at least a tidy profit after they are no longer of use to you. Mercenaries do not make high wages. You already own a ship for transporting the men."

"Still, it is a rather daring thing to do."

"That, my lady, is the secret of success in warfare—surprise."

"I'm grateful to you." She spoke humbled. A gamut of emotions: irritation, disappointment, anger, worry and stress had followed the silence from Mexico. "If I seem unappreciative it is because I've been in turmoil since my husband left. Please understand."

Rafael assumed a tone one would use with a child. "My dear, don't torture yourself. You have an arsenal of friends eager to help you. There are times when even the strongest of us must be comforted—or would perish."

Only concern for Bart led Anne-Marie to Rafael and Rafael sensed this. He knew this was not time to force himself closer. That would only drive her away. There would be plenty of time to advance his cause once he had a few dollars in his pocket—and more than a few if Bart should never be found. Admittedly, he had gone further with Mimi than he had intended. He still needed Mimi. "I am a friend wanting to rid you of your burdens, not add to them. I am certain that I can help you as possibly none other."

He rose, suave and elegant, sleek as an Arabian stallion. Bright burning eyes, capable of hiding no end of sophistry with gem-like vigor, seemed to make him brim with strength and confidence. To Anne-Marie now he appeared dashing and powerful as a Grandee stepping down from some heroic Spanish portrait ready to save her lost husband. He stood apart, a towering presence, capable of anything, no matter how far fetched, dangerous or extravagant. Both Bart and Tim had recognized his capabilities, which she had stubbornly misinterpreted and denied. Apparently, Latin males had a sticky, pushy lather about them that women had to push aside and ignore in order to appreciate their real worth. She had been wrong, but she had been learning. Now, thankfully Rafael was putting things on a plane that she could accept.

Moving slowly to her desk drawer, the silence being broken only by the rustle of her taffeta skirt, she withdrew a handful of bills and pressed them into Rafael's hands.

"What have we here?" he asked.

"Some money. We must start somewhere," replied Anne-Marie, having handed him the munificent sum of one thousand dollars. "I cannot permit you to advance money for this. I have no idea what you have already spent through friends in Mexico." She could see the pulses beating hard in his throat. He was reluctant to take money from her, she supposed.

Gently he raised a hand and pressed his fingers to his lips to stem any protest on her part. "If we are agreed on what must be done, I must begin at once."

"We are agreed."

Only later did she remember that she wanted to talk this over with Tim and write her father.

The following afternoon, refreshed, Rafael paid up three months' outstanding bills at Russell House.

Something in Mexico had gone radically wrong and he had no recourse but to go into a different plan. In mustering a guerilla band it would be simple to siphon off money. One had to be flexible, he reminded himself, enormously relieved to have some money in his pockets again. Due to the rising unrest in Cuba in what was a struggle for independence from Spain, Cubans were flocking to Key West. He could pick soldiers from this group. The young bucks won't be too interested in rolling cigars, the one industry in Key West open to them, he decided. They're all peons anyway, thought Rafael, whose sympathies lay squarely with Spain.

Anne-Marie walked to Consuelo and Tim's house to discuss Rafael's plan, only to be sidetracked by more exciting happenings.

"I was goin' to fetch you, Miz Ramsden," greeted a beaming excited Pearl, meeting her at the door, then leading her upstairs to Consuelo's bedroom. "Miz Clayton's baby is coming."

"You've called Dr. Burbury and the midwife, haven't you?"

"That's what Mister Clayton is up to right now," replied Pearl.

They found Consuelo pacing the floor.

"So, something exciting is happening," said Anne-Marie kissing Consuelo's harried brow.

"I'm afraid so. Have you any suggestions?"

"Yes. Pearl, run to Johnson's Drug Store, the one across the street from Russell House and buy some Tokoine tea. Charge it to me. Now hurry," ordered Anne-Marie.

"It will relax your nervous system. Meanwhile, I'll get your bed fixed. We will need some oil cloth, and some old papers, and a clean old quilt that can be washed easily."

Finding the common household items presented no problem and then Anne-Marie made up Consuelo's bed as she had seen it done when her children were born. First she made up the bed normally, then came the oil cloth sheet, then the newspapers and lastly the quilt. By the time this was done, Pearl arrived with the tea.

"You'll have an easier time if, at this point, you stay on your feet. It will help if you are thoroughly irrigated. Keep drinking tea every thirty minutes. You will perspire, too, but that's also good."

Thoroughly frightened, Consuelo promised to comply. "The pains started early this morning, but only in the last half-hour have they been regular. What's keeping Tim and the doctor?"

"Don't be so anxious. Nothing is going to happen in the next few minutes, much as you would like to have this over. Everyone will be here in plenty of time," soothed Anne-Marie, reaching for her friend's hand.

"No more children for me. One is enough. I can tell. This is going to be very painful. It is already, and I don't like it."

"Hush and drink your tea. Then I'll walk with you. Think, the endless months of waiting will soon be over." She was going to add: Your life will never be the same again, but that sounded too frightening, so she didn't.

"I handle pain badly. It's due to my Latin blood. Warn the midwife and Dr. Burbury of that." Fear rode in her eyes.

"Don't worry I will. Now fill your lungs by inhaling through your nostrils, breathe as deeply as possible and exhale slowly in the same manner."

"Where do you suppose the doctor is?" worried Consuelo, looking uncomfortable yet trying to follow instructions. Anne-Marie wiped her brow.

"I'm sure he's on his way, but this is going to go on for a while. Babies are not in a rush—especially the first one."

Finally, they could hear Tim, Dr. Burbury and the midwife downstairs. "Your team has arrived. Now, don't you feel better?"

"No," replied Consuelo, sharply. "What are they waiting downstairs for? I'm having the baby, not Tim."

"I'll go send them up," said Anne-Marie, anxious to escape the room.

After the briefest greeting to Anne-Marie, Dr. Burbury and the Black midwife, who came lugging her own midwife's chair, low as a child's, climbed the stairs to Consuelo's room.

Within a few minutes Dr. Burbury was back downstairs. "The baby is well positioned. With the midwife here, I won't be needed—if at all—for a while, at least for several hours yet."

Tim paled. "You're absolutely certain?" Judging from Consuelo's discomfort and trying to hide his anxiety, he found the 'several hours yet' hard to believe and worse to anticipate.

"Oh, absolutely," replied Burbury, "or I wouldn't leave. Your wife is a vociferous, colorful patient—one of my favorites. Now, take my advice and take a walk, a long walk, Mister Clayton."

The doctor's departure was followed by a series of screams resounding down the stairwell. Tim felt certain the baby would arrive sooner than the doctor had anticipated. This inexperienced opinion was based on the tenor of his wife's discomfort, probably the most unreliable indication of an imminent delivery.

Anne-Marie found herself running up and down stairs, attempting to comfort first one and then the other in the Clayton family. Finally, Dr. Burbury returned to look in on his patient.

"Can't you give me something for the pain?" begged Consuelo.

"Not at this point. It would slow down your labor and be dangerous for the baby. You're not ready yet." With his stethoscope he checked both heartbeats and smiled approval. Consuelo's pulse was good. "Close that window, Pearl. We don't want a draft on Missus Clayton. I don't want her to get a chill." With an affectionate pat he moved toward the door.

"Where are you going? Don't leave me!" cried Consuelo.

"I'm going downstairs for a minute to reassure your husband. I won't leave the house. You have the best midwife in Key West with you." Burbury edged from the room.

"It won't be much longer now," said Burbury to Tim who was pacing the floor, astounded by the doctor's calm and wondering if he would ever enjoy sex again.

"There's nothing you can give her?" asked Tim.

"Birthing is a natural process and whenever possible we should let nature take its course. It's the way we all got here." The doctor shrugged.

Then Anne-Marie stepped into the room. "The midwife wants you, Doctor," she said quickly, relieved to leave Consuelo in more experienced hands. She felt exhausted.

Two steps at a time the doctor took the stairs while downstairs Tim and Anne-Marie waited, tuned to the muffled voices above. Finally, a new and different wail rose above the scuffling feet and Dr. Burbury appeared beaming at the head of the stairs. "Tim, you have a beautiful baby boy. He's perfect."

"I'm so happy for you—and so will Bart be!" cried Anne-Marie.

Wiping a tear of relief and feeling less than foolish knowing that everyone in the house had shared the same nameless stress, Tim fought for words. "A boy! Isn't that great? Wonderful! And thank heaven that's over!" At last the months of waiting, pain, travail, and worry were in the past. He and Consuelo were inviolable.

Anne-Marie stepped to the door. "Where are you going?" asked Tim.

"To chill a bottle of champagne," she replied.

"One's been chilling for three weeks!"

Dr. Burbury was soon downstairs leaving the cheaning up to the midwife. Pearl gave her mistress a few drops of *pulsatilla* in camomile. Then she prettied her mistress, wan and tired but glowing with a radiance of supreme relief. Insulated by love, happy beyond belief, Consuelo showed off her production: a ruby red, surprised, kicking bundle of joy. Then they let the mother rest.

"I'm sorry Bart is not here to share this day with you, Tim," Anne-Marie said later.

"It's an important day in our lives. We're naming the boy Bart." He chuckled, "I would have liked his support."

"Rafael came over yesterday—now it seems weeks ago. He wants to take a small army to Mexico to look for Bart."

"Off hand it sounds like an expensive proposition, but I can see merit in it," replied Tim.

"Not necessarily. We should be able to sell the guns and horses profitably to offset the cost of the mercenaries once we find Bart. At first it sounded far-fetched to me, too, but considering the political climate of Mexico, it may be the only way to find him and perhaps save him. If it's money or Bart's life, money must be paid, no matter how much."

"How many men is he talking about?"

"A hundred."

"You already have a ship to transport the men and an area to train them There's plenty of Civil War surplus going begging: guns, cots, tents, mess kits, horses, *et cetera*. It's feasible, Anne-Marie."

"I think so, too."

"Write your father. I think you need a wiser head than mine at the moment, but I will help you all I can. Today is ending so beautifully, I find it difficult to contemplate reservations." A euphoria, stemming from overwhelming gratitude over the gift of a son and the support of all who sustained him, settled over Tim. In this benevolent spirit he pledged his support of Anne-Marie—a course of action that would effect his life greatly. "Once I'm sure no complications arise after the birth, I would be able to go to Mexico with you, if you decide to go yourself."

Anne-Marie almost confided that she was pregnant, but decided to wait for another day. By the time they had finished a patio dinner and their coffee, the night was black. Enormous stars and fireflies, like mischievous candles, taunted the diners with their phosphorescent beauty. "I am not yet ready one hundred percent to trust Rafael," said Tim. "But, by all means listen to all he has to say. Don't give him a nickel until everything has been carefully considered."

"Tim, be realistic. If he were to outfit a band of mercenaries for me, I would have to put money in his hands," replied Anne-Marie, speaking in defense of Rafael, yet not mentioning that she had already given him money—and possibly too much. Perhaps, I've been a fool, she thought.

"I told you I'd help. You have a brother-in-law and your father. Here are three men you know you can trust. For starters, let's have a meeting with Rafael tomorrow."

"Fine."

At the meeting Rafael saw that he was going to have to reckon with Tim Clayton. It would not be a one-man-show with Rafael in star billing. Anne-Marie wanted Tim to handle purchasing. Fluent in Spanish, Rafael could best handle hiring, payroll and training. Rafael was disappointed, but his jurisdiction was not without opportunities for extortion, especially if the training were extended a few weeks longer than absolutely necessary. The rolls could be padded. Sick pay could be siphoned off. It would be wise at this point to present a highly cooperative attitude. He would talk an honest game. "I'm no mathematician and I would like someone to check my figures at every turn," he insisted.

"That can easily be done. Anne-Marie's brother-in-law is an accountant."

"Perfect," responded Rafael. "We'll make a great team. We must keep everything on a business-like basis. I'm happy to donate my services, and I think we should get moving right away."

"We can't let you do that," interjected Anne-Marie.

"You have heard my terms."

Anne-Marie appreciated Rafael's enthusiasm. Tim was more cautious. "I think he doth protest too much," said Tim later when he and Anne-Marie were alone. "After all, he can't afford to work for nothing, so why play the grand don?"

"He suffers from too much pride, I'm sure."

"Let's avoid mistakes. Ability doesn't come necessarily with European manners. It remains for Rafael to prove himself. Certainly, we should give him a chance."

Tim's jaundiced eye made Anne-Marie resolve to be careful. Her anxiety could make her careless.

"Write you father to ship a hundred Colt revolvers," advised Tim. "They are made in Hartford—if we can't get them from surplus." The change of subject was welcome.

The subject of guns, however, was to come up again at their next meeting. "I've asked Father to purchase the revolvers as you suggested, Tim," said Anne-Marie.

"I'm unfamiliar with that pistol, having handled only European weapons," confided Rafael. "But, I understand the gun uses a new metallic cartridge called a 'bullet' and it can be fired a number of time before reloading."

"It's quite an advance," explained Tim. "The hammer must be pulled back by the shooter's thumb to cock the hammer and rotate the cylinder around to where there's another cartridge. Then all that's needed to fire is a light pull on the trigger. It's an incredible gun."

Rafael was slightly ruffled when he learned that rifles would come from Krupp in Essen. War clouds were brewing in Europe between Prussia and France over Luxembourg, which Napoleon III hoped to annex. Apparently, the Germans would have superior weaponry. Krupp was now manufacturing breach loading, cast steel guns and selling them to everyone but the French where Rafael's sympathy lay.

Rafael was also uncomfortable because in his own field as a military man he saw that he was out-dated and valuable as last year's almanac. The years in Mexico had cost him his expertise. He must remain silent at least for a while—a far cry from the commanding authoritative role he had envisioned for himself.

Anne-Marie was unaware of his deficiecies, but highly conscious of her own. She determined to learn as fast as possible.

That night she wrote her father: *"Dear Father, Because I know how distressed you will be, and how you will so foolishly blame yourself over Bart's disappearance, I am concerned for you. The fact is, to relieve us all, we must enter Mexico with a band of mercenaries to try to find and extricate Bart. This is not your fault. I make my own decisions and take responsibility for them.*

"As my agent, please put David on the payroll commensurate with his past earnings. I'm sending the yacht north for David and for an order of Colt revolvers and other supplies I am listing here including army surplus items to be purchased. David can see to it with your advice. We are going to have to sell all our U.S. stocks and bonds. Before September 21st, sell everything that we own on the New York Stock Exchange. I know you enjoy managing my accounts, but these are my orders.

"When we are finished with this expedition, the arms and horses that we must purchase can be sold profitably to reduce our costs. In other words, I don't think the expedition will cost as much as it seems at the moment in the long run. However, I want cash available. This is my decision, not yours, and I implore you, please in no way feel that you have been responsible for this turn of events. Regardless of anything you said, Bart would have gone to Mexico. You simply convinced me that I should let him go gracefully. David should bring the cash with him. Your loving daughter, Anne-Marie."

It was a difficult letter to write. Jason had been trading for her on the stock market, and he had done very well for her. She hated to sell, but she had no choice. Heaven only knew how much the expedition would cost and ready cash had to be available.

At the same time that she mailed a letter to her father, she dropped off a note inviting Rafael to dinner were he free. He arrived punctually, flowers in hand, flattering words on his lips. He was his charming best, which was what Anne-Marie needed.

"I'm sorry, but there are only the two of us tonight," she explained. "I can't be the gay scintillating hostess, but I know Tim would not want to leave Consuelo and I am not up to other Key West society. I thought you would be interested in hearing that we are moving ahead."

"You are doing the right thing."

"You'll find my brother-in-law helpful. He and Bart never got along well, but I never felt that was entirely David's fault. People with a head for figures can be boring…"

Despite Anne-Marie's perfume that left Rafael enveloped in a cloud of aphrodisia, the mention of an accountant brought him down to earth. She was involving Tim and now David, both of whom would complicate matters for him. Her remark reminded him of an envelope, which he handed her.

"This is an accounting of the money you have given me. When you are finished with it, I'd like it back because I've not had time to copy everything."

"That will be no problem," she assured him, slipping the envelope between two books.

For the remainder of the evening he was a delightful guest, amusing her with card tricks and anecdotes which took her mind off the enormous project before them. Once during the evening he was tempted to draw her close and came precariously close to breaking his resolve not to rush her, but his prior judgment prevailed. Sometime during the evening the envelope with his accounting went back into his pocket and out of Anne-Marie's house the same way it came in. Two days later she turned the house upside down looking for it, but it had vanished

She said nothing over having lost the accounting. He assumed this to be an indication of weakness.

For some days Anne-Marie had been at loose ends. She did not want to intrude on Consuelo and Tim, totally engrossed in their newborn and at the same time suffering from a lack of sleep. Her pregnancy did not show. She was also ill-prepared to deal with other friends not wanting to discuss Bart's absence nor her plans to spearhead a military mission to

Mexico which had to remain top secret. It was natural that she turned to Rafael to discuss their common interest.

"We have the perfect place for housing and training the men, Los Clavelas on Cayo de Las Matas—the Key of the Plants. The estate is now stripped of all fine furnishings. Here ships come and go unobserved. There are warehouses for storage. It would be difficult to imagine a more idea secret training station and it belongs to me."

"I must see it. Can we go tomorrow?"

"I have already sent *Los Girasoles* north or we could…"

"I'll get a boat. We can make a picnic. We'll go tomorrow."

"On second thought, I'd rather not take a stranger there at this point, but I do have an old skiff that I'm sure we could handle."

"Perfect."

The following day with a spanking breeze Anne-Marie and Rafael sailed easily to the key in less than two hours. As they entered the hidden inlet, two of half-dozen workers tending the grove helped them tie up.

"You can see here we have a perfect protected basin for loading and unloading," explained Anne-Marie, "and a large house to quarter the men."

Los Claveles, meaning The Carnations, loomed before them. The large stuccoed stone structure was now closed by tall, slender louvered doors, looking uninhabited as it was.

Slowly they proceeded toward the front terrace where Wade Stiles, wearing a ring of keys on a chain clipped to his belt met them. With a smile, Anne-Marie explained their presence. "It is necessary for me to show Mr. de Palma the property, Wade." Seeing a disturbed expression on the caretaker's face, she added, "Now don't get worried. I'm not thinking of selling."

A relieved smile crossed his face. Wade led them through the empty house, opening doors or windows where necessary to let in light.

"Wade is my most trusted employee," she whispered to Rafael.

Wade led them back outside, and carefully locked up the house. As they left the terrace to inspect a building that could be used as a barn, Wade suddenly drew his pistol and fired within inches of Rafael's foot. The Spaniard wheeled around to face Wade. "What in the devil do you think you're doing?" shrieked the Spaniard, the color in his face rapidly rising. "Don't you ever fire a gun near me again!"

"Look behind you, sir," replied Wade placidly.

De Palma turned to see a rattlesnake. Its body the size of his arm, possibly eight feet long, head blown off, now in death throes. The fiery pink color on de Palma's face blanched to white.

"I beg your pardon, sir," said de Palma, with a weak smile and swallowing hard.

"They usually rattle to give you warning," Wade replied. "I thought I would spare you that."

"That's one of the biggest I've seen on the island," said Anne-Marie, also awed. "Fortunately, Wade is an excellent shot. I believe you brought a picnic…"

"I did. Hopefully the cook at Russell House will not disappoint us. Excuse me for a minute while I get the basket," replied Rafael, anxious to be off for a moment's composure, at the same time watching his footing.

"I apologize for frightening your, guest, Ma'am," said Wade.

Anne-Marie laughed quietly. Now it was amusing. "I see that man will have to learn not to speak too fast."

Soon after they finished eating the excellent repast of dainty rolls, sliced cold meats, fruit and teacakes, Anne-Marie requested they leave.

Once underway, de Palma suggested that Anne-Marie should buy an old cattle boat to transport the horses. "The men can be transported on your yacht. I'll look for an appropriate ship."

"Tim Clayton will be able to assist you. He knows as much about ships as my husband."

Rafael seemed glum.

*   *   *   *

Upon returning to the hotel Rafael found a note waiting for him from Mimi. "*Please drop by this evening,*" it stated, nothing more.

Clearly, she had seen or heard something and she was angry. Once again he would have to mend that bridge—he supposed.

Having not been invited to dinner, he arrived rather late. Mimi's daughter Suzanne was out of town and obviously the servants had been dismissed for the evening as Mimi met him at the door. "I want to talk with you," she announced coolly, leaving him to hang up his hat himself.

"Is there anything that I can do for you?" he asked, flashing a smile that was lost on her back.

"Yes!" replied Mimi. "You can stop throwing yourself at Anne-Marie Ramsden."

"Mimi," intoned Rafael. "I don't know what you think you've seen or heard, but the accusation is preposterous!"

"This is a small town that thrives on gossip. Today I dropped by the Russell House to personally deliver an invitation and learned that you were on a picnic. Then, if you can believe it, I saw you with my own eyes, sailing off with her. I know you've been seeing her—but I chose not to mention it." After an indignant toss of her head, Mimi continued, "Between ladies and gentlemen a certain decorum should be observed—especially when certain bounds have been exceeded."

"My dear, you have something all wrong. I am doing my level best to locate her husband—at her and Tim Clayton's urging. For all practical purposes I have been employed for expertise on Mexico. Today I did have a picnic lunch packed, and I sailed with her to examine a piece of property. It was purely business. At the piece of property we met a number of other people. I wish I could tell you more, but I am committed to secrecy—for reasons of my own security I might add. If you force me to discuss this with you, you could seriously endanger me. Therefore, I humbly ask your trust…" Rafael's eyes fell to the floor.

Mimi, completely taken aback by his honest admittance found herself defenseless. "I'm sorry," she murmured. "Perhaps I have been unfair…"

"You have," he whispered, reaching out to her, enveloping her in his arms. Lifting her face to his, he kissed her. The lingering kiss and a gentle caress of her bosom broke down any remaining barriers. As soon as her response signaled, Rafael led her upstairs where he helped her undress and rid himself of his clothes. Falling on her, and with a lambent, languorous rocking motion, he locked himself into her, plunging in a never breaking the seal between them. His own fluids, slowly and carefully released met hers to produce a fire as passion engulfed them.

Rafael, like a young stallion, was capable of bringing Mimi to a pitch of madness over and over again. Her jealous turmoil during the afternoon had stoked the fire; his meek indignation and blameless innocence provoked the pathos to fan the flames. Intimacies varied the union so that the evening became one of the most sensual, hedonic and salacious encounters of her life.

Later curled in his arms as he slept, Mimi reviewed her lover's words. What was the secret work in which Anne-Marie was involving him that was so dangerous? She would have to find out.

Despite what Rafael had said, it was hard to imagine that Anne-Marie would not be interested in him. Captain Ramsden was equally good looking in his own way, but he was so…so unpolished, so boyish, unsophisticated. Also, it was highly possible that Bart Ramsden might never come back…What then?

Anne-Marie Ramsden had better not dare to trespass on her territory. Not if she knows what's good for her, thought Mimi.

CHAPTER NINE

Although Bart felt he was viewing the most harrowing landscape imaginable, it was also the most magnificent. Isolated deep green ravines shut from one another by orange mountain walls casting deep purple shadows, rose from the sky as sheer stone cliffs. During the night he and Ramona had traversed along a hairpin curve which descended and then climbed again. Between them and the ranch stretched a *barranca* or deep canyon, filled at the bottom with rampant, lush tropical vegetation. Here strange palms, grasping strangler figs, bamboo, lacey poincianas and jacarandas, mahogany and the giant cieba, crowned by orchids and bromeliads, vied for space in the sun.

In the uppermost, practically soilless reaches, scrubby pines, cacti and temperate vegetation clawed the land in a perpetual struggle for footing and water. Height twisted from rocky height, disordered, hostile, and terrifyingly beautiful. Above it all a brilliant sky capped the startling view.

It was a marvel to Bart that they had not toppled to their deaths during the night. "God, how have we survived?" he asked.

Ramona had no answer.

Impassively, he looked down at his figure. The ill-fitting boots, rough baggy pants, faded wool poncho, the whole sight of himself was alien. Yet there he stood in a strange land with all the strange smells and sounds, where even the sky was weird and violent. A livid bright sun fell on his face, as unreal as the land it lit.

Well, they had survived. That was something. He looked to Ramona and exhaled a sigh of relief. "Are you all right? It's been a long hard night for a woman in your condition."

"I'm fine, but I'm worried about traveling in daylight. Remember the horses see much better at night than we do."

"The horses will need to graze and you must be hungry," said Bart.

"No hungrier than you."

"For days you've been stuffing me. I've built up a reserve of fat. But, I have not broken the breakfast habit."

"I don't understand how you could get up out of a sickbed to travel so well. You must have been playing ill." She spoke without chagrin, but Bart thought that he detected a note of doubt. He hastened to reassure her.

"And where would we be now if I had not?"

"I hate to think."

"Then don't. Just pray. Praise the Lord and the whole kit and caboodle of saints. We need all the help we can get to survive this treacherous route that leads only to a road. I even find myself calling on God more than usual." Certainly the number if expletives he had uttered during the night as he stumbled about bore that out.

"One feels insignificant in the country. You can see much further— not just down a narrow twisted street. Here my mind is much clearer. I feel closer to the gods of my ancestors who still inhabit the land." For a moment her placid face seemed to glow as if she had a lamp within her that he had not seen.

"And who are these gods?" he asked, thinking of the ferocious, stylized grotesque figures upturned by the archaeologist Claude Charnay. David had brought his attention to Charnay's memoirs and photographs when they attempted to research Mexico. So little had been published in English on the country, that he had explored every possible reference for background.

"Do you mean Quetzalcoatl and Huitzilpochtli, the blue humming-bird? Or perhaps the rain god Tlaloc? The lord of the dead is Mictlantecuhtli and Tlalocan is reserved for those who die by drowning. There are many more Indian gods." She clicked off the strange sounding names as if they were close personal friends, but as she spoke, her eyes never left the path.

"Who was the goddess of fertility?" he asked, feeling that she was the one who had done them in.

"Xilonen."

"Maybe you'd better stick with the saints," said Bart. "On second thought, they seem more reliable."

Three hundred years of Jesuits, Franciscans and Dominicans, living in this country, preaching the Gospel to people gifted with extravagant imagination, had not accomplished what the world had thought, he mused. All that the Friars taught delighted these people. Dutifully and lovingly they embraced it all. Every fetish of the Roman Catholic Church was merely added to their prehistoric cults. Behind each bejeweled, silk-robed Madonna and saintly apostle lurked the spook of an Aztec god.

"The Aztec gods are more reliable where there are no churches. In the cities people go into the churches to find the holy spirits. They hover there. Ask any priest. Here they are everywhere," she explained.

"You amaze me, Ramona." Her simple resolution of two religions presented no conflict.

With the light they began to have trouble with the horses, accustomed to other hands. The animals were sensitive and moody, unfamiliar with the weight, feel and smell of Ramona and Bart. Thus when Bart swung abruptly onto his horse, its reaction was instinctive. The horse reared.

"Look out!" cried Ramona as soon as she saw the animal's impending reaction.

Her warning came too late. The instant the animal felt Bart's weight it exploded into action, rearing straight into the air and then down with a force that threw Bart over the horse's head. He landed in the dust as the frightened animal pawed the air. In an instant it was over. Ramona rushed to Bart's side, her voice quavering, "Are you hurt?"

For a moment or two Bart could not breathe, much less speak. Knife-like pains shot through his ribs. His lungs seemed ready to burst for want of air. At last he felt the onrush that lightened the blackness which had become nearly total. "I think so," he said, finally, his voice filtered to a coarse whisper. As Ramona bent over him fearfully, his face turned green. Then slowly his color returned to a flush of pink. "Maybe he just knocked the wind out of me," he said as the worst pain subsided.

"You shouldn't have leaped on him like that. You can't do that to a strange horse."

"The horse isn't strange. I've been beside him all night," he replied, slowly picking himself up, still cringing with pain. "I don't have a lot of experience with horses. Usually, I travel in a buggy. There have always been horsecars or trains or stagecoaches when I wanted to go somewhere."

"Once you are thrown, you should climb right back on again," said Ramona. "You must show the horse that you are the master."

"But, apparently, I'm not."

Ramona smiled a rare smile in agreement, a little half-smile that oddly appeared to Bart to be a sneer, so unaccustomed was her face to the expression. And why not? For some time now he had been the master of nothing.

Still, again with great effort he mounted the horse. This time the animal did not revolt. Bart's ribs ached and he feared that one or two were broken. Breathing was difficult. As long as they were on an ascending grade the pain was tolerable. It was on the descent, even into small gullies, when his weight shifted backwards to maintain balance, that he felt he was being sawed in two or hacked to death by a sword, stab by stab, step by step. He rode behind her, hiding his pain.

At last with a little distance behind them and a patch of pasture before them, Bart dismounted. It was then Ramona could see the perspiration on his face that, in the cool air, indicated the extent of his pain. With traveling this difficult by day, what would staggering through the next night be? Neither dared contemplate it.

"The horses must rest," said Ramona, tactfully shifting the responsibility to the sturdy animals.

"We have struggled all night. I wonder if we have covered five miles. We are probably, as the crow flies, no more than half a mile from where we started." He was thirsty. He thought of the little wooden box that he always carried on ships that included a vial of morphine and wondered where that box was now. Someplace far away, unfortunately. He was tired and weak. The rough dryness in his mouth tasted of clay. He heard, "Don't be discouraged. We are descending now and I know that it is hard for you, but there is water ahead. We will soon come to a few farms. Perhaps we can get something to bind your chest that will make traveling easier." He turned to her unbelieving.

"Perhaps we should separate. I can only hold you back. Can't we meet at a designated point?"

"I will not hear of it. You would become lost. Together at least we have two pairs of eyes and two horses."

"Then we must both get off this trail, or two fast men will be able to catch us moving on foot."

"I agree, but it is the only route to the road that I know."

Ahead they spied a place where the earth was covered with pine needles that would not show tracks. "Coatlicue, the goddess of Mother Earth, will help us. So will the maize spirit, Cinteotl, as soon we must have food."

"Forgive me if I can't keep the strange names straight. But you might also appeal to Saint Christopher. He might be more generously inclined toward me. Traveling Catholics I have known wear his medal for protection."

"True but we are in Indian country and not in the shadow of a cathedral where his influence would be stronger," Ramona reminded.

They tried to rest, but they could not. Darkening banks of trees, like an assemblage of umbrellas, offered little protection, and that only from above. The feeling of being followed and hunted was enough of a threat to keep them on the move, skittering like insects from a suddenly overturned rock.

Ramona did find a few mushrooms she knew to be safe. "You can tell they are not poisonous," she advised. "They have a few worms in them." The peppery flesh also contained a little water. They both knew they would have to find water the following day, and preferably not in the form of rain that would make the earth slippery.

Discouraged by the constant pain in his ribs, he was grateful for any distracting conversation she offered. She had favored Jaurez as a leader, but with surprising apathy, as if he were too good to last and doomed to fail. When she talked about the people she revealed amazing insights. The exploited Indian or *mestizo*, the Spanish-Indian mixture, although enslaved, malnourished, and wholly absorbed by the inhumanity of masters, still retained some free and creative communion with self, soil and God. This was what was important to the Mexican and could not be taken from him. These people could be exploited economically and yet they were not even aware of it. From the Aztecs the great majority of them had inherited a fatalistic philosophy that nothing could or would be changed. They had their food, shelter and their gods. The rest did not count.

Sitting and resting, then hurriedly struggling over the countryside, Bart and Ramona made small progress. Time did not work in their favor. Bart stared at her immobile face and wondered if she saw this. She complained of nothing. Silently, he complained of everything. Hungry and tired, when darkness came they attempted a little more speed. Ramona walked with a stick, testing the ground before them. Sighting the North Star, Bart kept them from walking in circles. Finally, exhausted, they curled up together for some sleep.

With sleeping habits gained from years at sea, Bart awakened often during the night. Revived, coolly and calmly he analyzed their predicament. He was slowing her. She would have to go ahead alone to get help and particularly water or they would both die. They could part on a conspicuous spot on the ravine and mark it with stones. She could use the marker as a beacon to return to. Meanwhile, he could hide nearby. She would have to agree. With that resolved he slept better.

*   *   *   *

The day following Ramona and Bart's flight, Pepito and Jiminez slept late. Upon awakening it did not take long to discover their escape and figure out exactly the route that would be used. From high points, sporadically, Ramona and Bart's progress had been observed. With provisions and without the encumbrance of horses, the bandits were able to descend from the opposite side of the *barranca* where they could cut off their prey. Miles ahead of Ramona and Bart they waited.

Patience was a deeply ingrained habit as was spying. The only difference was, this time they were not waiting for a stagecoach.

*   *   *   *

Dawn found Ramona and Bart on the move again, but soon, when their progress slowed appreciably, Bart revealed the night's resolution. Again, Ramona disagreed, but when they found an ideal spot that could easily be identified to return to, she acquiesced.

"I'm holding you up too much. I'll be the death of us both, please," he begged. "I have not recovered as much as you thought. With exposure I'm losing strength fast."

A lifetime of doing as men commanded prevailed on Ramona now.

"If anything happens to me, my wife will take care of you and the child. There's not a particle of doubt in my mind about that. She is an extraordinary person with an overblown sense of responsibility. A letter addressed to her in Key West would be delivered. She would be hurt, and she might not forgive me, but she would help you." His voice dropped off suddenly, but his eyes did not move from Ramona's. "I'll be waiting here for you."

Three stones were set as a marker.

"I will speed," she replied, overcome by the charge. She moved to embrace him, but then remembered his painful ribs. Their lips were too dry to kiss so she pressed her hand to his cheek and swallowed hard. Then mounting her horse, she looked down seeing his thin worn face and sunken eyes. The thought occurred that she would never see him again. He would not remain in one place as he had promised, she knew. He would soon be delirious and what could she do?

From his perch almost completely hidden behind boulders, but offering a bird's eye view of miles, Bart soon saw that he had made a terrible mistake. With incredible ease her route and progress could be followed. It made no difference that every once in a while she left the trail and disappeared into pines, he had only to wait and she would emerge. He could judge exactly where by the length of time elapsed. Clearly, he could not sit and wait for her. He would have to move and always under cover of vegetation.

With excruciating effort he broke off branches to twist into the poncho he wore to camouflage himself and the horse. It was a poor disguise, but from a distance it might work. Occasionally the plant cover caught on something, causing him to struggle to keep from toppling from the saddle. Then suddenly the sky blackened. Within seconds the wind picked up loose leaves with a rampant fury. Sand, swept into clouds, swirled past. It seemed only a few minutes until the rain came down in torrents. Gratefully from suppliant hands, he drank while the horse lapped at the swirling muddy water sweeping down the mountain. Soon small rocks and dead brush avalanched toward them. Seeing no let up, he positioned the horse on the windward side of a tree, using the tree as a brace for the animal while he, dismounted, found a leeward spot for himself. Large boulders, dislodged by the torrents, rolled past them, Clumpy dry hunks of earth that resembled stones, melted before his eyes, dissolving into slimey mud that would be washed into the jungle at the base of the mountain.

Then, as quickly as the rain started, it ended, leaving Bart thoroughly soaked and chilled to the bone.

He dared not move until the earth dried somewhat. Slippery cadent earth gave way with every step. Finally, feeling that he could lose no more time, he rebuilt his weather-beaten camouflage and crept along the mountain, clinging from bush to bush. Climbing slightly he could look back to the spot where he and Ramona had left the three stones as a marker. The stones had been swept away as had part of the trail where freshly revealed unweathered rock indicated a landslide, clean as a knife cut.

The spot would never be found again. Had he sat there and waited as promised, he would not have either. Closing his mind and accepting his fate, he pushed on, unthinking.

Ahead the *barranca* veered to the left, westward.

Bart was anxious to reach this cross-point for a daylight view of the terrain ahead. It was a high point and might reveal Ramona's route. Since the deluge he had been concerned about her and hoped she had positioned herself as he had. Refreshed by water, he picked his way along. Unless some habitation appeared, the next day he would have to spend some time hunting food. He could think of little else.

Night came too fast. He lay down a moment to rest, staring across the *barranca* for any sign of life. A magnificent eagle nesting in the top of a pine tree caught his eye and as he sat regarding the bird's posture, the sun dropped from sight. In the fading purple light he selected a campsite, the best he could see—a rock blind with a little grass. Beside the rock, lying down, he felt somewhat hidden. Thinking of Ramona, a brave and distant receding figure, marveling, he fell asleep.

With dawn, moving as rapidly as he could, he headed for the cross-point, sometimes riding, sometimes walking depending on the rigors of the terrain. Once in a near daze, he fell and rolled like a stone. The incline was so steep that only at the last minute was he able to break his roll by grabbing a stem on an old dead gnarled bush. His feet were already at the overhang. The pain of the fall and subsequent rolling were almost blinding and he wondered how he had been able to cling tightly enough to stop his fall. Once the pain quieted and he could think rationally, he recognized the danger of broken ribs puncturing his lungs.

Strangely, he was no longer hungry and it was not because the raw meat of desert animals was revolting. It would be very hard killing a snake or iguana with a rock when he had so little force in his arms. Their effort at the bush had strung them out, he thought. He had seen no berries, but the hunger had gone away. In moments when he was completely still, holding his breath to stop the pain in his chest, he felt euphoric. In rational moments this alarmed him.

Reaching the cross-point, he could see the end of the *barranca* and discovered that the great ravine was T-shaped. A fresh bird's eye view of miles opened up to him, but he also knew that he would be in view himself. Descending a short distance as quickly as he could, he took advantage of cover where he could wait to see Ramona, surely now on the other side of the canyon. He sat waiting for a spot moving. Once he thought he saw her, but she did not emerge further along, so he decided that he was mistaken. Because it was too difficult to watch his footing while looking for her, he decided to stay still a little longer. His eyes seemed drawn to one area where he thought he had seen some movement. Suddenly, he saw her. At first she was moving rapidly on the horse and his heart gave a great leap of relief. There she was, her heavy brown and red shawl flapping behind her! She had made it through the night!

Marveling at the distance she had covered, he congratulated himself on the decision to send her on alone. Then for some reason, obviously to do with the ground, she slowed.

From the distance she was a tiny figure, but it was unmistakably Ramona. The colors and design of her *serape* had been emblazoned on his memory as few other articles of clothing ever would be. Then suddenly two men jumped in front of her horse, grabbing the reins. What looked like a brief struggle ensued, both to hold the horse and pull her from it. The girl was no match for the men and Bart could see they were taking the horse from her. Each man took an arm and walked the struggling figure, her feet hardly touching the ground, toward the cliff. Horror-stricken he watched as the two men swung and tossed her over it like a discarded rag doll. He sat frozen. She seemed to fall downward slowly, as if she were floating, almost soaring, slightly teetering, her arms and legs spread wide as if to extend a glide. Unheard by Bart her scream to some unknown god echoed through the canyon, reverberating faintly minutes after she was gone. Then both men mounted the horse and trotted down the trail.

Bart sat stunned. He decided he had been hallucinating. What he thought he had seen could not have happened. He had been imagining due to lack of food. He could not have been an idle witness to two men murdering a girl. No. He would have done something. But how? What? The odd vision of Ramona sailing eastward persisted like a recurrent dream, but there had been no awakening. Also, he remembered every detail. He doubted if that were true of hallucinations. Perhaps it had happened. A sky that had boasted only one eagle now contained a dozen vultures dipping to earth. What were they doing?

Somehow his mind could not fasten on what he had seen: nor could he let it go: nor could he look again toward the canyon. He veered from the *barranca* fleeing the scene, leaving the trail.

A high plateau was widening before him. The going was not a whole lot easier, but it was less calamitous, he thought. Boulders and old dead stumps bore watching, but he saw no drops that meant sudden death even though in despair and fearing starvation there were moments when he would have welcomed a rapid end. Now his mind wandering, he rode along, an automaton. In turning his back on the *barranca* he was turning away from water, he feared. The green trees at the bottom of the canyon meant water, he had supposed, small streams coming in from somewhere. Still, he had changed course as was a captain's privilege.

Suddenly, in this almost delirious state a little wattle hut with a thatched roof and a riotous garden of flowers rose like a mirage before him. Cacti hedges washed by a recent rain glittered like knives and a maize field turned to waving sheets of gold. A brown woman swept invisible dust from the well-stamped earth of her doorstep with a single leaf of a giant palm. Bart approached the house and collapsed.

Some days later he awakened in the hut. Beside him in a rough cotton dress the brown woman squatted on a *petate* making tortillas. Quiet brooding eyes had been watching him, knowing that his fever had broken and that soon he would awaken. The only sound was the rhythmic patting of the cornmeal in the pale palms of her hands.

She and her family had cared for him since the day he stumbled on their home. Now for the first time her patient's eyes were fluttering. Immediately she rushed to the yard to call her husband and the children to give them the news. They all came to look.

The two parents and five children gathered around his pallet to stare. Finally, the bolder children smiled, allowing a little of the uncontainable excitement to escape.

Bart grinned wanly and nodded his head in thanks. His hosts looked to each other with what Bart felt were kind and pleased comments. After a few minutes the mother shooed the children outside, but in no time they were back, their eyes glued on the stranger.

They spoke no Spanish but an Indian dialect. Within a few hours they found their tongues, overcoming an initial shyness, having met their first stranger.

During the days that followed—melting into weeks—they shared their simple meals of corn and beans, with the inevitable spicy chilies, while he recuperated. Chilies came in various shapes and colors: long, short, fat, small and green, yellow, red or terra cotta. Peppers decorated the hut until they flavored every meal. Bart watched the mother roast them on a rack over charcoal until the skins were charred. Then she wrapped them in a rag for a few minutes before removing the skin and seeds. He soon learned to avoid the *piquin,* that were mighty hot but enjoyed the *poblanos.* The chilies grew in the backyard and the children munched on the hottest ones as if they were strawberries. Bart could only guess that they—while very young—had been desensitized to the irritating chemical in chili. He stayed with the red pimientos that were sweet.

Once the mother prepared a chicken, spiced with what she called *achoite,* and obviously relished, which she cooked underground in banana leaves. It was an important day, but Bart never learned why.

From the Indian family he learned considerably about the maguey. He watched them extract honey from the hollow in the center of the plant. He tried to help them crush the giant twisting green leaves, separating the fibers on a stone with water to produce hemp to make cloth and rope, but this task proved too strenuous for him. The spines were used as needles. White tender shoots nearest the earth were cooked and eaten. Dry leaves provided a gentle smokeless fire. The central stem of the plant when old and dry provided rafters. Survival in this part of the world, hard as it was, would have been impossible without this plant, Bart rightly decided.

Finally, he felt well enough to leave. He had no money to pay them—which they knew; no gifts to leave them other than gratitude, which sufficed. When he departed he embraced them all. Still, the children trotted behind him on his horse almost a mile until he reached the road. There he did his best to memorize the spot, hoping to come back one day to pay them for their care.

He had lost all knowledge of time, having no idea how long he had been kept by Ramona or how long he had been ill. He rightly assumed he had pneumonia before he fell on the Indian family. Days had drifted into weeks and weeks into months. To add to his uncertainly, he was in a land without seasons, without landmarks other than a snow capped mountain, Orizaba. Moreover, there were no road signs. He headed westward.

Wary even of his shadow, he turned every few minutes to look behind him. His horse was his prized possession. Most riders had only mules and any outlaw who came across him would try to steal the animal. The natural urge was to race, hoping to reach Còrdoba, but he knew this to be unwise, even if he were sure of where he was. He would have to conserve the horse's strength for an unexpected sprint if necessary. At times the road passed through fields of maguey, which was comforting now that he knew the value of the plant. Most comforting was the knowledge that some habitation was within a few miles.

Once he turned to see a pack of riders. Immediately he threw his horse into a gallop, and, having the fastest animal, he escaped. They need not have been outlaws, but the chase indicated they were. Finally, he approached a beautiful hacienda, obviously the main house of a plantation that probably controlled hundreds if not thousands of acres. The inhabitants would be Europeanized and no doubt hospitable to a well-mannered stranger no matter how tattered and dirty he looked.

He was right. Even the servant who announced his presence to the elderly *haciendado* was cordial and surprised. Like many people who live in remote regions, *El Señor* welcomed a stranger who could bring news of the outside world. His was an old and wealthy Spanish family, and naturally his sons and their wives preferred the social life in the capital to life on a country estate. The rigors of travel held the lonely old, white-haired man to the homestead, letting his children come to him as they did on holidays and vacations. After only a few minutes of conversation, Bart heard "*Mi casa es su casa,*" or "My house is your house."

Like a breath of fresh air gently seeping into rooms that have been closed, Bart's conversation was to brush the dust and cobwebs from Señor Quesada de Peraz's hungry mind. A bath, shave, fresh borrowed clothes, a comfortable room were made available and for the first time in months—as Bart had just discovered—he felt human again. Refreshed, dressed and descending the gracious stairway, he felt like a viceroy.

Quesada had carefully selected a menu for the day, which he wrote out in order not to forget what he was about to enjoy: *Sopa al estillo Sévigné, Los patés con acetuna, Los filetes de gallinas, Los chicharos á la francesca, Los coloflores á la francesca, Los pollos con truffas, Pudin de sago, Crema de todas las frutas, Conservade peras, Queso y mantiquilla,* with accompanying wines and coffee.

"Many times in the past few months I wondered if I would ever taste food like this again," Bart confessed, past the soup and into the tuna pate. "Please, forgive me if I seem to gobble." The frail, rheumatic, spidery old gentleman ate slowly and sparingly of each dish so that Bart had to slave to pace his appetite or feel like a peon.

"My cook will love you," replied *El Señor,* smiling. "It is thankless to cook for an old man."

Bart understood. *El Señor* only nibbled at the peas and cauliflower, ignoring the chicken stuffed with truffles. His skin seemed to Bart transparent. Underneath, his flesh glowed with pearl-like pinkness except around his mouth where wrinkles gathered into many tiny vertical streams.

"My Indian hosts fed me as well as they could. I feel only gratitude toward them."

"By any chance did they give you *gusanos de maguey?* It is an Indian delicacy dating to pre-Conquest times. When the maguey dies, its fleshy leaves become infested with great burrowing grubs or *gusanos.* I've tried them."

"Fortunately, the food was not so exotic, but at one point I would have relished them," Bart replied honestly.

"These are difficult times for Mexico. Like most elderly people, I'm pessimistic. Violence breeds violence. Jaurez has an ingrained hatred of the military, but in this country it takes an army to keep a man in power. We are not yet ready for the democracy you enjoy. After a leader has been chosen, the loser does not shake hands and let him lead. The losing party continues opposition—with violence."

"I did not enjoy the democracy I saw in Washington some time ago." Bart went on to explain his efforts to obtain a pardon for Dr. Mudd. "All were willing to concede that he was an innocent man, framed as a scapegoat, but I presume he's still rotting in prison. Political considerations were admitted to be the stumbling block."

"No, I'm happy to tell you he's been freed. I read about it several months ago. General Grant is now your President. But, anyway, exceptions prove the rule," replied *El Señor, now* happily into his pudding.

"Forgive me, but you have given me a wonderful piece of news. Have you any details?"

"I'm sorry. That's all I remember."

"That's enough to make me sleep well tonight." He did, confident that his friend Dr. Mudd was now enjoying his family.

The next morning Bart found himself eagerly awaited by his host, anxious for more conversation.

"I'm greatly concerned about this country. President Jaurez has crudely snubbed the military on important occasions so that our overly proud generals are seething. In this country that is foolhardy. Even my youngest son is concerned." He patted a letter that had just arrived.

"Let me ask you something, Señor, and if I'm out of order, please ignore the question. How have you managed through forty years of civil war to retain your holdings?" Bart was thinking of his Civil War, knowing the destruction in the United States. "Only four years of civil war destroyed the South where most of the wealth was."

"I will speak to you frankly: through what you *Americanos del Norte* call graft, but extortion is a better word. We also have *guerrillos* or our own private armies, and the ability, somewhat from experience, to judge which way the wind will blow. There has never been just one solution, but there has always been one at a time."

"And you managed to find it…"

"Many have not been so lucky," he whispered. "Corruption in government is a pox on this age. But I am interested in your life. Other than an education in Europe which afforded me limited travel many years ago, I have traveled only vicariously."

For a moment Bart thought of the cloudy waters in unfamiliar ports and the thunderous pounding of raging seas. Floggings and disease long behind him were recalled like cruel hangdog faces. "Señor, I have seen the worst and the best of this world and I can say to you that I have seen the same here: It can all be encapsulated within a radius of fifty miles from where we sit right now, I do believe. I'm judging by your table and gracious hospitality and the murdering bandits who roam your roads."

"You will see, this is a land of contrasts."

"I have."

Unsettled by painful recollections, Bart wanted to change the subject, but *El Señor* sat expectantly, hungry for words. When none were forthcoming from Bart, he furnished them himself. He had particularly enjoyed the renaissance and a return to the grandeur of his youth, which had occurred under the Empire. His tales were engaging.

"But I must tell you of the poor Indian family that took me in, nursed me, shared their tortillas and frijoles, saw me well, and once more on my way. I was overcome by that kindness. I wondered if it could happen anywhere on earth but in Mexico. My presence here today echoes that spirit of hospitality."

El Señor smiled a sweet, sad smile. He was more than pleased with his houseguest.

That there was extraordinary strings attached to this hospitality, Bart would soon discover. Additional clothes were ordered for him to replace those he wore, borrowed from one of the sons of the house. His saddle, by now in a wretched condition, was being rebuilt. Disturbingly, he learned that a visit of only a few days would be highly insulting to his host. In this house the concept of time was anything from what he had experienced. The clothes, saddle, an escort, letters of introduction, and money to travel would be ready—*mañana.* His company, meanwhile was the price.

Mañana stretched interminably. After two weeks, Bart was beside himself with anxiety to be off. He could think of no way to escape gracefully. The old gentleman had been more than generous and trusting, and should not be offended. Bart was the first American Señor Quesada de Peraz had met. He had greatly altered his host's opinion of the United States and its people and favorably, too—so even the honor of his country was at stake. The paradox struck Bart as ludicrous in its way. In effect, he was as imprisoned by kindness as he had been by force both on Dry Tortugas and on at the ranch. The fact that he was showered with attention and choked by kindness by a sweet-scented old man was all the more defeating.

Worse, he had not written Anne-Marie, having supposed that he would be leaving the hacienda immediately. After being absent almost four months without writing, he could imagine how a letter would be received stating, "*After a dreadfully difficult time, I've had a delightful visit with a charming old gentleman whom you must meet—and to whom I owe several hundred dollars…*" No, that was not to be contemplated.

El Señor had not met or even heard of Jared Russell. Bart rightly guessed that by now Anne-Marie would have learned that he had been helping Jared's family, and that, therefore, he had a dual purpose in coming to Mexico. That there would be a good many misconceptions, he never dreamed. He innocently hoped that Anne-Marie—or Jason better yet—had been helping Alma. At this point there was nothing that he could do about her anyway. He knew that Anne-Marie would have been worried about him, but he could even reason himself out of too much discomfort on that score. The Good Lord knew that he had spent hours, during the days when he went to sea, telling Anne-Marie that he would not and could not predict a return date. When he was gone, she was simply not to worry.

The journey from Veracruz to Taxco should have taken no more than ten days. He had noted that a few years earlier Maximilian and Carlotta, with an entourage of eighty souls, nobles and servants, had made the trip to Mexico City in two weeks, a trek obviously slowed by a liberal sprinkling of speeches, delivered at endless banquets put on by over-zealous committees. The fact that Bart had been a most unfortunate victim of circumstances which caused his delay made no difference. Like fattening a steer waiting for the slaughterhouse, he was sorry.

Again that evening he told *El Señor* that he would have to leave the following day. "I absolutely must. My wife must be worried sick. Even if I leave this house barefoot, I must go."

"Oh, I would never allow that!" replied Quesada firmly, "However, on the following day there will be great fiestas in Córdoba, Orizaba, Puebla…. The roads will be full of people and it will be entirely safe for you to travel. Your new suit, boots, everything will be ready."

Bart could hardly believe his ears.

"Señor, I beg you to understand. Your hospitality has been magnificent. I will never forget it—and you. The day after tomorrow I will travel as you suggest."

That was not to be the case. That night Señor Quesada de Peraz died in his sleep. After having been a guest in his house for over two weeks, Bart could hardly have been so lacking in respect as to depart before the funeral mass to come five days later.

Apart from the requirements of etiquette, he was ashamed that he could be annoyed.

Priests and embalmers came. A carpenter made measurements for the coffin and the wake in the house began. A constant procession of footsteps and whispers accompanied the wailing of mourners from the hacienda chapel where *El Señor* rested. Judging by the human traffic, everyone in the district came to pay his or her respects.

The house smelled of trampled flowers and burning candles. A great black sheet hung outside over the main entrance. Bart could do nothing but wait for the carriages of descendants from Mexico City summoned by the wire from Córdoba. They would want to hear of the patriarch's last days and of his good spirits. They would need an explanation of his own presence.

Finally, from the city, in veils and top hats, looking like tired black crickets, the mourning family descended from a caravan of carriages drawn by horses also draped in black.

Bart told them about the happy visit he and *El Señor* had had and of the gentleman's peaceful demise. The weeping soon gave way to eating, which in turn gave way to screaming as *El Señor's* sons and daughters and their spouses fought over their inheritances. Bart slipped from the house. With the delay he had lost the company of the revelers going to the fiestas so once again he was at the mercy of the dangers on the abominable highway.

Chapter Ten

On the terrace at Los Claveles, picking at Rafael's picnic prepared by the cook at Russell House, Anne-Marie felt it was decision time. She was no longer insulated as she had been by Bart or her father. Her life now called for aggressive action. She would need Wade's cooperation above all. Beckoning to Wade, the caretaker, she explained the reasons for her visit.

"I'm going to bring about a hundred men to this key who will go to Mexico to find my husband who has disappeared there. They'll have to train here. Most will bunk in the main house. On the grounds they'll be trained in horsemanship and riflery and then be transported. You will remain in charge of the property. Rafael de Palma will be in charge of training, and during the next few weeks we will often be here. Please set up a small room for me and one for Mr. de Palma. I hope it won't be chaotic, but in any event it won't be for long. We'll need absolute secrecy. If your workers have a vacation coming, let them have it now, so they won't be talking elsewhere about what they've seen here. I have complete faith in your judgment and ability to handle this. Have you any questions?"

"I'll handle whatever comes my way, Ma'am. I reckon we can use a little excitement. I think our cook can handle can handle the food…How's Miss Samantha? It's about time she learned to ride. I remember you learning—right here."

Wade was a native Conch. His parents came from Green Turtle Cay in the Bahamas with a great exodus seeking freedom. They were a hard and hearty bunch who made their living from the sea—a simple, honest dependable people.

"Miss Samantha is doing very well aside from catechism, but she'll get that soon. The Sisters of the Holy Names of Jesus and Mary from Canada have recently established a girl's school in Key West."

"Count on my support here, Ma'am," replied Wade, retreating.

As Wade returned to his work as overseer of the grove, which was predominantly citrus, but included pineapples, coconut, bananas, mangoes, avocados and papayas marketed in Key West, Anne-Marie breathed a sigh of relief. She had many times before thanked heaven for Wade's presence. The project before them would require the kind of loyal help he could give.

Aware of a bright prickly sun on her back, she suggested to Rafael that they start back. "We must get to Key West before it gets dark. There's a stretch to cover." No habitations would light the shore and inevitably at sundown the wind would die.

"I'm sure you're right," agreed Rafael, never interested in taking unnecessary risks.

Once at sea, he became communicative. He had been greatly impressed with Los Claveles. It was hard to imagine a more ideal spot to house and train a group of commandos. Seclusion and security were assured. But one thing had disturbed him, which he did not want to admit to himself. Gradually he was coming to the realization that he wanted Anne-Marie herself as his own. In the beginning he had wanted her money and power, but now she was gaining a grip on him emotionally that he could not escape. Love in his opinion made foolish slaves of men and he wanted no inhibiting chains. He had been playing the role of the great lover and he was beginning to live the part as if it were real. Now he recognized that it was. If they found her husband he'd have to kill him. Anne-Marie would be his. Mimi would be easy enough to get rid of.

"I'm sure it was difficult for you to return to your former home today and to find it stripped, empty of everything except memories," he said sympathetically.

"You made it easier than I had anticipated. I don't know how to explain it except that comparative strangers are often easier to talk to than close friends."

Rafael knew the remark was not intended as a reproof, although it was. "It will be harder to find a bunch of riffraff swarming over your castle walls."

"The place is solidly built. They can't do much damage."

"You'd be surprised."

"Perhaps, but then, what does it matter? Such things can become unimportant. The important thing is to be alive and well. Still we strive for certain things that tantalizingly elude us." She was thinking of her husband.

"You speak of how I feel about you," he confessed.

Anne-Marie felt her face quiver slightly. Any romantic involvement with Rafael was impossible. It was more than she could handle. "Please, never speak to me this way again. I'm married to another. I belong to him with all my heart. Even if he is lost—particularly if he is lost—I am not interested in another commitment. I still love my husband. No one can have what truly belongs to another."

"Yes, you can, by taking it."

"Those are calisthenics with words," replied Anne-Marie, a little frightened. "I believe I have made my feelings clear." She shuddered.

He sat beside her, rudder in hand, steering them toward a destination. Below rolled up sleeves, dark curly hair on his arms flattened in the breeze and the black hair on his head danced in curious disarray. The strangeness of him so, looking windblown and ungroomed, offered a new and different picture she found hard to equate with the debonair, polished socialite whose play she had, she hoped, just put down. She felt she was seeing him for the first time. By going into this project as he had suggested, he would be moving into her life with ever-increasing proximity. He seemed for the first time a real man. She would have to handle him with an iron glove.

"Just what sort of cattle boat do you intend to look for?" she asked, anxious to get away from personal matters. For her ships fell into categories easily described by one or two words, such as square-rigger, schooner, brigantine, sloop or yawl.

"I don't know," he replied, unwilling to admit any lack of knowledge and be trapped because of it. "I think it will depend on what we can find."

"Tim Clayton was at sea for many years. He knows ships and their capabilities. We should make no purchase without consulting him."

"I don't want to impose on him anymore than we have to."

"Don't worry about imposing. He's very concerned…"

"I may have to go to Tampa to find what we need. To drag him there seems like an imposition of the first order."

What Anne-Marie thought to be safe ground was growing shaky.

After a moment of silence Rafael began again, his tongue sharpened. "Madame, possibly you won't need me at all on this project, considering all the other capable hands that will have to be consulted at every twist and turn. If you want an errand boy or a lackey, I would suggest that you hire one."

It was a childish power play, born of macho instincts of the Latin male, which Anne-Marie recognized, but at the same time she could sympathize with Rafael's position. He had been appointed head of the expeditionary forces, and then step by step his sphere of influence was being reduced and he felt hurt.

"I couldn't begin to handle this without you. And when I think of the risk you take entering Mexico, I am truly terrified. Rest assured this is your project and I will stand behind your decisions."

Rafael's ruffled ego apparently soothed, Anne-Marie said no more, but a good many apprehensions lingered—in fact they seemed to be multiplying.

*   *   *   *

In 1869 Cuba belonged to Spain. Ever since 1843 a series of uprisings against Spain's oppression had raised sympathizers—with one's own interests fueling this compassion—but, the time had not been right for revolt and all attempts at independence had been crushed. The most recent and serious uprising had occurred the year before when Carlos M. Cespedes, a distinguished lawyer and wealthy planter, gave the cry "Cuba Libre" from his estate. He was joined by thousands of patriots and on October 18th 1868, he took possession of the city of Bayamo, his birthplace, having defeated a Spanish garrison. The victory was short lived, and the Bayamo forces were defeated, but the cry

"Cuba Libre" rang like bells throughout the land.

Spain, not having sufficient troops in Cuba to comfortably oppose the increasing unrest, raised companies of volunteers from the lowest class. The cruelties and atrocities of these volunteers continually fed the influx of fleeing Cubans to Key west. Señor Vicente Martinez Ybor, a wealthy manufacturer of cigars in Havana, fearing the caprice of volunteers, opened a branch factory in Key West. As soon as he did this, he was suspected of treachery by the Spanish government and put under surveillance. For Señor Ybor, this was the last straw. He then moved his entire business to Key West and came here with his family. His factory, El Principe de Gales, assured escaping Cubans of a means of livelihood as well as a warm reception in this country. It was from this labor force, particularly the younger and more venturesome men, that Anne-Marie planned to recruit her mercenary force. How these troops would react to training under a Spaniard, she had not contemplated. As always, she must take the really knotty problems to Tim

"I've cleared everything with Wade," she explained, "But I'm worried about the Cubans training under Rafael, a Spaniard," said Anne-Marie, glancing obliquely at Tim, feeling the weight of Rafael's temperament and pride.

Tim hunched a shoulder. "The thought is not a new one to me, but this is going to be his problem to work out. Certainly, he is aware that there is not a single member of the Cuban community here who does not look forward to a new revolutionary movement in Cuba against Spain, and, so far, he has managed to dance around it and be at least socially acceptable."

"He avoids any discussion of politics," volunteered Consuelo, a new-comer to the conversation bearing a pot of tea. "Let's hope he can keep it up."

"And if he doesn't?" asked Anne-Marie with noticeable trepidation.

"He'd be a fool, and you would be well to be rid of him. Surely he realizes that he would have a hundred guns at his back," said Tim. "It would take only one to improve his understanding." Tin chuckled.

Anne-Marie felt her blood run cold. "Perhaps I'm in for more than I bargained for. I hope for an operation in which not a shot will be fired. I'm ready to take risks with my own life, but I'm panicked at the thought of jeopardizing others."

"It's his decision, Anne-Marie. I take the man as an adventurer—and a gentleman. He strikes me as a man with leadership qualities: strong, well educated, shrewd and well able to take care of himself. Possibly, he thrives on excitement. I wouldn't sit up nights worrying about him—if I were you. I'd keep a weather eye on him which you will have a month to do. You'll have plenty of time to resolve the imponderables. At the moment he has a commodity, knowledge of Mexico, which he is willing to give away or sell, and which you will need. I'm sure you know his price by now…"

"I'm not sure what the price will be. That's another thing I want to talk over with you."

"Setting a price when you don't know the value is like buying a horse without looking into its mouth," said Tim.

The smell of salt on the clean and moving air that perpetually sweeps through every little alleyway in Key West, into each garden, through the small crowded houses and spacious mansions alike, filled their nostrils. Anne-Marie drew deeply, filling her lungs, emptied by the problem of Rafael. They sat on Clayton's front porch, Anne-Marie and Consuelo in wicker chairs and Tim on a wooden swing. The swing swayed so gently that Tim advanced and then receded, never far, but the distancing Anne-Marie found disconcerting. "What stipend would you recommend, Tim?"

"One based on performance."

"Tim," interrupted Consuelo, "How can you expect Anne-Marie to put a price on Bart's head? That's what you're doing. Now, let's be more helpful."

Consuelo understood; she was a curator of understanding for others, and very slow to pass a derogatory judgment.

Tim was quick to speak up. "Please, don't misunderstand. I'm not trying to be obscure: I'm trying to be helpful. I know nothing of Rafael's financial status or his wants. I only know what a dollar means to me, which is different from what a dollar means to Consuelo, and vastly different from what a dollar means to you, Anne-Marie. Let's ask him again what he feels would be reasonable. That's a primary rule of business. But, let's nail it down. The sooner the better."

"I'll talk to him about this with you present," she replied. "You realize, of course, that I'm up against the same problem with you. How do I pay you? How can I ever…"

Before Tim could reply she continued, "I can offer you nothing but a blank check signed with love. Fill in whatever you'd like." She threw back her head laughing.

Consuelo blanched remembering something from the past. Consuelo herself had stood at the construction site of Anne-Marie's new home. "Think of what we share as a blank check of love," she had told Bart, and he had replied, "It is signed."

Nothing immoral or adulterous was contained in the exchange, yet it had sealed their mutual trust with something more than one had in the bank. For this reason Consuelo would approve her husband's quest to find Bart. She had what she wanted, her beautiful all-absorbing child. Now she was realizing how demanding a newborn could be. Tim's involvement in helping Anne-Marie spared her from feeling neglectful of Tim. Still, it was significant that both she and Anne-Marie had used almost the same wording to express their affection for the husband of the other. Both women had a great capacity for understanding others, especially each other and Consuelo was ready to bet a fiver that much of Anne-Marie's consternation was not over Bart but because of a worrisome relationship with Rafael de Palma. Both women would have regarded this with no little alarm. She would have to speak openly with Anne-Marie, but not with Tim present.

"Come upstairs with me for a moment, please, Anne-Marie. I need your advice on the nursery." Consuelo rose and extended an upturned hand to hurry her along. Although surprised, Anne-Marie went.

Upstairs Consuelo led her guest to a small sitting room. "I wanted to get you out of Tim's hearing. I know Rafael had pursued you, and he is also pursuing other women in this town. I want you to be careful."

For a moment Anne-Marie was silent, unsure of her response. "He's an attractive man. Once or twice when Bart was around, I remember loathing him. Now that I need him, I'm embarrassed to find my attitude changing."

"I'm certain that you'll find Bart alive and legitimately detained. Maybe in some ways I know Bart better than you do, because I can be objective about him. You live in a small town where you have the position of an empress, so every eye is on you. Women are jealous of you—women you consider your friends. Be careful that you do nothing foolish."

"I also believe that Bart is alive, but it is hard for me to believe that no communication has been possible, so I'm worried and angry."

Anne-Marie stood and rose to a window, swirling her skirt with a flourish that expressed ire, but at the same time a desperation that touched Consuelo, softening, warm, dark, plaintive eyes. "I miss him terribly—I've even forgotten the damned episode with Zipporah. But I'm curious. What are my so-called friends saying?"

"Nothing worth repeating," Consuelo replied thinking of a recent meeting with Mimi, "because I have only noticed an attitude of envy."

"I know you would not repeat gossip," said Anne-Marie.

"I wouldn't repeat it and I would try to stop it, you know…"

Slowly the women descended the stairs, both troubled. Consuelo felt her loneliness as sharply as she would have felt her own. Anne-Marie felt the weight of wagging tongues.

Privately, Consuelo had told Tim that she felt relatively certain that Bart—in some little rat hole of a village in Mexico—was in jail. As a prisoner without funds even a postage stamp would be hard to come by, much less a quill pen, ink and paper. Furthermore, he could be serving a sentence of many years' duration. That he would eventually escape, Consuelo also felt certain. "Some pretty woman will get him out," she had told Tim. Silently, Tim had nodded.

CHAPTER ELEVEN

Anne-Marie correctly anticipated that Jason would be chagrinned over her instructions to liquidate her stocks and bonds, but not for the reason she assumed. She supposed that he would be disappointed with his own loss, his delight in having a fortune to play with, and, of course, he was. But also, Jason felt **within his bones** that Bart Ramsden was alive somewhere. Bart was adventurous, and writing was inconvenient. It would never occur to Bart that his wife might spend a fortune to find him by sending an army after him! Good Lord, no! When Bart was ready he would show up with a good excuse under his wide two-pointed captain's hat. But in the meantime his wife had written him instructions to turn her paper holdings into cash. Whoever heard of such a thing! Hundreds of thousands of dollars were to be put in a valise and hand-carried all over New York City and finally via the pirated Caribbean waters into the wilds of Florida. The girl was mad! Still, it was her money and as her banker and agent he should follow her instructions without quibbling. She had no conception of how difficult it would be for him to walk from bank to bank, trying to make immediate large withdrawals. If the word got out he would be cartooned pushing a wheelbarrow of money down Broad and Wall Streets. She had written, *"Sell everything."* Did she have any concrete notion of what the expedition would cost? He hoped so. He dearly hoped so.

Emily was quick to recognize her husband's displeasure, which, because it started with his own daughter, she, Emily was unjustly blamed. When he was pleased with the children they were his; when not, hers.

"I thought your daughter had some sense in her," raged Jason.

"If she were only here you could talk some sense into her," replied Emily, wistfully. She was saying precisely what Jason knew she would say, and besides he believed it himself.

"If you're going to make suggestions, can't you please suggest something I have not already thought of," he glowered.

"Yes, I might," replied Emily, drawing herself up, her gray eyes losing their softness, her nostrils quivering. "You must do as she says, but I do believe it would be wise of you to withhold a little and keep it here in the event everything is lost. I'm talking about a reserve."

"Stocks have been rising steadily. There's no sign of a let up. I hate to sell on a rising market and not a peak. It's not good business. Holding fifty or a hundred thousand here is no problem. I'm concerned with my credibility as a banker. Such sudden massive withdrawals put enormous pressure on banking houses. Some banks demand thirty days notice or impose a forfeiture of interest. I'd hate to be put in this position knowing how inconvenient it can be for a bank." He crumpled his napkin and rose to pace the floor.

They had been having dinner. The great dining room seemed unsuitable for two, so Emily served the meal from a teacart by the fire hoping the cozy atmosphere would lift Jason's spirits.

She knew Jason could handle his colleagues. The real reason for his distress was a loss of power and prestige. He'd have to go back to being a little township banker. New York bankers would ask questions, and as a Quaker he could not lie. Jason had been brought up a Quaker, but he had married a Methodist with whom he attended church instead of Meeting House. He'd have to say, "I have not pretended this money is mine. It belongs to my daughter and she wants it. That's that." The fact that she wanted it to support an army was too outrageous for comprehension. His dreams of financial wizardry were at an end. Emily could say little except that she was sorry. She looked so tiny and smitten, he believed her.

"I'll get David to accompany me. He must be informed. That ship with a fancy name will soon be picking him up. Imagine sending fifteen or twenty men to pick up one man! It's wasteful."

"They're getting paid and fed whether they work or not," replied Emily.

"I guess there are lessons to be learned here, such as easy come, easy go."

That night he wrote David: "*Prepare for a most important mission that for your own safety should be undertaken in secrecy. Prepare for an absence of several months. I don't know how long Anne-Marie will need you. You can depend on her generosity. Also the day after tomorrow please find the time to accompany me to New York. It will prove an unusual experience.*"

Jason's driver delivered the letter and waited for a reply. David was, he said, always at his family's service.

On the early morning train into the city Jason explained to David the details of the day's agenda and for the coming week. "Everywhere we go today, men will try hard to keep the money in their hands and to dissuade us from doing what we must do. We may not be able to get everything today, depending upon how many big draws the banks have had in the last day or two."

"Do you plan that we stay with Uncle Elbert?" asked David, enormously curious about the whole operation.

"No, I don't want to bring the family into this. We'll stay in a hotel."

David braced himself. He hoped his wife's small allowance was not endangered.

During the 1860's American industry had expanded from one-man enterprises into large units of corporate organizations. Two new trends of finance had developed—trends which meant business for the Stock Exchange: a swing of control to bankers and capitalists, and a demand for capital to move into larger spheres of operation, such as the building of railroads and the financing of industry. December 1867 had marked the first stock ticker and the end of the 'pad shovelers,' the swift runners who ran from office to office with quotations of stock prices. The offices of David Grosbeck & Co., where Jason made his headquarters in New York, were a frenzy of activity.

"May I see you alone, Grosbeck," said Jason.

"Certainly," he replied, certain that Jason was about to buy more gold. 'Uncle Daniel' Drew, Jay Gould, and 'Jubilee Jim' Fiske were steadily buying gold through their brokers. The price had risen to $143 per ounce.

In Grosbeck's office Jason gave the order, "Sell."

"Gold is bound to go higher," replied Grosbeck. "You don't want to pull out now, Frazier, and miss an opportunity of a lifetime. We have a lock on the gold market."

"I have my instructions. It's my daughter's money and she wants cash."

"But, surely as her father you can dissuade her. You're hurting us badly by pulling out."

"I'm sorry. I can't change her mind. It's personal. I'll take large bills."

Grosbeck's disappointment was clear. From a large safe he extracted over $280,000 in greenbacks. "I can't tell you how I hate to see you do this, Frazier, for your daughter's sake. Gold is gold. Only a few years ago you know what this paper was worth." Grosbeck carelessly tossed the packets of bills through the air. "This country goes on and off the gold standard every time you turn around."

Meekly Jason and David put the money in a case and with eyes averted bid Grosbeck goodbye. They left him sitting behind his desk, shaking his head in disbelief.

On the street Jason turned to David. "I feel like an ingrate. I'm sure Grosbeck thinks I'm moving to another brokerage. I bought gold at his suggestion—and a confidence—because he told me Drew was buying gold. He'll never give me confidential information again. I have seriously weakened their position." Silently they walked the remaining few blocks to the New York Stock Exchange at 10 and 12 Broad Street.

The exchange had been located on the second floor, but it had recently expanded to the ground floor encompassing what was known as the 'Long Room.' Previously the room had been occupied by George W. McLean and Associates, but because McLean had refused to bar non-members, the exchange took over the space. The 'Long Room' opened at 8:30 and closed at 5 PM. Trading continued on the steps and on the sidewalks until dark or later, depending on the enthusiasm of the moment.

Tables ornamented with inkstands ran lengthwise through the great room. Here members sat scribbling memoranda or following bids and offers as each security was called. Everyday the President of the Board called out each stock from a list. Following the name of me stock he inquired, "Any bids, gentlemen?" At this moment brokers having any stock to buy or sell signaled the chair and called out their offers.

Today trading was heavy and the chimney-pot hats and bowlers bobbed up and down as their owners yelled excitedly, "Take 'em!" meaning the shares were sold. The American flag hung above the presiding officer. Nearby sat a man feeding each bid into a ticker tape machine. This marvelous new invention could transmit each transaction as far away as England.

The commotion was greater this day than Jason had ever seen before. Men rushed about wildly, conferring with each other and then moving on, reminding Jason of a nest of ants. Bids ran higher and higher. An unmistakable enthusiastic frenzy, electrifying in its impact built steadily and reverberated through the room. Finally, Jason caught his broker's eye and signaled for him to come speak with them. Drawn and taut the broker hurried over.

"I have a number of securities for you to dispose of," said Jason, thrusting the sheaf of elaborately printed securities, magnificently illustrated with reclining female Roman figures or thundering locomotives resplendent with flourishing scripts and gold seals into the tense broker's hands. "My daughter is getting out of the market. Get me the best price that you can and meet me tonight at the Fifth Avenue Hotel, if you will, please."

"I hope you're not permanently leaving us," replied the broker. "There's a fortune to be made right now." A dead but well-chomped cigar between his lips made his words almost indistinguishable.

"I hope not for long," Jason replied as the frenzied broker spit and did not miss a brass spittoon.

"I have some beautiful buys for you," warned the broker, hurrying to escape what he considered a loser.

From the great exciting world Jason was being severed. Dragging David from the room, turning his back on the world of opportunity buzzing under a canopy of swirling cigar smoke, Jason sighed. Outside the human traffic cleared, but not Jason's despondency. He said nothing, but David understood.

"Keep in mind what goes up comes down, Father Frazier," said David, looking for words to cheer the older man. David understood the scene was hard to leave. He had been fascinated. Only a small hand signal from the gallery to a broker and in turn from a broker to the President of the Exchange meant an expenditure of thousands of dollars. Jason thoroughly enjoyed this form of gambling, legitimized as 'playing the market.' It was a sport.

"I must say Bart has taken an inconvenient time to drop from sight. Who in the world could be advising Anne-Marie at this time?" David asked.

"Apparently some foreigner with experience in soldiering in Mexico. I doubt that he knows much about finance. Once you get to Key West I hope you'll keep me informed."

The thought that anyone other than Jason might be advising Anne-Marie financially alarmed David. Jason would see that his wife May was taken care of; a stranger would not be so interested in her need. "You can depend on me, sir."

The whole experience of handling gigantic sums of money in loose expendable cash stunned David. They were carrying real money, not precise inked numbers on a balance sheet that needed only to tally with a journal and ledger, which one never saw.

The next step was the Chemical Bank where Jason presented a bankbook to a teller. "I'd like to withdraw these funds," said Jason.

The young man's eyes widened as he glanced at the balance. "You will have to speak with an officer of the bank, sir."

"Indeed," replied Jason. Within seconds they were ushered into a private office.

"I'm extremely sorry that you are dissatisfied with the Chemical Bank," said a paunchy, gray-haired officer over his spectacles. "If anyone has been discourteous or if any errors have occurred, I assure you, the situation can be remedied."

"I've been very satisfied. You have a fine bank. But, this is my daughter's money and she wants it," replied Jason stoically.

"You realize that we are entitled to thirty days notice, Mr. Frazier?"

"I do. I'm a banker myself. This is not a large sum for a bank of your size, I trust."

"The money is available, of course. I regret losing you as a valued customer." His tone was cold as if he assumed the money would be redeposited next door.

"If another banking house is offering you more interest, we will meet their terms," he added.

"That is not the case. I hope before long to redeposit most of this, if not all of it with you," assured Jason.

Similar incidents at the New York State Bank and Jay Cooke's bank followed. Fortunately Jason managed, through the promise of future business, to avoid heavy penalties for early withdrawal. By this time David was carrying over a million dollars in large bills.

After meeting with the broker from the stock exchange, who had finished selling Anne-Marie's holdings at Gallagher's Evening Exchange adjacent to their hotel, Jason and David had a few hundred thousand more to secure in the hotel safe.

"This has been a day of absolute folly," said Jason at dinner, dourly picking at his food. "Not that I would want my daughter to prefer money to her husband. I simply cannot believe that there is not a saner more sensible way to find a man than hiring an army to go after him."

David simply shook his head, awed by the whole proceedings, including his own part about to begin. This money would be put in his hands for safekeeping. It was more trust than he wanted, or point of fact, than he deserved.

That night David could not sleep and there was no equivalent of Zipporah to distract him, especially with his father-in-law in the adjoining room. He tossed and turned, unaccustomed to the hard mattress, pillow and stiff sheets. How easy it would be to jump ship in Charleston and flee with the money. He agreed with Jason. Bart would be found alive or would turn up when it suited him. He did love May, he supposed, but she would be replaceable. Then he thought of his two sons, Clay and Whitney. Should he absent himself with the dollars he would never be able to see his sons again. That would be a tremendous sacrifice. Still, the temptation to skedaddle was unnerving. He visualized himself lolling on a beach, surrounded by beautiful women on some exotic foreign shore. On the other hand, perhaps he could endear himself to Anne-Marie sufficiently to earn a vast sum working for her. He would weigh everything. With the thought that Anne-Marie would, in all probability, never prosecute for May's sake, he fell asleep.

The following morning Jason wanted to visit the Gold Exchange. "You simply can't let go, can you, sir?" asked David, smiling. The old man had gold fever all right.

Jason scowled. "If you had invested in gold, on margin, of course, and had made over $200,000 in a few month's time, I dare say you would appreciate my sentiments." David agreed.

What Jason did not know was that Gould and Fiske had cornered the market in gold.

Gould's first idea in forcing up gold prices was to stimulate the export of grains, which he transported on his railroads. As Europe was on the gold standard, Gould calculated that the farmers would take advantage of the high grain prices and sell abroad for gold. Through A.C. Corbin, President Grant's brother-in-law, Gould was able to keep informed on the President's views and intentions. Furthermore he was able through Corbin to bring pressure on the President to do nothing about the situation and let the free enterprise system work.

However, finally the President saw through the scheme and realized that Gould's interest was not in how much the farmers might get for their crops, but how much Messrs. Gould, Drew and Fiske might get for their gold which they had been quietly and steadily buying, producing an artificial demand.

By Thursday, September 23, 1869, the Gould-Fiske group had over $12,000,000 in gold. The price continued to climb. Soon it reached $155 an ounce and according to the *New York Herald:* "The revengeful warwhoops of the furious Indians, the terrific yells issuing for a lunatic asylum, would not equal in intensity the cries of speculators in the Gold Room."

Jason and David stood transfixed, no longer a part of the action, while about them men joyously counted their gains. A wide-eyed broker kept steadily building up the price, offering $160 for "any part of a thousand." Men continued to buy.

Having sold all Anne-Marie's gold the day before, Jason told David, "I'm sick. Let's get out of here."

David led Jason back to the hotel where they picked up their luggage, including a valise of money. They caught the afternoon train for New Jersey.

What Jason did not see—later that day—was a notice tacked on a bulletin board which read: The U.S. Treasury will sell, at 12 o'clock tomorrow, four million in gold and buy four million in bonds. Proposals will be received in the usual form. It was signed David Butterfield, *Assistant Treasurer.*

Corbin had informed Gould that it would be only a matter of hours before the government would offer to sell gold. As fast as they could the Gould-Fisk clique was selling gold under the cover of maintaining the appearance of buying. Smash! The gold corner collapsed. Within minutes the price fell to $133, while a hair-brained broker was carried from the room still gurgling $160 "for any part of a thousand."

The roar of the battle and the screams of the victims resounded through New Street, but Jason and David did not hear.

This occurred in the Gold Exchange. Nevertheless, its influence was felt on the floor of the stock exchanges where stock prices fell disastrously. Because of fear and tension, panic spread. On September 24, 1869 back in the Gold Room woes of anxiety gave way to torments of realization. For hours people stood gazing at the indicator that displayed the record of the struggle. Firm after firm failed. Fortune after fortune was lost. Suicides followed the ruin. Such were the penalties paid.

It was not until the following day that Jason, now resigned to return to small town banking, with infinite boredom opened his newspaper. The headline: "**Black Friday**" jumped from the page.

Within the hour David rushed in waving newspapers like tattered flags. "Father Ramsden, have you seen these?" he cried, more excited than Jason had ever seen him. "Read these and weep—for joy!"

"Yes," said Jason reaching for the *Herald.* "I'll be damned!"

CHAPTER TWELVE

Rafael de Palma opened a recruiting office downtown under the name of the International Explorer's Club of Key West. At first recruiting went slowly. Upon Tim's advice, Rafael claimed Mexican citizenship and not Spanish. The recruits, who had no idea of the difference between accents of Spain and Mexico, accepted Rafael's claim. Lured by wages, which were twice what the cigar factories were paying, a handful of Cuban patriots enlisted. From these Rafael selected Esteban Navarro, who had surfaced as a natural leader, to become his Field Marshal in charge of recruiting, quartering, logistics, training and everything else that Rafael could throw his way, thus freeing himself for what he considered more important considerations. With Navarro in charge, they soon had a full complement of men. Anne-Marie dared not wonder exactly what the men were being told as to their objective, but anyway the ranks were filling.

It was Consuelo who visited Wooleye, an almost blind proprietor of a waterfront saloon, and induced him to prevail on one of his clients, a veteran forger known as the 'Scribe,' to prepare fake passports for Anne-Marie's recruits. These were not copies of passports, but they were an official looking, elaborately decorated, artist's rendition of 'Right of Entry Permits,' in Spanish, purporting to have been issued by the Mexican government. Complete with enough flourishes, scrolls, ribbons and wax seals, the forgeries were designed to impress even the most intelligent bureaucratic immigration officer. Each entry permit carried a false name and number and credited the bearer with all courtesies extendable to an agent in the Department of Foreign Secret Service of the Mexican Government. No ambassador could have boasted more impressive credentials.

"A work of art!" shrieked Anne-Marie, as Consuelo produced the first sample from the 'Scribe.'

"Certainly worth framing," said Tim, tapping the sample. "A Holy Writ from the Vatican couldn't be more impressive. This paper would get a murderer into heaven."

"I'll settle for Mexico," added Anne-Marie, laughing.

David arrived with Anne-Marie's money excepting a small reserve. "*Paternal instinct prompts me to hold a little back,*" wrote Jason, "*prompted by your dear mother.*" David had had no opportunity to defect. A great steel safe was hoisted aboard *Los Girasoles* carrying the greenbacks and Colt revolvers, purchased according to Anne-Marie's instructions in Hartford. Once the ship was underway, Jason wired Anne-Marie the combination. "*Under no circumstances give the combination of the safe to* **anyone.**" Jason continued, "*But I must confess that you have a good deal more business acumen than I gave you credit for when you ordered me to liquidate. Keep the safe in your home, not in a little wooden office. Trust your father's judgment on this matter.*"

Discreetly David did not reveal Jason's misgivings over the liquidation. Certainly, it was to his advantage never to embarrass the old gentleman, always solicitous of May and his welfare.

Army surplus cots, horses, and equipment were purchased from Fort Taylor, right in Key West, an enormous convenience. Immediately this equipment was transported to Los Claveles, now the army camp and training ground. Even David who had considered Anne-Marie's plan to enter Mexico hair-brained, was agreeably surprised with the ease with which her resources lent themselves to the scheme. With the honed instinct of the way one con-artist recognizes another, David had reservations over Rafael. Anne-Marie's beauty and wealth were bound to attract, and certainly she was lonely and vulnerable. Her pregnancy did not yet show, and she had not confided in anyone on this score. David had no interest in protecting Bart's interests, but he was comfortable with the status quo. De Palma was a new unknown entity who had considerable authority and power. He could be a threat. The family fortune warranted a watchful eye; Jason could not have chosen a more interested, greedy and alert deputy.

David, of course, noted Zipporah's absence, but awareness of his indiscretions with her muffled any queries he might have made as to the whereabouts of the pretty servant. Wisely, he decided he would learn in time.

Rafael had not been as successful in skimming off money as he had anticipated. After the first dozen horses, which Rafael had purchased, seemed high, Tim succeeded in getting the rest as surplus war material including the saddles. Food for the army came cheap. The simple diet of predominantly rice and black beans, which the Cubans preferred, supplemented by abundant fish caught by the caretaker's men in the waters off the key, demanded little cash. The grove provided fruits. Besides, petty thievery was hardly Rafael's art, the proceeds not warranting the risk. He was hampered by a vexing and burning desire to be constantly in Anne-Marie's presence, which left little time to cement his relations with Esteban Navarro and to commit larceny. Consequently, he spent most of his time going back and forth between Los Claveles and Key West. There he found Anne-Marie always with David—never alone.

Tim, Rafael and Anne-Marie sat this day around a portable table at Los Claveles, now strangely different as a military compound, not a civilized dwelling. Tim had spent the morning supervising target practice and reinforcing the importance of keeping weapons clean, particularly the new breech-loading, cast steel rifles imported from Krupp's factories in Essen, Germany. David, Anne-Marie and Rafael worked on inventory. A merciless tropical sun bore down on the earth, denuded by men's boots so that not even the sandspurs survived. Any number of new paths, leading to hastily constructed latrines, a riding area, target areas and the beaches, where men bathed and washed their clothes, exposed a substrata of limestone rock now rubbed raw. Clotheslines that once hung with exquisite baby clothes and hand-sewn linen shirts now carried a motley assortment of rough, faded, tattered shirts and pants. Musky, heavy masculine odors, a combination of gunsmoke, oils, sweat and even manure supplanted the more refined scents of civilian occupation—those of minty geraniums and orange blossoms, blending with Anne-Marie's perfumes, ocean salt, Epicurean cooking or simply freshly baked bread. Even Anne-Marie, who had sat quietly reading or fanning herself in fluffy bouffant cambric, always within reach of a breeze, now wore khaki men's pants with a man's shirt hastily fitted to her by seamstress Clarke, and stomped around the compound in heavy boys' shoes doing her own errands.

When Estevan Navarro approached, she volunteered to help some of the men who were not adept at riding. "We may get into territory where jumps are necessary, Señor, and some of the weaker riders need specialized instruction. I can help them."

Esteban hardly would have scoffed at his employer, but the thought of a woman teaching a man anything about riding a horse—or anything else for that matter—struck him as ludicrous. Also, although he was impressed with Anne-Marie as a lady of property, as poor men are impressed by wealth, he found her suggestion so outrageous that he had difficulty replying.

"It's kind of you, Ma'am, but I think that is something a man could more easily handle, and I'll see that your wishes are carried out."

"Oh, but I'd like to," countered Anne-Marie, totally unaware of his reasons. His bafflement was matched by that of Rafael and Tim, who were equally startled by her suggestion. Almost as a chorus they protested, sure that she was joking.

"I'm serious," replied Anne-Marie, now rising and moving toward a window where she could call to Wade. "Please, bring me my horse."

Stepping outside with the men dutifully following, but still dismayed, Anne-Marie mentioned to several of the men, all weak riders, "Usted, usted, usted y usted, please get your horses and come with me."

Of course they would obey, but they looked at Esteban for orders. His nod indicated that they should do as the lady asked. At that point David joined the group.

Anne-Marie then asked Wade to put up her long-stored cavaletti or series of riding hurdles. While Wade busied himself with this project, Anne-Marie, her horse in hand, began in perfect Spanish to talk to the men about horses. She began with how the horse is made, talking about the skeleton, the muscles, memory and communication.

At first the men seemed tolerantly amused but before long their interest grew. Even Tim who spoke a little Spanish and David, who spoke none at all, stood absorbed watching the reaction of the men. Rafael withheld approval, but Anne-Marie was unaware of any of this. Once for a moment she had a panicking thought: what if her horse has forgotten their months of work? What if she fell and seriously injured herself and the baby? She could be the laughing stock of the island. By now more and more of the men had gathered around the riding area, curious as to what was going on.

"You must become one with your horse, and I do not mean only when you are riding horseback. Ride in the saddle at all the gaits but without reins and without stirrups, until you are independent of them. This is hard to do because the saddle is slippery, and the rider does not sit so close to his horse. Ride entirely on balance. You could ride many hours this way. It is not tiring." Anne-Marie's voice was now raised enough so that all could hear. She looked at Tim, now catching a light of approval in his eyes. Still, the proof of the cook would be in the pudding. She would have to perform perfectly. She could feel the tiny beads of perspiration on her forehead and palms, and her hands seemed to be soaking. A commotion within her churned and finally settled in her knees, which then felt weak. As if for a circus act, she gathered strength to perform. After a last loving stroke, she gave her horse a short pat and mounted swiftly.

At first she reined back, getting clear of the men, then she demonstrated the walk, trot and gallop. Then praying that her horse would not shy, she approached the cavaletti. "Carefully set your horse so that as he approaches each obstacle it will be easier for him to jump than to avoid it," she instructed.

The first hurdle was only eighteen inches, but soon Anne-Marie was taking her horse over three-foot hurdles as easily as stepping over a log on the ground.

"Maria Santisima!" cried one of the men as Anne-Marie made a particularly high jump and then quickly made several changes in direction.

"Bravo," came a chorus.

Careful to stop before her horse became tired, Anne-Marie had earned the respect of the men and then was free to correct some of the faults she had observed. "I notice that you ride too far forward, too crouched. Don't keep your legs so far back," she told one rider. To another she said, "And, sir, you ride too straight with your weight behind the balance point." Pointing to another she said, "You ride very well. You can help the others." He beamed with pride.

Finally, she removed the horse's saddle and to the great surprise of all present she stepped out of her own heavy shoes. Then she jumped on her horse, rode bareback for a minute, and then still moving drew herself up to a standing position on the horse's croup, or rump, and rode around the circle. "Now note how I fall," she said, knees bent, lightly jumping to a patch of soft sandy ground.

The men, feeling they had watched a circus act, were ecstatic. "Bravo! Bravo!" they cried.

"You really surprised me," said Tim. "I found the lesson a remarkable experience. Where did you learn to ride like that?"

"Right here," she replied.

"You were magnificent," said David. "I thought I was acquainted with all my little sister-in-law's talents!"

Rafael had watched the demonstration with mixed feelings. There seemed to be no end to her abilities and he was not sure he liked that fact. Such women were difficult to handle and control. "That was quite a performance. You surprised us all."

"I didn't mean to be performing, but I soon saw I had to. These men have to be trained. I may be the only one who can teach them. I wouldn't want to repeat that lesson tomorrow, but now the men believe that I can help, which is the important thing. Was I wrong?"

"No, you were superb," Rafael conceded. "If you shoot as well as you ride you will put us all to shame."

"There's no chance of that. I've had no interest in guns."

The rest of the afternoon was spent working with five men most needing instruction. By nightfall she knew much had been accomplished. Others had remained to watch and asked for help when she had time.

Rafael had his room in the main house. Anne-Marie, David and Tim occupied staterooms on *Los Girasoles,* tied up in the basin. The ship's cook had prepared their meals in the style to which they were accustomed, served by the steward. Rafael and Wade naturally were invited to join them. This evening they were all rightfully tired, Anne-Marie especially. Recognizing an equally strenuous day to follow, Anne-Marie suggested they retire early. Rafael and Wade returned to their quarters and those remaining bid each other goodnight. A few ravenous sand fleas hastened their resolve.

Anne-Marie could not sleep. Long unused muscles ached while her brain raced excitedly over a thousand and one details that during the wee hours grew in outlandish proportion. The ship, shielded from the sea by a fringe of tropical hammock and mangroves, was cut off from the prevailing breezes so that her cabin seemed oppressively hot. After hours of tossing and turning she remembered the nearby ocean and how pleasant night swims had been when this was her home. Certain that everyone on the island was now asleep, she quietly, still in her nightdress, left the ship, walked along the wharf and easily picked her way to the sea. There she lay down on the beach, cushioned by the sand, allowing the gentle cooling waves to splash about her. Here the night was beautiful.

She allowed her nightdress to become soaked, but then, remembering it was the only one with her, she hung it on a dead branch to dry. Naked, she swam back and forth close to the shore in relatively shallow water stretching every aching muscle. Slowly the aches subsided. Then she returned to lie on the beach, letting the cool surf break around her, the water sluicing past with only the gurgling sound of rushing bubbles to mix with the low crush of collapsing waves. Here was another world. Tormenting doubts that Bart might not be found alive subsided. The mind-boggling logistics of transporting one hundred men and most of their food across Mexico and back—and then seeing them safely out of the country—receded like flickering stars. Lesser problems: Alma, Zipporah, the Doyles, Rafael and her father's frustrated hobby of money-making receded like tiny burned out comets, evaporating into space, little more than sparks from a seaman's pipe.

She gazed up at the broad, luminous, peppering of light, the Milky Way, swathing the heavens. The four major stars that form the Great Square of Pegasus were setting in the west. On the east the Seven Sisters, daughters of Atlas turned into stars to form the Pleiades, wrapped in faint nebulosity, rose on the shoulders of Taurus the Bull. High in the eastern sky Orion the Hunter with belt and sword, and Leo the Lion, for countless centuries man's banner of courage in the equatorial, lent their awe inspiring distant fires to bolster timid hearts. Following Orion came the Great dog, Canis Major, whose eye, Sirius or the Dog Star, was the brightest star in the heavens. Anne-Marie's eyes went back to Taurus. There was her planet Jupiter, a great bright white spot, ready to cast its benevolence upon his children. Sighting Jupiter seemed like a good omen.

Her knowledge, stemming from Bart, his books and navigational papers, neatly stowed in the ship, the *Catherine*, seemed part of another life. Brushing the water from her skin, letting the soft breeze and starshine dry her, she strode the beach. Finally refreshed, she put on her nightdress and returned to the ship ready to sleep.

She was not the only one on the island who could not sleep. Rafael tossed and turned in his small room that offered privacy but little air movement. His mind, unfettered by details of the expedition so adeptly handled by Esteban Navarro, centered on Anne Marie and her day's achievements which shook his own self-esteem. She lay peacefully sleeping, isolated and insulated from him by two men acting as watchdogs, while he suffered alone, burning with desire. The more he thought of her, the more impossible sleep became. Finally, acknowledging the futility of trying further, he slipped into a shirt and pants. Instead of walking through the house and rousing any of the men sleeping on cots in what was once the dining salon, he went out by the kitchen door and walked toward the ship, bathed in a soft night light. As he approached the wharf, he grew bolder and speciously curious as he sauntered along the rough planking. The tide had risen so he had only to crouch to peer into her dimly lit stateroom, made discernable by the ship's smoking lamp just outside her quarters. Her bunk was empty! He stood transfixed, staring into the vacant master stateroom, now growing in vacuity with each sweep of the gently swaying light. For a couple of minutes he stood dead still thinking that she might be using the head, but nothing moved and there was no sound. Who was she sleeping with? Blinded with jealous rage, seething with hatred against both Tim and David, slowly he retreated to the main house. Once he stopped and turned, wondering if any of the other staterooms might be lit, but saw that the rest of the ship was in darkness. Totally shocked, he returned to his room to pace the rest of the night away.

By breakfast time Rafael had gained sufficient composure to join Anne-Marie, Tim and David on *Los Girasoles.* Anne-Marie sensed a coldness in his attitude toward her, although his impeccable manners blanketed his withdrawal. Confident that his mood would soon pass, she returned to help the riders, but she was aware of his unexplained absence. That afternoon they would return to Key West, so it was important to use the time. Once there, one big problem remained to be solved: they still needed a ship to transport the horses.

The sail back to Key West also was strained for Anne-Marie due to David: He hardly let her out of his sight except when she went to her stateroom, when, of course, no one followed. It left no opportunity to query Rafael over his coolness except in the presence of the whole group. Finally, to all of them she confided, "There are a number of things we should discuss. For starters, I'm concerned over being able to recognize our troops once we get on the road. They will not be in uniform, so we may have trouble keeping together."

"Why not some sort of distinguishing scarf?" suggested David.

"What a splendid idea! Señor de Palma, would scarves meet with your approval?" Her face was soft and pliant. She would abide by his opinion.

"Mr. Doyle's suggestion seems quite practical," replied Rafael showing no warmth.

"What would the disadvantages be?" she pressed, still looking at Rafael.

"I see none, off hand."

"Having uniforms made would delay the expedition and certainly make talk in Key West, not to mention the expense," David added.

"Which brings us to the point of your services, Señor de Palma," interjected Tim. "Anne-Marie is most anxious that you be well recompensed for your time and the great risks that you are taking, which is certainly difficult to put a price on."

"I have told Madame that my services are a gift to my friends."

"That I cannot accept, Señor," interjected Anne-Marie. "It's too much."

"Then, if you absolutely insist, and we are all in this together, I suggest that you award me the same as Messrs. Doyle and Clayton."

"But that is hardly fair as neither Tim nor David take the same risk as you do entering Mexico. David is family. You could be shot if discovered. Compensation to them embraces other kinds of services as well as this project."

"I'm sure your demands are heavy," said Rafael sardonically.

Anne-Marie was unruffled. "You misunderstood. Tim and I feel the nature and brevity of this project is not the same as a long-term proposition, and we would like to set a fee that would be pleasing and acceptable to you, regardless of the outcome. You are enormously generous, but we all need money to live. There is a limit to what I can accept from you." Her tone was friendly, but the last sentence was severe.

"I can see that you should have a little sister at home that I might marry," replied Rafael in a tone of retaliation.

Anne-Marie sat in stunned silence, smothering any revelation of her shock. With David and Tim present, such a childish display of temperament was uncalled for. Slowly, she gathered her wits. "My sisters are all taken, Señor, so regretfully, I'm forced to offer you less."

Sensing that the conversation was getting nowhere, Tim changed the subject.

"It's difficult to conceive how the ship will look stripped of the fine furnishings to accommodate the troops. We'll be packed like sardines."

"Slavers this size carried over a hundred and fifty men from Africa," replied Rafael.

"I'd buy another boat before I'd run anything like a slaver. I remember them well. You could smell them for miles." Anne-Marie rose. "Please excuse me. I would like to change before we dock. The ladies of Key West would frown on my male attire. I wonder what they would say if they knew I was teaching a bunch of mercenaries to ride."

The normal hubbub in the harbor of Key West as they docked proved a welcome distraction to Anne-Marie's irritation with Rafael. Consuelo was there, a minor center of attraction with the baby in a great elegant Victorian baby carriage, surrounded by on lookers. Spongers and fishermen were unloading their catches. Captain Ben Baker, owner of the *Rapid* and nearly always the master wrecker at every wreck on the reef, supervised the unloading of his latest salvage operation, drawing a good share of the curious. 'Crazy Jim' hustled through the crowd crying, "The Indians are coming," but no one paid any attention. Jim's family, the Williams, had been living at Indian Key at the time of the Indian Key Massacre, and although they survived, their young son had been driven insane. He wandered the streets of Key West harmlessly making guttural sounds, which developed into screams about the Indians when crowds were present. Anne-Marie's driver and carriage waited in the background. A perfunctory thank you and a reserved goodbye were all that Rafael received from Anne-Marie when she took David's arm and her wounded feelings to walk toward Consuelo.

"How good of you to have spared your husband for a few days," said Anne-Marie, embracing her friend and then turning to ogle the baby, who already appreciated attention. Rafael approached to greet Consuelo, but having been dismissed by Anne-Marie he dared not linger beyond the amenities demanded by polite society.

"I think we had a very productive trip, which I'm sure Tim will describe fully," said Anne-Marie, now looking for Tim who had also disappeared. "Where is Tim?"

"I found an old ship that I think will be perfect for transporting the horses, and I sent Tim over to talk with the owner," whispered Consuelo. "He should be back in a few minutes."

"How wonderful! That was the last big problem we had."

"Ramsden luck! How perfect everything has fallen into place for you," said Consuelo.

"My luck is matched by my friends and is largely produced by them, too," said Anne-Marie.

Within minutes a beaming Tim rejoined the women. "The ship is perfect for our purposes. We can buy or charter it, which may be the wisest choice, but I'll leave that to you. We will meet with the owner tomorrow at ten o'clock."

"I would imagine Bart would prefer to say which ships we buy, but we can decide tomorrow. Join us tomorrow evening, Consuelo, and I suppose I should ask Rafael, too. Mother always said the number at dinner should not be fewer than the Graces nor more than the Muses."

"If the Graces are busy, try the Fates," said Tim with a wry smile.

Anne-Marie had to laugh. "I'd love to stand here subjecting myself to your husband's wit," she replied turning to Consuelo, "but I simply must wash my hair. I went swimming late last night, and I'm still powdered all over with salt."

"I thought I heard considerable traffic on the wharf," said Tim.

"I was not considerable traffic. I was barefooted and could not have made a sound. I was gone at least two hours, swimming away the day's muscle strain, not to mention considerable anxiety. I didn't see anyone."

"I guess one of the men suffered a restlessness also, but you must be careful."

"Don't worry, I will," she replied, finally on her way laughing and scratching.

That evening she and David were alone. "This may be the last quiet evening we have to talk for quite a while, David. Several times I've considering asking you to come to Mexico, but I truly feel I need you here more. I don't like risking my sister's husband, but more importantly I may need a pivotal point where there is someone I trust implicitly. I'll send you as many wires as possible letting you know where I am. We can do this in code. You can also keep Father informed as you think best. When you judge the moment is right—from messages I send—send Captain Sands to pick us up."

"I'll do what you wish. Frankly, I don't have as much confidence in de Palma as you do, so I would like to be around to protect you, but you will have Tim."

"Why is it you don't trust him? I didn't at first either, but then he proved himself quite capable. I'm impressed with the men he had hired, for example."

"Nothing specific, but for a starter, I doubt that he is interested in finding Bart. Besides, no man trusts another with his little sister."

She had to smile, then he continued on a more serious vein. "Today I took the liberty of doing something before locking up the rifles and giving the key to Tim." David then produced a leather pouch, no larger than a purse. "I feel it important that you remain in absolute control. At some point this control could be taken from you—by anyone. This pouch contains the firing pins from the Krupp rifles, and the rifles are worthless without them. The men will have their pistols, but pistols are inaccurate and of little value except at close range. When you want to activate the rifles, you can, but only you can. No one saw me do this. For your own safety, do not confide in anyone." Then he dropped the small but heavy pouch in her lap.

At first Anne-Marie was astonished at his initiative, but before he finished speaking, she felt grateful for what he had done.

"All the firing power in those guns lies in your lap. You earned the respect of every man yesterday with your riding ability. I could see it. They loved you. But, I realized that you know nothing about guns. You don't need to know anything as long as you have these."

"That was clever of you. Perhaps I am too trusting…"

David's revelation confirmed something quite pleasing. He had more sense that Bart had ever given him credit for.

Under newly washed and flaming copper hair she seemed to David the epitome of innocence and naivete, the perfect victim for a scoundrel. David had made an interesting discovery beyond his initial suspicions. He was not certain, but he also thought Rafael was padding the payroll. He counted the names on the roster and then tried to count the men he saw, but Los Claveles was a large estate and he honestly could not be sure of the discrepancy, which amounted to about ten percent. At this point it would have been wrong to have alerted Anne-Marie, so he resolved to alert Tim. It would be easy enough to make a check as the men came aboard. If there were a discrepancy, David knew it could be attributed to French leave—some of which they should expect. Having thought it all over, he opted for discretion. More importantly, he needed to endear himself to Anne-Marie by considering her welfare, so he continued in a personal vein.

"I want to spend some time everyday with Samantha. She will miss you, but at least one member of the family will be available."

"Oh, David, you have no idea how much I appreciate that. Children should not be left entirely to servants, and I have not been the most dutiful mother. It's not that my heart is not in the right place. There have been so many demands upon me."

"Little Sister, I know you've always done the best you can. Don't underrate yourself. All will run smoothly here."

"I'd like you to look in on Consuelo when you can. With a baby to occupy her, she won't miss Tim as much; still a little adult company would keep her spirits up."

"I'd be glad to oblige. She's a charming woman."

"Feel free to entertain here. Our social life is not very exciting, but Key West boasts any numbers of characters."

"Have no qualms," he replied, certain that the next month would be much more comfortable for him than anyone could anticipate.

The following day they supervised the stripping down of *Los Girasoles.* One small cabin was left intact for Anne-Marie. Tin, Rafael and Esteban would share its equivalent; as only two would be occupying the quarters at the same time, one man remaining on duty at all times.

Anne-Marie and Tim kept the ten o'clock appointment with the owner of the *Forward* and within five minutes had arranged to charter the ship, complete with crew to transport the horses to Mexico. That evening Anne-Marie announced that preparations were complete and they could leave as soon as Señor de Palma was ready. Smiling graciously she told him, "While we were gone Consuelo found the *Forward*, and this morning Tim and I arranged for her charter to transport the horses. Whether we sail tomorrow or the day after depends upon you, Señor." He was startled.

"I would not think of inconveniencing you for a moment," replied Rafael, rising to the occasion, but decidedly unhappy feeling out of control.

"Then we will leave as soon as you can load. Delay will only alert the authorities and add countless problems," said Anne-Marie.

"You're right," said Tim. "We gain nothing by indecision. Indecision is like the stepchild who doesn't wash his hands and is called dirty, or who washes his hands and is accused of wasting water. Let's go!"

Consuelo joined in, "The sooner you go, the sooner you'll return. Let's get this behind us. Then I will thank you, Anne-Marie, to keep your husband at home. I think I've spent a decade trying to save that man."

Tim reached for his wife's hand. "I would say that my wife is joking, but of course she is not." They all laughed.

"We can leave tomorrow," announced Rafael.

"Then let's have a toast," said David.

"What better," replied Anne-Marie, calling for champagne. When it arrived she raised her glass with a signal for others to follow:

"Here's to a trip to Mexico

To find a man who had to go.

Here's to you, Tim, staunch and true,

And to Consuelo, don't be blue…

Here's to David holding the fort,

No matter what, he'll be a good sport.

And here's to Señor, who masterminded it all

May all your endeavors never lead to a fall."

"Hurrah," they all cried, buoyed by the spirit of camaraderie and adventure.

They are all risking something to save my husband, thought Anne-Marie. Self-sacrifice must have its own rewards as they were all risking something and perhaps not knowing what. The next month would affect their futures for a long time to come. The thought was awesome. She reached for another glass of sparkling wine to erase it.

"Have we thought of everything?" she asked.

"Everything that we can do anything about," replied Rafael.

"If only the horses don't get shipping fever," she cried, covering her eyes with a hand for a minute.

"I think you'll find seasickness a bigger problem," said Tim, sagely.

"I never knew horses got seasick," Anne-Marie replied, incredulous.

"No, but men do."

And they did.

Los Girasoles, by the need to sail at the same speed as the *Forward,* not to become separated, was seriously inconvenienced. The novice sailor/soldiers had to learn that a sailing vessel seldom travels in a straight line, but shifts course to catch the wind with a tack that demands attention or one is likely to be sick all over one's shirt. So, for six days and nights, despite a good wind, those not sick stepped over moaning, groaning bodies—men who hoped in one moment to die and feared in the next that they might. The only cure, Tim advised, was to sit on the shady side of an old church in the country and listen to the church bells.

Anne-Marie and Tim had strong stomachs, which was fortunate as they were the ones most willing to tend those ill. Gradually, the *mal de mer* abated and the men were able to rouse themselves and wash their clothing prior to landing, but the smoother passage had also meant less speed.

Anne-Marie devoted her time to cutting and hemming the red scarves, which she wanted the men to wear in the field to facilitate keeping them together, also to keep them from shooting each other—God forbid—should any shooting occur. The scarves she counted carefully, but several times she noted her count was off. "I thought I had finished forty," she told Rafael. "I can't even count anymore."

"Some of the men may be overanxious to get their hands on their own. Men do have romantic notions, you know, and they have watched you sewing a particular piece…"

The night before departure, David had also gotten Tim aside to confide his hunch that Rafael's roll might not be accurate. When the boarding began, Tim positioned himself with the roster in hand to check off those embarking, but soon Rafael found something more important demanding Tim's attention. He himself relieved Tim of the roll check. Knowing his insistence would only commence the voyage with bad blood, Tim acquiesced readily enough to Rafael's wish, but this seemed to confirm David's hunch. Tim agreed with David that there was no point in worrying Anne-Marie with the unconfirmed judgment. Tim did notice eventually that he was handed an amended and accurate roll. Ninety men included the crew.

Throughout the voyage Anne-Marie dared not examine her bedraggled once beautiful ship. Instead, when she looked away from her sewing, she gazed longingly at the *Forward*. At a distance it seemed tidy in comparison.

"Have no fear, Madame," said Captain Sands. "No real damage has been done to your ship. The crew will have it clean as a whistle before we even near Key West."

*　　　*　　　*　　　*

There was no way that Rafael could have left Key West decently without saying something to Mimi—at least if he ever expected to live in Key West again. Mimi had been doing her best to worm out of Rafael exactly what he was doing. Certainly the International Explorer's Club of Key West, where Rafael spent most of his time when in Key West, was a front for something. His deepening suntan also revealed outdoor work, which seemed inexplicable. Further, he seemed to be interviewing men. The work was, by his own admission, dangerous, secretive— therefore illegal—and under the aegis of Anne-Marie. At first Mimi thought the business was smuggling Bart out of a Mexican prison. Later taking Rafael's Spanish blood and patriotism into consideration, she decided Anne-Marie might be fomenting another Mexican revolution. She would regain her husband and Rafael would regain Mexico for Spain. Was that too farfetched? Not with Anne-Marie's money. Also, Tim, another foreigner was involved.

Wisely, Rafael wrote and mailed an explanatory goodbye letter, which enabled the expedition to set sail from Los Claveles before the letter was delivered. It read:

"My dearest Mimi, This note must suffice as I dare not visit you tonight due to the hour. A sudden voyage will separate us for a few weeks at most. I beg you not to mention anything you may have guessed regarding my recent occupation. It could endanger my life. The last few weeks you have made my life bearable. We must be grateful for what we have had together. Who knows what the future will bring? Your loving friend is in haste, R. de P."

Mimi flew into a rage. It was an ambiguous note, at first saying a few weeks and then carrying overtones of a permanent separation. Why such haste? Clearly, Consuelo had been avoiding her on the pretext of being occupied with the baby. I must pump Consuelo, she thought. If it weren't for the fact that Rafael's life might be jeopardized, she would go straight to the authorities. She would wait a little while. Anne-Marie Ramsden had better watch out. She had no business playing with other men's lives.

*   *   *   *

Anne-Marie's feelings of insecurity, heightened by Bart's departure and prolonged silence, had peaked. Her achievements had strengthened her. Now she was the center of attention of almost a hundred men, all appreciative of her beauty and ability, but containing this—as best they could—under the pressure of dire threats from Rafael. Still, there were moments when Rafael, Tim and Esteban were not present and the men could look at Anne-Marie in admiration and lust. Rafael's insecurity in the face of unbounded masculinity in competition grew by leaps and bounds. Hiding this insane love-madness took every ounce of will power he possessed. He could think of nothing but love for Anne-Marie and his determination to have her. So totally absorbing was this obsession that throughout the voyage he could hardly enter a discussion.

Anne-Marie assumed that his silence was due to a hovering seasickness that he did not want to admit.

Every night Tim firmly insisted that she bolt her door. "There are almost a hundred men aboard this ship with one thing in mind, Anne-Marie." His counsel was sobering. And, at the sound of the slightest scuffle in her stateroom, Tim would have broken down the door. "You know Captain Sands has the authority and duty to punish a rapist. He could make him walk the plank…Let's not let anything like this happen."

Anne-Marie shuddered.

On the sixth day they saw land, and a magnificent sight it was. The outline of the rugged mountains that skirt the city of Orizaba was clear. The clouds, hovering around the base of the mountains and obscuring the lowlands near the coast were rapidly rising. The summit of Orizaba, covered with snow, towered above everything. When the clouds rose and covered the lowlands, the undulating, finely diversified land in deep luxuriant verdure lay before them.

The landing and entering into Veracruz, dreaded for weeks, went so swiftly and easily, Anne-Marie would laugh about it all of her life. The three custom's agents and immigration officers froze in astonishment and fear as the group, led by Esteban Navarro, crowded into the building. The officer in charge, having noticed the pistols and clothing of ruffians, stretched a trembling hand to receive the "Scribe's" impressive forgeries. After a few minutes of reading he began bowing to superior forces, fawning. Frantically the agents began stamping the papers, wanly smiling as they murmured, "Bienvenidos! Bienvenidos…Vaya con Dios…"

They were not that welcome. Only one glance had established that the entire police force of Veracruz was outnumbered at least ten to one, and Maria Santisima, an officer in charge could read, couldn't he?

One agent, fear having brought on an irresistible bodily urge, quickly stepped outside only to be surrounded by more men, busily unloading and saddling horses. He wished he had remained indoors. Within half an hour of the first step on Mexican soil, the excited troops were riding out of town toward Orizaba. They traveled on an awful road with darkness descending. Finally, they camped, just off the roadside, having passed the sand hills and ponds of stagnant water which formed the backyard of Veracruz, knowing there was little chance of any normal traffic until the next morning.

"We must get away from Veracruz as fast as we can," warned Rafael. "Or the whole troop could come down with yellow fever. The next town is Córdoba. Many have made it there only to die."

It took customs agents two days pouring over a *Book of Protocol and Procedures* to discover the hoax—there was no Department of Foreign Secret Service—and to report it to the governor in his castle. By this time the number of invaders had multiplied to possibly a thousand men—as they told it—certainly bound to take over the country. Consternation grew when no one could even guess from which nation they had come.

Unfortunately, Anne-Marie was not privy to this information or to a later report that would go to the governor as they hurriedly left the city. Once during the night she awakened to the sound of hoof beats which for a moment she imagined as a possible at attack upon their rear. It was only a muleteer working a coach, a great lumbering broken down machine drawn by ten mules, pushing to get home. But from then on, the possibility of an attack could not be discounted, she knew.

Chapter Thirteen

Bart approached the ancient city of Puebla de Los Angeles in a better physical and metal state than he had enjoyed in months. The road, clearly evident, traveled by both people and animals, was well established so there had been no danger of taking the wrong fork or turning at crossroads that ran nowhere except to some distant and isolated hacienda. Inns along the way had offered tasty nourishment, and by now he was well accustomed to Mexican food.

The city spread out on a plain, cradled by a rim of mountains, the most spectacular being Popocatepetl and Ixtaccihuatl. Known as the city of tile, glistening in the sun glazed tiles were everywhere in varied hues, adorning the eighty-some belltowered churches as well as homes. The roads within the city were wide and clean, sloping from curb to center, where, to Bart's surprise, in some of them ran streams, while others seemed to be flooded for sanitary purposes. Struck with the beauty of the Spanish Colonial architecture, the parks and plazas with their flowers and fountains, the colorful tile work, and intricate wrought iron decorating buildings, Bart secured his horse and entered the post office.

The first order of business was to telegraph Anne-Marie that he was alive and once more a free man. He had been gone over three months. She would learn the details later, but he assumed this news would be comforting.

In the post to his dismay (and almost the first thing he saw) was his picture on a poster offering one thousand American gold dollars for information leading to his whereabouts. Seeing no need whatsoever now of paying anyone this exorbitant sum, he removed the poster and rolled it up. As he did it a toothless old beggar hastened across the street and entered an office. Bart shortly felt a hand on his shoulder and heard, "You are under arrest. "

Polite protestations in reasonably fluent Spanish to no avail, he was led to the office of the prefect of the police. A title, Jefe de los Cuerpos de Policia, marked the office door.

The jefe, a large, well-mannered, friendly man, listened to Bart's explanation, but saw things differently. There was no reason why he should not receive the award himself by notifying the United States' envoy to Mexico; after all, he knew of the captain's whereabouts.

"But, the award is no longer valid," protested Bart. "There's no need for me to pay a reward telling me where I am, and this is what will happen."

"The reward is offered by your wife, not you."

"It's the same thing."

"Not at all. May I see your papers, please. It is necessary to establish who you are," explained the jefe.

"I'm sorry. I have no papers. They were taken from me when I was kidnapped."

"Oh, Captain, that is unfortunate. I'm afraid I have to detain you here, for your own safety, of course, until this matter can be cleared up."

"I have committed no crime…"

"You have removed public property." He smiled. "What hotel are you staying in, Captain?"

"I just this hour arrived in Puebla. My first concern was to wire my wife. I've had no opportunity to register."

"Then you are a vagrant."

"That's the most ridiculous charge I've ever heard in my life," snorted Bart, fighting to control mounting anger. "I have done absolutely nothing unlawful in this Goddamned country."

"You are insulting an officer and debasing the sovereign nation of Mexico in addition to removing public property. These are serious offenses, Captain." The prefect's manner remained calm. He was a man capable of dramatizing any experience to the hilt, well geared to making the right effect, swift to act and certain of his power. He moved about the room that was his own little stage.

"And, under the laws of this sovereign nation, I am certainly entitled to counsel," replied Bart angrily, but at the same time aware that everything he said would be used against him in a rapidly closing net of extortion.

"Of course," replied the jefe, stroking his heavy moustache. "I will attend to that at my earliest convenience. In the meantime, I trust you will not be too uncomfortable. We have suitable quarters for our higher-type malefactors." A stroke of his chubby hand was the signal for three subordinates to escort the victim into a small but clean barred suite. With a resounding clank the iron door closed behind him.

Flabbergasted over this turn of events, Bart paced the floor, wearing off steam. Clearly, in an agitated state he would get himself only into deeper trouble. He could do little but await a lawyer, selected by the prefect, and doubtless one who would charge an inordinately high fee. Heavy iron grill-work at the windows made escape impossible by these openings unless he could bribe an underling to provide a hacksaw, certainly a possibility, but one that could take time and more privacy than there was likely to be.

A framed notice on the wall informed prisoners of the menu that could be ordered and paid for from a nearby restaurant if prison fare proved unacceptable, which Bart was certain it would be. Certain other services desired by gentlemen, including laundry, boot polishing, shaving, and manicuring were also available at a price. Doubtless with a percentage to the jefe, Bart supposed.

Anne-Marie had been ill advised in posting such an extravagant reward. In the United States a thousand dollars would feed a man for three years. This buying power was at least quadrupled in Mexico. For such a sum the prefect would be willing to go to great lengths. Bemoaning Anne-Marie's action, he walked to the window. Outside in a courtyard an old Indian was feeding his horse, he noted gratefully. At least it had not been stolen.

Wanting desperately to write Anne-Marie and allay her fears over his well being, he knew this was impossible. The only address the prefect had was one through diplomatic channels. Anne-Marie's home address, when obtained, would only lead to private extortion. Certainly, within a few days he could break free. For the time being he could only dream of his wife. To consciously dwell on her long, only made him lonely.

Firmly resolving to remain docile and to observe prison routine, Bart also decided he could play the prefect's game. He could wait until surveillance was relaxed when he could overpower unsuspecting guards. But first he would have to fool the prefect as to the direction he would be taking or he would be apprehended again for a much greater crime. Acting too fast would be a mistake. The prefect was also playing a dangerous game in which he certainly had not had time to work out the details. Undoubtedly, he was hoping to make a fast coup. Drawn out negotiations, during which Bart could talk to others, would spell trouble for the prefect as surely he had underlings who could benefit by unseating their supervisor. Distasteful as imprisonment was to Bart, to a great extent he had learned to handle immobilization. He had served time at Fort Jefferson, one of the world's worst prisons. He had been held near Orizaba by ruffians. His career had imposed the confines of a ship where for weeks at a time he could not move more than a hundred feet. His quarters here were better than many he had endured. His bed, consisting of a frame spanned by interlacing small ropes supporting a thin horsehair mattress, was cleaner than he had expected. Certainly the present was tolerable, but it was also conceivable that the prefect would try to break him with much worse conditions. He would have to be alert to threats, although he seriously doubted that he would be subjected to torture. The prefect would not dare go that far. Throwing himself down in the bed, he slept.

It was late evening before he awakened, called a guard, and requested a dinner to be brought in with an accompanying wine. About an hour later a young girl arrived at the prison with a tray. Suddenly, his blood ran cold as he looked to the door and in the dim light thought he was seeing Ramona. A gap in the grillwork was large enough for a tray to pass, and with a closer inspection as he took the tray from her, he saw that the resemblance was only superficial. Also, she was much too well dressed for a servant. A wan smile broke slowly across his face.

"You startled me," he explained, now embarrassed over the mistake.

The girl regarded the tall, blue-eyed prisoner, clean-cut and nice, and wondered what he was doing in a jail he seemed too good for.

"I am sorry. I have brought you a specialty of our city, *chilies en nogada*. It is stuffed peppers topped with red pomegranate seeds, green coriander leaves and a white sauce. According to legend the dish originated here to honor our newly won independence. Perhaps, for a man in prison, it is not appropriate, but it is the best dish on the menu today."

"I'm sure it will be delicious. If I looked startled when you arrived it was because you reminded me of someone far away. But, I don't know why I'm telling you all of this except that you so kindly explained the dinner."

"And for dessert you have *gaznates,* wheat shells that are fried in sesame oil and then filled with cream and coconut. I hope you enjoy your meal. Will you be wanting breakfast tomorrow?"

"Oh, yes, do bring something."

"The guard will take your tray. Sleep well," she said, departing.

Bart looked to the empty doorway, feeling bereft by her departure. How nice she was.

Finishing dinner, he gave the tray to the guard, retaining the bottle of wine to ease the night. Eventually, he moved to his bed and lay there in a semi-stupor counting the red bricks that formed a gentle ceiling arch leading to the adjoining room. When the candle in a square glass lantern suspended from the ceiling died, he fell asleep.

Breakfast was not served early in Mexico and when the young girl arrived he was ravenously hungry. In the bright sunlight that bounced around the barren white walls, he could see her much better, and wondered how he could have mistaken her for Ramona, she was so much prettier and livelier.

"I cannot understand what you are doing here," she said. "You don't look like a criminal, but I have seen your face before."

"On a poster in the post office."

She laughed. "Of course."

"And your chief of police wants the reward."

"Which you do not want to pay because you know where you are."

"Exactly."

"Our public officials are crooked. However, I cannot continue to bring you all of your meals. My father owns the restaurant and I brought your tray last night because we were short of hands. Normally, a waiter comes. I came back today because you seemed like a nice, kind type and I was curious about you. You will be out in a month or so…Everyone occupying these quarters is."

"A month or so," cried Bart, horrified.

"Usually only politicians are here, and they take care of one another. Hasta luego, Señor."

"Adios," he replied, again regretting her departure.

Within a few minutes the prefect arrived and Bart could hear him barking orders, until finally a lull settled in the offices, and he appeared at the iron grill door.

"Good day, Captain. I hope you had a good night."

"I fault your hospitality only in that it is confining."

"But, by your own choice."

"By my own choice I would be on my way to Veracruz and home. Despite untenable delays, I have completed my mission. I have enjoyed you beautiful country. If your policy of mañana, tomorrow, were one of hoy, today, you Mexicans would rule the world."

Flattered by the North American's evaluation, the prefect was willing to chat. Bart obliged, satisfied that he had got over one point, his destination. He would never need to refer to this again, and should not. If he made his escape they would look for him on the wrong road.

"If you have any playing cards, and would like a game, you know where you can find me," said Bart, smiling.

"Do you play *Conquian?*" inquired the prefect.

"Yes, as well as several variations such as Rummy."

"And *Ambigu?*"

"Or Brag," replied Bart. "I'm also fond of Backgammon."

"My pleasure."

So began the afternoon games that at first took place on two narrow tables separated by the wrought iron door. Later, the prefect would enter Bart's room. Bart played an artificial game, allowing the prefect to win most of the time, but not by a suspiciously large margin. Carefully Bart restrained his normally bold and aggressive game for a defensive, conservative play, slow to make up his mind. In fact, had Bart not been absorbed in the deception, he would have been bored to distraction with his own game. Throughout the play the prefect kept up a patter urging Bart to give him a letter which would assure him the reward.

"I'll think it over this evening," said Bart with pseudo-characteristic indecision, bound to taunt the prefect.

"A wise decision," replied the prefect, certain that Bart was nearing capitulation.

"I'm not sure it is," mumbled Bart, more than a little amused with what he was doing, and pleased, too. The prefect seemed to squirm.

"You are wasting your life here. A young man like you should be out in the world, accomplishing things or at least having a good time. You are only postponing what you will decide to do later."

"Perhaps you are right."

"Of course, I am. You will only miss our fiesta in the next day or so."

"Is that right?"

"Yes. It's an important one, based on one of our oldest legends. A Mexican fiesta is a work of art! Music, dancing, costumes…"

"And the legend?"

"The legend is the framework, and it varies all over the country," the jefe explained. "There are three leading characters: the General, the Bandit, and the Bride, the Bride being played by a man, of course. As the legend goes, once many years ago, a Spanish general came to Mexico and married an Indian girl. They had two children and were very happy until the Spanish authorities passed a law forbidding marriages between Spaniards and Indians, requiring Spaniards to put aside their Indian wives. The men took the boys, and the daughters were relegated to the women. The general took his son back with him to Spain, where his education was neglected so he became a bandit. The bandit was forced to leave Spain and return to Mexico."

By this time Bart was becoming interested in the fiesta as a means of escape. "Very interesting. Continue, please."

The prefect obliged. "The girl was put in a convent which the bandit happened to pass. Looking up at the balcony he saw the beautiful girl and fell in love with her. He threw her a letter. Never having seen a love letter before and overcome with passion, she jumped from the balcony and ran away with him. Meanwhile, the general was sent to Mexico to capture the bandit, which he did, just before a priest was about to marry the couple. Just as the girl flew to her lover's side, in the shuffle she lost her locket, which the general recognized. In it was a miniature portrait of her mother, whom he had loved deeply. Then the general knew the girl was his daughter. In some unexplained manner the general also then recognized the bandit as his son. He then had to reveal that they were brother and sister, and, of course, could not marry."

"It sounds like a great fiesta," said Bart.

"I hope you can attend," replied the prefect.

That evening the young girl came again with Bart's dinner. As she slipped his tray through the door she observed that Bart's guards were paying no attention to their prisoner who was on friendly terms with their boss.

"Do you have any idea how I can find a man to help me escape?" he whispered.

"Possibly."

"With only a little rope a horse could pull the iron grate off the door to the courtyard and then the grate off my window."

"I know a young man in need of money," she replied.

"Will this do?" Bart handed her a small pouch.

"I will see."

Bart fervently hoped that the girl would bring his dinner tray and reassure him, but in her stead came a waiter. Never did the chilies seem so fiery. Then he glanced down to a tortilla to see scratched in the thin, flat cornmeal bread the words "*Dia de la fiesta*," or day of the fiesta. Heaving a sign of relief, he downed the damning evidence.

The following morning Bart was certain the fiesta was going to start. People came out of their houses in costume, each group with a band of musicians. They walked around a little, enjoying the music, but then disappeared. The fiesta was off. Bart's hopes fell. The following day the same thing happened, but the fiesta simply didn't catch on. Bart's distress grew.

He spent a restless night worrying over the wisdom of attempting an escape involving a young man who might be putting his neck in a noose if the scheme were detected, dependent on a fiesta that couldn't get off the ground. The following day, a Saturday, meant reduced vigilance.

Instead of ordering wine with his dinner, he would also ask for a bottle of stronger tequila, which the guards surely would enjoy sharing.

He also had one more ploy to use on the prefect, who was certain his fish was nearly hooked, and who was spending more and more time playing cards with his prisoner.

"The trouble with you is, you have no gumption. You have a good memory for cards, but no spunk. You sit rotting here when all you need to do is give me a letter and you are free as a bird," said the prefect who instead of playing cards returned to his office.

Bart turned to his window. At first he could see only one musician. Then came an Apache in a magnificent feathered headdress. The soldiers appeared. Women wore long, full, red flannel skirts and white shirts with green yokes trimmed with spangles, draped with many beads. Then another batch of musicians appeared. The fiesta was on!

Bart called to the prefect, who hurried to Bart's door, certain Bart had decided on the letter. Instead, Bart had decided the time was ripe for a lie. "Señor, I wonder if you know that just before I was arrested, I telegraphed to my wife informing her that I was safe. I supposed that by this time she would have notified the authorities and I would be free."

The chief's face fell. "Why didn't you inform me of this earlier?"

"It didn't seem too important," replied Bart, now certain that the post would be closed because of the fiesta and the records could not be checked.

Certain that he had a dunce on his hands, the prefect stormed from the building.

Bart walked to his door with the bottle of tequila and called a guard. "I'm afraid this is too strong for me, but you may enjoy it," he said, extending the bottle through the bars. "It is too bad you can't attend the fiesta, but this may help."

Eagerly the guards accepted the unexpected bounty and began to drink.

From his window slightly above the crowd Bart could distinguish the leading characters in the drama that would soon be enacted: the

General, the Bandit, and the Bride. The line of costumed participants gradually lengthened forming a procession headed for the plaza. Some way like costumes had joined together, Apaches in one group, devils in another, musicians in another. The procession, circling his block and having gathered speed, slipped from sight while excitement increased in the crowd.

Within a few seconds the faintest noise in the courtyard indicated that the courtyard gate had been opened. Suddenly a tossed rope came flying through the air. Quickly, Bart grabbed it. With an expert seaman's knot he attached it to the iron grill barring his window. Within seconds a young man in a devil's costume attached the other end of the rope to the saddle of his horse and gave the horse a sound whack with his whip, pulling the iron grill work to the ground.

Meanwhile, the procession, feeling the need for some concrete action, rounded the corner and the General and the Bride disappeared into Bart's building, the Town Hall. Immediately, they came out on a balcony above the Bandit on horseback. The Bandit took a letter from his pocket and with considerable effort in three attempts, got the letter into the waiting hands of the Bride. After a brief reading, the Bride leaped gracefully into the saddle of a waiting horse, a veil hiding her drooping mustache and her dress hiding a pair of men's trousers. In a second the crowd cleared a path. Sensing that this was the moment, Bart jumped to the ground, mounted his horse, fled the courtyard, trotting into the nearest cleared path, pursued by the Bandit and a Bride, who in turn were pursued by a General and his soldiers.

The chase went merrily through the streets with terrific noise and total pandemonium, ending up at the plaza. After many weeks of being pent up, concentrated energies and excitement found release in the reveling participants.

One and all assumed that Bart, the advance rider, was simply clearing the way for the three participants in the drama. Sighting the two great volcanoes that gave him his direction, Bart departed from the stage, which had ended at a small hut at one end of the plaza. Here people clustered waiting for the last act. Soon the Bandit, the Bride and the General entered the hut. Following tradition, a moment later flames broke out on the thatched roof, prompting the trio to exit. With the hut ablaze, and one last blast of music, the carnival had reached its fiery climax. When the bonfire died, the crowd dispersed and straggled home.

Bart, of course, had missed the last act. Never having caught sight again of his benefactor or the young girl who hired him, he galloped from the city.

Bart felt reasonably sure the episode in Puebla was closed forever. Surely, no charges had been filed against him. Monday morning the prefect would discover no telegraph had been sent weeks earlier before he was apprehended. Possibly, after the fiesta an alert had been sounded on the road to Veracruz that might or might not keep a few bureaucrats busy for a few days. His losses at cards to the prefect would cover an outstanding bill at the restaurant, but that was life. Perhaps one day he could make amends himself. Once more he was a free man, beholden to a lovely girl he could not name.

CHAPTER FOURTEEN

The first night in Mexico had been limpid and dark with all sounds muffled by the resistance of thick, damp, still air so Anne-Marie could not tell if what she heard were snores of seventy-six (by an accurate count) sleeping men, cries of nocturnal animals or restrained laughter of some, who like herself, were too keyed up to sleep. She alone had a private tent although she shared it with bags of rice, flour, coffee, beans, cases of ammunition and whatever had to be kept dry. The bivouac had been hastily hacked out of a jungle that although bounded by a road, defied containment. Had not the road been steadily traveled by day, within a few weeks it would have disappeared entirely into the fast-growing, encroaching tropical rain forest on both sides. They were in the Tierra Caliente, a steaming, bug-filled, hot land where nature ruled and only the Gulf of Mexico made habitation endurable.

Anne-Marie had avoided Rafael's eyes, even though she knew his were upon her, burning the back of her neck like the incessant fire of a summer sun. Occasionally, she had tried to throw him a friendly reassuring glance—one swift and unromantic. Always an incalculable fiery passion, a dark power in him that Anne-Marie felt, seemed ready to burst out. This Tim and Esteban attributed to tension over the expedition, which naturally would weigh heaviest on him, but which Anne-Marie rightly felt had much to do with her personally.

By late the second night they made the blue-gray hills. The short tropic twilight long before had given place to darkness. The men had eaten and finished their meal with cigarettes and coffee. Around the campfire they had laughed over the landing and departure from Veracruz. After the voyage, the first two days in the saddle had been exceptionally tiring and, as the men stretched or moved, their joints creaked. The horses, tethered near at hand, chomped their oats and maize. Suddenly, a long mournful howl came through the night, repeated in a chorus. Terrified, Anne-Marie rushed from her tent to the dying campfire.

"What was that?" she cried, looking to Rafael who was about to retire.

Again a long unearthly cry echoed through the canyon. "Coyotes, Madame. They are crying to heaven for rain."

With a shudder and sigh of relief Anne-Marie returned to her tent, wondering how in the world she would sleep were the cries to continue. They did, off and on, throughout the night. Furthermore it was still night when the first bird chirped and soon was joined by thousands. With half-light Anne-Marie could hear the men stirring, rising, coughing, stretching and shaking out blankets, saying little except in muffled low morning voices. Then suddenly with dawn a cacophony of sound burst forth as screaming monkeys and parrots, having discovered the night's invasion of their territory, protested the intrusion. Anne-Marie lingered in her tent, allowing the men to make their morning ablutions, unhampered by the presence of a woman. Finally, the smell of coffee indicated that the party had moved toward the work of the day, and they would soon be on their way. The horses would need water. Government troops might be in pursuit. Realities came to the fore as the animals receded under a broiling sun.

As Rafael had predicted, finding water for the horses was not a problem. There were watering troughs in every village, but watering took time. Many of the company were always standing around waiting, either before or after letting their horses drink. At such times they could make trouble, and this morning two men did.

A pretty girl, possibly only twelve or thirteen, caught the eye of one of the men, eliciting flirtatious and fresh remarks. Suddenly, an irate father, having heard the remarks, rushed from his doorway waving a machete and demanding apologies. He was soon joined by a throng of villagers. A serious confrontation might have followed had not Rafael come forward. "Señor, with such a beautiful flower for a daughter your concern is understandable. My men have behaved badly, but they join me in begging her pardon. I hope you will accept this small gift as a token of our remorse." Rafael spoke with flourish. He then gave the man a *peso* and four *reales*, which amounted to a dollar and a half, which was gladly accepted. Rafael's indemnity, polished manners and soothing apologies soon quieted the father as well as subduing his men.

Despite strict instructions that there was to be no marauding or pillaging, the men had to be constantly restrained from stealing. "You must pay for what you take," insisted Anne-Marie, "or you will be punished."

Still, sometimes the men, like a pack of unruly boys, enjoyed a little terrorization of the women in markets as a communal sport. One old man almost lost his whole burro load of bananas, but Anne-Marie happened to see the incident and paid the man well for the crop. Soon it became evident that she, Tim, Rafael and Esteban would have to ride widely separated in order to maintain control. Even at that, the big problem would be disciplining the men after infringements were detected. At the next rest stop that they took to refresh the horses, Anne-Marie confided to Tim her concern over the men stealing.

"Probably, we must expect a little of this," Tim replied. "If it gets too bad, we can divide the men into blocks and appoint a chieftain who is responsible for maintaining order in his own block. Those caught stealing will be given the dirty work to do. That might cure them."

"How would Bart have handled this?" she asked.

"For one thing, he had experience that told him where troubles would develop. This is all new to us. Troublemakers tend to find their own kind, which makes them more dangerous. Bart was always separating these men with different watches on his ship—a system we don't have. Bart used to say that a man is judged by the company he avoids."

"We'll have to return over this same road and the villagers know it. We don't want roadblocks and vigilantes waiting for us, which would be the case if we can't control the men," insisted Anne-Marie. "It worries me."

"Why don't you talk to the men tonight when we make camp? I think they will be more inclined to listen to you than Rafael, Esteban or me. They respect you for your talents that have nothing to do with your being a lady."

"I'll try."

"You get stronger everyday," assured Tim.

The confidential exchanged was observed by Rafael and he was quick to move toward them.

"I was telling Tim that some of the men's behavior has upset me, and he feels that I should talk to the group tonight, Señor."

"You can. Of course," Rafael replied. "I doubt that it will do much good. Men will be men, and sometimes they are not nice." His eyes met hers, and Anne-Marie felt he also was offering a note of apology for his own earlier behavior.

"I think I should try anyway."

"I think we should get going," said Tim. It occurred to him later that he was doing what Bart did so effectively: separating two people with divergent opinions before either could take too strong a stand.

After dinner that night of *Moros y Christianos*, Moors and Christians, or black beans and rice, Anne-Marie moved to the fire where all could see her.

"I must speak to you," she said, drawing on a well of courage that might or might not run dry before she finished, so uncertain was she of the right approach needed to reach the men.

"Some among you have not been *caballeros* or gentlemen worthy of wearing my colors, your red scarves. Do you know what they stand for? I will tell you: the blood of Cubans that for so many years now has spilled fighting to put down oppression and terror. Gentlemen, remember why you were forced to leave your homeland and come to Key West. You cannot behave like Spanish oppressors in this country, stealing form poor peons." She paused, suddenly remembering Rafael's nationality, which stilled her brain and tongue for a minute only. She had said it.

"Disreputable behavior could bring down the whole Mexican army upon us. If our passage brings attention from the newspapers so that towns fear our approach and lay waiting to attack us, we will have no chance for the success of our mission. A few could bring us all down. The street markets where we must buy food will disappear to side or back streets. Gentlemen, fear can do many things; piggish actions of a few could mean ruin. We could all land in prison."

She moved closer to the fire, capturing like a magnet the beams of reflected light, which then radiated from her as if she were the light source. Her eyes glowed. Her dazzling copper hair shimmered. Perhaps they saw her as an ancient mythical goddess; they were silent.

"We must support one another. Your leaders don't want to take severe measures, but we shall if the safety of the troop demands it. You hope to survive this with money to start life anew in the United States, to build your own businesses, to save your families, to find a new life of freedom and security. I can help you do that. But, your destiny lies in your own hands. Gentlemen, I tell you, it does not lie in mine."

Letting her voice die with that last sentence she stepped from the fire, disappearing into the surrounding darkness. The men sat entranced. For a long moment everyone remained in silence, somewhat embarrassed, but she had made her point. The sincerity in her voice and manner was infectious, and above all, highly inspiring. By the time Tim found her, her face was chalk white.

"If you are considering running for mayor of Key West, you earned quite a few votes." Tim grinned from ear to ear.

"Thank you. I felt a little like Jeanne d'Arc…That is pretentious, isn't it? I don't mean to be so…" Her eyes were wide and misty.

"You were short and sweet and put your message across well. Tomorrow we should see considerable improvement," replied Tim, making her feel good.

"I've been frightened of burning bridges behind us," she explained.

"I admire your perspicacity, but you also may have stopped the men from burning the bridges in front of us."

A few minutes later Rafael appeared, quick to offer his shaded compliments. "I'm glad I didn't have to follow your act, Madame. It was most effective."

"But it was not an act," she stammered. "How could you make such a statement? I am disturbed by improprieties committed by these men!" Her eyes narrowed to slits in defiant anger.

"I simply had had enough when you talked about red scarves," snarled Rafael. Turning from her abruptly, he disappeared in the night.

Anne-Marie looked about anxiously, fearful that some of the men might have been within hearing distance, and thus would learn that Rafael was a Spaniard. She must be careful. Luckily no one was in earshot.

Remorseful, she cried after him, "Rafael de Palma," not daring to raise her voice, yet fearing his anger, she wanted to make amends. She took a few steps after him, but rough terrain proved more than she could rapidly cover. Despairing, she made her way back to her tent. What should have ended as an evening of pride of accomplishment, satisfaction, and a minor but important victory of spirit had been twisted by Rafael into a dismal defeat. Her own rudeness she minimized. She met Tim, unwilling to retire until he saw her safely in her tent.

"I offended Señor de Palma."

"I suspected as much, but he will recover."

"Please Tim, no quips about pride."

Tim laughed. "All right, but remember every silver lining has a cloud."

"Tim Clayton, must you always exasperate me!" she cried entering her tent. Still, Tim saw the smile she could not hide. There was no way that she could be angry with that teasing man.

By morning Rafael's wounded pride had apparently healed. Later in the day he had to admit that the change in the men was astonishing. In a swift but orderly procession without incident, they had passed through village after village, always in the shadow of Orizaba, in terrain rising and lowering on an abominable road. They had made remarkable progress.

That night Anne-Marie moved out of her tent to sleep in the open as did the men. "I'll sleep better. I think the shelter afforded by the tent draws too many insects."

"It could be safer for you," said Tim, actually thinking of snakes and being unwilling to put fear in her mind.

Rafael overheard both remarks and when the opportunity permitted he said to Anne-Marie, "In case you were worried, I doubt that any of the men would have entered your tent."

"I wasn't worried about the men. I was worried about the insects!"

"Hum," replied Rafael. "Am I, by any chance, considered am insect—an ant, a mosquito, a beetle, a spider or a scorpion?" His tone was frivolous and sarcastic.

Surprised, Anne-Marie laughed, studying his expression. "You could be a scorpion, now that I think about it; yet on the other hand you are capable of weaving a beautiful web."

She was standing by her horse. Knotted at her throat was her red scarf that shot its color up to her face so that she appeared to be blushing, which she was not. "The statement was not meant for you."

Rafael seemed to relax. She went on to say, "The success of this venture seems to rest more upon restraint than anything else. We must all exercise restraint."

"Those who restrain their desires do not have many—or they are weak enough to need no restraint."

Obviously, they were not speaking the same language. She threw up her hands and walked away. She did not want to be callous with Rafael. He was much too serious, due, she assumed, to the risk he was taking by entering Mexico, and for this she knew that she must be grateful.

Behind that sweet innocent face and a beguiling smile of a compliant child, Anne-Marie had a will of iron. She was stubborn. When she was a child her great desire for approval and love had masked her determination—most of the time. But, as a young, rich, beautiful woman, she was learning the extent of her powers—and she used them.

Córdoba lies in the foothills of the eastern Sierra Madre range, a place of refuge from the threatening malaria and yellow fever in the plains below. Still, there was a tropical charm, pleasing to the whole company. There were coconut trees, coffee groves, tobacco and banana plantations, and gardens with every fruit that ripens under the tropical sun; oranges, lemons, guavas, bananas, pineapples, cherimoyas, mangoes, avocados and granaditas flourished around the small vine-covered houses. Within the square of the market Anne-Marie noted what had to be one of the most beautiful gardens of the world. There a tangled mass of fruits and flowers overhung winding walks, with fountains and pagodas for resting-places at almost every turn. It being Sunday the town was filled with people from Amatlan and other villages roundabout who had walked to town carrying their shoes. They dressed in the gaudiest cotton in all colors of the rainbow—or the plumage of the birds of their primeval forests—for their Sunday outing to attend church and meet their friends. Beads of coral, laces they had made, and ornaments of silver completed their attire.

Tim bought a day old paper from Orizaba and chuckled. The news was almost entirely local but one item, which undoubtedly had come in by wire, and was of great interest to the leaders although brief and dreaded. "Officials are investigating reports from Veracruz and Puebla of an invading army, not in uniform, judged to be in excess of five hundred men, that disappeared outside the city. The army was entirely composed of cavalry units, thought to be in support of invading foot soldiers that possibly have used a different port of entry."

"Well, they know we're here," said Anne-Marie. "I expect we may have to begin skirting towns and at night we may have to camp further off the road. This will add to our difficulties."

Tim concurred.

Skirting villages, they soon learned, was doing things the hard way. It was much easier and time saving to go in and out of towns fast on the post road. Orizaba rose above the richly colored mountains, dominating the landscape with breath-taking splendor. After crossing a small desert area, the road entered mountains with deep ravines where unexpected gorges and streams were exceedingly dangerous. The few sleepy Indians, worried only about having their produce stolen, presented no danger. But this area was notorious for armed robbery, hardly a threat of Anne-Marie's troops, but a curse to many. They made the steep ascent to the rocky plateau of the city of Orizaba without incident. Here they passed the maguey or sisal plantations, which Rafael assured them often contained thousands of acres.

"One plantation is said to be as large as the state of New Jersey," said Rafael. "Here it is hard to say who we'll meet. Republican government forces can be anywhere and these wealthy landowners have their own defenders."

"If we keep moving, they may not bother us. Unfortunately, they know the terrain and we don't," added Tim, realistically.

Occasionally, they met mail-coach *diligencias,* drawn by teams of mules, obviously a good deal more terrified of them that they were of the coach riders.

"Wave as you pass," Anne-Marie ordered. "Let's hope they forget they've seen us. I have a feeling, however, that we are unforgettable."

"Let's hope they don't read the papers," said Rafael.

"Getting a newspaper became an important daily event." Another report stated: "Investigation continues concerning reports of an invading army on horseback sighted near Orizaba this week. Details are sketchy, but villagers have reported seeing as many as a thousand men. President Jaurez has ordered all garrisons in the area to be on twenty-four hours alert. Troops from the northern states are expected to reinforce troops in Veracruz, Puebla, Tlaxcala, and possibly Morelos."

The most serious and disturbing incident on this stretch concerned a fight between to men, Martin Carrero and Luiz Herrera.

Martin, a handsome young man, Anne-Marie had liked immediately. He was a good rider and attended to his chores without shirking. But he also liked to gamble, and even though he lost rather consistently, especially to Luiz, he was good-natured about it. Both men were always ready for a bet on anything. Evenings they pulled out a tattered deck of cards or rolled dice to pass the time, usually with several on-lookers.

The too steady losses at cards began to make Martin suspicious; he knew he was smarter and he played his cards better. It occurred to Martin that Luiz had a tipster who looked into his hand and then signaled to Luiz whether he should continue betting or pass. After Martin decided that this might be the case, he held his cards tight to his chest so that no one could see his hand. Following this practice, Martin won.

The next time they played cards, Martin returned to his old practice and lost. It convinced him that Luiz was cheating. They were playing late when most of the men in the troop were asleep, when Martin, rightly or wrongly, made his accusation, "You're a cheater!"

Martin threw down his cards. Luiz demanded an apology, virtually the only option open to him. Not only was it an insult of the first order, but if believed by the other men, it would mean ostracism by them. A punch in the nose would not do.

Martin then stood up, looking down at three men who were behind him, he accused them of taking part in the swindle. With this, he incurred their wrath, deserved or not.

Luiz then cast insulting aspersions on Martin—and his mother— which awakened many of the sleeping men, who, not having heard what had led to the disturbance, but who tended to be sympathetic to Martin, joined in the fracas.

Anne-Marie awakened to a brouhaha of terrifying proportions. By this time Tim was also awake, concerned mainly with keeping Anne-Marie out of it. "In a fight, only the peacemaker gets hurt," he cried, holding her back.

"Someone has to stop them," she begged in a rising panic.

In the melee she could see only a tangle of bodies swinging at each other with forces capable of breaking jaws, flattening noses, and rendering men unconscious. For some minutes the fight went on involving at least half of the company. Finally she saw Rafael take out a pistol and fire into the air. The crack of the pistol brought the fight to an abrupt halt.

"This will be dealt with tomorrow," said Rafael. "Each and everyone of you is sentenced tonight to silence. Not one word is to be spoken or whispered until tomorrow or I personally may kill you."

To a man they obeyed.

"Until we talk tomorrow and learn how this started, there's nothing to be done," said Tim. "Señor de Palma, we owe you a debt of thanks. Now, let's go to sleep."

Still, it would be hours before Anne-Marie could close her eyes. It was impossible to estimate what the fight would mean. Were the men dividing into two warring camps?

Were they simply working off excess energy? Relieving tensions? They all had pistols; my God! They could have dueled—and still might. That was the traditional way Latin men handled insults.

Hours later, one terrifying recollection lingered: she knew that without any doubt Rafael would have made good his promise had the men not obeyed. He was a Spaniard. Did they guess it?

CHAPTER FIFTEEN

Taxco virtually hangs on the side of a mountain overlooking a valley that is broken by a *cordillera* or chain of mountains with a low zigzagging skyline. Far beyond a higher range, the Sierra Madre del Sur, ends the view. Finally, Bart had reached his goal months later than he had expected.

Following a narrow cobblestone street that twisted and turned above the Prisca Cathedral, the *Zocalo* or central plaza, and the main part of town, he found himself before a magnificent villa. The house, belonging to Señor Ramon Alvarez Ramirez y Berra, part owner and manager of the mining company in which Anne-Marie had a major interest, had not been hard to spot. It rested on land chiseled from the slope by terracing, and, like almost every other building in the town, had its back to the mountain. A long many-arched façade ran along the street and overlooked the valley.

Bart stood before a heavy wooden door, a door within a larger carriage door. A bell with a rope hanging from it announced his presence and summoned a manservant who ushered him into a carriageway and up two steps to a waiting room on the right. Meanwhile another servant relieved him of his horse. Bart was offered a chair and was left to await the master of the house. The wait was considerable giving him the opportunity to examine every detail of the room.

A centered massive iron candelabra hung from chains over a heavy round table with elaborately scrolled wrought-iron legs, flanked by two massive high Spanish chairs. A long bench, padded with red velvet cushions, lined the street wall. A box-like desk, also supported by an iron base, stood against the wall separating the carriageway. Three sets of tall, slender, matching double-doors gave access to the room, and one of these sets now open afforded a view of the inner courtyard. Here was a garden centered with a circular pool, dominated by an iron etagere. At least half a dozen parrots sat on stands or laboriously flapped around the court, squawking and squabbling intermittently over their roosts. Bored with counting the rafters and floor tiles, Bart was experimenting with raising and lowering the candelabra, when to his embarrassment, Señor Ramirez appeared.

"Señor Ramirez, I am Bartholomew Ramsden. Forgive me for tampering with your ingenious lamp, but I am intrigued with its operation."

"Think nothing of it. It is clever, I agree even though I designed it myself. I regret keeping you waiting so long, Captain, but nowhere near as long as I have been waiting for you," he added good-naturedly, signaling for Bart to take a chair.

"Holy Toledo," exclaimed Bart with a gesture of amused despair. "You could have no idea, but the important thing is, I am here, finally. Perhaps I'll wake up once again in another jail, but if this is a dream, I'll stick with it. It's a good one." Both men laughed.

Ramirez, a short, squat, middle-aged man of Spanish blood, was obviously a gentleman. A great bushy handlebar mustache, gathered to a fine point at the tips, could have provided the inspirational curlicues seen everywhere in the wrought-iron work. Strong piercing eyes, hedged by ungovernable black eyebrows, dominated his portly face. A massive chest abruptly lost substance at the waist and continued to dwindle to culminate in dainty feet. He looked to Bart like a bullfighter, who in retirement, had turned to weight lifting—an estimation that was only half true.

"The important thing is you are here, and I sincerely regret the inconveniences you have suffered in my country," replied Ramirez. "We have been through very difficult times. Only a small percentage of our foreign mail comes through and often none goes out. After all, you can buy a meal with stolen postage stamps on one letter to the United States. Months ago I did receive a letter saying you would be arriving within a few days…"

"Señor, we have received no correspondence from you in almost three years, and as you know, my wife has a considerable investment here. This is the reason for my presence. What is the problem—not that I haven't seen some?"

Ramirez laughed, shaking his head in bemused bewilderment. "For all practical purposes, I have had to severely cut back all production from the mine. Despite President Jaurez, Mexico is a lawless state. The biggest thieves of all are the police. Our mining equipment is antiquated, dangerous, so unsafe that in all conscience, I feel I am tolling a death knell sending men underground. Having risked the men, shipments never arrive. The silver is still there, safe in the ground. I ask you, Captain, what else am I to do?"

"Determine the reinvestment that is necessary; call on your stockholders; get government protection. Your situation cannot be unique. Many companies must be in the same predicament. Or, together hire your own militia to insure that your shipments reach ports."

"Are you speaking of joining with competitors? They may be the ones who were stealing our production."

"I am suggesting that alone very probably you can do very little, but that owners together, organized, can do anything. In the long run the answer is *power*. Get yourself into a position of power."

"It is an interesting idea…"

"It's not mine. Ten well-armed men can guard ten bars of silver or ten thousand. What is not economically feasible with small shipments can be another story when the mines operate through a cooperative."

"I can see we have much to talk about, Captain. Last year's books are locked in that desk behind you." Ramirez pointed to the long, squarish cabinet. "I want you to see for yourself how bad things are. Naturally, you'll be my guest while you are in Taxco. I regret my wife and our children are not here. My wife is visiting her father who is ailing."

"I'm sorry."

"I'm sure you would like to get settled. Tell me, how long can we hope to have the pleasure of your company?"

"I'm most anxious to return to my family, but now that I'm finally here, I'd like to accomplish something. I think I can be of service to you. But, I must get a letter off to my wife."

"Splendid. Our housekeeper will show you to your room. At two o'clock a meal will be served, the *comida*." Ramirez checked his heavy gold watch and from a chain inserted a small key that wound it. "I'll see you within a half an hour," said Ramirez standing. "If that is convenient with you?" Of course, it was.

Bart's quarters were light and airy with a magnificent view overlooking the town and the valley. Everything a guest might enjoy had been provided. On a high dresser stood a variety of scents, lined up like soldiers, all in 750-ml bottles. Bart passed up what appeared to be local or Spanish and French colognes for the familiar freshening '4711' Eau de Cologne, which he sloshed over his cheeks and neck. A well-appointed desk and chair beckoned, but also reminded him of the desk downstairs in the entry. Obviously, that was not a working desk, and the books therein would not be an accurate set of books, but a second set, or possibly a third. There, over a fine glass of brandy, tax officials could be met in privacy or bribes could be made. For the moment, sunshine poured into the courtyard, dousing the garden with a thin, clear shadowless light. Bart turned from the task of writing, and with a sad poignant sense of futility, threw himself on the bed. There would be time to write during the siesta when he hoped to be more certain of his impressions and less painfully aware of how much he missed his wife.

The *comida* amounted to a traditional daily feast of six courses with a change of plates for each course, and a continuous stream of hot tortillas passed in napkin-lined silver baskets. Two maiden aunts joined the men for the meal. Their continuous mutterings over the servants' shortcomings during the mistress's absence cut appreciably into Bart's conversation with Ramirez as soup followed soup, although the second soup was actually a dry soup, a highly seasoned rice dish in an elaborate sauce. A course of chicken was followed by one of goat, which had been well roasted. Fried beans came before the pudding. After coffee and fresh fruit, the ladies excused themselves with glances that seemed to Bart to say, "We know what is expected of us and resent it, but we will comply."

"They've had a difficult time lately," explained Ramirez. "The present regime has been hard on the church. Priests have virtually vanished, going into exile or business. Many have married. Religion has always been a large part of their lives, and now this solace is severely restricted."

"Stand still and silently watch the world go by—and it will," remarked Bart.

"If they would only be silent, I would be delighted to have them do that," said Ramirez in genial despair.

Still, a certain callousness was evident in Ramirez in Bart's opinion, judging from his manner in addressing his relatives and servants. Not that he was rude or even detached, but there was no real warmth behind a studied mask of good humor. It seemed that he was determined that nothing could or would be done to turn the mine problems around. Defeatism characterized every word, yet Bart felt certain that the man was self-centered enough to take care of himself. Excuses were passed around like tortillas and clearly Bart was expected to gobble them up.

"I know this is time for your siesta," said Bart, "and I would not think of detaining you. Will you be free in a couple of hours?"

"I am at your service." Ramirez suppressed a yawn. With bows they parted, and Bart retired to his room to write Anne-Marie.

The task was easier now. Having arrived safely, an end was in sight. Also having eaten, his spirits had risen; the sick loneliness within him had abated and he could think of his wife in clearer terms, those that he could more easily describe.

"*My dearest wife,*" he wrote. "*Incredible as it will seem to you, this is the first opportunity I have had to write. Somehow I've survived sickness, prisons, robbery and hunger to arrive today penniless in Taxco. I beg you to forgive my absence and the concern I have caused you. Believe me, it can all be explained. I have missed you beyond words. A thousand times I've closed my eyes so that I could be with you—that being the only way.*

As you might imagine since arriving I have had only an hour or two to form any reasonably sure impressions on the purpose of this visit. Therefore, I hate to say anything other than the fact that my natural optimism is met by pessimism, pound for pound. There should be no problem now in writing you frequently. We must only hope that my letters arrive. I will do whatever I can with dispatch, all the sooner to be back with you and Samantha. I'm counting on you to relieve the worries of our dear families as to my well being—at least physically. I will close this letter now before my love for you and my hunger to hold you close drive me to desperation. Yours always, Bart."

Carefully addressing the letter and aware that he had no money for stamps, Bart moved to the bed, prepared with a turned-down sheet and blanket for his siesta, and slept.

The afternoon's business was close in tone to that of the morning. The books were open to him, but as Bart had surmised, they showed rapidly dwindling profits followed by rising losses until Ramirez, closing vein after vein, brought the business to a trickle. The high point of the meeting arose when Bart announced that he wanted to go down into the mine. Ramirez had not been into a mine since he was a boy, and then he had been thoroughly chastised for it. He could not conceal his shock.

"You don't want to go down there. You'll get filthy. A mine is no place for a gentleman. I've told you, it's dangerous. You shouldn't even think of it."

"Señor Ramirez, if I am going to solve some of your problems, I would like to do it from the ground up."

"I could not think of allowing such a thing." Indignation had turned his cheeks into two red apples.

"How long has it been since you've been down into the mine?"

"Some time. I'm kept informed by a foreman. I can judge the yield from the surface. What counts is what is brought up."

"Let's go tomorrow anyway." Bart saw the futility or pursuing the discussion further for the moment.

"There's little to see beyond a mill and a pile of dirt." The captain would have other thoughts about going down into the mine once on the site, Ramirez felt certain.

"With whom do you compete?" asked Bart.

"I will show you," replied Ramirez, leading Bart to high double-doors that led to a terrace. There they could look down on the town over a mass of red tile roofs. Ramirez pointed out the Prisca Cathedral on a small central square. Adjoining the church was a house.

"Under the church is the first important mine here. Josè de la Borda, a prospector, discovered the vein. Eventually, he made some forty to fifty millions, in dollars, mind you, from mines in Taxco, Tlalpujahua and Zacatecas. He built the church at a cost of over a million, even paving the square. He used to live in the adjoining building, but then also gave that to the church as a home for the priests. He moved to Cuernavaca where he built another home and a magnificent garden with terraced slopes, lakelets, cascades, and fountains. Those were the good old days. The company he founded now mines lower down the mountain near where we are." Ramirez pointed to a small building, the mill, and its patio or paved yard where the crushed material was treated. "Bands of a dozen mules or mules and horses harnessed together are driven up and down from morning until night, over the *torta*, until it is a slushy mass. Mechanical appliances can't seem to take the place of the equine mixers," he explained. "Years ago the trampling of the *torta* was done by barefoot Indians, so we've made some progress."

"What is the *torta?*" Bart asked.

"The ore as it comes from the mine, mercury, water, salt and copper sulfate."

"Apparently the principal agents then are mercury and horseflesh or rather mule flesh," said Bart.

"Exactly."

Bart had other questions, but soon Ramirez turned to questioning him about his journey across Mexico—diverting questions which Bart was compelled to answer. Ramirez listened with a great deal of interest. By the time the dinner, a *merienda,* was served at six o'clock, he was favorably impressed with Bart's ingenuity and perseverance. The man might prove more difficult to handle than he had anticipated, he decided. The meal was a tea-less high tea of chocolate, *atole* or a sweet milk and corn in a broth, and cakes—and was, in short, filling.

"After that big meal in the middle of the day I never thought I could think of food again, but this is most pleasing," said Bart. "Experience, particularly most recently, has taught me never to refuse food as I could not know when or from where the next meal might come." They laughed.

"You continue to amaze me, Captain. Your frankness is most refreshing. In this country pride would prohibit a gentleman from ever mentioning hunger or imprisonment. Is this characteristic of your people?"

"It is true of those I admire. My pride seems to run in an inverse ratio to my fortunes. When I had very little money, I had much pride; now I am married to a wealthy woman, I have no need of pride." Bart pulled out two empty pockets. "Thanks to you, there is food in my stomach and a roof over my head. Why should I try to fool you and lose your respect?"

"Many would."

"What many people do or think is seldom troublesome for long. Any group of people without a leader is soon dispersed. Perhaps in time a strong leader emerges. But then we are back again to one individual, Señor, which is another story. Vultures hang together, terrified of life or action. The eagle hunts alone, looking for movement. Beware of the eagle," he mused.

Bart's first errand the next morning was to visit the Bank of Mexico. There he arranged for adequate funds for approval by telegraph by the Minister of the United States to Mexico. If he saw that it was necessary to come down on Ramirez, to leave his domicile, he would need money in his pocket. Ramirez was helpful. This piece of business accomplished, Bart announced he would like to see the mine at once.

"But, Captain, we will be due at the house shortly for the *comida,*" stalled Ramirez.

"My apologies for the inconvenience, but I would like to visit the mine, that burial ground of good intentions, as I have come to think of it. I believe now is as good a time as any."

Recognizing that protests would serve nothing, Ramirez complied.

The mines of Taxco were practically in the town as the site offered not only the ore but also the necessary water supply. Still, they took the carriage over the bumpy road during which time Bart had a further opportunity to question Ramirez about his earlier impressions. "You say the main hindrance to operating profitably is thieves. Where do they hang out?"

"In the hills between here and Mexico City."

"Do you have any idea who they are?"

"Of course, I've been approached. They want money, exorbitant sums for protection. It's an old racket."

"Sometimes a good one," replied Bart, "if the cost is not too great and if they are really protecting."

"We would only be robbed again, further down the road."

"Not necessarily. There is honor among thieves, especially if it is to their advantage."

Ramirez seemed unusually flushed, more than the rollicking carriage warranted. "It is impossible to deal with these ruffians. One can't imagine a cruder bunch. They live by plunder. The police can't begin to cope with them."

"And the less silver that is moved, the less they have to steal. Right?"

"Exactly." Ramirez seemed to find the thought confusing.

Ramirez and Bart stepped down from the carriage before a small, dirty, office building near the mill shop and stables. Clearly, Ramirez had not visited in months, even years, judging by the lack of interest his presence generated. Obviously embarrassed, he began barking orders in a falsetto voice as if he had a whip in hand. For a few minutes Bart said nothing, but quietly observed the scene, permitting Raminez to blow off steam and regain his composure. Finding nothing to observe within the office, Bart walked outside, Ramirez at his heels.

"Now I'd like to go down into the mine," said Bart, heading for an entrance a few hundred feet away at the base of a mountain in a desert of trampled earth and stone, a wasteland of mutilated earth.

"You'll need a lantern," shrieked Ramirez, horror struck.

"Then please have one brought me."

"It's hot down there. You'll ruin your clothes," added Ramirez, fairly dancing, raising a cloud of dust at his feet. "You can't go down there alone."

"You said I would need a lantern," Bart replied coolly. "And, if I can't go alone, lead the way."

Knowing he was trapped, Ramirez led the way. They descended a circular core bored into the earth a little more than a yard wide. In the center of the black hole ran a pole on which little triangular wedges were nailed to form a ladder. Occasionally cross pieces of wood from side to side steadied the pole and kept it centered. Bart soon discovered that pole had been laid upon pole to gain the depth necessary, penetrating deep into the earth. Here and there tiny caverns had been cut in which the men were working, chipping away at the silver-bearing ore. Bags of ore carried in pouches on the men's backs were then carried to the surface and dumped. The air was almost suffocating so that although the workers were not exerting themselves they panted constantly like mongrel dogs. Into this sea of blackness they slowly and carefully descended. The small, caverns cut in the sides of channel had little or no supports against collapse. Occasionally caverns were sealed off.

Finally, in a larger deeper cavern where Bart could stand, he removed his coat and shirt, tossing them over one shoulder. Carefully observing the consistency of the rock in which tiny particles of silver glistened in the dim light of the lantern, Bart compared various caverns in which the men were working. He said nothing, but clearly they were working where the ore was low grade, but easier to work in.

"Let's go up now," said Bart to Ramirez, who was panting more rapidly than the miners. Slowly, so as not to miss the precarious footing and slip into water that had accumulated in the bottom of the channel, they climbed to the blessed air above. During the night, Ramirez managed to explain, men would come in to blast what would be an inferno of powder and smoke.

Bart was aghast at what he had seen, but he remained silent. Once in the sunlight he used his shirt to wipe away the sweaty dirt from his bare torso and his ears and hair, while Ramirez also busily mopped himself with his handkerchief. Before Bart could dress, Ramirez had seen the deep crosscut scars that horizontally laced Bart's back, shoulder to shoulder.

"What happened to you?"

"Flogging at sea," Bart replied. "Before I learned when to fight."

Ramirez paled visibly. Clearly, Captain Ramsden could be a dangerous man.

Throughout the trip back to the house, Ramirez maintained a constant patter, designed to divert Bart, but at the same time relishing being safely on the surface and having an ordeal over with. Moreover, he thought the captain knew nothing of mining and certainly everything that he saw would confirm what he himself had said: mining was an unprofitable, dirty business.

They were, of course, late for the *comida* and would be later yet as they needed to bathe. The maiden aunts, shocked at seeing their filthy condition, and dismayed at learning they had gone down into the mine, were so distressed that their fine, dark moustaches actually quivered. A hard stare from Ramirez had been wonderfully silencing as the men repaired to their quarters.

During the meal the aunts remained silent until Bart brought up the subject of bandits. "I'd like to know more about them and I'd like a confrontation with them," he announced.

"Impossible," replied Ramirez as the ladies gasped.

"Why not? They're just people."

"Little better then animals."

"I'd like to meet with them—here." Bart's tone was decisive. "I need to think about this further, but I believe this could be a decisive step."

"Do not think about it further. We could all be murdered," replied Ramirez. Doña Mercedes, the elder of the two aunts, looked as if a bad stench had descended on the room. Doña Carmelita reached for her chained rosary, tucked in her bosom.

"We can see that we survive," crooned Bart. "We have a rough road ahead to turn this business around, but we are playing for high stakes. I want to hear what our enemy has to say."

Ramirez paled. "If you are asking me to have these people in our house…"

"I would appreciate that. Let's fight on home ground where we cannot be ambushed."

The two aunts fled the dining room for the third floor chapel to pray.

"I regret the distress I've caused your family, Señor, but I have had a difficult time in just arriving. My wife has a large investment here. I do not intend to give it up."

"Then you may have to remove me, Captain."

"As a guest in your home I sincerely regret this state of affairs, and I can remove myself immediately if it would make you more comfortable. If, however, it is necessary as a major stockholder, **I will remove you.** I sincerely hope you will not bring me to that. Señor, at this point I do not have all the answers to your problems; I may have a few. As an adversary, you would only add to my problems, so I hope to work with you, not against you." Bart stood, pushing back his chair.

"I am going to take a walk now. I will return late enough not to interfere with your siesta. Please, think it over," said Bart.

Bart strode from the house leaving a speechless Ramirez to his troubled thoughts.

Pleading chants for divine intervention wafted down through the courtyard to mingle with the screams of the parrots. The cool pungent air in the street still carried the redolent traces of charcoal burners and vendors that had only recently vanished into doorways and alleys for a pause in the day's occupation. With the shops closed, the streets were deserted. With a rolling stride, gripping the cobblestones in a manner such as all sailors walk to maintain balance, Bart moved about the city, his mind racing faster than his feet.

The first problem was one of deliveries. Once they were assured, production could be improved immeasurably. He thought he saw what Ramirez was doing: dropping production by ordering rich veins boarded up, doing nothing about abominable working conditions and safety measures, letting profits drop, letting the value of the stock fall until he could pick up the whole company for a pittance.

Bart knew he needed a good engineer and a better accountant. Ramirez was already a part owner, but one who could cause a lot of trouble if he, Bart, were to try to get ride of him entirely. At least for the time being, if at all possible, it would be better to work with Ramirez. He hoped he had frightened him. He had not removed his jacket and shirt to expose his mutilated back to no purpose.

Christ, the man was clever. Anyone who could design the candelabra in the *officina* of his home to raise and lower so easily could design machinery to move ore. He could also devise a means of getting air down into the earth. Ranirez was lazy, but he had talent that with persistence, discipline and a few carrots could be tapped.

At least two hours later Bart returned for the confrontation. A trembling servant admitted him. Without doubt, the household had been in consternation from Ramirez right down to the lowliest servant who shoveled manure from the stables. Ramirez, acutely distressed, struggled for composure as he capitulated. "Welcome, Captain, I am at your service."

"Señor Ramirez, I am at yours."

"If having those bands of banditos here will satisfy you, I will comply. When would you like to see them?"

"Now—the sooner the better."

"I will send a messenger," replied the startled Ramirez, seeing no other avenue open to him. The captain meant business. He was allowing no time for chicanery. "You realize you are endangering my family?" His voice was sad.

"Your wife and children are out of town, and I think your two maiden aunts have an infinite capacity for survival," opinioned Bart.

"Would you mind if we made this appointment after dark, sparing me the disdain of my neighbors?"

"Not at all. I understand your position, Señor. I don't want to talk to them anymore than you do, but this business is in a crisis, whether you recognize it or not."

That evening, appalled by the necessity, Ramirez opened his doors to ten bandits and then let Bart take charge. To Ramirez's chagrin, Bart requested that a servant bring wine, befouling his fine crystal.

The scrubby guests were led by a swarthy, heavy set chief, named Paco, younger and cruder than Bart would have thought. The introductions were curt.

"I am interested in buying protection for our silver production. Señor Ramirez tells me that thieves have preyed upon us. We are making a number of changes, which will result in a much higher production, and which will be rich enough to demand protection. It is my impression that you offer protection?"

"Correct, Señor. We will be happy to oblige."

"Now that we are in agreement, what is the price?"

"Eight *reales* a day per man." A gloating grin broke over Paco's face, while fulgent, black eyes glittered over the anticipated success. A stupid, extravagant gringo was obviously taking over from Ramirez. He would probably pay anything.

"That's two pesos a day. Let's discuss an intelligent price." Bart sipped his wine but kept his eyes on Paco.

"I have starving people to feed. The awaited land reforms have not yet reached us."

"I'm sympathetic to your starving people, but I also notice that you wear silver buttons." This remark was designed to encourage Paco's henchmen toward quietly suggesting a compromise.

"These few buttons would not feed many long," said Paco, crudely punctuating his reply by breaking wind.

Bart ignored the retort and continued. "Of course, there are a number of options open to us. We can halt production entirely until the government takes firmer control, but I find governments inordinately slow. We can mint coins on the site and sell to the government at a ridiculously low price and let the government use its army to protect the silver. We can merge with other mines to ship collectively and split protection costs.

Surely you understand that we must make a profit. The more successful we are, the more money you will make. I suggest that you choose a reasonable sum and cooperate. We hope to make many improvements, and so will you. Your people are living in caves. Some have little to eat and wear. They can hardly keep healthy." He paused.

Bart's eyes moved about the room. This was not the first time that he had been compelled to win over a scruffy bunch. As a young sea captain occasionally he had faced a crew of hostile men testing to see how far they could push an untried authority. The flash of this sensation caused him to tower up with sudden height, meeting each man's stare with unwavering calm. In the silence his fearless posture summoned respect. Bart turned to Paco and under his stare felt him waver.

"What guarantees do we have that these are not empty promises?" asked Paco, now evidencing interest in the proposal, which made sense. The gringo had more brains than he had supposed.

"What promises have been made previously?"

"None."

"Then why doubt mine when you see that it will be possible to keep them? There are many ways to skin cats. For instance, my genial host is a mechanical genius. Look at the clever system he has devised to raise and lower this lamp." Bart moved to the candelabra to demonstrate how with one finger he could raise or lower the heavy iron fixture. "He will devote considerable time to engineer a system to mechanically move ore. We are hiring a chemist to cut waste. I suggest you consider what we have told you about our intentions. Deal with us reasonably and you can share in our good fortune."

The eyes of Paco's men were on *numero uno* as he spoke for them. "Six *reales* a day is the best I can do."

Feet shuffled. Bart looked to the floor and saw that the men's feet and legs sported a ludicrous combination of coarse sandals and puttees. The sight made Bart smile and this gave his reply, inadvertently a powerful impact, a sarcastic twist.

"Evidently, you do not understand. I said you must be reasonable. I can bring in laborers from all over Mexico for half that price, and they would be glad to come. Where would you be against them?"

Again the room grew silent while the men waited. Slowly the terrified prayers of the aunts and servants upstairs in the chapel, muffled to a low singsong chant, drifted to the *officina.* Still, no one spoke. Then outside the church bells all over the city began tolling the hour, one after another. Finally, the pandemonium subsided. Bart wondered why he had not noticed the bells before. Too absorbed, he surmised, which was rather dangerous. It was inconceivable that he could have become so locked into himself that a racket loud enough to summon every angel in the city could go in one ear and out the other and not strike one chord of response. It was the fastest way he knew—in negotiating with a crew of thugs—to get a knife in his back. He would have to be more careful. Waiting for an answer, he gathered his wits. Finally the answer came.

"Four *reales* and a *cuartilla with* food on the road," offered Paco.

Ramirez wondered if Bart were familiar with the *cuartilla,* a copper coin that was worth about three cents.

"Four *reales* and a *tlaco,*" offered Bart, the *tlaco* being yet a smaller one cent coin. "I must say you Mexicans make change a nicety. You split *tlacos* only with a hatchet!" The bandit seemed pleased with the compliment. "Only while on the road," cautioned Bart, who wanted to give a little and that in particular. Ramirez nodded his approval to Bart.

Paco then accepted the sum without even glancing at his minions for their consent. The deal was evidently a good one for them, Bart thought. With satisfaction they would keep it.

"One more glass of wine and a toast to a better life," said Bart, standing to pour the wine. When the bottle was empty, Bart gave his order by a lifted eyebrow to Ramirez to procure another. With Ramirez out of earshot, Paco spoke out. "You drive a hard bargain. But what assurances will we have that your policies will continue after you return to your country?"

"If the profits drop, I'll know something is amiss."

"You might investigate rich veins now sealed…"

"Naturally, I have been down in the mine myself, and I know much must be done—and by trained engineers."

The negotiations and toasts over, Paco and his men departed in good spirits.

As soon as the company disappeared, the aunts descended, still shocked but now curious. It was time for the light ten o'clock supper, the *cena*. Once seated, Bart's remarks silenced them. "I would like to thank you for your support, Señor. I am aware of how difficult my ideas have been for you to accept. If more capital is required for the changes I feel to be necessary, the company will have to be reorganized: Let's try to avoid this. I suggest that we cast the next blocks of silver in one thousand-pound units. That should make theft difficult."

"But, I don't understand. Why then are you hiring protection?"

"The protection will also repair the road wherever necessary to get the heavier coaches through."

"Devices, which you know you can construct, will greatly reduce labor costs. Even the cheapest labor can't compete with a machine that lifts ore rapidly. More difficult will be a ventilation scheme to change the air, which we must also devise. We will keep our promises to these people with jobs, but they soon may be doing different jobs than they are hired to do now. We will employ a chemist and secure an outside-certified bookkeeper for more modern accounting methods. That way you will always know exactly where you stand, wining or losing. I'm afraid you have been working in the dark without sufficient figures as guidelines."

It was an adroit means to give notice that Bart had not been fooled, that Ramirez's cheating had been recognized and ended.

Any embarrassment Ramirez felt, he kept to himself. Obviously, he would have to devote full time to the business. Still, the thought of mechanical invention, doing what he enjoyed, thrilled him, and Bart watched with satisfaction the growing smile on Ramirez's face.

"Patents which you acquire through the company, if sold elsewhere, will also pay one-third royalty to you personally," added Bart. He supposed that might be regarded by his wife's father as over-generous, but Ramirez was a clever man, a talent which might not be readily found elsewhere. Ramirez on his own ground could be a jewel of enormous value handled right.

"Captain Ramsden, I am deeply moved. I misjudged you, and you have done me a great service—greater than I could have asked. Thank you for your trust." Ramirez swallowed hard, aware that he had had a close call, but that he had survived. Tears of relief bathed the emotional man's eyes. The two aunts, totally unaware of their nephew's problems since Bart's arrival, with haughty disapproval of the dictatorial ways of the *Norte Americano,* lifted their lengthy, rustling skirts and carried their ignorance with them to the next room.

"I apologize for their uncivilized behavior. When my wife is here she keeps them under control."

"They do not understand, and I do not hold you responsible for such an affliction. As you say, their old world is collapsing and they are helpless."

"Their chief concern now is that, without a resident priest, they may die without benefit of the last rites. I am sure they are now praying for my soul. It is good that someone does…"

"The present state of the Catholic Church in Mexico will not last long," said Bart, thinking of Ramona and her mixture of Aztec and Christian gods. "Perhaps as a foreigner I have a more distant and less emotional view of your people."

After one last glass of wine in the salon where the great fireplace cut the evening's chill, Bart bid his host goodnight.

After Bart retired, Rameriz remembered Bart's letter that he intended to steam open and read. Now he decided that it could probably be safely mailed—without reading—as he had promised. Then he turned his attention to designing a chain belt with odd-shaped buckets attached, which could be pulled by two men on the surface turning a wheel, with no hands holding below.

Bart awakened late in the night and stepped quietly to his balcony where he could see Ramirez's light still burning. Satisfied that good of some kind was already coming from his day's efforts, he returned to instant sleep.

During the next few days a number of conferences including miners followed. Safer blasting, adequate shoring and protective helmets, for example were explored. "You will spoil these men," cautioned Ramirez.

"Rubbish! We're trying to keep them alive, and they know it," countered Bart. "Experienced dead men are no help. We're after increased production. Businesses can be too shortsighted. This expedition has already cost one half year of my life. I'm determined to make it pay, if not tomorrow, the day after. I don't want to have to come back here to do this all over again!"

His severe and determined expression would have told Ramirez that he meant it, even if Ramirez had not known it anyway.

Two weeks of concentrated effort, that included several round-the-clock sessions with a smithy passed, so that finally Bart decided he could safely depart with Ramirez now fully engaged and work would continue. To see the end result of his efforts would take more weeks than he was willing to spend. He wanted to get home. He had written two more letters to Anne-Marie explaining the work, which he had given to Ramirez for mailing. Ramirez, totally absorbed in his projects, had been innocently negligent. The day after Bart left he remembered to mail the three letters to Anne-Marie.

Bart had certainly remembered—whenever he had struck up a conversation with anyone new—to ask whether or not Jared Russell had been seen. Once he was given what might have been a positive report. An alleged astute professor from Princeton, New Jersey, had been seen collecting rock specimens from many points along the highway. He had traversed Mexico, inquiring about tequila production, while arriving in a small cart pulled by a donkey. For his own protection he never said where he was going. It was assumed that continuing westward he would reach the Pacific Ocean. Having heard this, Bart knew Jared would have reduced the hazards to those of the confines of a ship—considerably less than those cross-country, but involving a lot more time.

Bart had to smile, thinking of his quiet, studious friend, who had chosen a perfect disguise that tallied with his hobby. Clippity-clop, Jared would have pushed along, oblivious to time or danger or anxious family and friends...

CHAPTER SIXTEEN

After what would be known thereafter to Anne-Marie's men as the "Battle of Puebla" or the previous evening's brouhaha, they were completely subdued. Apparently, the scrimmage had been the result of pent up tensions needing an outlet. When it was over the men did not remain in two warring camps, but settled into the usual routine of travel. A few sore muscles, sprains, cuts and bruises remained as silent reminders, but more painful was Anne-Marie's disdain of their behavior.

"How a bunch of grown men could behave so childishly, no, so stupidly, is inconceivable. Have they no heads on their shoulders?"

Tim and Rafael understood and let Anne-Marie grumble without comment. However, Luiz and Martin did no more gambling.

As curious as Anne-Marie was to see Mexico City, the intellectual center of the New World, twice the size of New York City with wide avenues and beautiful buildings, she dared not enter the city with her army. So, from Puebla they traveled northwest to San Martin Texmelucan, almost to Los Reyes and then cut southwest, below the floating gardens of Xochimilco with their lovely great cypresses which had rooted below the lake to form gardens, to the post road to Cuernavaca.

The circuitous route to Cuernavaca was old (Cortez built his first palace in this city), well traveled and not difficult. Cornfields, inconveniently dotted with great boulders and dappled with shade trees, formed a strange rural landscape. Trees themselves, devoid of leaves, had been made into open-air silos and were laden with drying corn-husks. Now the great plain of Mexico, rimmed by a string of mountains, stretched for miles before them. Cuernavaca and Taxco lay ahead.

The road ran through the center of Cuernavaca, a prosperous city of gardens with familiar vegetation, not unlike that of Key West. The company flew past. They dared not dawdle fearing the possible pursuit of government troops.

With the city behind them on the last night before reaching Taxco, late when most of the men were sleeping and the campfire had almost died, Anne-Marie saw from the shadows that Rafael was beckoning to her. Thinking that he wanted to speak to her privately about something, she slipped from her bedroll to join him.

The cool night air, thick and misty as a cloud, hovered around them so that walking was difficult. Politely taking her hand, he led her some distance from the group.

"You wanted to speak to me?" she queried, stopping in an obvious refusal to go further.

"Yes," replied Rafael.

Then suddenly his arms were about her, his lips seeking hers while crying out, "I love you. I love you." Holding her tight he whispered, "I am dying for love of you."

Pushing herself from his arms with one great shove, effective only because it was so sudden, Anne-Marie fled. Terrified, she fairly leaped over the ground, finally coming near enough to the camp so that Rafael could not, dared not, pursue her. Shaking with rage, she found her bed. A few minutes later she heard him approach and say, "I'm sorry." Still as a possum, she fought for even, measured breath.

"The incident, coming as it did so close to their goal, was unnerving. She owed so much to Rafael, and he could only construe her behavior as unappreciative and cruel. If Bart were not in Taxco, what would she do?"

The next morning she acted as if nothing had happened. Rafael followed her lead.

Travel became difficult as they entered the foothills of the Sierra Madre range. Hairpin curves and rickety bridges tormented men and horses alike. They seemed to be forever climbing with too few descents in which they could gather strength. Occasionally there were shortcuts feasible only because they could travel single file. These were pointed out by Indians with directions that were hard to follow. The road was always described as good. Passable was well nigh impossible. Still, the route was beautiful, the air cool and food no problem. Young Indian boys stationed by the roadside under shade trees offered iguanas for sale, secured on leashes as dogs might be, along with cactus fruit and other delicacies of the region.

Less than an hour's ride to Taxco they encountered a terrible rainstorm, making the route suddenly precarious, sending down stones from the mountain and swelling the River Huajintitlan. Now Rafael headed the caravan—blessedly far removed, thought Anne-Marie—as she and Tim were the last in a long line. As soon as the rain had cleared, Tim discovered that two men were missing. Anne-Marie made him count again, which confirmed his discovery.

"Stay here with the men and I will ride back for them. They must have become separated during the rain," ordered Anne-Marie.

"I can't let you go back over that so-called shortcut alone, Anne-Marie. I insist we all go back," said Tim.

"No everyone can use the rest."

"Then I'll go with you. It may not be far," Tim insisted.

Taking only a few men they started back. It was not far before they found the rain had seriously undermined a footbridge they had crossed.

"Give me the lightest horse," demanded Anne-Marie. "Take two ropes from the two end posts and secure these posts with four lines to those two great trees. They will make it safe enough for me to cross, but certainly not the rest of you. I have an idea where the men have become stuck. If that mountain were not there we would be in calling distance.

While I'm gone, stiffen up the bridge on the other side so that the three of us can get back to you."

Tim disapproved, but Anne-Marie insisted. He had to set an example by following orders. Rafael at the head of the column knew nothing of the problem or certainly he, too, would have protested.

Anne-Marie was losing patience. "Gentlemen, I am anxious to get to Taxco. Please, do as I ask, and save us all time."

"At least, take along extra rope. It may be needed," said Tim, now resigned to doing as he was ordered.

With the bridge stabilized, Anne-Marie crossed easily, covering twenty-feet with no problem. She had been right. Exactly as she had thought, one man had become stuck avoiding a sudden cascading stone and slipped into a small gorge during the landslide.

His buddy stayed with him, but without ropes, there was no way to pull out the other horse. They knew someone would come back, combing the trail for them, but they were surprised to see Anne-Marie.

"The problem is a weakened footbridge that the men are repairing. I'm the lightest person in the company, and, as you know, the one who gives the orders." She smiled and added, "Although they didn't like it."

With the extra rope and two horses pulling, the men soon had the corralled horse free. As rapidly as possible they returned to the footbridge and a flock of relieved faces.

"I don't know what possessed me to let you go back alone," said Tim, mopping his brow with the back of his hand in relief, once Anne-Marie was safely on their side of the bridge.

"Good sense," she replied.

"I must admit, it was a good job," Tim admitted.

The story of the incident fell on Rafael like a pitcher of cold water, and his reaction was different. "With all due respect to your authority, there are limits to a man's patience. Your going off alone was more than we should have to bear." Clearly, he was angry. "If Tim and I do not follow your orders, the men won't either. This puts us in an untenable position. We would appreciate some consideration."

"I'm sorry, but it seemed the wise decision. Forgive me…" Her eyes, troubled by the rebuke, met his. "The men must see they will not be abandoned."

Of course, they did, and her feat was not as dangerous as either Tim or Rafael had contended. It had, however, enormously endeared her to the men and it had not undermined authority.

Rafael did not add that he thought she had been grandstanding and to a captive audience of underlings, but his disapproval was there to rob her of her small moment of triumph. Hating the fact that she could not keep peace with the man, she rode off to exchange the small horse for her own. Each step brought small but significant accolades in the form of gently tossed bouquets of smiles from the men. Forcing a smile, she returned each salute.

Rafael's discomfort reflected a growing tension over their arrival in Taxco where he knew they might hear that Captain Ramsden was alive and safe, destined to return at his own convenience and claim Anne-Marie. Everyday with her had only strengthened his desire and determination to make her forever his. His possessive nature could accept nothing less. Each day he had grown more and more determined. With a desire bordering on fanaticism, he followed her movements and gestures, which in a twisted way he misinterpreted and resented. This he dared not reveal again, knowing it would turn her from him.

Anne-Marie, all the while busy as a mother hen with her chicks, had sensed this, but much went over and past her, so concerned was she with the details harassing them all. Trying to soothe his ego over and over again she turned to him for information. Only he could explain the simple lifestyles of the people they passed, trudging along the roads, leading their burros, or sitting on steps with a hand out begging. He identified the black and white poplars, the giant tulip trees, the delicate colibris that quivered on trellises so quickly passed by, and amate trees whose bark had been used to make paper since the time of the Aztecan empire. Whatever peaked her curiosity, Rafael could satisfy, if only in fleeting conversation. A dozen times a day she had reined in her horse and galloped to his side to ask a question. Then satisfied, she returned to her position to move with the caravan

Occasionally, slipping through a village at night, from a doorway they could catch the strains of a *habanera*, such as *La Paloma,* played on guitar or mandolin, and Anne-Marie hungered to dally and join the enticing group. The sweet romantic strains, so different from anything she had ever heard, were strangely touching and opened a new door of musical experience understood only by Rafael among her circle of friends. Certainly, her troops knew this music, but she did not.

Leaving the men on the outskirts of Taxco, Anne-Marie, Tim and Rafael entered Taxco, leaving Esteban Navarro in charge. At the top of the town they found the home of Señor Ramirez. A servant, startled by Anne-Marie's strange clothing, admitted them and led them to the *offic- ina* where a few weeks earlier Bart had cooled his heels.

Ramirez did not keep Anne-Marie and her party waiting, but came beaming immediately. A warm ebullient greeting preceded his announcement. "Three weeks ago the captain departed. How sad that you have missed each other!"

Anne-Marie seated herself quickly, her knees feeling suddenly weak. "Is he all right?"

"I presume he's fine now. He had a terrible time getting here. He had been ill, imprisoned for weeks, held as a hostage, robbed…" Ramirez went on to describe the wraith of a man who landed penniless at his door. "I mailed a number of letters to you, but obviously they arrived or would have arrived after you had left. You look as if you, too, had a dif- ficult journey. I apologize for the traveling conditions of my country."

Anne-Marie sat in stunned silence. Overwhelmed by her great relief, she fought for air. The eyes of the men were upon her, wondering if she would faint. Relief was followed by bewilderment. What should she do now? The heavy wooden table resting below Ramirez's ingenuous chandelier steadied a trembling hand. The shimmering tile floor, patterned like a quilt, seemed to dance before her eyes. Finally, she found her voice.

"Forgive me, Señor Ramirez, I have not introduced Mr. Timothy Clayton and Señor Rafael de Palma from Key West. These two gentlemen have led my expedition across Mexico to find my husband. We have traveled here with over seventy men, knowing the hazards of travel. The men are outside the city."

"There will be no problem taking care of them. I'm glad that you are here so that you can personally report to the captain on our progress. He introduced a number of changes, which we are just beginning to implement with considerable success. One of the changes was constructing some housing—simple, of course, but now roofed in——where your men can sleep. The three of you will be my guests. *Mi casa es su casa.*"

"You are very kind. We accept with pleasure."

"Madame, I am delighted," replied Ramirez, clasping his hands together in excitement. "I have much to tell you. I'm sure you would like to refresh yourselves and rest a little. I'm astonished that you have brought a small army with you."

She turned to Rafael. "That was Señor de Palma's idea."

"Could your men be connected in any way with the rumors in our newspapers concerning an army's invasion?"

Anne-Marie smiled. "Very possibly. These rumors interrupted our plans to remain in telegraph communication with home. Consequently, we did not learn what had happened to my husband until now. You have given us a wonderful piece of news."

"I'm grateful for the opportunity. Certainly the news could have been very different."

Tim then offered to return to the men to lead them, with Señor Ramirez showing the way, to their housing. "I'll also bring your things, Anne-Marie, and yours, too, Señor de Palma."

"That would be good of you. It will be wonderful to be clean again," said Anne-Marie, speaking for herself and Rafael and nodding a goodbye.

Elated over the news and vindication of Bart, Anne-Marie wished desperately that she could only but see him. Bart is alive; Bart is alive, she said to herself over and over again. Music rang in her ears. They had arrived safely and they had found a welcome. Her feelings warranted sharing. She turned to Rafael. A cold silence enveloped him while his mind raced. His unpleasant expression, drawn and taut, signaled trouble, immediately dispelling all feelings of relief and pleasure. Dear God, what now? She rose and walked to the doors facing the inner garden, needing an escape.

"How beautiful this courtyard is," she managed, stepping outside.

Neatly tended flower beds, separated by walkways, paved with stones artfully graded with little runnels to carry off excess water, circled a central fountain. Anne-Marie found herself gazing at the stones, studying unimportant details, in order to let her mind slowly digest Ramirez's news. The knowledge that Bart was alive had changed everything. The world was suddenly beautiful. It was so lovely to be alive. Then she looked to the *officina* and saw Rafael's face, still pale and tense, as he struggled to hide the emotions churning within him.

Blessedly a servant arrived who could lead her to her room where she could avoid his eyes.

She had been completely honest with him. She had never intentionally encouraged Rafael. She loved her husband. Rafael's obsession for her was now putting a terrible burden on her. The man was a fanatic. Her calm and cool New England upbringing had not prepared her for his mad passion. He was frightening.

By the time she had bathed and washed her hair, Tim and Ramirez had returned, bringing more suitable clothing which was delivered to her by a maid. It was time for the *comida,* only slightly delayed. During the last three weeks her waist had expanded which had gone unnoticed under her men's clothing. Slowly, her pregnancy was beginning to show, and now her dress would not close. The gap, she discovered, she could hide with a shawl, and did. Gowned, refreshed somewhat by the bath, she went downstairs. There her party was introduced to the aunts, who through Bart had gradually become accustomed to *Norte Americanos.*

Anne-Marie's beauty and polish—and tales of her enormous wealth certainly exaggerated by Ranirez—had a quieting effect on the two spinsters. There was also much to talk about. A young chemist who Bart had engaged had made improvements in the milling. One large shipment of silver had arrived safely in Mexico City. Ramirez's mechanism for raising ore out of the ground was operating. There were a few bugs to be worked out, he said, but in principle, it was excellent—if he did say so himself.

"Production is up. Labor costs are going down, although we've hired protection. In a few days a large shipment bound for Europe will be ready," he announced.

"We can see that it gets to Veracruz," Anne-Marie volunteered.

"No problem at all," added Tim. "The men are armed, and we should be able to dodge the armies looking for us." He laughed. "All we want to do now is retreat."

They all laughed excepting Rafael who managed a wan smile before asking the value of the shipment.

"In excess of fifty thousand dollars," replied Ramirez. "And, unfortunately, we cannot ship in thousand pound blocks as the captain suggested because the shipment goes to several different houses."

Only when the shipment—an old order that should have gone out earlier—was discussed, did Rafael's interest revive, but no one noticed.

"You could not have arrived at a better time for us," exclaimed Ramirez. "Unless we deliver soon, we'll lose the order. I've been genuinely concerned about getting it to Veracruz."

"Your husband has truly inspired my nephew," said Doña Carmelita. "He thinks of nothing but the mine, and the plans your husband envisioned. I have prayed ardently for the captain's safe return."

"Indeed, our nephew is a new man," added Doña Mercedes.

"The captain is a man of action and very clever," added Tim, smiling at Anne-Marie. "And, as you can see, he is well matched with Madame Ramsden."

Always jealous of Anne-Marie's friendship with Tim, Rafael resented Tim's appraisal of Bart, and bristled. Besides, he thought, Tim's contribution to the expedition had been negligible. He, Rafael, had been the one Anne-Marie had leaned upon. Finding it impossible to hate Anne-Marie whom he desired intensely, and equally impossible for the time being to destroy Bart, Rafael turned his rage toward Tim. Then he remembered the night at Los Claveles when Anne-Marie was not in her stateroom. Undoubtedly, she had been with Tim, certainly not David. Glowering jealous hatred for Tim smoldered in his chest like the burgeoning volcanoes they had been skirting. He would have to act. There would not be much time.

"Tomorrow we must all visit the mine," said Ramirez. Anne-Marie and Tim were in accord.

"As you can imagine we have had no opportunity for sightseeing. We never left the highway," said Anne-Marie.

"Then certainly you must visit the beautiful Prisca Cathedral. It was built by Señor de la Borda who made a gift of it to the people. It cost over two million dollars. De la Borda and his wife had only two children, both of whom entered the church as a priest and a nun. With no heirs of his own, de la Borda threw a fortune to the church. It stands over one of the richest silver veins in the world. The altar is plated in gold. The people say, 'God gave to de la Borda and de la Borda gave to God.'"

"I would love to see it," replied Anne-Marie.

After Anne-Marie saw the working conditions of the miners, the hazards they endured, the pitiful housing for a pittance pay, she saw something else: After years of greed and exploitation, de la Borda may have become doubtful over his credentials to enter heaven, and thought to improve them by building a church. But she did not think of that until later.

That evening Doña Carmelita and Doña Mercedes, staid society members, sat in their parlor playing European classics on the harpsichord for Anne-Marie's entertainment. Later, out in the street young men strummed their guitars and sang the current popular love songs from Spain. The lovely melodies only made Anne-Marie hunger for Bart. Carefully that night, she bolted her door.

Meanwhile, Rafael struggled with a plan that included both robbery and murder. The plan was implemented the following morning while the household breakfasted, and, considerately assumed that Rafael was sleeping late.

*   *   *   *

In Key West Mimi read in the *Key West Dispatch* of an unidentified army invading Mexico. It threw her into a panic. Still, fearing for Rafael's life, she could do nothing but inwardly rage against Anne-Marie who had obviously lured her lover away.

CHAPTER SEVENTEEN

The prospect of being master of Anne-Marie's home for a month was highly pleasing to David, and he was thankful to be relieved of the need to traipse across Mexico. He had not looked on the journey as an adventure, but rather as a catalog of miseries and dangers borne of disease, bandits, and general discomforts. On the other hand, the social life of Key West in comparison to that of Pleasantville, New Jersey, shone brightly.

That Zipporah was not there had come as a surprise, and he was curious. He had promised to look in on Consuelo. As a confidant of Anne-Marie surely she had heard what had happened to the girl. Perhaps she could tell him. David had questioned Samantha and learned only that she and Concepcion had not liked her—reason enough for her dismissal. But, it also had been their belief that Bart was someway involved with the dismissal.

Having a confidential way with women anyway, David had no difficulty in approaching the subject. Enjoying a cup of tea on Consuelo's front porch, David stroked Consuelo's cat and launched his inquiry.

"I'm not surprised to find Zipporah gone. She was ambitious and unscrupulous. I found her forward with men, too. Anne-Marie was bound to notice and disapprove."

"I didn't like her either," concurred Consuelo, with a little laugh.

"I thought I saw her on the street the other day," David lied.

"That's unlikely. She moved out of the state," replied Consuelo, knowing that she had recently sent a money order to the girl in Charleston, and the girl was unlikely to jeopardize this income. "Are you sure you saw her?"

Consuelo was justifiably alarmed. Zipporah's whole story could have been a hoax, designed to bleed Anne-Marie.

"No, of course not, but whomever I saw certainly reminded me of her."

"I expect she is quite visibly pregnant by now," Consuelo remarked, thoughtful of male interest in Zipporah's figure. Instantly, she recognized her breach of confidence and attempted to recoup. "Therefore, she wasn't doing her work satisfactorily."

David, stunned, quickly changed the subject, at the same time relieving Consuelo.

David knew he had taken Zipporah to bed, and was pretty sure Bart had not. Consuelo's disclosure meant that Zipporah could have been carrying his child—a highly disturbing thought, and one that warranted further investigation. He would query Consuelo no more. He would write an old friend who lived in the same town that the girl came from. Releasing Consuelo's cat, he rose and excused himself with the need of a pressing errand—a letter to write and mail.

"The next time you visit I hope you will stay longer," said Consuelo, sorry to see her company leave.

"I'll be glad to. The mail packet leaves today, and I must get a letter off to my wife."

"You're a devoted husband. How nice!"

David returned home to write his friend—not his wife—requesting a simple character reference. A reply would take at least two weeks, but he would have an answer before Anne-Marie returned. "Damn," he muttered, truly upset.

His letter was safely on the boat before he heard the ship's horn announcing its departure.

Consuelo's revelation put a serious damper on his spirits and David found himself unable to dismiss the subject. After a restless night he decided to telegraph. The next morning he walked briskly to Baldy Smith's telegraph office on the north side of the island with a brief penciled message: DEAR FRIEND, EXPLANATORY LETTER FOLLOWS STOP PLEASE CABLE ANY PERTINENT INFORMATION REGARDING CHARACTER OF ZIPPORAH RICHARDSON STOP GRATEFULLY DAVID DOYLE.

Within two days he had his exonerating reply: ZIPPORAH DISINHERITED STOP PREGNANT OUT OF WEDLOCK STOP LETTER FOLLOWS.

Immensely relieved, David was free to enjoy his stay in Key West. He would now give a series of dinner parties. He could count on Consuelo's help as he would need to draw on her friends. Certainly, she would also enjoy a little social life.

Ten days would follow before David received a letter from his friend explaining that Zipporah had come from a good family, but she had been caught with a man in her bed, and admitted being pregnant. Instead of a shotgun wedding the fanatically religious father had thrown her out. Zipporah had disappeared. Apparently she had sought work as a domestic. Her plight was that of many a fallen woman. All of this would have been interesting had not other events intervened.

The first was Bart's unexpected return. After a race across Mexico, he had seven days on a brigantine in which to rest and recoup. His shock on learning Anne-Marie had taken an army to Mexico to find him was total. He was flabbergasted.

"Bart," said David. "For heaven's sake consider—she had no word from you in months. She also had a Spaniard, Rafael de Palma, whom I do not trust, urging her to take this action. I'm sure you can imagine Jason's chagrin that she would buy an army. Fortunately, Tim accompanied her or, of course, I would have. Actually, de Palma's plan was not bad. The men trained at Los Claveles. The whole operation was highly secretive. The horses and guns she can sell to the Mexicans when she is finished—with the sale offsetting their cost. She promised to cable me, which she has not done—but I think I have the answer to that. According to the papers, the Mexicans think they are being invaded by a foreign country's army—which they can't even locate. It must be Anne-Marie's army. If she has been apprehended, it would have appeared in the papers."

Bart paced the floor. "That woman has too damn much money!"

"That's another story," murmured David, shaking his head.

"Do you realize the danger she could be in? My God, I can't even turn to our government for help under these circumstances!"

"Don't underestimate your wife."

"I'm not. I'm facing facts, and that country—as I know it."

"If all's well, we'll get telegraphed instructions within the next few days asking Captain Sands to pick her and the men up."

There was also good news: Jared Russell had arrived safely home in the north.

The two men talked for hours. Bart explaining the unbelievable delays he had encountered before reaching Taxco, and once there, what he had discovered. With considerable pleasure David could describe his day in New York with Jason selling gold and stocks prior to the market's crash.

"Bart, whatever Anne-Marie's expedition cost in dollars, she more than made up for by selling out when she did. Jason was dumbfounded. You should have seen the old geezer when he learned of her luck."

"Let's hope her luck holds. She'll need it. And we're powerless to help..." Bart felt numb with frustration.

Bart's reunion with Consuelo was joyous. "What a sight for sore eyes you are," he said, embracing her.

"If you ever go off like that again, Bart, we will kill you. You have no idea what you put us through."

"My first recommendation is to get rid of any Mexican interests you may have immediately. The country is chaotic. But, Anne-Marie will see for herself. You look marvelous. Show me the baby…" She did.

Later that day Bart's letters to Anne-Marie, which had traveled on the same ship as he had, were delivered. Slowly, he was beginning to understand what had prompted his wife's actions.

Walking downtown the following day, Bart ran into the owner of the Russell House where Rafael had lived. William Russell was a curly-bearded man who always wore a frock coat and silk hat whenever he stepped on the street.

"Oh, Mr. Ramsden," greeted Russell. "How fortunate to run into you. Perhaps you can shed a little light on my problem. I know Rafael de Palma has been working for your wife. He left Key West without a forwarding address and without letting his rooms go. Do you think he intends to return?"

Prompted by pangs of jealousy more than anything else, but also cognizant of David's distrust of Rafael, Bart was not inclined toward charity or consideration for him. He could have relieved Russell by saying de Palma would soon return, but Bart was not so inclined, and assurance was not forthcoming.

"I haven't seen him in months. Does he owe a large bill?"

"Nothing too much, but if he's gone for good, we can use the rooms."

"I think it would be easy enough to evaluate what he left as to his intentions…" Bart replied, coolly.

"Yes, of course, but you understand I hate to go in alone. Considering that he worked for your family, perhaps you would be kind enough to accompany me."

Bart's attitude was enough to make William Russell assume that de Palma was no longer in good repute.

"I would be glad to," Bart replied, eager to discover anything he could about the man, his suspicions growing.

Bart's discoveries left him inwardly shaken.

Almost immediately he spotted letters from Mexico in Ramona's handwriting, a curious script distinguished by Latin curlicues quite unlike that of Americans. Pulling open an envelope, he learned that she was ready to help de Palma with a plan. Bart had no doubts as to what that had been: to hold him for ransom. She thanked him for money. Bart slipped the letter into his pocket, an act that went unnoticed. He turned to let his eyes fall on the washbowl and pitcher whose china pattern matched a cracked *pot de chambre* in a small room in Veracruz where he had first been held a prisoner.

"I feel certain that Señor de Palma will not return," said Bart, finally. He did not add that it would be unhealthy for him to do so, but that was what he had decided.

Later he remembered that in the tiny room where he had first been held, when he came down with yellow fever, he had noticed the very elaborate, hand painted, unusual pattern on the *pot de chambre*. Because it was cracked with a wedge broken out, Rafael had not bothered to transport it to Key West with his few small pieces of furniture. He left it with Ramona. Three worn uniforms, limp and tired, collecting moths, remnants of Napoleon's New World Empire, hung in a small cupboard. It was all the man had in the world other than possibly—Bart gulped—his wife!

Bart left Russell House and rapidly walked to the cable office. Then he returned to Samantha and David. The afternoon was spent numbly with Samantha, deeply worried over Anne-Marie. The evening was spent talking with David.

"I made a very disturbing discovery today. I have proof here in my pocket—there is more locked up in Russell House—that de Palma, in cahoots with a girl in Veracruz had me kidnapped. Later the girl saved my life as she nursed me through yellow fever. She died helping me escape. I wonder, did he have her killed? With my own eyes I saw her murdered, and I could do nothing about it. I was on the other side of a canyon…"

"My God, are you saying that Anne-Marie is in danger?"

"I don't know, but she could be…"

"What can we do?" asked David, throwing up his hands in a futile gesture.

A great wave of sympathy and understanding touched both men, bound as they were through their different relationships with Anne-Marie. Past distrust and animosity were forgiven and forgotten in their shared concern. David was unusually moved.

"Possibly the wisest head in Key West belongs to your friend Consuelo. I think you should talk to her."

"No, not at this time. We have laid too many problems at the feet of the Claytons already. Consuelo has a new baby and doesn't need this worry over something she can do nothing about. Surely, in the next few days we will hear where—in that Goddamned country spooked with Aztec gods—she is!"

"Now wait a minute," said David, "Let's think about this. Tim is with Anne-Marie. I have warned Tim that I thought de Palma was padding the payroll. Knowing this, he would be watchful. I'm sure de Palma hoped to find you lost. No, Bart, Anne-Marie is not in danger. I'm certain, Rafael hopes to marry her."

"And what does he do when they discover that I am alive?"

"Darned if I know. I did one thing that I hope will help her. I removed all the firing pins from the rifles and gave them to her in a little pouch. The guns are worthless without the pins. She's the only one who knows that."

"David, that was one of the smartest things you've ever done. Thank you!"

"I hope so. Now I'm afraid Tim may be in danger…"

"Now you see why I don't want to talk to Consuelo," Bart murmured.

It had taken David some minutes to come to what Bart had guessed immediately. But he did get there, thought Bart. "I sent a telegram to Ramirez this morning telling him that de Palma was behind my kidnapping and that he might be dangerous. Anne-Marie and Tim should be warned if possible. Of course, by my calculation they have left Taxco, but Ramirez may be able to intercept her, knowing exactly when she left and where she is likely to be now."

"What a brilliant idea!" said David. "Don't you think you should also cable the United States' Minister to Mexico?"

"Christ, David, she went in with an invading army on forgeries! How in the devil can I call on authorities? I guess I should cable Jason, but why worry him?"

"I've already done that," said David meekly. "Jason made me promise to keep him abreast of things." He felt stupid as, indeed, his remark had been. "We're both sitting here discounting her beauty, her winning ways and her luck. Luck rides the same horse she does. Remember the way she sold greenbacks just before the crash?"

"I'll try not to," said Bart, as the men took their worries to their respective beds.

The events of the next week were to have their impact for the rest of Bart's life. Because of his concern for Tim, and feeling this might be revealed to one as intuitive as Consuelo, Bart and David did not visit her for a couple of days. Then knowing that if they didn't they would be highly remiss, they did. Pearl met them at the door, saw them to the parlor and asked that they be seated. She left and returned a few minutes later to say that Miz Clayton felt poorly. "She has a real bad headache, and says she's sorry, she can't come down."

"It's unlike her to be sick," said Bart to David, looking questioning. He turned to Pearl. "Has she seen the doctor?"

"No," replied Pearl. "Earlier today she asked me to take over the baby. She looked peaked."

"Go upstairs again, Pearl, and feel her forehead. Tell me if she has a fever."

Pearl was happy to oblige. Bart rose and strode nervously about the room until Pearl returned. With Tim gone—and on his account—he was damned well going to see that Consuelo was well taken care of.

"She do have a bad fever, sir," Pearl announced.

"I'm going for the doctor. Put cold wet cloths on her head," Bart ordered, hurrying from the room, David at his heels.

It was almost half an hour before Bart found Dr. Burbury, who had been out on a house call. "Please, see her right away. We'll follow in our carriage."

They did and waited downstairs an interminable length of time before the doctor descended the stairs. Meanwhile they also learned from Pearl that Consuelo also was vomiting.

"I'm glad we acted as soon as we did," said Bart, tentatively.

The expression on Dr. Burbury's face generated no little alarm even before he spoke. Bart knew Burbury had known Consuelo all her life, and she was more than just as patient, a dear friend. "Is Mr. Clayton in the city?" he asked.

"No. He can't be reached at the moment. He's on a business trip in Mexico."

"Consuelo is very seriously ill, perhaps critically. Of course, I may be mistaken, so many illnesses begin with a fever, sore throat, vomiting, but her stiff neck alarms me. I fear meningitis…"

"I know nothing of the illness," said Bart. "It's serious, you say?"

"Very. I wouldn't think of leaving her, but I could use more medicine than I have with me." He began scribbling prescriptions. "Please pick these up for me as rapidly as possible."

Bart flew from the room to Johnson's Drug Store. On reading the prescription Johnson lifted an eyebrow. "Somebody pretty sick?"

"Yes," Bart replied, too distraught to think and too frightened to ask about meningitis.

He returned with the medicine, but it was almost two hours before Dr. Burbury came downstairs again. "She appears to be breaking out with a rash typical of the disease. I can't seem to budge that fever." Dr. Burbury seemed sick himself.

"Can I see her?" Bart asked.

"Captain, I suppose you **can** see her, but this is a contagious disease and you must consider the possibility of taking it home. She is heavily drugged. Right now she is resting." His expression was sad.

Bart was chilled to the bone. "Dr. Burbury, is she going to die?"

The doctor hesitated which was enough to make Bart feel his own heart crack open.

"Bart, we're all going to die, but yes, Consuelo may die soon—even tonight or tomorrow. But, meningitis is not always fatal. There are rare, very rare cases in which the patient lives. I'm afraid her next symptom will be further mental confusion."

Clearly, Dr. Burbury had little hope.

A myriad of poignant memories, visions of Consuelo's beauty, recollections of her valiant courage, her eternal wisdom, tucked into every circuitous whorl of Bart's brain, now taunted him, as they would for years to come. The loss of Consuelo would be even more unbearable for Tim. He turned from that thought and wept. Dr. Burbury also wiped his eyes.

"We're doing all we can, but I'm afraid it's not enough," whispered Burbury returning to his patient.

Tim would remember her well and happy. He was missing her last days, but he would be spared knowing she was going to die.

"Further mental confusion" hardly described Consuelo's delirium.

Now David sat alone downstairs waiting for an occasional word from Bart who hovered just outside her door. Aunt Hannah and Aunt Petrona, old Black citizens, the only trained nurses on the island whose services were for hire, had been summoned by Burbury, and they worked upstairs with him applying cold compresses to her body as rapidly as they could be applied and lifted, so hot was Consuelo. Voices were hushed, footsteps rapid, while downstairs the grandfather clock chimed off the hours.

Once a low heavy jungle beat reverberated through the night as the darkies drummed out an obeah, the voodoo they had brought from Africa. The obeah roused a chorus of barking dogs in howling protest. David viewed this as an alarming omen.

Upstairs Consuelo seemed to rally, recognizing Bart. Heartened by this, the doctor eased from the room, signaling the two nurses to do the same, hoping that Bart could strengthen her will to live.

Bart sitting by her bedside, held her tiny trembling hands in his own.

"I'm frightened. I know I'm dying, Bart," she whispered.

"No! No! Consuelo, You'll live…" he cried in desperation.

"Promise me that you will look out for Tim and the baby. Without me they will need you."

An emotion of crushing intensity bound his chest and sealed his lips, so that he could only reply by firming his hold, as if he could hold her here on earth, his beloved faithful friend.

"Anne-Marie needs you, too. Move closer to her." Her voice dwindled. "You have so much. Together you could have it all…"

Just before dawn Consuelo slipped into the inevitable coma as the disease ran its deadly course. When Bart came downstairs for the last time he told David, "She died in my arms."

Mercifully, David was there to make the funeral arrangements as Bart was too grief stricken to function. Pearl and the baby were moved to the Ramsden house.

Mimi, having been for many years Consuelo's closest friend, displaced only in the last few years by Anne-Marie, although stunned, presided over the wake. She answered the inevitable question, "Where are Tim Clayton and Anne-Marie Ramsden?" with the only answer she had been given, "They are both away on business trips." This generated a fresh flow of tears as each questioner envisioned the horrible homecoming. "And think of that beautiful baby boy…" said all.

Bart's sudden appearance and Anne-Marie's absence had mystified islanders, and no one got much of an explanation. Also the sadness of the occasion erased any suspicions that Anne-Marie and Tim might be together in a foreign country. Only Mimi suffered Rafael's absence, and Bart's reappearance was enough to stifle her intention of alerting the authorities.

Concepcion took over when poor little Pearl collapsed under grief and strain.

Bart retreated beyond the closed door of his bedroom, insulated and isolated by stone walls of his home. He had experienced a similar grief once when he believed Anne-Marie dead, which had been without proof. But Consuelo had died in his arms. This time there would be no respite.

The funeral was held in St. Paul's Episcopal Church with the Reverend E.O. Herrick conducting the services for an overflowing crowd. Consuelo was buried in the City Cemetery, which lay in the thickly settled part of the city. The custom prevailed in Key West of closing the doors of stores when a funeral procession was passing. With all the business along the line of the march suspended, the last tribute of respect was thus paid to the dead. With Consuelo gone, it seemed to Bart that even the world had stopped turning.

He walked out late at night to the corner of Passover and Winsor Lane where he could see her grave, days later still banked with a blanket of flowers, a remnant of the last tragic pageant in her name. Silently, he wept.

Chapter Eighteen

Anne-Marie had raced across Mexico seeing the topography but little of the life, and that of only the poorer classes. Rafael had tried to answer her questions, but she remained hungry for more intimate glimpses into the country and its people. Not only was Señor Ramirez's home a brief haven where the big puzzle besetting her for months was solved, but it also gave her a taste of Mexican home life, so different from anything she had experienced.

The comforts of a rich man's home: a clean bed, interesting food, music and conversation were a welcome distraction from the more pressing problems soon to be faced. Like Bart, she was intrigued by the strange foods and the odd times they were served, such as a *copa* of brandy in the early morning or the inviolate siesta, which nothing short of mortal danger would interrupt.

She found the class distinctions peculiar. Ramirez's aunts patly divided the lower classes into *gente de razon* or rational people and *gente intractible* or those who it was almost impossible to comprehend. *Banditos* fell into this class, apparently there were a lot of them in the State of Guerrero. House servants—it took three to do the work of one American—were regarded as underprivileged children, but rational people. A maid was always there to help Anne-Marie bathe, yet the maid was hardly willing to bathe herself, despite the outward appearance of cleanliness.

Within no more than two or three days one of the largest shipments of silver would be ready for delivery to Veracruz and it would be up to Anne-Marie's troop to deliver it. She would also have to make arrangements for the sale of the guns and horses.

She hoped for a safe and easy journey, but the Mexican army was still looking for her. To achieve her aims it seemed that no less than President Jaurez himself could help.

Both Tim and Señor Ramirez supported her plan to meet with Jaurez. Rafael did not. "I'm sure, Madame, your husband would agree with me. Bureaucrats are the same the world over. You will become embroiled in miles of red tape. You may also find yourself in prison."

"I don't see otherwise how we can break out of this country without bloodshed. I'm particularly concerned about you."

"I appreciate your consideration. Also, I may separate from the group from time to time—with your permission, of course—perhaps with only one other man. I would never be far away, but acting as a scout or following in the rear as a lookout."

"But, Rafael, you could fall prey to robbers…" she objected.

"I would carry nothing they would want to steal."

"Your horse!"

"I should be able to outrun anyone. But, I'm sorry, I can't approve of a meeting with Jaurez, President or not."

"Anne-Marie can be very persuasive," argued Tim. "How many times has she swayed the men?"

"She did not sway President Johnson when she sought a pardon for Dr. Mudd. It would have meant Johnson's neck. She may not succeed with Jaurez for the same reason. Presidents are not as powerful as one might think."

"Let's not argue. We have a day or two to decide. Let's visit the mine. Tomorrow is Sunday. We would not interrupt work," cajoled Anne-Marie.

Feeling certain Anne-Marie would not want to descend, Ramirez agreed. He was most anxious that she would be able to make a favorable report to her husband.

Rafael excused himself to walk around the town, an activity women of Anne-Marie's class would not do on cobblestone streets where there was precarious footing. Tim retired to write Consuelo, leaving Anne-Marie and Ramirez alone.

"Madame Ramsden, not because you will be traveling with a particularly rich cargo in a lawless country, but simply on general principles, I want to warn you: Don't trust anyone." Seeing her surprised expression he continued, "Don't be alarmed. I've seen nothing subversive among your fellow travelers, but I know some of the unsavory ways of this world. Greed does strange things to people."

"That is very kind of you. The last few months have taught me that people of different nationalities are difficult to judge. With you, we form a unique combination of Mexican, English, Spanish, Cuban and American people trying to work together. There have been problems. Perhaps I've been too trusting in an effort to understand and appreciate these differences. Do you understand what I mean?"

"Exactly, and that is the reason for my concern. A word to the wise…"

The following day they went to the mine. Only two guards and a superintendent were present. Ramirez, Tim, Anne-Marie and Rafael made up the visiting party.

The superintendent was testing a mass of mixed ore in the patio. He explained that if the mass, which was left untouched for several days, chemically heated up too rapidly, lime was added which cools it. If, on the contrary, the mass were cold, he would add copper and sulphuretted iron in a powder and a small quantity of salt. This he called a *magistral*. He put a small quantity of the *magistral* in Tim's hand with a little water. The heat created was such that Tim threw it away instantly, making them all laugh.

"Are you sure you haven't a stove hidden under there?" quipped Anne-Marie.

"The superintendent examines the amalgam every other day. That is why he is working today. He puts a little of the amalgam in a wooden bowl and then adds salt, quicksilver or *magistral* as he finds necessary to complete the amalgamation. He's our cook, sampling the soup," Ramirez explained.

Because Rafael and Tim expressed a desire to go down into the mine on one of Ramirez's improvements—a wooden elevator carried by ropes which now took the place of the old ladders—they turned next to this area, a few hundred feet away. By the length of the rope, wound around a spindle carried on a frame above ground, Anne-Marie could see that the descent would be a good many feet.

"You go first, Mister Clayton," said Rafael. "I'll follow." It appeared to be the polite gesture.

"Wait a minute," intervened Anne-Marie, thinking fast. "First, I would prefer to see that apparatus tested with a man's weight in stones."

"It has been tested many times, Madame," said Ramirez, proudly.

"Still, this I want to see. Indulge me."

Ramirez was happy to oblige. "Bring over those stones," he ordered a guard standing nearby.

Stones were loaded aboard and slowly the elevator, controlled by two guards at the crank, descended. Then suddenly the rope snapped. A resounding thud echoed through the chamber. The group was appalled.

"Madame," cried Ramirez, aghast. "We've been sabotaged! Competitors, of course. Thank heaven for your intuition!"

"I thank heaven for it, also," said Tim. "I doubt that I could have survived that." The hole was a black pit; the elevator laying someplace on the bottom, undoubtedly in splinters in water.

A shocked, greatly disturbed group returned to Ramirez's home.

"Thank you for your warning, Señor Ramirez. I took your advice to heart."

He was close to tears. "I'm so grateful that you did. The guards will be dismissed immediately. Of course, I'll investigate this thoroughly."

Within two days the shipment was ready, and Anne-Marie and her troop could be on its way. No further mention was made of the proposed visit to President Jaurez. It would be up to her to decide whether or not she wanted an audience. With fond farewells they took leave of Señor Ramirez and his family.

"You will forgive me if I go ahead as we discussed," said Rafael to Anne-Marie. "If we miss connections we can meet at Tres Marias—a much smaller city than Cuernavaca."

Still shaken by the near disaster at the mine, and with only Rafael's safety in mind, Anne-Marie was quick to agree. His presence reminded her of the perpetual problems he presented. Their brief separation only meant one less problem, when she felt she had so many.

"You know the route you must take, so you don't need me for that," said Rafael.

"I'd feel better if you weren't traveling alone. I think it might be safer."

"Then I'll take Esteban Navarro—the smartest of the lot. Perhaps the two of us together can make a plan to ease our way home."

To that Anne-Marie agreed.

Because the progress with the silver would be a good deal slower than Rafael and Esteban's, Anne-Marie decided suddenly to take a short cut. Tim felt it was riskly, but acknowledged that Anne-Marie had a point. The main road was so bad, it was hard to imagine one worse. "We have ropes and horses to pull the wagons free if they get stuck," she insisted. Reluctantly, Tim concurred, but Anne-Marie noted that he was unusually silent.

The way was much more difficult. Small barren plains and sterile rocky ribs (which intersected them), stony foothills and dry *arroyos* beneath higher mountains, made hazardous traveling. Once when they crossed a dry streambed fringed with mesquite and cactus, a dozen low dark forms darted suddenly from the shadow of the bank. In a twinkling of an eye, Tim fired. A large animal fell—others scattered.

"What were they?" Anne-Marie asked.

"Peccaries or wild pigs. We will dine well tonight," said Tim.

It was a good shot, and indeed, excellent eating, roasted at the bottom of the *arroyo* where they camped. That night they found a cave, snugly hidden in a wall of rock with a floor of the purest quartz sand, and a limpid rivulet flowing nearby. It made a perfect resting-place.

It was quite late when Tim signaled to Anne-Marie. She followed him a few feet to the perimeter of their camp. "I don't want to worry you, Anne-Marie, but perhaps I must."

"Never be concerned about that, Tim."

"Someone is trying to get rid of me in an unpleasant fashion."

"What do you mean?" she questioned.

"Just that. I'm afraid that rope was cut expecting me to descend. I would have dismissed this thought had not I found a rattlesnake, a Mexican type that is poisonous but has no warning rattlers which could alert its prey, in my baggage."

A look of shock crossed her face. "How did you escape it?"

"I have a habit of years' standing while traveling. I put a hair through the clasp on my saddlebag—or any valise I'm using—so that I can see if my baggage has been tampered with. The hair was missing, so I opened the bag very carefully."

"That's too awful. Have you any idea who could have done it?"

"Only a hunch."

"Who?"

"Rafael de Palma."

"Tim, you can't mean that. He hasn't been with us today. Why would he want to kill you?"

"He had an opportunity to visit the mine last night, and he came down late for breakfast. Only he and Ramirez both had such opportunities. I discount Ramirez. Rafael is in love with you. Perhaps he thinks that I stand in his way. It's the only explanation that I can think of, and it has been very hard for me to come to that."

"I know him well," she replied, her voice a shocked whisper. "Your arguments would be convincing if I could believe him guilty of such a thing."

"I long debated telling you my feelings, and perhaps one day I will owe him an apology. Still, I felt I had to warn you. He may be a very dangerous man."

Despite the clean and beautiful cave, Anne-Marie did not sleep that night. By dawn one thing was settled: She would seek President Jaurez's protection and his mercy if need be.

Later the following day they caught up with Rafael and Esteban Navarro at Tres Marias. As Anne-Marie had guessed, he was disturbed that she had not followed the route he had outlined. It seemed to her that he was smothering his surprise that Tim was alive, but perhaps that was her imagination.

*   *   *   *

Unbeknownst to Anne-Marie and Tim, on separating from them in Taxco, Rafael had been busy. Riding with Esteban, Rafael had suggested, much to Esteban's alarm, that Esteban join him in hijacking part of the silver, as much as they could carry, and, of course, the guns. Rafael knew an unscrupulous *ranchero* on the route who had his own band of defenders who could assist in the heist.

Rafael's suggestion had not come as a total surprise to Esteban. Rafael had been unusually attentive to him during the preceding days, dropping such obvious hints as, "Stay close to me, and I will show you how we can make a fortune," and "I'll take care of you, don't worry." Esteban was not a stupid man, and knew that probably this fortune could only come from Anne-Marie. Also, he knew that had he not played along with Rafael, someone else would have. Hence, he had pretended to be in accord. There was no point in confiding his intentions to Anne-Marie. At that point they were unsubstantiated. So, he decided to play along with Rafael until he knew more. One thing was certain, by riding with Rafael, Esteban could protect Anne-Marie better than at her side. It was impossible for him to plan what he would do until he knew what Rafael was going to do or how he would do it.

On the night that they spent alone upon leaving Taxco, Rafael revealed it: The *ranchero's* men would ambush Anne-Marie's troops. The great shipment of silver would be hidden in caves off the road until it could be safely divided.

Hearing the plan, Esteban bravely decided that he could break away from the men waiting in ambush to warn Anne-Marie. He could be killed doing this, but the shots would alert her party, and if Mexican marksmanship were true to form, he would not be hit.

Throughout the following day with the *ranchero* and his *guerrilleros* they waited impatiently for Anne-Marie's caravan, the *ranchero* growing more and more irritated with Rafael every hour. Finally, it became apparent that Anne-Marie had taken a different route, one to the north, shorter but harder. Furious, Rafael and Esteban were forced to abandon the plot for the time being, and he and Esteban took off for Tres Marias, leaving the *ranchero* to watch the road. Rafael's chances of getting his hands on even a part of the silver from the *ranchero* would be remote, indeed, if Anne-Marie were to appear on that road. At the same time, by not appearing in Tres Marias he might lose her for the remainder of the journey.

*   *   *   *

On meeting in Tres Marias, Anne-Marie announced that she was going to see Jaurez. Rafael made no effort to hide his disapproval. Stubbornly, she stayed with her decision.

"The men must remain safely hidden outside the city. I expect to spend tonight in the best hotel I can find. You and Tim are free to do the same. No one need know that you are in the city, Señor de Palma. If I'm thrown in prison, get the men home as best you can." Her tone was not defiant, but resigned. Both men saw that she could not be dissuaded. They elected to join her, but had hardly a word for one another.

At length they arrived at the heights looking down at the valley of Mexico City, celebrated in all parts of the world. Circled by mountains and snow-crowned volcanoes, the innumerable spires of the city and tile domes glistened in the sunlight. The whole fertile valley, enclosed by eternal hills, complete with lakes and flower covered islands, lay before them. The islands, a western Venice, with hundreds of boats gliding swiftly along its street-canals were to the south. Low houses with red barrel tile roofs and curious gigantic ahuehuete trees or towering tulip trees abloom with great clusters of red flowers, formed the bulk of the city, intersected by twisting narrow streets, broad avenues, and ancient aqueducts. Here and there plazas dotted the landscape. From afar it seemed like a model or toy city to them.

Entering the city, Anne-Marie selected a small hotel, even though she would have preferred the finest. She had but one respectable dress with her—and that would no longer close properly without a shawl—and no carriage for a suitable entrance. Still, the following day she knew she could be pretty and clean. Several times during the night she was certain Rafael tapped on her bolted door, but she did not answer. Eventually, the tapping stopped.

With dawn, curious street noises began. A man selling coal awakened her. A grease-man followed selling butter and lard. Soon a *cambinista*, a woman with a shrill voice wanting to exchange fruit for chilies, joined the overall racket. Mule-drawn open streetcars, curtained for inclement weather, carried people to work urged on by a driver crying, "*andale, andele*" or "Get moving!" Peddlers with needles, pins, shirt buttons, mats from Puebla, tape, sweetmeats, cotton-balls, salt beef and pork plied their wares, all at the top of their voices, expecting to haggle. The loudness tried Anne-Marie's sleepy patience with its surprising clatter. There was no recourse but to face the day.

Having breakfasted with Tim and Rafael, a meal as silent as the morning noises had been loud, Anne-Marie departed for the majestic square known as the *Zocolo,* laid off in the days of Cortez. Here she found the Palacio National, an immense building containing besides the apartments of the President and his ministers, all the chief courts of justice. Beggars were everywhere, the most frightening being lepers, holding out fingerless hands for alms. Inside the building, at every turn lounging soldiers and women in shawls stood about. To reach the President Anne-Marie was forced to go to one aide-de-camp after another, each passing her along, each unwilling to deny her access to his office. She was an obviously important woman, but without an appointment. She would speak only with the President. No one would risk crossing her.

Getting beyond the general public she was ushered through the famed Hall of the Ambassadors, lined with heroic portraits and lit by four enormous crystal chandeliers to the crimson and gold reception room. There she was asked to wait. Within half an hour, President Jaurez himself arrived. Anne-Marie curtsied and addressed the short, squat, morose, stern looking Mexican dressed in a black business suit. In him no strain of Spanish blood existed. He was a man known for his silence. He did ask her to be seated.

"Your Excellency, knowing you to be a just man, I am throwing myself on your mercy," began Anne-Marie. "I entered Mexico following the disappearance of my husband in Veracruz. He came to Mexico, legally, to investigate our silver holdings in Taxco. When three months elapsed and I had heard nothing from him, and our minister, Thomas Nelson, could learn nothing, I became desperate."

"I understand," he replied.

Anne-Marie then explained that she had organized a troop of *guer-rillos*, composed of Cubans fleeing Spanish oppression, trained them, brought them to Mexico on her ship, traversed the country, and in Taxco learned why her husband had not written. She then described in detail all she knew about her husband's experiences: the kidnapping, the illnesses and imprisonment. Jaurez let her speak.

"I have bought every morsel of food the men have eaten. I have not been a marauding cavalry unit supporting invading foot soldiers—as was reported in the newspapers. My men are now carrying and guard-ing a great shipment of silver bound for export. My men are armed. We carry one hundred of the finest Krupp steel, breech-loading rifles, some of the world's newest and finest weapons. I have a supply of excellent, well-trained horses. I have hoped to sell these guns and horses to your government for a fair market price. I respectfully ask your protection in leaving your country with the silver your country needs to sell."

Jaurez said nothing to make her confession and plea easier. His Indian face remained expressionless. His black eyes never left her face. For a moment she feared he would call a guard and have her thrown into prison. But finally he said to her, "My dear woman, your devotion to your husband, your persistence, and your ingenuity amaze me. Why did you think you needed several thousand men?"

"Your Excellency, I have only seventy-six."

"My generals do exaggerate. But you had no permission for these seventy-six to enter Mexico?"

"Correct. They are good law-abiding men who hope to establish themselves in Key West. They entered Mexico on forged papers pro-cured by me—and of which they knew nothing." Her eyes then fell to the floor. Then she explained her previous experience in trying to obtain a pardon for Dr. Samuel Mudd and how defeating the American bureaucracy had been. When authorities could not help her, she had taken an illegal means of getting her troops into Mexico. She rightly felt her husband's life had been at stake.

"Yours is an amazing story."

"Your Excellency, quite frankly, if I were to be imprisoned for my actions here, I'm sure my country would be supportive, were it necessary, to secure my release. But I am worried about my men who would have no such protection."

"Who said anything about prison?" asked the President.

"I was thinking of my crime against your country."

"It seems to be slight. Apparently you bear us only good will—despite your husband's unfortunate adventure."

"That is true. My intentions were good." Tears of relief and gratitude welled in her eyes. "I would prefer not to sell you the guns, but to give them to Mexico. Moreover, by doing so I will avoid trouble with the United States' government. But I greatly desire and would appreciate your army's protection in getting my men and silver out. The horses are negotiable."

Jaurez smiled. "I have spent an illuminating two hours with you. Please, return tomorrow and meet with one of my generals. There is one in whom I have deep confidence, Porfirio Diaz. I see no reason why we cannot work together."

As if flying with her own wings, Anne-Marie returned to the hotel.

Tim and Rafael were waiting for her. Not speaking to each other, they had buried their noses in newspapers in the lobby while marking time.

"The government will work with us," she cried joyously. "I will give them the guns. The important thing is to get everyone out safely and the silver on a ship bound for Europe." Her face radiated happiness. "Tomorrow I meet with the top general to iron out details. What a relief! Isn't it wonderful?"

Tim beamed at her. "Well done, Anne-Marie!"

"There seems to be no end to your prowess," added Rafael in an icy tone. His face was cold. Anne-Marie was stunned. What was wrong? Could he not smile? His own life had been at stake. And, had she not saved it?

"Hire a carriage, Señor de Palma. You know this city. Show it to us. This must be a day of celebration." The two men must put their differences aside. Surely they were ill founded, she decided.

Within a few minutes a carriage was there. Seated on one side of Anne-Marie, Rafael directed the coachman to take them to the Paseo de la Reforma and the Promenade of Carlotta to the Castle of Chapultepec, a short league, past the hoary cypresses and poplars. Here were the Gardens of Montezuma, his aviaries and fishponds. Above, at the castle where Jaurez refused to live, abhorring the castle as a symbol of European dominance, the apartments were lonely and abandoned, the walls falling to ruin. The interior was guarded by a few soldiers.

Here Rafael had lived as a part of the royal entourage in a small apartment. "Although Carlotta did her best to make the palace livable, the interior was never finished," said Rafael, speaking only to Anne-Marie. For a large tip a soldier escorted her party through a few of the other large salons and apartments with magnificent regal appointments since they were in the heritage of Viceroys as well as the latter-day Emperor. A monogramed "R.M." appeared to remind everyone that this was the palace of the Republic of Mexico.

From the terrace that ran around the castle, the view formed a magnificent panorama. Again, the whole valley of Mexico stretched out before them. "How it must have pained you to leave this beautiful city," said Anne-Marie. "It's the most beautiful place I've ever seen. It makes New York look like a cow town."

"Have you ever heard of Guadalajara?" asked Rafael, condescension in his voice.

"Should I have?"

"It is older and larger than your New York."

Returning to the city, Anne-Marie noticed the high-class women. A Spanish mantilla of black or white lace did a fascinating duty in place of a hat or a bonnet. High-heeled pointed slippers struck Anne-Marie as marvelously flattering to the feet although possibly painful. The women wore no corsets, paying for style with another coin. They passed homes of the wealthy explained by Rafael.

"I never knew such an elegant way of life existed," said Anne-Marie, awed by the trappings and splendor announced by curved balconies, tile terraces and elaborate grillwork.

Later Rafael ordered the driver to take them to a shopping street where one shop after another boasted a host of luxuries, articles and services: wines from France, Spanish wig makers, French jewelers and tailors, shoemakers, and fabric shops with the best from China, Italy, and England all for sale.

When the city closed down for the lengthy siesta, they returned to the hotel. Excited and enthralled with all she had seen and done, Anne-Marie retired to her room, but neglected to bolt the door. Having removed her dress, she stretched out on her bed, aware only how quiet the city had become. She was almost asleep when she looked up to see Rafael bolting her door.

"What are you doing here?" she cried, too startled by the intrusion to realize his intentions, although now wide-awake. Within seconds he was throwing himself upon her.

"Anne-Marie, I must speak to you," he whispered, his lips searching hers with a stream of kisses she did her best to evade.

"This is not speaking to me," she managed to utter angrily while attempting to push him away.

"Do not reject me," he begged.

"Don't you understand, I must…"

"Anne-Marie, all you have seen today, the magnificent villas, the luxury, a life of excitement is within your reach. Make your home here with me. I can make it a paradise…"

"How can you conceive of such a thing?" she stammered, again doing her best to push him off of her. "Here you are in danger. I have a husband and a child I cannot leave. Rafael, you must face reality."

"You are my reality." The words were like the thrust of a sword.

"I am not. How can I make you understand?"

Rafael stiffened and Anne-Marie realized a different mood. One no longer pleading, but cruel and demanding, absorbed him. His face, now pulsating and twisted with rage, was dangerously alarming. Suddenly, she realized that she was not dealing with an impetuous lover, but a madman. She dared not cry out, exposing herself to Tim and the hotel staff in such a compromising situation. She was no physical match for Rafael nor could she reason with him. She could not push him away, and to fight would endanger her life.

With the ferocity of a wild animal he attacked, ripping at her under-clothes while opening his trousers. Aware that resistance would only be more painful than submission, she endured his rape. When he was spent and collapsed, still upon her, she could only be thankful that she had not been choked to death, as certainly he was capable of such an act. Mercifully, when it was over, wordlessly he left her.

For a few minutes she lay in shock, then she absently turned to the ruin he had created in her clothing. Blessedly, a little packet with a needle and thread was with her. Each little stitch, at first awkward and undi-rected, helped steady her trembling fingers. Finally, the torn garments like herself, scarred but repaired could function. Slowly she achieved a measure of composure. Rafael had snapped. She was now certain, he was a thoroughly dangerous man. In this strange land there was nothing she could do but get Tim and herself back under the protection of her troops as soon as possible.

Facing unpleasant facts, swallowing humiliation, she found Tim waiting for her in the lobby, refreshed after a good nap.

"You know what we must do, Tim. We must telegraph Bart and ask him to arrange with Captain Sands to pick us up at Veracruz. I think by pushing hard we can be there in a week—about the sailing time they would need."

"I was hoping you had come to that. I'm anxious to get home. I've been dreaming too much of Consuelo."

"I'm sure you have. Let's do that right now."

From the central post she telegraphed: YOUR LOVING WIFE AND TIM HOPE TO BE MET IN VERACRUZ BY YOU AND SANDS STOP SEVENTY-SIX MEN MUST BE TRANSPORTED STOP HAVE MISSED YOU STOP YOURS ANNE-MARIE.

They walked through the Alameda, the city's most fashionable park, surrounded by a stone wall and a trench, stopping for a moment to enjoy a bit of a concert played by a military band. It was then she realized that she had not included Rafael in her count of seventy-six men. She would not go back to change the message. What difference would one man make?

Rafael was not present at dinner and Anne-Marie had not expected him. Noting that she only picked at her dinner, Tim spoke his mind. "You seem down, more troubled than you should be—as I see things now. Surely, the absence of Señor de Palma has not disappointed you?"

"I believe disappointed is hardly the word."

"Remember, he's a bachelor. He's probably enjoying a night on the town."

"True enough," she replied. Tim is still being generous with Rafael, she thought. "I've had to revise my opinion of him, and frankly, I'm frightened. I fear he is a dangerous man."

"So do I, but I think I can take care of myself." It did not occur to him that she might also be afraid for herself. He was aware of only two threats upon himself.

"Let's not talk about him. I'm concerned about meeting with General Diaz tomorrow. He may not be as kind as the President. I have not made him look good."

"Only this morning you were so happy. The world was at your fingertips. The difference in mood is striking. What changed it? Nothing is different."

Anne-Marie could not meet his eyes. "All of a sudden I have realized a lot of things. You might call it an awakening. Please, don't be alarmed.

The night before last in the cave I never closed my eyes. Street noises here began at dawn. Frankly, I'm terribly…tired."

"I can understand the let down now that a successful end to this journey is in sight," remarked Tim, now enheartened that she could look at him.

"So near and yet so far. Tim, we haven't seen the end yet, and the stakes have gotten oppressively high."

"Don't be discouraged. We're almost home." He gave her had a gentle pat. "With your luck we can't lose. Put on the charm tomorrow. It's unfailing."

She wished she could be so sure. Tim's lopsided grim and the wine helped.

*   *   *   *

General Porfirio Diaz was a powerful presence, a person valued more than any program or party he was destined to lead. Peasants and the city's poor called their generals by heroic names: protector, savior, deliverer or liberator. Clearly Diaz was a benevolent and paternalistic tyrant of mestizo blood. He was a man easily touched by Anne-Marie.

His men stationed in the capitol would follow her troops out of the Federal District, but always at a distance, so as not to alarm the populace at large.

"With binoculars we will keep you in sight at all times, and with a good deal of pleasure," joked the general. "The silver will be well protected."

At the border of the State of Puebla there would be a change of guard and again as they entered the State of Veracruz. The price for this support and immunity from prosecution would be, of course, the guns and ammunition.

*   *   *   *

Meanwhile back at the camp Esteban also had passed a sleepless night. He had not had an opportunity to warn Anne-Marie about Rafael. If he, Esteban, made accusations, it would only be his word against that of Rafael's. Anne-Marie had known Rafael for a much longer time and might believe his denial. So far, Rafael had been foiled, but surely, he would strike again. But how, when and where? After tossing and turning he decided to remain alert and say nothing until events showed him the way.

*   *   *   *

Anne-Marie's success with President Jaurez and the anticipation of additional Mexican soldiers to their company had pushed Rafael to the breaking point. Out of a jealous rage he had resolved to kill Tim Clayton. He would steal from Anne-Marie everything that he could. He would haunt her until the end of her days. He could not be toyed with by a woman in such a fashion. Wisely, he had announced his intention to travel alone or with Esteban much of the time so Tim would be expecting his absence. He still had a few days to accomplish his ends.

Anne-Marie's rejection during the siesta had been the last straw. He left her and went to an apothecary for a white powder. Entering the stables of the hotel, he sprinkled this powder into the empty feedbag of Tim's horse. Then, as Tim had suggested, he found diversion in the city in one of the lower class theaters. The Teatro National, or the grand opera house, had been sold out.

The theater that he found was dark, dirty and smelled of unwashed bodies and clothing. The first actress, hardly a favorite, was wooden, never distressed in even the tragic scenes nor faintly pleased in the pleasant ones. She flubbed many of her lines. A prompter spoke so loudly that the audience knew in advance what the actress would say.

Everyone smoked—even in the galleries, in boxes, and even the prompter throughout the whole performance so that smoke curled eerily through the theater. There was no applause. None of this detracted from Rafael's enjoyment. He was otherwise engaged, reveling in plans for revenge.

He returned to the hotel late enough to avoid meeting Anne-Marie or Tim. He asked to be awakened before dawn.

The next morning Anne-Marie had had her successful meeting with General Diaz and had telegraphed Bart. Now she checked out of the hotel paying for three rooms and stable fees. At the desk she asked about Rafael, and was informed that he had departed early. For that she was grateful. She hoped that they would not meet again until she boarded her ship, *Regina de los Girasoles*, in Veracruz. Bart would be there.

The horses had been watered, fed and curried, and were ready to march. Anne-Marie tipped the stable boy well for his care and trouble. With Tim she rode back to the outskirts of town where her men were waiting.

"Just because we have an army behind us, Tim, we cannot discount treachery. Please, take no chances," she pleaded.

Tim nodded in agreement.

When they began the journey, Rafael was still missing.

CHAPTER NINETEEN

Bart's telegram from Key West to Ramirez warning of Rafael's treachery had disturbed Ramirez mightily, but by then there was little he could do. Anne-Marie and her men had left Taxco before the message arrived, and possibly now they were near Mexico City. He knew they were rushing homeward, and was naturally reluctant to delay them by putting authorities on their trail. It never would have occurred to Ramirez that Anne-Marie would get an immediate audience with the President, and that Porfirio Diaz would be assigned to protect her within the limits of the Federal District of Mexico City and later in the State of Puebla.

Bart decided that the news of Consuelo's death should not come to Tim by wireless. He would break the terrible news to Tim himself; he would not foist that heartbreaking job on another. The knowledge would not get Tim home any sooner, and the man would be spared a few days of grief.

With Anne-Marie's request to be picked up in Veracruz in hand, Bart walked to the ship, *Los Girasoles*, to talk to Captain Sands. "How soon can you be ready to sail? Madame is ready to come home."

"Give me an hour, sir," replied Sands.

"Do you suppose you could possibly arrange a second ship to sail with us to transport the men? With the sad news we bring Mr. Clayton, I would hardly wish an arduous voyage on him—beyond what it is bound to be. A second ship would insure him some privacy."

"I'll do so, sir."

"We will sail then as soon as you're ready."

Because of the salvage operations based in Key West, finding a second vessel capable of transporting seventy-six men presented no problem to Sands. A dozen or so ships were in their berths, but sufficient food would have to be stowed for the return journey.

Sands reconsidered. "Give me two hours then."

Sand's eyes were already on Sylvanus Pinder's ship. Pinder himself, robust, handsome and jolly, would be an ideal captain for such a journey and his ship could be chartered providing the trip was legal.

Precisely two hours later, Bart and David set sail with Sands, Pinder close behind, prepared as planned.

A five or six day interval had to be filled by reading, sitting, or walking about deck, looking for ways to kill time while nevertheless, hating its passage, which at its end, would require the telling of the tragic news. Bart stared at the water, so clear he could see great sharks surfacing, only later realizing what he had seen, so lost was he in sorrow. Bart hardly heard an accomplished raconteur, one of the sailors, an ugly active little fellow who spun long endless stories of his own invention, to which the crew listened with interest and amusement.

Unfortunately, about twenty leagues from Veracruz, a *Norte* hit them. Bart knew it was coming without looking at the barometer, which fell as rapidly as Bart's face. Rain came down in torrents. Their entry into port would be delayed although they could see the cap of Orizaba, called by Mexicans the mountain of the star, Cital Tepetl. A temptress, thought Bart, so near and yet so far.

Then the *Norte* was followed by a southwind, and *Los Girasoles* was forced to turn away from the coast with Pinder's ship close by. The southwest wind held implacably for three days. Then again the barometer fell, causing all hands to prepare for another *Norte*. This the sailors called a *Norte chocolatero,* because it came so fast the shock tore a sail. Towards evening the wind calmed, but both ships, tossed about by a swelled sea, became a purgatory. David was too sick to move from his stateroom. Twice he was dumped from his berth. For three days in sight of Veracruz they were tossed about, moving further from the city every hour. Even the sailors began to look miserable.

Finally, the wind blew from the right quarter. *La Brisa,* the breeze that ideally followed a *Norte,* rose and stuck with them. The ships finally went steadily on their course at eight knots an hour. Again Veracruz was in sight.

David emerged pale and haggard.

"I've known at trip from Key West to Veracruz to take as long as twenty-five days when a steam packet could make it in three," confessed Sands. "So, I don't feel too badly about ten days, Mr. Doyle—except for your discomfort, that is."

"Had that been the case, I would have tried swimming," said David.

Bart, ever aware of his dreadful task, felt drowning had merit.

*   *   *   *

Anne-Marie and Tim, leading their caravan, moved from the Valley of Mexico toward Puebla. It was late in the day before they rested, and Tim offered his horse the feedbag during the rest stop. Mounting to continue he soon told Anne-Marie, "My horse is acting peculiarly. She pays no attention to the reins and seems disoriented."

"She does seem a little drunk. Trade with me for a little. Maybe it's you."

"I haven't been drinking. Why would I suddenly not know how to ride?"

"I didn't say that, but I do know horses. You sailors and carriage-riders worry me the minute you put your feet in the stirrups," she quipped.

"Well, if you insist, see for yourself," replied Tim dismounting. She was a Half-Bred, a good-looking, strongly built, free-going mare usually quiet and obedient.

As soon as they changed horses, Anne-Marie knew immediately something was wrong, and wondered what strange sickness the horse could have contracted. "Tim, I see what you mean. How long has this been going on?"

"Only for the last few minutes."

"In other words, since the horse ate from the feedbag?"

"Yes."

"I fear we're both thinking the same thing." They had not seen Rafael since Mexico City, and exchanged concerned expressions. Anne-Marie no sooner got the words out than the horse took off, leaving a cloud of dust, with Anne-Marie attempting to bring the horse under control.

Tim turned quickly, hoping to catch Esteban's eye to signal him to take over control of the caravan, but the rear of the group was not in sight. Unwilling to waste another second, he took off in hot pursuit, trusting that one of the men foremost in the column would inform Esteban.

Anne-Marie had some experience with racing horses. Occasionally for diversion she had raced along the beaches at Cayo de las Matas, the key where Los Claveles was located. There it was possible to race halfway around the island. Her instructor fortunately had warned her that horses sometimes break away frightened by a snake or wild cat. "Above all, don't lose your head. The cure is quite simple. As soon as the horse bolts, get in galloping position. First, sit forward, leaning a little, speak to your horse, and pull back hard in a series of pulls on the reins. If the horse doesn't stop, just ride. The horse will get worn out and reach a point where it cannot run another step. It may be so tired that you will have to get off and walk it home."

The advice was well and good except the horse wasn't running from fear alone but from something else. Also Anne-Marie knew that a frightened horse would head for the highest point, a hill or a mountain, a primal equine instinct that had meant survival to its ancestors, no doubt. Here a mountain range was in full view and the horse would soon react to the sight. As long as they were on the road, the race would not be difficult; once she left the road it would be a different story. Within a few minutes the maddened horse became aware of the range and cut sharply, heading for the rising land, ignoring all other commands.

The course was now difficult. The horse took jumps she would have otherwise faltered at or even shied from. Under the circumstances, the rider can easily fall and break a leg, neck or back. Tim never could have managed, Anne-Marie knew, and was consoled by that thought. Only with intense concentration was she able to stay in the saddle. Unless the drug wore off soon, there was a danger that the horse would drop dead, and perhaps she, herself, one way or another, with her horse.

Fortunately, the rising terrain enabled Tim and her troop to hold her in view most of the time. Meanwhile the tension of the ride was tiring Anne-Marie to exhaustion. As the climb grew higher she saw, from the corner of her eye, cliffs from which a maddened horse might leap, killing them both. Only luck had put such precipices out of their erratic path. The high almost barren terrain also spared Anne-Marie the worry over low branches.

The mare was worth trying to save. The heavy load of silver took all of their horses; there were no extras and the loss of even one horse would slow down and even halt them altogether should another horse fail. More horses would be hard to come by in the squalid shabby villages on the outskirts of the capitol. Slow little burros were all the country offered as beasts of burden.

The wild ride was also viewed by other eyes. One of General Diaz's scouts, riding ahead of the Mexican troops, had seen the horse sprint from the caravan, but he was too far behind to be sure of what happened. It could have been a runaway horse or a runaway rider, he reported back to his general. Rafael had also observed Anne-Marie's troop from a distance. Much to his dismay, Anne-Marie and Tim had switched horses, which he had not counted upon. Once again Tim Clayton had thwarted him. Ignoring Anne-Marie's danger, he cursed Tim's charmed life, his hatred mounting.

Gradually, Tim's runaway mare, wet with sweat, reduced exertion and began responding to commands, if only in a fickle way, it seemed to Anne-Marie. Both horse and rider were close to collapse. Finally, heaving and trembling, the horse stopped, allowing Anne-Marie, also shaking, to dismount, tottering on her feet. The mad ride had taken no more than fifteen minutes or twenty minutes, and it would take far more time to return to the group, yet both had to rest first.

Clearly, thought Anne-Marie, they had been stalked by a killer. Tim was the prey. He was safe as long as he stayed with the group, but if he rode off alone in pursuit of her, and surely he would, he would be in terrible danger. Sick with worry, leading the horse as fast as she could, she came back down the mountain, her own steps halting for brief moments as she stumbled right and left.

Fortunately, Rafael, skirting the road, hiding from both the caravan and the Mexican troops, could not go after Tim without exposing himself to either General Lopez's men or Anne-Marie's troops, both of who had stopped to await the denouement. Tim, at first moving at a decent pace, then restrained by the need to look for Anne-Marie, finally spotted her and galloped to her side.

"What are you doing away from the group?" Anne-Marie asked livid with rage. "You're being stalked by a killer, Tim. I can take care of myself. These are my orders. You stay with the group from now on. We must keep you surrounded. This very minute you are in mortal danger!"

"How about the danger you are in?" replied Tim, his radiating concern he could find no words for, yet he was well aware of her anger.

"But, only by mistake. I was glad I was on that horse, not you. That ride took everything I know about horses, and if I had not spent the last two weeks in the saddle, getting into condition, even I never could have survived it—with all my experience."

When they rejoined their group, Anne-Marie ordered the men to surround Tim at all times. "We have good reason to believe someone is making attempts on his life. That horse was drugged by someone in Mexico City."

"I would like to speak with you," said Esteban. "It cannot wait any longer."

Ordering a rest period, Anne-Marie drew him aside. "What is it, Señor?"

"Rafael de Palma is behind this. He wanted me to join him in stealing your silver. He even had a *ranchero* waiting to ambush you outside Cuernavaca. I pretended to go along with him, feeling that only in that way I would have wind of what he was doing, and could be certain of it, and could best protect you."

"Why didn't you tell me this earlier?" cried Anne-Marie, her eyes ablaze, her mouth agape.

"When did I have the chance? Until Mexico City, after Tres Marias, de Palma stuck to you like flypaper. He was a friend of yours. It would have been my word against his, and I feared you would believe him. So, it seemed best for me to stay close to him, hoping to learn what he was about, and to protect you in that way. Please, believe me…"

She had no reason not to. "I do, Señor Navarro. Thank you for your loyalty. I'm sure de Palma promised you a great deal of money."

"Money isn't everything, Madame. You have promised us all something more than money. You have shown us a courageous way to live. You are willing to fight for what you want, and to do it the right way. I admire you. The others know it and agree with me."

"Thank you for your support. I'm sure you are being stalked right now. You may be in danger even for talking to me in broad daylight. So, let's dally no longer," said Anne-Marie, suddenly conscious that three hours had been lost and that now one more man had to be guarded.

*   *   *   *

General Diaz put down his binoculars. "The lady is back with her troops," he said to his aide. "She is very beautiful. I regret having to turn her over to another garrison at the border of Puebla." He smiled, a bit wantonly.

"You want those guns badly, don't you, sir?"

"I'll get them. Someone will blunder between here and Veracruz."

The aide-de-camp laughed. Diaz was Mexico's most brilliant general—a crude peon but a brave one. Once Diaz had escaped from prison in Puebla by lowering himself out of a window on a knotted rope. His wife, Doña Carmelita, a fine lady, had been polishing his rough edges, substituting wine for *pulque*, putting him in white tie when the occasion demanded, and teaching him to use silverware instead of tortillas to scoop up his beans—and the like.

"I know. Someone will blunder, and you will get the guns," replied the aide confidently.

*   *   *   *

The next three days passed uneventfully, but the nearer they came to Veracruz, the more anxious Anne-Marie became, fearing that Rafael would strike again, and this time, from necessity, more daringly. Protective measures, although they slowed the caravan, were thus far effective.

Rafael had come to the decision that he could not steal the guns, ammunition and a sufficient portion of the silver without covering his act with a smoke screen of some diverting event. He could not depend upon Esteban Navarro, who now rode close to Anne-Marie. The guards had been increased to guard the silver cargo, and the increased watch continued all night long. Riding time during the day had been reduced in order to give the guards time to sleep, and then, disconcertingly, sometimes they moved at night. Keeping up with them while always riding out of sight ran him ragged. He grew desperate. The most effective diversion would have to come from a fire, and the fire, to be effective would have to be set in the *Tierra Templada,* the high dry land, where they were now, not in the *Tierra Caliente* close to the coast. He would have to move fast.

Finally, Anne-Marie's troop camped at a perfect location for Rafael's purposes near a poor farmer's wattle hut with a thatched roof. Shortly before dawn, Rafael struck.

A small brush fire drew the attention of the guards, giving Rafael time to steal the guns and to hide them nearby. He was aided by two well-paid local henchmen, quickly recruited from a bar for this purpose.

The events of the night were to be so tumultuous; Anne-Marie would never discover exactly how Rafael accomplished his aims. She, Tim and a few more of her men were awakened by the screams of a terrified farmer, who with his wife and four children had fled their home when their thatched roof had been set afire. The farmer blamed Anne-Marie's campfire for the disaster, attributing sparks from their camp as the cause of the fire that made their home a blazing inferno. Concern for the poor man's plight drew Anne-Marie's full attention. Exploding ammunition deliberately thrown into the brush fire by Rafael added to the furor.

The brush fire, wide spread, had also alarmed the horses and their fear was compounded by the burning hut and screaming humans. The exploding ammunition that went off like strings of firecrackers completed the pandemonium. Whinnying and screaming horses, rearing and kicking, straining at their lines, added to the general terror.

In the chaos, a small part of the silver was stolen.

The explosions brought the Mexican army racing to the encampment, adding to the disorder. It was dawn before the situation could be assessed. Most important, the guns were gone. It was the guns, and the guns only, that insured the safety of their departure.

The Mexican forces, now from the State of Veracruz, were headed by General Lopez, an arrogant man who resented this assignment, and, being unsympathetic to Jaurez, felt that the prized guns were fictitious, and that Anne-Marie had bamboozled his government. The presence of her troops, almost a month earlier, had proved an embarrassment to him because he had been unable to find them. Now he was certain that the fire and explosions were a cover for having no guns. With icy reserve he listened to Anne-Marie's description of the pre-dawn event.

"I am committed to seeing you safely to your ship in Veracruz, Madame," said Lopez, "but the terms are explicit. You are to supply us with a hundred rifles."

"I know the terms," replied Anne-Marie. "And, the bargain was made with your country in good faith. What happened was most unfortunate. You have no idea how upset I am, not for myself, but for my men."

"The guns cannot be far from here," interjected Tim. "If we spread out our joint forces in a wide line, combing the countryside, surely we will find them where they are hidden, because they must have been hidden hastily."

Knowing refusal to cooperate would bring criticism, Lopez felt forced to comply, although he was convinced that a search would be futile and said so.

"I believe our man will not be between here and Veracruz," said Tim, "but he would have fled in another direction, possibly northward or southward, but most likely to the west."

"If it is west, I cannot help you. That is another general's territory," replied Lopez. "He and his troops would now be headed back toward headquarters in Puebla."

"Then I am certain that is the direction that de Palma took," replied Tim. "He had to have seen the switch in government support units. I will take some of our men and search in that direction."

"No, you can't do that! That man is after you. I won't hear of it," said Anne-Marie.

"I'm sorry, but this time I can't follow your orders. I'll take a number of men with me. He never practiced riflery with the men at Los Claveles, remember?"

"Please, listen to reason, Tim. I beg of you. This is not the time for you to take any risk!"

"I don't intend to. Like you, I intend to get our men back safely." Tim was adamant. With a large party of men they would sweep westward. General Lopez and his men would sweep forward to the east.

"Then I will go with you," said Anne-Marie to Tim.

"If you insist, but I feel it would be far wiser for you to stay here in charge of the men guarding the main body of silver."

"We have Esteban," she countered.

"Every minute we stand here quibbling valuable time is being lost. Rafael de Palma will not be traveling with the guns, but he will be traveling as fast as he can. I'm ready to trust Esteban, but I'm not willing to trust anyone completely."

"Please, Tim, we have to trust him."

"Rafael could not have accomplished what he has without help. If you are certain of Navarro's loyalty, let him stay here to protect you," said Tim.

"I feel as Mr. Clayton does," interjected Lopez. "We are wasting valuable time. I will sweep eastward. If the guns exist, you, Mr. Clayton, or I should be able to find them."

The general's doubts pushed Anne-Marie. She had little choice but to listen to the two men. Reluctantly, she saw Tim depart with half her company in one direction and General Lopez in the other.

She turned her attention to the farmer who had lost his house and part of his corn crop that had burned. The distressed family sat together silently waiting for Anne-Marie's attention.

The wattle hut had not burned to the ground. Anne-Marie surveyed the ruins. The one room was a mess of ashes. A bundle of canes, where the children had slept, had not burned. The room smelled of cooked meat, and Anne-Marie soon saw why. *Tesaje,* or beef cut in long strips is dried in the sun. While it is curing it must not be exposed to rain or dew, so it is always put under cover at night. The bedstead was festooned with it. The beef also hung on the rafters that had been singed in the fire.

Anne-Marie not only offered to pay for the damage, but put some of her men to work cleaning up the mess. New thatch had to be cut, and under the farmer's direction repairs were begun.

General Lopez's men, riding in a line only a few feet apart, soon discovered fresh earth. The burying had been done rapidly where there was a drop in the terrain so that shovels were not even called for. Very soon the three cases of guns and ammunition were uncovered. The general ordered a case ripped open and was quite pleased with the beautiful firearm handed him. Bright Krupp steel glistened in the sunlight. Carefully he examined the weapon that would not only offer his troops accuracy, but would avoid the clumsy reloading of muskets presently in use.

His muskets were, indeed, clumsy to use, and loading was not simple. After each firing the barrel had to be swabbed out to remove any hot residue before the gun could be recharged, a procedure that took valuable time, skill and care. This done, measured powder was poured down through the barrel. Then a piece of wadding was added and packed with a ramrod to force the powder into a compact mass. The musket ball could then be added, which had to be shoved into the barrel. Finally, a little more powder was poured into a priming hole to ignite the gunpowder in the musket chamber. Only then was the gun ready for aiming and firing.

Lopez had heard of Krupp's new guns which used bullets, but he had never seen one. Ordering an ammunition carton broken open, he inserted a bullet, and with the gun pointed skyward, pulled the trigger.

Nothing happened.

"This gun seems to be faulty," he said to an aide. "Hand me another."

The same thing happened. After trying several more, the general was furious. "These guns are worthless," he declared. "Pack them up. I shudder to think what that woman is foisting upon our country."

"Shall we give them back to her?" asked the aide.

"No," replied the general. "No, indeed. They will stay in our hands for whatever they're worth—which may be only evidence."

Meanwhile Tim's group moved westward, traveling as rapidly as they could while still combing the countryside. Rafael had a headstart of at least thirty minutes, but reduced by the fact that earlier he had had to travel in darkness. Now both had the advantage of daylight, but Tim knew that Rafael was also slowed by the purloined silver, bound to be as much as he dared carry on his back and on his horse. It would be heavy. At times the route was circuitous, climbing around *barrancas* that made spreading out impossible, and always infinitely easier for one man than a group. When they reached an area where clearly a man could hide, Tim gave up the chase.

"This is impossible. We could spend days looking for a man here and never find him with bloodhounds. I think we should go back. We are wasting time."

The men agreed.

Tim's posse turned to face a string of foothills on the right and a mountain range on the left, dominated by the snow capped Orizaba, the highest point in Mexico. Mimosa and other vegetation among boulders above them offered a thousand places where a man and a horse could hide and patiently wait until they disappeared.

"Let's get on the road," said Tim, nodding toward the high land surrounding them.

Suddenly a pistol shot rang out and Tim fell from his saddle. Every man's eyes turned on Tim in horror, and then to the surrounding landscape above them where not even a leaf moved.

It was a perfect shot through the head, killing Tim instantly.

Every man present would have given his right arm for the privilege of felling the killer who was now scurrying down the other side of a hill, where, hidden by vegetation, his horse was resting after the race of escape. The horse was laden with two saddlebags of silver. A backpack of silver lay on the ground nearby. On foot, Rafael had climbed to the high point to survey the route ahead. When he looked down to his surprise and delight he had discovered Tim's group. At some point driven by the rough cross-country terrain to the road, they had missed him. He was near enough for a deadly aim.

Fearing for their own lives, the stunned men started back. Tim's horse carried his body face down over his saddle.

Rafael, now certain that his shot had been fatal, elated over his successful revenge and bounty, grew careless. Had he been willing to lie low, his whole operation would have been successful; but instead he weighed himself down again with his silver-laden backpack and saddlebags and moved slowly off. The terrain that had previously aided him, now for a brief second revealed him.

Tim's men turned often to look behind, and one of them caught sight of Rafael to their left. "There he is!" he cried.

Immediately most of the men wheeled their horses to the left and set off in hot pursuit. Cutting far from the road racing south Rafael met the Tuxpango River. He had no choice but to cross it. On the opposite side dense vegetation would protect him, he thought.

Plunging into the river on his horse, he heard a pistol shot. The horse below him stopped swimming. He was swept by the current downstream, deeper and deeper on his floundering horse. Terrified, Rafael left the horse and attempted to swim, but the silver was a burden he could not lose. It sank him. He had made a fatal mistake.

Tim's men saw what was happening and followed the river some distance until the silver laden horse, only wounded surfaced. The horse's large body was rammed against a ford that formed a small cascade—many abound in these hills—which held him until the men could pull him free. Rafael never surfaced and never would. Only a small stream of bubbles traced his grave.

Leading the injured horse, which the men had relieved of his cargo of silver, they headed back to the highway. It did not take long for the men to catch up with those escorting Tim's body.

When the united group approached, Anne-Marie was arguing with General Lopez who had refused to turn over the recovered guns. Her back was to the road.

"You have no right to hold the guns, whether you believe them worthless or not," she insisted, her color high. "They belong to me."

Lopez scoffed.

A sudden changed expression on everyone's face caused her to turn. She saw Tim's body, and the color drained from her face.

Blessedly, Esteban was there to take charge as Anne-Marie was beside herself with grief. They were still eighty-two miles from the sea. Carrying Tim to Key West for burial was impossible. Esteban rode immediately to the city of Orizaba to arrange for a hearse to pick up Tim's body. Knowing the rules of the Catholic Church, Esteban affirmed that Tim had been a Catholic and arranged for the funeral.

Anne-Marie's sad party moved to the city where they would spend the next two days preparing to lay Tim to rest.

"La noche triste," moaned the men. It was a dismal night.

Anne-Marie remembered that only a few days before Rafael had described to her another *noche triste.* Cortez, the Conqueror, had stood atop another great temple and looked down on Mexico City that he would make his own. "The streets and canals were the same then," said Rafael, "except for a few newer streets where canals had been. Most of the houses were of reed. The Spaniards remained in the city until July1st, 1520, when their barbarities caused the people to rise up in their might and drive them out. The defeat was called 'La Noche Triste.' Cortez wept." Now Anne-Marie wept.

Orizaba, whose name means 'Joy in the Waters,' was a beautifully clean resort city in La Joya Valley. The owner of the hotel and his wife where Anne-Marie stayed were helpful in advising Anne-Marie, being sympathetic to her plight. They sent a modiste and her daughter to sew all night long to make her a suitable black dress.

The service was held in the stone Chapel of the Rosary, in the handsome parish church of San Miguel. It was a strange ceremony for Anne-Marie, this Latin mass. She was the only woman present. Her *caballeros* in their red scarfs also now wore black bands on their arms. With General Lopez's men they crowded the flower-filled chapel.

The church contained a magnificently inlaid chest of ebony and ivory for the storage of sacerdotal robes and vestments, and so to this Anne-Marie donated money to add to the collection in Tim's name. She was aware that it was an odd gesture, considering how disinterested in clothes he had been, but it pleased the church. She also arranged with a sculptor for a mausoleum to hold the coffin and mark his grave.

"There should be a number of benches nearby where people can sit and peacefully wonder who the man was to warrant such a fine resting place," she said. "I will come back. His wife will have to be pleased with everything." Yet how could she be? she thought.

At last they paid their farewells to Tim and returned to the road. The procession was somber and orderly without a single act that might have offended Anne-Marie. Without the men to think of she would have remained in Orizaba longer to supervise the planting of the grave, but the city abounded in exquisite gardens. Many could do a better landscaping job than she, she knew. Her thoughts were those of procrastination. The dreaded meeting with Bart and Consuelo must come as soon as possible. She prayed for strength to meet them. To have loitered would have been wrong.

Upon arriving at Veracruz, Anne-Marie, General Lopez, and Esteban Navarro continued on to the governor's castle, which was not within the city, but commanded the entrance to the port. There she learned that no foreign vessels had entered the port due to the inclement weather, which was sure to change soon. To Anne-Marie's relief General Porfirio Diaz appeared as President Jaurez's emissary.

After greeting Diaz, she explained, "General, your colleague, General Lopez, has my guns, but he does not have the firing pins, so, of course, they won't work." She then explained the tragedy that had detained them.

Diaz was outwardly furious with Lopez for withholding the guns, but secretly rejoiced over the blunder—a blunder which he had predicted—and which enabled him to claim the guns for his own troops.

"I knew something terrible had happened the moment I saw you in black," said Diaz. "Please, accept my sincerest sympathies. It was our duty under the agreement to protect you and your men. You are a General, Madame, and, as you see, when you lose a man, the life of general is a hard one. Rest assured everything possible will be done to expedite your departure. Neither your ships nor men will be delayed."

"I am much obliged to you, General."

"Your men will be quartered here in the castle where there are also apartments for you with a view of the harbor. You will be able to see your ships the minute they arrive."

"That is more than kind of you," she replied, grateful for so much real kindness.

To be relieved of a burden that once loomed so great—getting the men out safely—now warranted appreciation. How needless her worries had been, and yet how awful would be her impending disclosure.

Requesting a simple supper in her room, Anne-Marie begged to be excused. The elegant apartment and elaborate bed was not unwelcome, and a comfortable bed she had, with mosquito curtains. At least I haven't lost the baby, thought Anne-Marie, and that is a wonder. Another child will be a pleasant surprise for Bart—after the grief.

Her sheets and pillows were trimmed with lace, but she never noticed them. Despite the sultry heat, she escaped into a deep sleep.

CHAPTER TWENTY

It was mid-morning the following day that *Los Girasoles*, accompanied by Sylvanus Pinder's ship, entered the harbor of Veracruz.

A crowd of all ages and sexes, drawn by the many ships held off shore by the bad weather and intrigued by the spectacle of seventy-some men wearing red scarves, assembled to see what was going on. Curious eyes soon settled on a beautiful woman in black taking leave of dignitaries.

Not that the spectators were not a curious group themselves. They were of all complexions and peculiarly attired. Some wore pantaloons; others—as if to make up for their neighbors' deficiencies—wore two pair, the second slit up the side of the leg in an odd Mexican fashion. The men wore large hats trimmed with silver or beads. Some of the women's dresses were only rags; others had holes deliberately cut to let in air. All were jostling, crowding and nearly throwing each other into the water, giving space only to an occasional leper.

Anne-Marie moved through the throng, which separated to let her pass. Finally, she could see Bart coming toward her, arms outspread, unsmiling with David a few paces behind. Where was Consuelo? Why hadn't he brought her?

He was uncharacteristically dressed wholly in black!

In a moment great comforting arms held her. "How did you know?" she asked. Then it dawned on her, he could not have…He had been at sea.

"What has happened?" she asked, her voice trembling.

Bart looked around, his eyes searching for Tim. "Where is Tim?"

"We've lost him, Bart. He's dead!" Tears welled in her eyes. "And you are wearing black. Why?"

"We also lost Consuelo. She died two weeks ago of meningitis." Holding her body so as to support her, Bart led her rapidly to her ship, away from the crowd.

Aware of Bart's sad message, David, Captain Sands, and the crew left Bart and Anne-Marie alone in the salon. But David had overheard Anne-Marie's explanation that Tim had died also, and went to find Esteban Navarro.

"Can you take charge, Señor Navarro?" asked David. "Because of Madame Clayton's death we brought a second ship for the men. I don't think the Ramsdens should be troubled with anything more now. I would imagine they will want to sail as soon as possible."

"Certainly," replied Esteban, "I'll let you know just as soon as we're loaded and ready to sail. As you might imagine, the men are also grieved. They were fond of Mister Clayton and in addition, giving up their horses this morning was a sight I never hope to see again. They had become attached..."

"I'm sure," said David, understandingly.

"Lest I misplace this, here is the money in gold for the horses and the Colt revolvers. It would take me a lifetime to make good the loss, should it disappear," said Esteban, handing David a heavy leather pouch.

"I'll see that Madame gets it."

After a tactful interval, David entered the salon to find Anne-Marie and Bart sitting close together, Bart's arm around her, her hand in his. She rose to embrace David.

"Bart has told me how helpful you have been. I'm grateful, David."

"I only wish I could have done more."

"You know how close the Claytons have been to us—especially to Bart. It was intolerable to think of one without the other."

"Fate can be strange—and occasionally kind. It is good to see some comfort in this loss." Then David remembered the money, a heavy weight still in his hand. "This is yours. Don't drop it. It would injure a foot. I heard it was very hard on the men to give up their horses."

"Perhaps I shouldn't have sold them." Unsure she turned to Bart. "But I didn't know how the expedition would turn out, and a promise is a promise."

"You mean to the Mexicans?"

"Yes."

"You've done right."

"I'm no longer capable of decisions. Also, we are expecting another child, Bart. Under this black dress I am bulging," Anne-Marie announced.

Bart was delighted. Otherwise, the voyage back to Key West was uneventful, marked by a growing rapport between Anne-Marie and Bart. Their losses had driven them into much closer understanding. At night, sharing one berth almost until dawn for a few minutes they were overwhelmed by a fire, all nerves aglow, all thoughts blotted out. Then later they remembered.

"Strangely, early, when I most hoped that you would take some action, you would not have, I knew, because I had not been gone long enough to alarm you. I'm sure you saw how difficult a simple thing like writing a letter is in that country. You have letters from me at home, which arrived before I left. I also have a letter found with Rafael's things, now packed up at Russell House. It clearly indicates that Rafael, from the very beginning masterminded holding me as a hostage. You were right about him from the start. He was a scoundrel."

Anne-Marie shuddered. "You weren't the only one fooled, my dear."

"And Consuelo and Tim will not be meeting *Los Girasoles* anymore as we pull into the harbor," added Bart, remembering and reaching for his wife's hand.

After an easy voyage to Key West, Captain Sands' well-trained crew insured a neat docking, and soon they were ashore.

It was good to be on firm land again. Key West seemed so pretty—and clean and civilized—with its many handsome mansions and well tended little cottages, many built by ships' carpenters, even some put together without nails but by wood dowels. The freshly painted woodwork bespoke widespread prosperity, and the climate assured some measure of comfort even for the poor. Coconut palms waved in the early morning breeze as Anne-Marie, Bart and David walked to their house, hurrying to see Samantha.

The little girl was asleep in her bed. It seemed to Anne-Marie as if the girl had grown a foot in her absence. "How could she have grown so fast?" Anne-Marie whispered. Then containing her awe no longer, Anne-Marie unable to wait, awakened her with a kiss, and Samantha jumped into her mother's arms.

"Mother, I got a baby brother while you were gone," cried the happy girl. "Come see."

Anne-Marie looked to Bart, who tagged along into the newly established nursery where Consuelo and Tim's baby lay sleeping.

"Hush, don't wake the baby," ordered Samantha, something she had heard a hundred times. Of course, the baby awoke, much to Samantha's delight. He, too, had grown and smiled at Samantha.

"He's mine," Samantha announced.

Soon Pearl, sleeping in the next room, awakened by voices, hurried to her charge.

The news of Tim's death had to be broken to Pearl. "It's almost a weight off my mind. I so dreaded him learning what had happened," said Pearl sadly. "I'm grieved out, Miz Ramsden. I'm plum grieved out."

After a few minutes, seeing that the maid intended to cope with her duties, notwithstanding, they left Pearl and Samantha to attend to the baby's morning toilette, obviously now a routine.

Once in the hall Anne-Marie said to Bart, "I think we should adopt the baby."

"I've hoped you'd suggest that, but the decision will be yours. I must say, it would make me happy to have a son."

Anne-Marie patted her stomach. "And maybe you have another here, but you know I wanted a larger family."

Downstairs they found David reading three weeks' mail. He was also in a good mood, warmed by letters from his family. It had occurred to David that his brief fling with Zipporah might have been laid in Bart's lap. If this were the case, he saw an opportunity to make amends.

"I have a letter here from a close friend who lives in the same town as Zipporah," said David. Anne-Marie stiffened. The ordeal with Zipporah was something she wanted to forget. Having learned that Bart was safe in Taxco, she determined never to mention Zipporah to him. She would pay every month as impersonally as she paid other unpleasant bills.

David continued. "He says Zipporah was caught *flagrante delicto* in bed with a man. She admitted she was expecting, but the man refused to marry her. The father threw her out."

"I guess that explains her behavior on the ship," said Bart, obviously an innocent by his casual tone. "She always seemed to be glowering at us. I was relieved to get back from Mexico to find her gone."

Zipporah as a subject ended there. How right Tim had been, thought Anne-Marie. She had convicted Bart without a trial. It was a painful lesson, but in light of her present happiness, she could afford to be merciful and generous even to someone who had wronged her. Again, she had made a promise...

"I must go to Los Claveles this afternoon with David to pay off the men and clear up everything with the caretaker. I'm sure the men are anxious to get back to Key West with their riches. I hope the saloons don't take it all. Some, I know, are pooling their resources to start businesses. One group wants to start a Cuban newspaper. They want to call it *El Republicano.* Señor Jaun Reyes will be the editor. Bart, will you come with us?"

"Only if you need me desperately. I have many legal things to attend to regarding the adoption of the baby and the handling of his property. It will take months to complete, but we have to get started sometime."

With David on her ship she sailed to Los Claveles.

As she had anticipated, the men were packed up, their few possessions on Sylvanus Pinder's ship, awaiting her arrival. Esteban had prepared a payroll sheet and had it on hand. From a table in the kitchen David counted out each man's wages. With everyone occupied, Anne-Marie walked through her house, none the worse for wear. Cots and gear were neatly staked in what had been the drawing room, a tidy mountain. She walked through the great dining room to the servant's quarters and to the small room that had been occupied by Rafael. It was musty and dark so she opened the shutters to admit light and air. The narrow bed was made army-style—tight. A white mosquito net that hung from the ceiling was neatly tucked under the mattress, all the way around the bed. A small table was bare. She opened a cupboard that contained a few clothes. Then she tore the bed apart, lifting the mattress, turning it over. She found what she was looking for: a corner where the mattress had been stitched, neatly and securely. She ripped it open. There she found several envelopes and papers. The accounting that had so mysteriously disappeared from her home was there. In the envelopes was money that she knew had been stolen from her.

She pocketed the money and then stood in the window ripping the letters to shreds, furious with herself for being fooled for so long. No curiosity even existed over the letters from Ramona. They, too, as tiny scraps fluttered across the yard in the breeze. She had seen enough. She remade the bed, closed the shutters, and joined David in the kitchen.

She shook each man's hand and personally thanked them all, wishing them well. Many pleased her with appreciative comments. "I learned a lot from you," and "We are going to miss you."

She had a special thanks for Esteban. "If you need a loan to start your business, please present your plans to my husband. We'd like to help you."

Finally, the men could sail back to Key West on Pinder's ship that would slip from the secluded basin into the open ocean. Anne-Marie returned Wade's keys and thanked him for his forbearance with the disturbance to his turf, the grove. The paths worn by the men were already disappearing as the rapid tropical plant growth took over. "The project took everyone's cooperation. There's no more need for secrecy, Wade. Give your men a vacation and take one for yourself with pay."

"You should do something with this place, Madame. It would make a fine resort hotel."

"When Bart will put time to it," she replied smiling.

There was much to talk about that night at dinner, and much that was left unsaid.

"I went through de Palma's things today at Russell House. I was sure he would have siphoned off money from the expedition's funds. I hoped to get a lead—if only a bankbook—but I found nothing. I also got the adoption papers moving. Perhaps you should buy Clayton's house. If it were available perhaps your parents could be lured to Key West for the winters," Bart explained.

"David and May could visit with their boys," Anne-Marie added.

"I'm getting anxious to see my family. There's not much that I can do for you here now. Do you realize you actually made money on this expedition?" asked David.

Bart shook his head in disbelief.

It was decided that David would take funds north to put Jason back in the investment business again. "Won't he be happy?" Anne-Marie already knew.

"Indeed, he will. You took his marbles away," said David.

Once again Anne-Marie indulged David in a trip home on a private yacht. "You don't have to do that. I can take a packet," said David.

"Hardly, with a fortune in hand. Bart and I have much to do here. We won't miss the ship. You'll have a much more pleasant voyage."

When they waved goodbye to David, standing together on the wharf, Bart acknowledge with surprise, "My God, I'm afraid I'll miss him!"

He would. David had someway softened the loss of Tim.

Clearing personal possessions from the Clayton house was a heartbreaking chore. Anne-Marie bought Consuelo's jewelry from the estate. "Someday the boy may want the jewels for his wife," said Anne-Marie, "and I can't think of a stranger wearing them." Ball gowns were packed away as being unsuitable for the poor. Linens were saved to be handed down.

One evening weeks later, Anne-Marie wore Consuelo's opals. Bart could not take his eyes off them. She never wore them again. They're not for me, she thought, despite Bart's denial that they saddened him.

Still the presence of a baby in the house was felt immediately. He was a joyous healthy child. When little Bartholomew was awake the house rang with laughter. Even Bart was often on Duval Street, pushing a magnificent Victorian pram, accepting praise for 'his son,' while Samantha, dashing in and out of every store, lured acquaintances to see 'her baby.'

"I think two Barts in one household is confusing. Would you object if we called the baby Clay?" Anne-Marie asked.

"I wouldn't mind at all. I never wanted a junior, and was pleasantly surprised with a namesake. Nothing you do offends me," said Bart. "Clay is short and sweet."

Los Girasoles sailed back and forth bring Emily and Jason and Bart's parents for a sojourn in Key West. They not only enjoyed the respite from the cold northern winter, but also viewed the improved relationship between Anne-Marie and Bart.

A tad over the expected time followed before a beautiful dark-haired baby girl was born. She was named Olympia. "She's a beautiful brunette like your grandmothers were until they got older," Bart told Samantha. "You're going to be a busy girl with two little ones to mother."

Anne-Marie's convalescence after the birth was short. Soon she was out in the garden with the children or taking short walks with the two necessary carriages. With Concepcion and Pearl they usually passed the tightly shuttered Clayton house, no longer a place of sadness but an embodiment of change, a focus of so many eventful years. The house had been a sanctuary for both Bart and her, laying their worries on the doorstep, like the morning paper, the pitcher of milk, or the fresh Cuban bread. The house where Clay was bred stood as a testament to love abounding.

One other detail needed airing, and finally Anne-Marie asked Bart to explain his relationship with Alma Russell. They happened to be walking past the Clayton's house. "I'm ashamed to say I went through your desk, desperate for information as to your whereabouts in Mexico, and found several letters from Alma begging for money. It sounded as if she were carrying your child."

Bart threw back his head and laughed. "Woman, what an imagination you have! Jared and I thought we'd like to import and bottle tequila. I doubted that you would approve, and so I didn't mention it. Jared crossed Mexico, and having learned that doing business there was well nigh impossible, he then sailed home, but from the Pacific side of Mexico! I had promised to send Alma support while he traveled never dreaming of the route he'd eventually take. I hear he collected a lot of rocks for Princeton. But my dear, I haven't laid eyes on Alma in four or five years."

Anne-Marie looked up to see a dark-haired female approaching with a scruffy pony. A woman's glance scanned the house, and noting the closed shutters, turned to take her begging or her cheap wares to sell elsewhere. She looked like a gypsy, although there were none in Key West, but Anne-Marie remembered the gypsy of her wedding day and her alarming prophecy. "You will have a mortal enemy in a dark-haired man. You will travel far. You will be rich. Oh, I see great wealth for you.

You will wear magnificent jewels. You will know rulers and noblemen. But I fear for your firstborn. I fear for your husband's children."

With a lighter heart than she had known for months, right there on the street, Anne-Marie kissed her husband.

Epilogue

In 1872 President Jaurez of Mexico ran for reelection. However, an unsuccessful military revolt led by Porfirio Diaz tarnished his victory. Soon after Jaurez died of a heart attack.

Not long after Anne-Marie and Bart traveled to Orizaba to check on Tim's grave, now marked by the completed mausoleum. The plantings had flourished and both were pleased with the care given the plot. They also were comforted to find it a popular resting place, enjoyed by the townspeople who often sat on the benches admiring the view of the beautiful valley. They took carriage rides, driving to the cascades and gardens of the area, enjoying the flowers, ferns and orchids at be gathered at the wayside. On returning to their hotel one afternoon Anne-Marie learned that Porfirio Diaz and his wife were in the city and sent him a note. An invitation to dine with them followed.

Through enormous profits on sugar plantations as a *haciendado* General Diaz was now a very rich man, enjoying a vacation in the attractive resort. A splendid dinner was ordered by Doña Carmelita for their North American guests. Anne-Marie was prepared for the occasion, having beautiful clothes with her, and with Bart at her side they made a striking couple.

"I'm sure you know that you have a very courageous wife," said the general to Bart. "But, I wonder if you know that she rewrote history?"

Bart laughed. "I fear that you may be exaggerating, but it would be pleasant to hear, especially coming from you—the man destined to become the next President of your country."

"My pleasure," responded Diaz, smiling at Anne-Marie across the table.

Diaz drew a long breath. "At the time of your unfortunate venture into this country, the Mexicans were chafing over the territory lost to the United States as a result of your war with Mexico. We had been forced to accept the insignificant sum of fifteen million dollars for the area encompassing California, Arizona, New Mexico, *et cetera*, a lot of land. Feeling among the generals against your country ran high. For some months we had been massing troops near the border planing to reclaim a large portion of this territory when your wife entered the country with her army. Reports on the number of troops were, of course, grossly exaggerated."

"Still," continued Diaz, "We assumed her cavalry unit was supporting foot soldiers. Divisions were recalled to our southern states—Puebla, Veracruz and Morelos—to repel her invasion. For weeks she evaded us. Then one day she appeared before Jaurez at the Palacio National, throwing herself on his mercy. "Give her protection," ordered Jaurez, clearly disgusted with his generals. As you know, we made a bargain.

"But, as soon as I saw her superior guns—Colt revolvers and Krupp rifles—I knew any attempt to wage war against the United States would be foolhardy. We would have been pitifully unprepared, and it would have been a foolish maneuver. Our plans for aggressive action were shelved then and there. Time passed and our wounds healed."

"That's an amazing story," said Bart, with a chuckle, looking with new eyes at his elegant, beautiful wife.

"Remember," said Diaz, regretfully, "because of a nail a kingdom was lost."

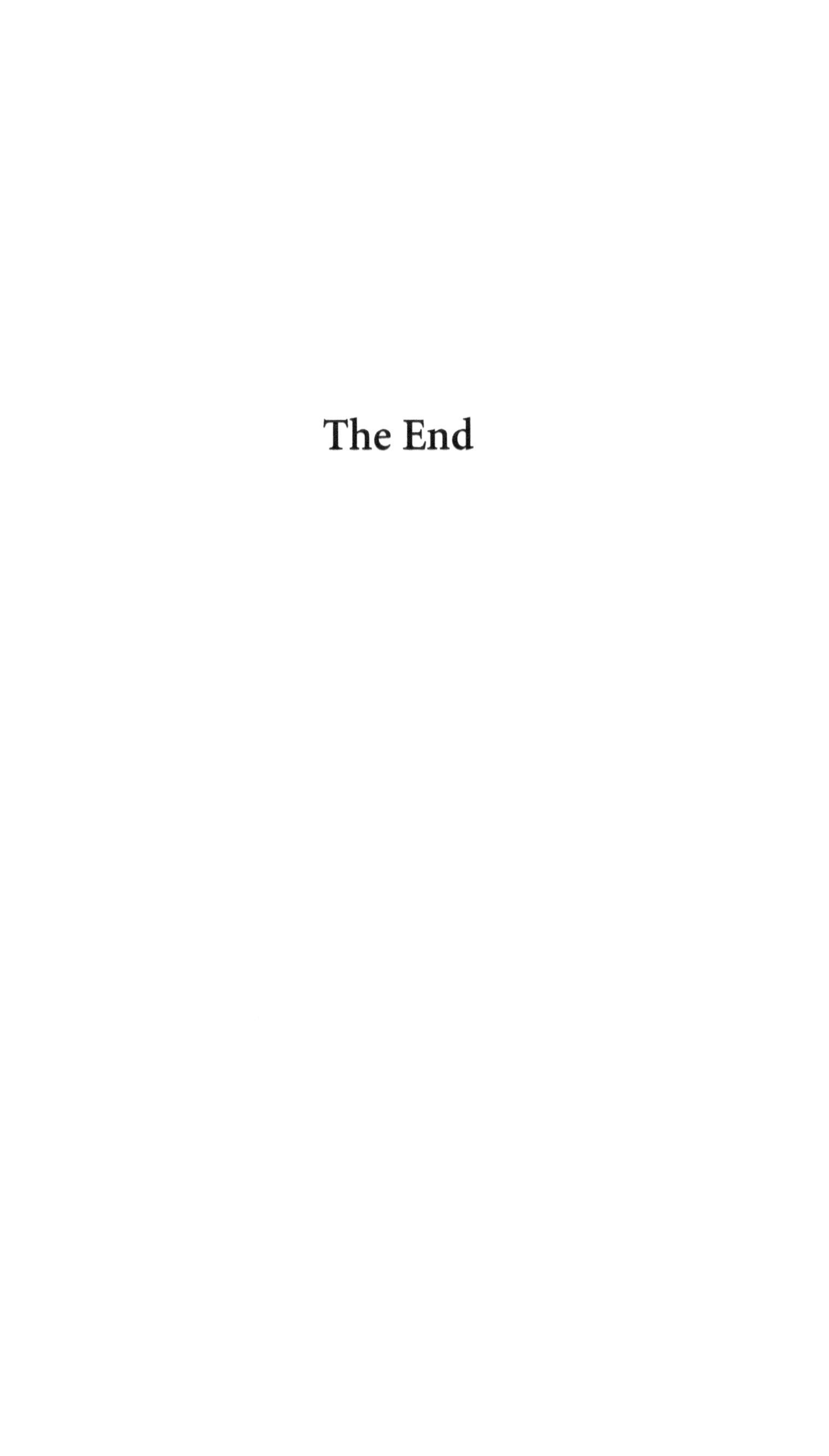

The End